MARSHAL BOOK 2
SUPERSTAR THE HARBINGER

BY HARVEY MINNICK

Order this book online at www.trafford.com
or email orders@trafford.com

Most Trafford titles are also available at major online book retailers.

Author Credits: The Coming Of Marshal

Printed in the United States of America.

ISBN: 978-1-4269-6499-2 (sc)
ISBN: 978-1-4269-6500-5 (hc)
ISBN: 978-1-4269-6502-9 (e)

Library of Congress Control Number: 2011905738

Trafford rev. 09/14/2011

 www.trafford.com

North America & international
toll-free: 1 888 232 4444 (USA & Canada)
phone: 250 383 6864 ♦ fax: 812 355 4082

MARSHAL BOOK 2
SUPERSTAR THE HARBINGER

MARSHAL BOOK 2
SUPERSTAR THE HARBINGER

CHAPTER ONE

ALIEN AFTERMATH

It is a bright and sunny day in Washington DC. There is a large crowd of reporters camped out on the Capital steps. Connie Banger, a reporter of Asian descent, is fidgeting before her cameraman, who admonishes her saying, "Connie! Stop squirming around, you look fine. You'd think you had never done this before."

Defensively, she snaps back, "I want this to go better then yesterday, I let Dauntless get away."

"You got her to say hi," Tim replied.

"Some piece of reporting that was," Connie replied sounding downhearted.

"Why don't we shoot the promo now and get that out of the way?"

She cheers up, "Good idea."

"Why don't you lead in with something like, the alien attempt to take over the Earth has been foiled?"

"No one says foiled anymore."

"How about, the Earth is safe for now?"

"We don't know that. You've been reading too many tabloids. Let me do the reporting." She clears her throat and he raises his camera signaling her to begin. "This is Connie Banger reporting from our nation's Capital. Congress is in its second day of hearings to determine what happened in Chicago."

A short distance away, Heather Carter, a drop dead beautiful twenty something blond with wavy hair, sees the crowd of reporters and makes her way around to the side of the Capital building, and makes her way in through the entrance near the Congressional cafeteria.

1

In the cafeteria, three high school age boys in white shirts and ties are mesmerized by the sight of sunlight flashing off her shapely legs as she walks down the dark hall. Her entire body seems to magically sway back and forth just a bit as she tosses back her hair with a flick of her hand. "OH YEAH!" The youngest of the boys gushes.

"That's her!" Another boy announces as they all jump to their feet and rush to meet her. As they confront her in the hall they realize, "You're not Dauntless!"

Heather stops and stares at the boys blocking her way. "Never said I was. But can you tell me were they are holding the hearings? I'm kind of lost."

One of the pages starts to answer and then it comes to him, "Hey! Wait a minute, you, you're in the picture with Dauntless! He pulls a rolled up newspaper out from his back pocket and shows it to her.

Amused by all of the attention, she takes the paper and looks at it. "Yep! That's me, BUSTED!"

"You know her! What's Dauntless like? Is she coming back today?" The younger boy asked.

This put her off just a bit not being the center of attention, but she quickly perked up saying. "No, she's back in Chicago, you know, … doing hero stuff." She hands the paper back to the taller boy adding, "You'd like her, she's nice."

"What are you, some kind of secret agent?" The youngest asked.

She smiled and stooped over a little to be face to face with him. "My, aren't you the smart one. If I told you I'd have to kill you and we don't want that do we?" She gave his cheek a tweak and continued past them down the hall.

"WOOO! I think I'm in love."

"She even smelled good," he gushed. "Just like vanilla."

Later, Heather is sworn in before a Congressional fact finding committee. Mr. Morvan, the committee's chairman, is seated at the center of the bench before her with several other members of Congress. After making the necessary greeting he asks, "Agent Carter, I know you were assigned to investigate what happened in Chicago. What are your findings?"

She adjusts the mic in front of her and answers, "That's a big question. I cannot tell you anything about how the UFO came to crash in Chicago, I wasn't involved with it at that time."

Mr. Morvan leaned forward and spoke into his mic. "We know the UFO was actually an alien space ship carrying alien prisoners to a prison planet when the Russians shot it down. We have also already heard from

Dauntless and know how she became so strong. We are more interested in what happened on the day of the anti-matter explosion that nearly destroyed Chicago."

Content to be the center of attention again she explained, "I don't have the alien technology that General Solo used yesterday, so, you'll have to bear with me. From my interviews with MaCos Ex, one of the surviving escaped aliens, I have learned that they had three anti-matter bombs. They were going to set one off destroying the city of Chicago as a show of force. They were hoping the anti-matter blast would signal other aliens to come and help them take over the planet."

"MaCos Ex, the alien engineer, and Mogo were captured by Dauntless as they tried to escape. Adack, the pirate leader, was captured by Marshal and Major Otis at Ground Zero. Marshal couldn't disarm the bomb that was about to go off, so he fashioned a spear throwing stick out of a tank gun barrel, and used it to toss the bomb as far away as he could."

"He did all of that while being poisoned by the radiation?" Morvan asked.

"That's right, the radiation literally burned his body up as he threw the bomb. You must understand that I wasn't actually there for most of my report, no one was. It took place over too big of an area for any one person to have experienced," she replied.

"Yes, of course we understand that you have interviewed many of the people involved during the course of your investigation. That's why you're here, please continue," the chairman directed with a wave of his hand.

She paused to ponder the events of that day, and the images came rushing back to her. She could see them in her mind as if it was just happening.

There was a partly cloudy sky over Chicago as a small spark raced up from the cities' Southwest side. As the spark arched over the city it flickered and grew in intensity until it was brighter than the sun. The second sun just cleared the line of tall buildings bordering the cities' lakefront. About two miles out over the lake the new sun started to fall. As it was about to plunge into the cold waters of lake Michigan, the new star starts to go super-critical giving off a blinding flash. A giant orange ball forms beneath the surface of the lake and the water starts to churn and boil off.

Two miles to the west, a blinding flash removes all of the color from the snarled traffic on Lake Shore Drive. Office workers shielded their eyes before they burst into flames. Every painted surface bubbles up and blisters or bursts into flames. Trees burst into flames. Seconds later, the trees are whipped about and the cars on Lake Shore Drive are tossed aside landing on one another. Every East-facing window is shattered and blown in, over 100,00 of them.

On the city streets the people were first alarmed by the shadows cast by the flickering flame as it passed overhead. There was a bright flash off to the East and a gust of hot air came rushing down the east west streets. The tall building on the cities' lakefront shielded the city from any further damage inland.

Miles to the north, Lufthansa flight 109, a Boeing 747, is on approach to O'Hare. The flight crew sees the spark come flying up and descend into the lake. They marvel at the flash and brace themselves as the shock wave races at them. The 747 was ripped to shreds by the shock wave. Another 747, a mile and a half further back in line sees the flash, as the German wide body is vaporized before them. The pilot turns to his first officer asking, "Did you see that?"

"They exploded!" He replied as he reached to activate the radio. He added, "I'll call the tower." As the first officer starts to make the call, an unseen force slammed the 747. The stricken jet remains intact, but all of its systems failed and it starts to descend towards the lake.

A mile and a half back yet another jet is on approach. "What's going on? They're going down too fast," the pilot wondered out loud.

"Was that a nuclear blast?" The co-pilot asked, as their ship was buffeted by the shock wave. The third jet was sent into a gentle dive toward the lake.

"We've lost everything! We're going in. Tell them to get ready to make a water landing!" The pilot commanded as he struggled with the controls. The co-pilot tries to raise the flight attendants on the phone but there is no response.

He turns to go back. "It's not working!" He runs into Jennifer who is the chief flight attendant coming through the door to the cockpit. "We're going down, get them ready for a water landing." Her pretty face went blank as the meaning of his words sank in, and she turned to go.

A bright flash and a gust of hot wind pass over two high school kids kissing while sitting on the sand at Foster Avenue Beach with their backs against the breakwater. Gradually they become aware that something is not right. The sound of FFFFF filled the air. They could not hear the panicked screams of 200 people coming towards them.

Forty seconds later, the 747 glided down into the surf. The airliner skipped along the lake's surface until its engines caught the waves sending water spraying everywhere. The 100-ton glider slides up onto the sand of Foster Avenue Beach, just missing the breakwater. The forward hatch of the airliner cracks and swings open. Seconds later, an escape slide is inflated and one of the crew is standing in the doorway looking out at the kids on the beach. Jeffery, the high school boy, stands up pushing his long oily hair back out of his eyes. He summed it up in one word. "Woo!"

On the cities' Southwest side, not far from Midway airport on Cicero Avinue. is a crater, covering nine city blocks, which is surrounded by devastated buildings. This was the scene of the UFO crash and more recently, the scene of a pitch battle between the Army and aliens trying to take over the Earth. At the center of the crater are the wrecks of two army helicopters and a burning tank. Major Henry Otis, U.S.Army, stands in his battle dress uniform with his old .45 ready in hand. After surveying the area he turns and asks Dauntless, "are you alright?"

Dauntless, a 21-year-old buxom blond in a tight, high collar white coat with blue pants and black boots, is holding a badly burned body. Visibly shaken, she answers the Major, "he's dead, burned to a crisp."

"Yes, I can see that, there's nothing we can do for him. But we have to think about the living," he said as he came over to her.

"But he saved all of us," she said fighting off tears.

"He was a hero, he died a heroe's death, and now it's your turn to step up and make him proud," he said trying to sound reassuring. It wasn't working. She broke into tears and started sobbing uncontrollably. He was unaccustomed to this and at first didn't know what to do. Soldiers aren't supposed to cry. Finally, he embraced her and tried to commfort her. "There, there, get hold of yourself Lieutenant Holmes. We have work to do."

She regained her commposure and after wiping her eyes asked, "but what can I do?"

He took her by her arms, and trying to sound more fatherly than like her commanding officer said, "You're in the super hero business now. Go, you'll figure it out when you get there. Take the Blackhawk and go save some lives."

Brandy Holmes not only looked like one of those comic book goddesses, now she was one. Not truly a godess of course, but divine in form and nature. She was all woman. Also known as Dauntless, she is a newly commissioned 2nd Lieutenant, and Earth's only superhero. She recently acquired the strength of ten men and great speed. She has been equipped by the government with special tools that she carries in her utility belt, and has a uniform made of alien materials recovered from Marshal's crashed UFO. It will heal most injuries almost instantly.

She goes over to the only remaining helicopter with its engine running and turns to ask, "what about the prisoners?"

"Dump em out. I'll guard them until some help shows up," he replied waving his side arm in the air. She promptly turned and pulled two nonhuman semi-conscious aliens out of the chopper and dumped them on the glassy ground. As the chopper took off carrying Dauntless to the cities' lakefront, the middle-aged officer walked over to the aliens and commanded them, "don't try anything. One false move and I'll shoot all of you right here. Now get over there with Adack so I can watch you."

As the chopper lifts off, Dauntless discovers she's not alone. "Dr. Cooly! What are you doing here?"

Dr. Beverly Cooly, a very well built 30 something red head in a white lab coat, glasses and oversized belt buckle, came out from the back of the chopper. "I never left. I was here when you jumped out, remember?"

"But what are you doing here?" Beverly didn't normally go on missions; she was usually left behind in the lab or medical facility.

"I'm a doctor, I'll be needed where you are going."

Brandy steeled down in the webbed seat and tapped the badge on her uniform to open a comm link. "Ok, Buster, let's get going."

"Where to Mama?" The voice of the chopper pilot crackled in her headset.

"Mama? Buster you make it sound like I'm some old lady. Do I look like an old lady? You had better get your eyes checked, are you sure you can see ok?" Dauntless joked.

"Ok Lieutenant, is that better?"

"Yes, but Dauntless would be better." She looked over to Dr. Cooly and sighed. "I don't know why they can't get my name right."

Beverly offered her explanation. "They made you an officer and a Gentleman, remember?"

"Where to?" The pilot asked again.

"Head for the smoke," Brandy replied, pointing off in the general direction.

Back on the ground in the crater, Adack, the goatheaded alien in a fancy pirate coat, is coughing up blood as he manages to slide a manhole cover off of his body. "ARGG! What you say tharr? How about getting me some medical attention?"

Major Otis hastily comes over and trains his sidearm on Adack's head. The muscles in his hand are flexing, trigger finger itching to pull the trigger. "You're the one responsible for all of this. Why shouldn't I just shoot you and let Dr. Cooly dissect you in the lab?"

"Let's make a deal." Adack was getting desperate, he could sense the anger in the human.

"A deal? Why should I? You have nothing to bargain with." Henry was becoming agitated with his prisoners. He knew he should hold them but he was dearly tempted to shoot them.

"I have advanced alien technology," Adack offered.

"Correction, we have your advanced alien technology."

"AY! But most of it is scattered all over this here crater. You don't know how to make em work do yah?"

"We can figure them out," the Major replied.

"Ay maybe, but my boyO MaCos tharr can fix anything. I wager he can even bring that tharr Marshal back to life for yah," Adack countered seeing a faint glint of hope.

"Is that true?" The major asked as he backed away and lowered his gun.

MaCos Ex, the multijointed pigfaced alien engineer looked to his leader for direction. "Go ahead and tell em. Call it a show of good will," Adack said encouraging him to talk.

"It is possible. The Marshal uniform may be able to regenerate his body," MaCos hesitantly said.

"But it was destroyed with him," Major Otis said, both intrigued and suspicious.

"Yes, but you have a working copy or was that just a cheap primitive copy Dauntless was wearing?" MaCos asked.

"Then I guess we really don't need you do we?" The Major said once again turning his attention to Adack.

"But my boy MaCos tharr won't help you without his dear old Captain, will he?"

Major Otis, seeing a chance to employ an old military adage to divide and conquer replied, "MaCos, we can make a deal but not with Adack. He's going back into the freezer.

Looking back and forth MaCos answered, "I think we can come up with some sort of arrangement."

After thinking about the events of that day for a few seconds, Heather poured herself a drink of water from the pitcher that was on the table near her, and went on to explain about what had happened on that most eventful day. She did not make any speculations about Major Otis and the deal he made with the aliens or make any accusations. She just recounted the facts as best she knew them. After finishing, she turned to see General Solo in the audience. He gave her a nod of approval as the chairman spoke. "So, Major Otis took it on to himself to make deals with enemy aliens?

"I was not, and am not, privy to the details of the arrangements made with MaCos Ex," she replied defensively. "And I don't know who, if anyone, authorized it. But it seems to have been a good idea, judging by how things turned out," she added.

Mr. Morvan looked back and forth at the other members of the committee before dismissing her saying, "Thank you Agent Carter, your testimony has been very enlightening. This committee stands adjourned for today." He tapped the counter with a gavel and everyone stood up and started to go. General Solo came over to her saying, "you did a good job."

One month later in deep dark space outside the solar system, a three engined cruiser glides over a frozen rogue planet. Our sun appears as only another very bright star. On the bridge of a starship, five small blue-gray aliens sit at control consoles arranged in a semi-circle with their backs turned to the captain seated above and behind them.

The screen in front of the ship's Sensor Officer is alive with various displays, and a steady flow of information. The data continues to stream in and then suddenly jumps for a second. The screen flickers and returns to normal. He adjusts some controls and studies the results. He scratches his chin. The small thin alien turns away from his control console and excitedly addresses his captain. "Captain, I have just detected an anti-matter burst."

An even smaller gray female with a head three times too big for her body answers him. "So, what's so important about it?"

He nervously responds, "it's coming from a primitive planet in the next solar system. They shouldn't have anti-matter yet."

The Captain ponders this for a second. "How far to this planet?"

The Sensor and Nav officers confer briefly before the Navigator reports. "One cycle at 30LSV."

"Are you sure about this planet?" She asks.

The Navigator checks his commputer display again and answers, "yes Captain. It's definitely a primitive planet; in fact, it's a protected one. Planet 1981 is a primitive paradise with a dangerous primitive culture rated at

5.2 on the Harvo techno rating, heavy industry and nuclear power but no space travel."

"Hmm, 1981?" The captain paused before continuing. It could be a distress call or maybe a research ship has gotten itself in trouble. Mr. Yoso, it looks like we're going to Earth. Helm, set a course. 30LSV if you please. Mr. Der, prepare a briefing. I'm going to get some sleep. Yoso, you have the Comm." She gets up and starts to leave.

The Sensor officer stops her to ask, "Captain, how did you know it was Earth?"

She stops and gives him a puzzled look before answering, "don't tell me you've never heard of Earth?"

"Of course I've heard of Earth, but we don't have clearance to go there."

"Kram, we're not going there, we are just going to check out the anti-matter explosion. If they have developed anti-matter technology, the no contact rule may be lifted. And that would mean a lot of credits to be made."

The next day, the alien starship is in orbit 400 miles above the Earth. Kram reports to his captain, "there are no distress calls but there is an alarming amount of low frequency radio traffic from the humans. They seem to be filling their airwaves with pointless chatter."

Der adds, "there are no unaccounted for or missing vessels."

"If no one is missing, it must have been the humans. They must be getting close to anti-matter technology," the captain said as she turned to Yoso. "Nothing to report, enter it in the daily log to be sent off. We'll send a packet once we're clear of this solar system." She then turned her attention to the Helmsmen. "Get us back on course, 60LSV once we're out of the solar system, and the packet is launched."

The ship effortlessly turns away from the Earth below. The three hyper drive engines glow dimly and the Earth falls away.

The cruiser glides majestically past the asteroid belt and the gas giant and on out of the solar system. Small breaking engines come to life for a couple seconds and the ship stops and remains motionless. A silver tube is lowered below the ship, between it's two lower engines. An orange ball of electrical energy starts to form under the ship between the engines. The ball grows bigger and lightning bolts start to arch off of it. There is a flash, and an orange streak is seen leading away from the ship. "Packet's away!"

CHAPTER TWO

DAUNTLESS TO THE RESCUE

Six months later, a sleek shiny commuter helicopter glides along the Chicago skyline. Below, the rebuilt lakefront towers sparkle in the morning sun. Inside the well-appointed bird is Major Otis in his class A uniform and half a dozen dignitaries from the UN. The Major directs their attention out the right windows. "As you can see, most of the damage has been repaired. The Zeta radiation from the anti-matter explosion only had a 15 second half life so there was no contamination problems to deal with, only the fire and blast damage."

A Chinese gentleman interrupts, speaking with only a slight accent, "I heard that there was a citywide failure of all electronics."

"That was mostly limited to the lakefront. The tall buildings shielded the rest of the city from most of the effects of the blast," the Major explained, and then went on saying, "everything with a commputer chip that was exposed to the radiation was fried and has had to be replaced. That's about 40,000 cars and uncounted electronics. The damage was in the billions."

"Just how many casualties were there?" The delegate from Brazil asked.

Otis paused before answering. "From the first impact when the UFO crashed, there were about 12,000 killed and another 25,000 hurt. The anti-matter blast killed another 27,000 with an additional 100,000 injured."

"Why so many? America is an advanced nation. I heard Dauntless was on the scene to save many people," asked the man from Japan.

"She did," Otis answered defensively, adding, "but she could only do so much. Most of the casualties were in moving cars when the blast hit. Their cars were thrown about and caught fire. Many more were hurt by flying glass and the fire department couldn't get in to help them because everything was clogged up with wrecked cars and burning cars. It was a nightmare."

"Then you were there," he said as his thoughts went back to the Hiroshima survivor he had met as a Government official.

"Yes. I was in the crater at the time."

"I thought we were going to meet Dauntless," Mr. Lee from China said.

"She has been called away. You know, a hero's work is never done. But she will be joining us later, I can assure you of that," the old soldier said, trying to lighten up the mood.

"What about Marshal?" Lee asked.

"Yes, you'll be meeting with him as well."

Lee continued to press the soldier for more information. "How is this possible? I heard he was killed, surely American medicine isn't that advanced?"

"He was, but now he's better. I can't explain it, I don't know the technical end. I'm sure Dr. Cooly will be happy to explain it all to you when we meet her later. Just don't expect too much out of him, he's still convalescing and his memory hasn't returned yet."

"What about the alien technology?" Lee's question piqued everyone's interest.

"You'll be seeing it at Ground Zero and at HERO HQ."

"How far is it from Ground Zero to where the anti-mater blast went off?" The man from Ireland asked in his high-pitched voice.

"Marshal tossed the bomb a distance of nearly eight miles." This was a line of questioning the Major was commfortable with.

McGee sat back in his seat. "Amazing."

The room was dark, very dark and quiet. PING! "Planet fall, we will be docking at Halla station in three kilocycles. Announcing planet fall, we will be docking at Halla station in three kilocycles. All passengers going below should have their travel documents ready before reaching the gate." The announcement stopped and the muffled sounds of a cruise ship could be heard in the darkened cabin.

A deep disembodied voice broke the quiet darkness of the room. "Huh? I told the Steward to call us when we had 200 kilocycles."

A female voice answered back, "he did, I sent him away."

"WHAT! This is my stop! Lights on!" The small cabin slowly light up. A hulking blue skinned alien with black hair sat up in bed. The smaller silver female that had been sleeping on top of him was sent tumbling over in the bed. As he got up, the bed linen fell away exposing his muscular body in all its glory. He was in the au naturel, all 6'8" of him. He looked as though he weighed 400 lb, but he actually tipped the scales at 650lb of solid muscle. "I just have time for a quick exposure."

The girl in bed rolled over onto her elbow asking, "What's the rush? The ship will be in dock for a full cycle."

Marshal explained as he dashed into the washroom, "I am expected to report at the constabulary Headquarters when I arrive." A few seconds later, she joined him in the sonic shower. His body was already tingling all over from the effects of the sonic waves. She startled him, causing him to jump at her first touch. "What are you doing in here?"

She started to caress him cooing, "I thought that much was obvious."

He grabs her by both arms and picks her up and carries her into the cabin room. Setting her down on the bed, he quickly turns and takes his shiny black belt from the dresser. He takes a pill out of one of the many pouches on it and hands it to her telling her to take it.

She holds the pill in the palm of her long thin hand and asks, "what is it for?"

"It will counter out the effects of my pheromones. You are obviously under the influence. I don't have time for this," he said as he returned to the washroom.

She sat there looking at the pill. Finally, with a sly little smile on her face, she shrugged her shoulders and tossed the pill over her shoulder. She looked at the belt on the dresser. There was a massive hand gun in the holster. She shook her head in the negative and jumped up to join him again.

White clouds swirl about a tan planet as Halla station orbits high above. There are several small vessels of different designs docked at the station. A shuttle comes up from the planet's surface as the large liner silently pulls up along side the station. The multi-decked liner comes to a commplete stop only a few meters from a gate. The gate unfolds and docks with the giant ship.

Welcome music plays as the passengers and their luggage make their way down the concourse. There are many different types of aliens, some exotic types like the feathered Horons and scaly lizard men from Reptillicus 6. Most of the passengers are Grays, either tall or short. Some even looked human.

There is a short delay in the terminal as the passengers make their way through immigration and customs. Medium sized Grays in green uniforms are checking everyone's travel documents as the newly arrived passengers and their luggage pass through the scanning tunnel.

Off to the side stand a group of five larger Grays, anxiously watching the throng of beings coming and going. They are a mixed group, with two having large almond shaped eyes and one with an oversized head, all wearing tight high collar coats, black belts with blue pants, and red capes; the uniform of a Federation Constabulary Officer.

The almond-eyed female looks around and asks, "where is he?"

"Shuttle for Government House departing from the blue gate," was announced overhead.

The intrepid group of peace officers turned and struggled to shoulder their duffel bags that were nearly as big as they were. As they made their way to the blue gate one of them was heard to say, "we can't wait for him."

Back in the windowless cabin, the silver girl is all curled up on the bed. She looks deeply satisfied. The door chime sounds and she leaps up from the bed. *He's come back!* She thought as she rushed to the door.

Outside the door in the passageway stands a red skinned female, she looks more than a little devilish with her pointed ears and upturned eyebrows. She wore the black jumper uniform of the ship's crew, with a cleaning apron over it. She was readying her cleaning cart when the door slides open. Both girls were surprised by the other. They just stood there looking at each other. The maid waved the cleaning supplies in her hand at the enthusiastic passenger as she started to explain. "Housekeeping." Two silver hands reached out snatching hold of the cleaning girl by her arms and jerked her into the room. The door closed behind her.

There they were, nose to nose, with the cleaning girl looking a bit apprehensive. "You'll have to do," the silver said with a hopeful tone in her voice.

The maid started to protest, but silver would have none of it. Cleaning supplies flew into the air as the maid was whisked over to the bed.

About half an hour later the shuttles from the green gate came in for a landing on Vail. As the shuttle comes to a stop, three ground crewmen rush out to attend to the vessel. The hatch opens, and the passengers file out one at a time. Some are fumbling with luggage and others with small children with them.

Marshal, now wearing his uniform, towers three or four feet above the other passengers. He walks over to the ground crew unloading the luggage. The uniform of a Federation Marshal, with its white coat and high collar and distinctive chest flap going down the right side, and badge with red glider cape, grants him permission to go where he pleases. He picks his duffel bag up out of the pile. Tossing it over his shoulder, he makes his way out with the others.

Marshal makes his way across the busy steel and glass spaceport. Once outside, he is met by one of the redcaps who asks, "Can I get you a sedan off…" He stopped mid sentence when he spotted the Marshal badge on his uniform. "Sorry, can I get you a sedan Marshal?"

Marshal hesitated before answering. "Sorry no, I'm working with limited funds. Can you direct me to the Constabulary Headquarters?"

The redcap chuckled to himself and pointed at a stone and steel building towering 40 stories above the rest of the city. "You're going to Government House. That's it over there. Can't miss it."

Seeing the building was less than two klicks away and that he had virtually no money left, he decided to walk. *He was already late, what difference would it make? Besides, it would give him a chance to see his new duty assignment,* he thought.

With his duffel bag on his shoulder, he started to make his way through the busy streets of the city. The smaller residents gave him a wide berth as he walked among them.

The street was awash with activity with people coming and going. Most of the locals were Grays, but there were a few exotic types as well, but none were as big as Marshal. There were many different vehicles on the street, mostly sliders, but there were a few carts from the outlying region that were drawn by Dramms, a kind of cross between a camel and a yak.

The older buildings were of the adobe style seen all over the universe, but there were newer prefabricated ones of steel and plastic and glass as well. Rounding a corner, the street was lined with sidewalk cafés all covered with awnings to protect the patrons from the intense sun that beat down. As he walked he thought, *perhaps I should have taken a sedan Oh well, it's too late now.*

As he walked on, Marshal was noticed by two old Grays sitting at the corner café. "Did you see the size of that one?" The first one said.

"They're getting bigger and bigger all the time," his companion quipped.

"Must be something in the water."

Marshal walked on up the hill. A tall (5 foot) green bean of a child came running out of the restaurant on the corner, with a Gray waiter in pursuit. Marshal reached out his left arm, his only free hand, as he was carrying his duffel bag on his shoulder with his right. He caught the fleeing child by his arm as he passed. The child suddenly came to a halt and his feet swung skyward, but he did not fall. Marshal had hold of him. The child, actually a teenager protested, "Hey, let go of me!"

When the green bean finally realized what had hold of him, his eyes opened wide and he turned a paler shade of green. He was not accustomed to anyone being that much taller than him, let alone a Marshal. Marshal was nearly two feet taller and a good five hundred pounds heavier than he was. The giant blue roadblock asked, "what is going on here?"

A few seconds later the out of breath Gray arrived saying, "he and his friends skipped out without paying their bill!"

"Do you have the credits to pay for you and your friends?" Marshal asked as he gave the boy's arm a little squeeze.

"YEOOW! Yes!" The boy winced in pain.

"Then pay the man and don't do it again," Marshal sternly commanded as he let go of his arm.

"My arm!" The juvenile commmplained rubbing his throbbing limb.

"Let that be a lesson to you." Marshal admonished.

They all made their way into the restaurant as the two old Grays looked on. "Is that what they mean by the long arm of the law?" They both laughed, and settled back into their leisurely pastime of watching the world go by.

A minute or so later their dull gray eyes widened noticeably as the world came to them. The silver girl stood before them, she was looking about, looking for something, or someone. She was wearing a flowing silk dress of many colors. It was held up by a pendent and necklace around her thin neck. The sun was glinting off of her bare arms and shoulders. She spoke. "Have either of you seen a big blue Federation Marshal around here?"

"Big blue Federation Marshal? Was he as big as a Dramm?" The first one mused with a twinkle in his eye.

"Nearly," she replied, with her hands on her hips.

"He just went in Swaygos on the corner," he said as he motioned to the corner restaurant.

She thanked them and made her way up the street. As she walked away the two old men looked at each other and back at her exposed back. "Say! She's one of those Gammons. You know what they say about them don't you?"

"They're supposed to be the best," Edgar, the second one replied, as he shot a knowing glance at his companion.

"That's not all they say Edgar."

After giving it some thought Edgar added, "she must be part of the new floorshow at the casino."

"What makes you say that?"

"Just look at the way she moves, it's practically immoral!"

"Just how old are you anyway?" Choncy asked his lifelong friend Edgar. They looked at each other without saying another word. Looking back at the girl who was out of sight, lost in the crowd. They drank their tea.

In the restaurant, Marshal is standing at the corner of the bar with the owner trying to talk him into something. "I really shouldn't, I have no credits and I have to be going," Marshal protested, adding, "we're not supposed to accept gifts."

"Think nothing of it. It's your first day here. It's not a gift! The first drink for the law is always free here at Swaygos," the owner insisted.

"Well if you insist, I'll have a cold tea." Marshal relented.

The girl from Gammon stepped in the door, stopped and put her hands on her hips, fixing her gaze on Marshal. He turned as he took a sip of tea and spotted her. He tapped the badge on his chest and began to speak. "Federation Marshal in Swaygos in need of backup."

She sashays up to him and everything gets blurry. The voice of General Solo comes booming in. "Doctor Cooly! Can you hear me? Take that thing off!"

Doctor Beverly Cooly, a buxom beauty with auburn hair and a passion for oversized belt buckles removes the helmet she was wearing. It is an alien helmet with an amber visor. She fumbles about for a second and then puts the helmet down on the desk in front of her. She is in the laboratory at HERO HQ. General John Solo, a two star General in the Army, stands before her in his class A uniform with all of his ribbons and badges on. He is not happy. She picks up on this and struggles to find the words to explain." I was using the helmet trying to find anything that might help Marshal with his memory loss. And I think I may have found something," she said with a hopeful tone in her voice.

He was not impressed. "This is not the time to be doing that. The delegation from the UN is on their way. And I would rather not share the fact that we have an alien device that allows us to see what they have experienced."

"But General, think of it as a learning tool," she implored.

"Yes, I do. And I want us to be doing the learning. Is that understood?" The General shot her a look.

"Yes General." She stood up and placed the helmet back in its container.

"Then put it away until they're gone. Major Otis and Heather are at Ground Zero with the UN people. They will be here soon." He turned to go.

"I thought Dauntless was going to meet them," she said as she handed the case containing the helmet to a soldier that had just stepped up.

"She was, but she was called away. Something about a fire," the old soldier answered as he left.

She put her glasses back on and saw her reflection in a darkened commputer screen. "Oh, my hair's a mess." She started to work on it.

A sleek helicopter circles just South of Midway airport. Below is a construction sight spanning nine-city blocks, surrounded by rows of demolished homes. The helicopter is carrying the UN delegation. Inside, Major Otis directs their attention out the windows on the right side of the cabin. "Below us is the UFO crash sight. All of the ground in the crater was melted by the intense heat and turned into glass and covered everything with a thin layer of glass."

At the center of the crater below them, construction crews are busy at work putting up a building, as armed Air Force Guards look on from the perimeter. The Major calls their attention to this. "That is where the UFO is. We couldn't move it so we decided to build the research center on top of it. As you can see, work is still going on."

The Chinese delegate asked, "that is all very interesting Major, but will we be able to actually see any of the UFO?"

"Yes Mr. Lee. You will be able to see and touch the alien equipment."

Mr. McGee asked, "do you mean to tell us that Marshal threw the anti-matter bomb all the way from here to the lake?"

"That's right Mr. McGee, with the use of a bent tank gun barrel he tossed the bomb from the center of the crater over those buildings to the East and into the lake where it exploded just under the surface. I saw him do it."

"Remarkable! This Marshal of yours must be one truly remarkable individual."

"Indeed he is," the Major agreed with the man from Ireland.

"But that's just the point I wish to make. This Marshal is not yours. All of us should have free and untethered access to him and the alien technology." Mr. Lee was anxious to make his point.

Major Otis started to answer but paused to think his reply over. Before he answered the pilot interrupted saying, "prepare for landing please, fasten your seat belts."

"Mr. Lee, I am just a simple soldier. It is up to the government to decide what to do with the technology. As for Marshal, he is not our prisoner. He is still receiving medical treatment, and when he has recovered it will be up to him to deside where he goes." Having said that, the good soldier fastened his seatbelt.

At that time several miles to the North not far from the HERO headquarters, smoke billows from a tall apartment building. A news chopper circles the scene as an Army Blackhawk helicopter joins them, cincling above the fray. Dauntless stands inside with the side door open surveying the scene. Smoke is blocking her view.

"Are you sure the General approved this trip Lieutenant?" Buster the Pilot asks.

"How many times do I have to tell you to call me Dauntless when I'm in this uniform?" She asks as she holds on to the doorframe while they go around.

"Sorry, but you didn't answer the question." He pressed her for an answer.

"Major Otis said I could take the chopper," she answered, leaving out that he said it over a month ago.

"Are you sure you're not just trying to get out of dealing with all those suits and brass hats?"

"Would I do something like that?" She answered as she hung out the door straining to get a better look at the situation below. "Don't answer that!" She barked before he had a chance.

As they fly around she sees there are indeed families on the top two floors trapped by the smoke and flames. "Look! There's people waving at the windows trying to signal for help. Buster, there's people down there. The Fire Department can't get up that high. This looks like a job for a superhero!" You could hear the excitement in her voice. She didn't want to be the Earth's first superhero. She had planned on being the city's first female detective, but a quirk of fate had changed all of that. She really didn't care for all the superhero hype but she did like being able to help people. And this was something she could do.

"Do you have anyone in mind?" Buster joked back.

"Get me on the roof," she ordered as she prepared herself to jump.

Looking down, the pilot could see all manner of things on the roof, big things like AC vents and smaller stuff like TV antennas and dishes, barbeque grills and patio furniture. "There's too much stuff! I can't land."

"Just get me close and be ready to drop us a basket." She turns to the crew chief and gives him the thumbs up sign. He nods to her.

"Are you going to do what I think you're going to do?" Buster wanted to know.

"I've done it before. This'll be easy. The building isn't even moving," she said with just a hint of false bravado.

"Here we go again!" The crew chief shouted.

The chopper comes in and hovers above the burning building. The downdraft from the choppers rotors pummels the rooftop. The young lady, known to the world as Dauntless, jumps out of the helicopter and lands on the roof. She falls 20 feet and bounces back to her feet and looks around. The roof is not burning, but smoke is coming up in cracks. She makes her way over to the door. Before she opens it she realizes that it is hot. Can't go that way. She taps the badge on her chest and tells the chopper, "I can't go in that way. The stairwell is on fire. I'll have to find another way."

She looks around trying to find anything to use. She finds a pair of barbeque tongs and ponders them for a few seconds before tossing them away. "Oh this is useless! Time to get physical!" She goes around stomping her foot on the roof looking for a weak spot. Finding one, she begins to stomp on it until she breaks a hole in it. Then she kneels down and delivers several hammer fist blows widening the hole. Finally she just rips out a chunk of the roof.

She drops down through the hole and finds the apartment full of smoke. It's hard to see or breathe. She takes a small device out of her utility belt and puts the rebreather in her mouth. Moving on, she finds a family of three trapped by the fire. The carpet on the floor between them and her is burning wildly. The father is trying to beat back the flames with the curtain from the window behind them.

She goes over to the sink in the kitchen and turns on the water. "Oh, this is hopeless!" She returns to the family. It's really getting hot. She has to back away from the flames. Looking around she realizes that it's the carpet and furniture that are burning.

She goes over to a doorway where the carpet stops. She tries to get hold of the edge of the carpet but can't. She smashes her fist through the floor and gets hold of the carpet and rips it up and away from the family with a mighty heave, sending furniture and flames flying.

The family comes running and they all make their way back away from the fire to the room where she smashed a hole in the ceiling. "How do we get out?" The father asks.

"Uh.." this stumped her at first, and then it came to her. She spit out her rebreather to talk. "Ill lift you up through the hole and.."

"ME, NO! They go first!" He insisted.

"No, they can't make it without help. They need you up there helping pull them up when I lift them up. You have to go first, they're not strong enough".

"Okay," he agrees and she virtually tosses him up through the open hole in the ceiling. Working quickly, she passes the mother and daughter up to the waiting arms of the father. "What now?"

"I'll call the chopper. They'll let down a basket for you." Having made the call she returns to the burning apartment. *The fire is getting more intense every minute. And there' another family trapped below, but how to get to them?*

She tries the door out but the hallway is commpletely blocked by flames. "Well, I guess I know what that means," she said to no one in particular. She knelt down and started battering the floor with her fist. Eventually, she made a hole and was immediately met by smoke and flames from below. "I'll have to try elsewhere," she said as she backed away.

She made her way over to where the first family had been trapped. It wasn't easy; she had to jump over some flames. She smashes through the floor as before only this time, she finds a woman and her son terrified and looking up at her through the hole in the ceiling. As Dauntless enlarges the hole in the floor, the walls of the room she is in collapse and the entire room becomes involved with the fire. She jumps down just in time to avoid being hit by falling burning timbers.

"Thank God you came for us!" The woman said as she held her seven-year-old son.

"We're not out of it yet," Dauntless said as she looked around for a way out. Seeing nothing but walls of flame in every direction she picks up the couch and tosses it out and through the window, making it much wider. "There! That's our exit." She uses her badge to call the chopper, only to hear.

"Sorry Dauntless, we're still picking up the family on the roof. They're having trouble with the basket."

"Hurry up! We don't have much time down here."

Buster, hearing the concern in her voice, called back. "I'll be with you ASAP. And the next time you throw something out of a twenty-story window you might want to give those down below a heads up. You nearly brained a couple of them."

"Roger that! Have you got an ETA on the evac?" She said looking down out the hole in the wall she had just made. "Man! It's a long way down." The wall collapsed, bringing the fire even closer to them. The mother and child drew closer to one another. "HEY BUSTER, we really need that evac!"

"I'm working on it." She looked up and saw the chopper trying to lower the basket, but the flames had reached the roof and were forcing the chopper back. The chopper climbed up to avoid the flames, but the hot air off the fire was causing some serious updrafts and the basket was just dancing around at the end of the line.

Buster tried to get the basket to swing into them but Dauntless couldn't reach it. The rope got tangled on some of the debris hanging over the edge of the roof and it caught fire. The line broke as the chopper tried to free it.

"What are we going to do now?" The little boy asked.

"Don't worry, I'm going to get us out of this," Dauntless said, trying to sound confident. The problem was, she didn't know how she as going to do it.

"Can't you fly us out?" The mother asked.

"No, I don't have Marshals.. Yes I can! Sort of!" She activated her comm link. "Buster, get that great big bird of yours down here where I can see it! Hurry!"

Dauntless got her grappling hook and launcher out of her utility belt and readied it, wrapping the lanyard around her wrist. Turning to the mother she said, "put your hands around my neck and hold on as tight as you can." She then picked up the small boy in her left arm. "Hold on!"

Seconds later, the Blackhawk helicopter was hovering outside the hole twenty yards out. Dauntless pointed her launcher at the bird and fired. It went POOF and the hook sailed out, trailing a thin line behind it. The hook slammed into the soft skin of the chopper and stuck. She looks the mother square in the eye and says, "here goes nothing."

"WOOO NO!!!" Dauntless leapt out of the burning building and swung out under the helicopter. As they swung back and forth, the mother started to lose her grip and Dauntless wrapped her legs around her. There they hung safe, more or less out of the fire. Safe just as long as Brandy could hold on with just one hand while holding the boy in one arm while he was kicking and screaming and holding the mother with her legs.

The crew chief stuck his head out the door and saw Dauntless and friends hanging on by a thread. He encouraged the pilot to speed up their descent. Hold on she did, and the chopper let them down in the nearby park. After landing, the crew chief came over and told Dauntless that she was one lucky girl.

"Lucky? What makes you say that?" She wanted to know.

"Because, your hook was stuck on the door, and nothing was holding the door open on the tracks. It could have fallen off or closed and cut your line at any time."

She shook her head. "What can I say? Someone up there must like me," she said with a chuckle as she walked away.

CHAPTER THREE

THE UN VISIT

Meanwhile, at the Ground Zero construction sight, Pete Lewis, a tall, thin 20 year old with long oily blond hair and a poor excuse for a mustache infesting his upper lip, looks down from the air duct he is working on, and catches a glimpse of what looks like an alien to him. So he crawls further in and gets an eyeful.

His foreman had called all of the HVAC guys out a few minutes ago. In fact, all of the workmen had been called out. Why he had stayed, he didn't know. Maybe he just wanted to finish up what he was working on or maybe it was too much of a bother to keep quitting work whenever some soldier boy said to. There was too much hurry up and wait to suit him, for whatever the reason.

Below him is the central core of the UFO. A 25-foot metal disk with three rows of twelve hatches each. MaCos Ex, the pig faced multijointed alien working with the Army, walks up to a PC that is connected to the core. MaCos is wearing military fatigues and is escorted by two armed soldiers. Pete sees MaCos work the PC and one of the hatches pops open. Out slides a sarcophagus. The lid opens revealing a second lid inside, this one made of curved glass. Inside the sarcophagus is a sleeping or dead alien.

MaCos walks over to the sarcophagus and works the controls. The hiss of a vacuum seal being broken can be heard and MaCos opens the second lid. He removes something from the orange jumpsuit the alien is wearing and hands it to one of the soldiers and closes the lid. They close the outer lid and slide the sarcophagus back in the core and leave without detecting Peter's presence. That was about to change.

"HEY YOU!" An armed airman shouted at him. "What are you doing there?"

"Just trying to get out. I'm in a bit of a tight space," he called out.

The airman stopped him as he came down and asked to see his ID. Pete showed him his ID and security pass. "You were supposed to be out of here five minutes ago."

"Sorry, like I said, I was stuck in a tight place. It took me all that time to get out. I didn't see anything." *Oops!* Pete thought he had given himself away. But the airman didn't pick up on it.

Pete walks over to where the other workmen are gathered and takes a seat on a pile of sheet metal. The sleek helicopter carrying the party from the UN passes overhead and lands about 100 yards away on a temporary heli pad.

Major Otis is the first to get out followed by the six delegates. Mayor Weekly and the Vice President and other VIPs are there to greet them, including General Solo. The politicians make a few brief statements pledging mutual respect and access to the alien technology as it becomes available.

After the opening statements, General Solo introduced Heather to the delegates. "Hello gentlemen, my name is Heather Carter, I am Dr. Coolys assistant. Dauntless was supposed to be her to conduct the tour of Ground Zero and the holding facility. But she has been called away and is expected to return any minute now. I'll be conducting the tour in her absence."

"Will we be meeting with Dr. Cooly?" Mr. Hon Soo the man from Japan asked.

"Yes, at HERO HQ," Heather replied as they walked towards the construction site.

"You are the one that had sex with Marshal. I heard you were pregnant with his alien child,' Mr. Lee said, in an accusing sort of way.

This statement caught Heather by surprise and she stopped dead in her tracks and was almost run over by the small entourage. "I don't know where you heard that, but I can assure you that I am not carrying anyone's child." She directed them to look at her flat abdomen. *I wonder how they heard that?* This puzzled her but she didn't want it to show so she just kept on talking, something she was good at.

She led the small party into the construction zone past the bare girders and pointed out the UFO's core to them. "As you can see, the site is still under construction. The UFO remains are in the middle of the construction site. The core of the UFO is intact and there are 36 working cryo beds."

"So, you have 36 aliens," Lee asked?

"No, not all of the beds were occupied. And some of the aliens were killed," she said as she stopped before the core. She gestured to one of the hatches as she spoke.

"Just how many do you have?" Again, Mr. Lee was questioning her.

"I'm not sure we know exactly how many aliens we have here," she smirked and paused before continuing. "You see, we haven't been able to open all of the beds. Dr. Cooly might be able to answer that when you see her."

"Where are the aliens?" One of the African delegates asked.

"They are being held here in cryo," she replied.

"All of them?" Mr. Lee inquired.

"No not all," she paused. "Marshal is at the medical unit at HQ, you'll have a chance to meet him later."

"How is it that this Marshal is still alive?" Mr. Lee again asked.

As the question and answer session continued, not far away two Men In Black were observing the proceedings. "Just why are we here? They're going public with all of this?" Agent Bee asked.

His equally non descript friend Mr. Tee replied after giving it some thought, "these are still aliens and it is our job to protect the planet from any alien threat. Besides we have more experience dealing with aliens than anyone else."

Bee gives a nod of agreement. "This is just a side show, want to go for coffee?"

"Sounds good to me but it's your turn to buy." As they turn to go Tee notices, "Look who just got here." He points out Dauntless coming in the back way.

There is a minor commotion when Dauntless joins the party in her smoke soiled uniform. "Sorry I'm late. There was a fire and well, I guess you can figure out the rest."

"I was about to open one of the cryo beds for them to see," Heather chimed in.

"Go right ahead, don't let me slow you down," Dauntless replied as she backed away, being uneasy with all of the attention being cast upon her. She greeted the mayor as she joined the group.

Heather used the PC to open one of the hatches, the sarcophagus slid out as before. The lid popped open with a hum exposing the inner lid which was frosted over. She moved over to it and wiped the frost off with her hand. Inside was an alien in a tuxedo. "I'm not going to open this one because he has the ability to read minds and even take control over you. But if you look close you can see Mogo's third eye."

"Why is this one wearing a tux?" Mr. McGee asked.

"That is what he was wearing at the time we captured him. You may remember, he was the leader of the escaped aliens," Heather said as she stepped back to allow all of the dignitaries a better look at our unearthly visitor.

This did not satisfy Mr., Lee who posed the next question, "I understood that they had some sort of universal translator but his seems to be missing."

"You are right Mr. Lee. His has been removed. We are trying to use it to communicate better with Marshal. His communicator was destroyed when he was killed," Heather offered in explanation. The dignitaries looked confused. Heather thought it might be a language problem so she tried to explain again. "When Marshal was killed his translator was destroyed. But now he is alive and we are trying to use Mogo's translator to communicate with him."

As the others huddled around the cryo bed asking their pointless questions, Mr. Lee cornered Dauntless and asked her, "Just how strong are you?"

"I can lift a car."

"Full size or commpact?" The Chinaman was most persistent.

"It depends." She smirked.

"Is this the actual uniform or merely a copy for show?" He asked as they walked away from the core.

"It's the real thing," she reassured him. "It's all dirty because I just came from a fire. It will be on the news."

"Was it difficult to make?" His questions didn't stop.

"I couldn't say, I had nothing to do with it. We tried to make me a uniform at first but that didn't work out very well, then they figured out how to use Marshal's old uniform to make more of the material. That was before it was destroyed." She explained as they walked past other pieces of shattered alien technology on display.

"So, you have more of it. How does it feel?"

"Mr. Lee, you're a curious fellow, so full of questions. It's like satin except for the collar and cuffs, which are stiffer. I think Dr. Cooly has some to show you later."

After commpleting their tour, the party was led back to the helicopter for the trip to HERO HQ. As the chopper lifted off, the various foremen barked orders to their work crews to get back to work. "We're behind schedule!"

Two helicopters fly across town, a sleek commuter job with the UN people in it, and a second Army UH1 Huey with the rest of the party. Just inland past the park and Lake Shore Drive a few blocks in, just on the other side of the EL tracks, are several ten-story buildings. Off to the side is a T-shaped building with wings going to the North, South and West. There are flashing lights on top and three heli pads. They both put down on top of this eleven-story building in the middle of the Truman University campus on the city's far North side. They deplane and are met by Dr. Cooly who quickly escorts part of them out of the rotor wash from the choppers and into the elevator.

The Vice-President and General Solo and some of the UN delegates are left waiting for the elevator to return. The VP motions to a sign over the elevator doors saying, "so, the H in HERO actually stands for hero." The General was quick to agree. The sign read, WELCOME to Heroic Emergency Response Organization.

In the elevator, Mr. Lee works his way close to Dr. Cooly who is six inches taller than he is. "So, Dr. Cooly, you have brought this Marshal back to life. How did you do it? I must know, just how was this done?"

She looks down at him and her glasses slide down her nose. After adjusting her wayward spectacles she answered. "Well, uh Mr. Lee is it? It wasn't so much what I did but how we did it." This confused the man from China, so she went on to explain. "His uniform did it. It has restorative properties. All we did was put him in one. And he just grew back on his own."

"What have you learned about his internal organs? What is the source of his great strength?" Mr. Lee inquired.

"Uh, that's kind of an embarrassing issue. You see, we don't know much at all about him. When he was first brought in, we tried to X-ray him but found nothing. His flesh is too dense for normal X-rays machines. But we didn't know that at the time. Our X-rays showed nothing but a solid mass. That's why we started breaking him out of the glass that encased him. If we had known his organs were intact we might have dissected him before he awoke."

The elevator comes to a stop and they get out. As they make their way to operations, Mr. Lee pressed the good doctor with another question. "AH! But the uniform had been destroyed. So how could you use it to … as you say, regrow him?"

As they entered a conference room she turned to him. "Before it was destroyed, even before he had awoken from the crash, we had taken samples of the uniform. It wasn't easy, you see it repairs itself. We managed to cut a small swatch from it and it started to grow. Eventually, we had enough material to make a second uniform and that's the uniform we used to bring Marshal back to life. Are you satisfied Mr. Lee?" The auburn beauty was becoming annoyed with him.

In the hallway outside the conference room, General Solo pulls Dauntless aside, telling her "Lt. Holmes, go upstairs and bring Marshal down with you. But not before you get cleaned up." He was not pleased with his most junior officer.

"Yes sir, sorry sir," she replied as she turned to go.

The remaining part of the party filed into the conference room and took their seats at the great table. Beverly started to address them.

Brandy raced down the hall and ducked into the waiting elevator thinking to herself. *He's right, what was I thinking showing up like that? I know I wasn't thinking. That's not much of a defense.* As the elevator doors open, she rushes out and dashes down the hall to her room. Tee, the Man in Black, is sitting at the central desk and saw little more than a blur. WOOSH! "Morning Ted!"

"That's Tee," he corrected, as she rushed by, "morning Dauntless. In a hurry?" He replied to empty air.

She unbuckles her utility belt as she flies through the door to her quarters and tosses it on her bed. Next, the gloves came off. She was practically in the shower before she was able to undo her high collar and rip open the bib front of her jacket. One of her boots went flying, knocking a framed poster off of the opposite wall.

Two minutes later, Lt. Brandy Holmes was upstairs with wet hair and clean Army BDUs. (Battle Dress Uniform, the camouflage fatigues the soldiers wear.) *Being ten times faster than the average human does have its advantages.* She enters the medical wing and is met by Nurse Linda Chapel and the nearly seven foot tall blue mountain of rippling muscles known as Marshal. "I'm glad you're here, he's always happier when you're around," Nurse Chapel said.

He gets up when he sees her, smiling all over. "Come-on big guy, it's time to be going," she said as she patted him on the shoulder.

He turned to face her while he was trying to fasten his high collar. "Here, let me help you with that," she said as she reached up to fasten it.

As she touched Marshal's collar, he spoke. "Unable to locate sidearm and cape."

She snapped his collar and brushed off his broad shoulders. "You lost your cape and you gun is downstairs, you won't be needing it." She linked her arm with his. This brought a big smile to his face, and together, arm in arm, they walked down the hallway to the elevator.

Back in the conference room, a two inch scrap of silk-like material is being passed from delegate to delegate. "That is an actual piece of alien fabric. You'll notice that one side is white while the other is pink. The pink side is the inside of Marshals coat. It is covered with nanobots, tiny microscopic robots that sit dormant until activated. Then they go into action repairing anything they come in contact with," Dr. Cooly explained.

"Amazing! But how is this possible?" Mr. Hon Soo the man from Japan asked.

"We're not exactly sure what mechanism activates them, but they seem to read DNA when it comes to organic material and they simply copy inorganic material," the doctor said trying not to get too technical with them.

"So, what accounts for Dauntless' amazing strength?" Mr. Lee asked.

Dr. Cooly cleared her throat before answering. "Well, the nanobots in the jacket read and repair things. The jacket still had some of Marshal's DNA in it and she was in an unstable condition from the radiation burns when he put it on her. The cells that made up her body were badly damaged by the radiation and undergoing a state of mass mutation. We guess the nanos read both his and her DNA and made repairs that in this case turned out to be improvements."

Mr. Lee, being the last of the delegates to handle the cloth, holds it and asks, "so, this material can not only heal the wounds of anyone wearing a uniform made of it, but it can also repair and reproduce itself." When he was finished he sat back in his chair and dropped his hands by his sides.

At the back of the room, as Dr. Cooly answered him, Heather whispered to Major Otis, "did you see that? He put the sample in his pocket."

The soldier leaned over and whispered back to her, "it will do him no good."

"And earlier I thought I saw him put something under a table top. Could be a bug," she continued.

"Say, you are the sharp eyed one, aren't you." He smiled back at her.

"He's nothing more than a brazen Commie spy. I'd like to."

He SHUSHED her. "I'm on to him. Careful what you say. You might be heard," he cautioned.

"She flashed her bright eyes at him and whispered, "aren't you the sneaky one all of a sudden. Here I thought I was supposed to be the secret agent."

"Me, sneaky? I'm just a dumb grunt," he chuckled. They both quieted down when they noticed General Solo giving them the eye.

"We have a sample of the cloth for each of you to take with you. Uhh?" Beverly looked down and was confused by the absence of the sample, but quickly gathered her thoughts and moved on to the next bit of business. She motioned to a soldier in the background to come forward. He was carrying a tray and placed it on the table.

On the tray was a handgun different from anything they had seen before. The unearthly gun was bigger than any earthly handgun, and it was made of a ceramic material. Dr. Cooly motioned for them to pick it up, and of course, Mr. Lee was the first to heft the weapon. "It's heavy!"

"Yes it is. That surprised us at first, but when you stop to look at who was carrying it, a few pounds meant nothing," she smiled as she answered.

"What does it fire? Is it some kind of ray gun?"

"Ray gun? No, it fires a .75 caliber plasma bullet."

"How effective is it?"

"We don't know. The ammunition for it was destroyed when the UFO crashed. We have been trying to recreate it but we've had no luck so far."

"I bet you have," Mr. McGee commented. This drew a look from all of the people at the table. It was at that moment that Lt. Holms and Marshal arrived, still arm in arm. Marshal ducked to avoid bumping his head on the doorframe.

The room fell silent. The little Irishman at the end sensed that something had happened behind him. He turned around in his chair and looked up and up and still further up. Marshal was directly behind him, towering three feet above him. He sank deeper into his seat as Marshal held his hand up showing his empty palm in greetings. He said something in unintelligible alien gibberish and tapped his neck.

Brandy, standing next to him, reached up and pushed on the small silver diamond on his collar. "Just a second big guy, it's not working."

After a few more minor adjustments he tried again. "Greetings, I Marshal ZZT!"

They all looked around in confused amazement. Finally, Dr. Cooly explained. "Gentlemen please, we are experiencing difficulties with Marshal's translator. Please bear with us."

"Can he understand us?" Hon Soo asked.

They all looked to Dr. Cooly for an answer. She looked back at them and shrugged her shoulders. Then they all turned their attention to Marshal who looked back at them with a look that could only mean, what did I say? "I guess not," she ventured to guess.

"Why don't you fix it?", Lee inquired.

"You see, the problem is that we just don't know how it works. It works some of the time. All we really know is that it has to be in contact with him for it to work properly. And even then, this one is damaged and the translators from the other aliens don't seem to work either. It has us stumped," Dr. Cooly said trying to sound sincere.

"This is unacceptable! You promised us full access and you show us nothing but a piece of cloth and an empty gun. And now this! How do we even know he is really an alien and not just some kind of Hollywood trick?" Mr. Lee exploded.

The Vice-President stood up and addressed the group. "I can assure you that there has been no funny business, no substitutions made here. We're showing you what we've got. If you choose not to believe us, that's your loss."

Marshal menacingly walked over to Mr. Lee and opened the flap of his jacket, reaching in as if to pull something out of an internal pocket. He started to rummage around as if he was trying to find something that wasn't where it should be. Not finding whatever it was he was looking for, he held up his right palm exposing the bar code on it. He pointed to it saying, "Marshal."

"I guess he understood some of that," Beverly offered up as an explanation.

Brandy came over as Marshal tried to speak again and pressed her hand against his neck. "ZZT Jurisdiction ZZZT Federation constabulary ZZT!"

Brandy offered her take on the partial message, "I think he's trying to tell you that he is Marshal and something about being in his jurisdiction."

General Solo stepped in to calm the situation. "Gentlemen, you can see the immense difficulties we are facing here. We have the samples of the alien fabric for you that you can take with you. You can use them to grow more of the material yourselves or experiment on it, whatever you see fit. We're not trying to hide anything. We just don't have that much to share with you, that's all. You saw the size of the crater out there. You can imagine the size of the explosion and the damage it caused. It's a miracle we have anything."

Major Otis stepped up to the general's side and reminded him, "Sir, may I remind you of the award ceremony scheduled for this afternoon. It's almost time."

The General perked right up. "That's right gentlemen, it's almost time for the Vice-President to give Marshal his medal. Could you all please accommpany use to the courtyard for the ceremony?"

As they file out the door, Major Otis takes a sample of the alien fabric out of a heavily guarded case and hands it over to each of them. When the Chinese delegate steps up the Major has nothing for him. "It' seem you already have your sample," he said with a smile and slight chuckle. Mr. Lee stormed off in a huff.

After they left, Major Otis pulls Heather over to the side instructing her to, "go back and see if you can find anything Mr. Lee or any of the other delegates may have left behind."

"The nerve of that man! I'd like to kick him where the sun don't shine."

"But that wouldn't do any good. He'll just try something else, and being a diplomat and all, he'd just get away," Otis sighed.

"It's just frustrating," Heather lamented.

"Oh that wasn't so bad, it was probably just a distraction to draw our attention away from something else they're going to try," the soldier said trying to calm her.

"Do you really think so?" She inquired as she gave him a look.

"Maybe. Besides, it's not like they're the only ones trying to get access to the alien technology."

"Who else has tried?" This had piqued her interest.

He paused before answering, "let's see, there was the Japs and the Russians the Arabs and the Israelies."

"I can understand the Russians, but the others are supposed to be our friends," she said as she looked under the table where Lee had been seated.

"They're only our friends when it helps them," he said as he turned to one of the soldiers that had been guarding the case with the fabric samples in it. "Go get Sergeant Call and tell him that he and his squad are to sweep the entire HQ and the Ground Zero commmplex looking for bugs.

"Yes sir!", and the soldier was off.

Heather slid over to Major Otis and showed him a small button sized device she found under the table.

He took it and studied it for a few seconds. "Hmm, it's a mark 29. It's a Chinese copy of a Japanese bug. Short ranged, but able to penetrate some pretty thick walls. He dropped it into the pitcher of water that had been on the table.

"Ker plunk! That should take care of that." He smiled.

Heather gave him a close scrutiny. "You have idiot sticks (crossed muskets) on your collar but you know more about this sort of thing than any infantry officer would."

"Maybe that's because I was once an infantry officer and now I'm something else." He posed his response to her. "You're not the only one here with a secret, you're just from a different agency that's all."

"But now I'm all yours," she slyly smiled.

"That's a loaded statement if ever I heard one. Come on, we're going to miss it. You can check for bugs later."

They make their way outside to the courtyard, which has a small stage, podium, and seating for a couple hundred. Behind the small crowd is a small army of security personal and TV crews. As they make their way to the side of the stage, Otis spots a Man in Black and goes over to talk to him. "GEE, or whatever letter you are, I need a favor."

"I'm Dee."

"Of course you are. Listen, I need some of your MIB techs to sweep the HQ and Ground Zero site looking for bugs and anything else that doesn't belong. Can you do that for me?"

Dee nodded his head in agreement. "We're here to help. I'll pass it on. Consider it done."

Otis turned to see what had happened to Heather. She was fine, so he turned back to Dee and he was gone, lost in the crowd. "I wish they wouldn't do that."

He joined Heather at the side of the stage. The VicePresident was speaking. Heather turned to him saying, "they've started. Who was that?"

"Just someone I know from work," he replied.

The VicePresident finished his speech and turned to Marshal. Brandy prompted him to get up and step forward. The VP took the medal from its case and pinned it on Marshal. "For valor and gallantry far above the call of duty, I award you with the Presidential Medal of Freedom."

The VP motioned for Marshal to step up to the podium. He did, but was unable to get his translator to work. Lt. Holmes stepped up to the mic saying," My oversized friend here is having technical difficulties with his translator, but he told me earlier. Now let's see if I can recall his words. Oh yes, he has no memory of the events leading up to this, but he is greatly honored and that he would do anything in his power to protect the planets in his jurisdiction. Or something like that."

Finished, she laughed to herself and turned and led the big blue Aurorian back to his special reinforced seat. After the ceremony is commpleted and they are making their various ways out, a reporter stops Major Otis. "I recognize you. You were there when this all went down!"

"What if I was?" The Major replied trying to get past the reporter. But the mob of reporters and dignitaries and just plain people prevent him from making his planned escape.

The reporter posed a question. "Marshal has been killed what, two, three times? Care to comment?'

"I guess death isn't the career ender it used to be," he said half joking with the man.

"Huh? But he's from another planet! It's unheard of."

"Unheard of? This might go on all of the time on other planets."

"Can you be serious for a second?" The reporter persisted in asking.

"Unheard of? Hardly, what about the King?" He joked some more.

"What?"

"You know, Elvis, he's worth a whole lot more now that he's dead than he ever was while he was alive."

"That's not what I meant and you know it. He's been reported killed at least twice, some say three times. Others are saying it's all a hoax."

"A hoax?"

"Yeah, you know, he really wasn't killed at all or that it's not the same guy," the reporter elaborated.

"Look, the time he was hit by a train he wasn't killed. We never said he was. That was all on you guys getting it wrong. And he is most definitely the same guy. Do you really think there are more than one of him?" The Major answered as he finally got some separation from his questioner.

Later that night, in a basement apartment inhabited by two 20 something slobs, Pete and his brother Roy. Roy is munching on a greasy pizza and watching TV as Pete comes in carrying a paper bag containing an order of extra greasy fries and a killer roast beef sandwich.

Pete flops down on the couch next to his brother. "Whatchawatchin?"

"Fox news," Roy grunted.

"Oh man! You've just got the hots for the blond. What's she raggin about now?", Pete commmplained.

"Ah, the Chinese here in Chicago said something that got everyone all upset."

"What did they say?" Pete asked as he ripped open a packet of ketchup and dumped its contents on his fries.

"Somethin' about wanting to buy alien technology."

"Huh? I was there and I didn't hear em say anything about that."

"They said that the alien technology at Ground Zero here in Chicago is priceless, and that if the UFO had crashed in China that they would be willing to pay one million dollars to anyone for a piece of the recovered alien technology," Roy explained to his brother.

"Sounds like they just put a price on it."

"You work there, have you seen anything?

Pete answered as he inhaled his fries," yeah, they got stuff all over the place. Just today I saw one of the aliens open up one of those cryo beds."

"Wouldn't it be sweet if you could get your hands on some of the alien gold."

"Yeah, but the place is guarded. Even if I could get hold of something, there's no way I could get it out."

"There's always a way."

CHAPTER FOUR

HEATHER TAKES CHARGE

Two Gray peace officers are holding the silver Gammon girl by her arms. They have brought her out into the street and Marshal is also there. She is struggling to get free but they are holding on for dear life. The senior warden asks, "are you sure about this?"

"Yes, I don't want to press any charges. She can't help it. She's clearly under my influence. I gave her the antidote but she didn't take it," Big Blue explained.

"You do know she's a Gammon?" The Warden asked.

Marshal nodded yes.

"And you know what they say about them?" The Warden asked just to make sure.

"Yes," Marshal gestured with his hands as he answered.

"And you still...," the other Officer chimed in.

"Yes, but that was four cycles ago on the liner. Look, it's simple, I just got off of the liner and all she needs is a little time. Couldn't you just hold her for half a tick?" Marshal implored.

"Four cycles?" The warden was starting to see the light.

"Yes, four cycles in my cabin."

"Half a tick?" He asked as he thought it over.

"It could take that long to check her ID," Marshal added.

"Less than that if you can get her to take the pill." He takes another one out of his belt pouch and hands it to the warden.

"That's unlawful detainment! You can't make me take the pill!" She renews her attempts to break free.

"Yes we can. It's the same as if you were a deadhead and refused to take your equilibrium. If it is deemed for your own good and that you are incapable of making sound decisions for yourself, we can make you take the pill," the warden argued back, as a small crowd started to gather around them.

"That's the spirit!" Marshal added, "keep the peace now and avoid breaking the law later."

A few minutes later, Marshal is on his way down the street with his duffel bag over his shoulder. He towers over a sea of bald gray heads. As he rounds the last corner, he sees the Government House, a 40 story stone and steel building jutting up into the sky unchallenged by any of the nearby buildings. There is a low stonewall capped with a fence. Behind the fenced wall surrounding the commpound is a garden full of exotic plants and avian life forms. The gate guard took one look at Marshal and waved him in.

Inside the foyer, Marshal found it well lit and modern. He made his way over to the elevated constabulary desk and put his duffel down. Behind the desk sat the desk sergeant with a prehensile trunk and elephant like ears. Marshal handed his travel documents to the desk sergeant who took it without even making eye contact or looking up. "Federation Marshal shield number 8181 reporting," Marshal said in his deepest most commanding voice.

The tone and direction of the voice caught the desk sergeant's attention and he stopped and looked up. He dropped the pen he had been writing with in his trunk. He looks down at the documents again and tries to pronounce something on it. Marshal stopped him saying, "Don't even try."

The Sergeant grunted and said, "you're late."

"I was delayed," Marshal explained.

"The chief likes to meet all of the new shields. Report to him on the fifth floor," the sergeant instructed as he handed Marshal back his documents. He pointed to the elevator on the right with his trunk.

"Thanks Sarg," he said as he tossed his duffel back on his shoulder and headed for the elevator. Marshal sat on a bench outside the Chief's office. The chairs were too small.

In a minute, his five traveling companions came out and made their way past him.

"I see you made it." Marshal nodded in the affirmative.

The petite Gray receptionist told the Chief that the Marshal had arrived. She tells him, "just leave your bag there, you can go in now."

"Great moons of Spudmoor, what have they been feeding you?" The chief fell back in his seat as he first looked upon his newest marshal. The chief was a smallish Gray with a large head. He wore the same uniform as did Marshal, only Marshal's would make five of his.

"Just the usual," Marshal jokingly replied.

"Are there more at home like you?" The chief asked trying to get a feel for his new man.

"No, not many," Marshal shook his head as he answered.

"I guess not," the chief mused as he studied the documents. He had heard that they got a little bigger in the outer Southern quadrants but he hadn't actually been there.

"How do you pronounce your name?" The chief asked as he tried to get his mouth around it.

"You can't sir, just call me Marshal." It was true. The one thing all of the Gray races had in common besides being gray was that they all had little slits for mouths and were unable to pronounce his name.

"It says here you are Aurorian. I've never seen or even heard of one. Where did you come from? The Southern quadrant I bet."

"That's right, Aurora is a subject planet of the Andorian Star Emirate."

This caught the Gray's attention. "The Andorian Star Emirate? That's not even part of the Federation. They're over by the Kling frontier!"

"We are pledged. I am here as part of the Ohmahaw exchange," Marshal explained.

"I see you were in the Imperial Guard. Where do your loyalties lie?" The chief wasn't quite sure what he had here.

Marshal answered trying to alleviate his new commander's suspicions. "I was taken from my home when I was very young. I have no memories of it. While in the Guard, I was commissioned as an Ess Sea Ay Knight, and warranted to serve the Federation. I have pledged to serve, and serve I will." Marshal sounded very positive.

Looking back at the documents, the chief observed, "I see you're qualified... There's not much you're not qualified to do. Just what am I going to do with you? Obviously you'll never fit in around here," he pointed out. "You can't even sit on most of the chairs."

"I'll go where I'm needed." He sounded confident.

"Well said! I think you'll do well on the frontier or maybe deep space patrol. You have to be self-reliant out there. You'll be a natural. We'll get you a posting in a few cycles. My receptionist will tell you how to get to the temp billets.

General Solo sits at the head of the great table in the conference room. Major Otis, Dr. Cooly, her assistant Heather, Dauntless and Mr. Tee from the MIB are all seated around the head of the table. The Top Sergeant and three other Army officers and one Air Force officer round out the people in attendance.

General Solo clears his throat and begins to speak. "I've just returned from Washington. The Congress has finished their inquiry, and they have found that we are not at fault for the near destruction of Chicago, as they put it."

He turns his attention to Dauntless. "The VP and the undersecretary are not pleased with your conduct leading up to this Lt. Holmes."

"Sir?" She started to answer, but then her brain caught up with her mouth and she just sat there dreading what she would hear next.

He went on, "but they also commended your conduct as Dauntless. That, and the positive press, have secured our funding for this year. Well done." He turned to Dr. Cooly. "It seems the press can't get enough of our friend from the distant stars," he said sarcastically. "What have you got for me?"

She hesitated and pushed up her glasses before answering. "We, uh, we are still having trouble communicating with him. We don't seem to be able to get any of the translators to work on him. I've had MaCos working exclusively on it and even he can't make the repairs without the necessary tools."

Not happy with what he was hearing, the general leaned over to ask, "what tools do you lack?"

"Well, that's hard to explain, General sir. He needs some highly specialized tools that don't exist on Earth. We have been trying to make them but it's taking time. We just don't have the level of technology," she explained

Seeing the dissatisfied expression on his face she quickly added, "but we won't quit until we do sir."

"But in the meantime," he inquired?

She looked around the room for help. Receiving none, she ventured to say, "in the meantime, I have Brandy and Heather trying to teach Marshal English."

"Hmm, maybe we should bring in some help," he speculated.

"That might be a good idea," she conceded.

Major Otis chimed in to ask, "but who could we bring in?"

"There aren't many people cleared to work on alien technology." Heather added.

"How is the alien MaCos Ex working out? Any problems?" The General asked.

The Doctor and the Major traded glances before Major Otis spoke up. "No security problems sir. He hasn't tried anything. He seems to be happy as a clam. It's not like he can go anywhere and not be seen. He has no special powers or abilities. He's just an engineer with special skills. We can guard him with minimal security."

"That's right sir," Beverly quickly added. "I have learned some of Marshal's background using the helmet, but it's not commmplete. The helmet, like everything else, was damaged. Perhaps if he looked at it."

"What have you learned? Is there anything that we should be concerned about?" The senior soldier asked.

"Nothing to be concerned about, general sir. Only that he was in the Imperial Guard and a Ess Sea Ay knight before becoming a Federation marshal."

"Hmmm, keep after it Doctor. Do what you think is necessary."

"We, uh, I mean, I was wondering what about using the helmet to help Marshal regain his memory?" Dr. Cooly asked.

"Not until we definitely know what's in it. You and MaCos Ex can work on it." The General then turned his attention to Heather saying, "Heather, I want you to find us an English teacher for Marshal, one with a clearance. MIB might be able to help or maybe Dreamland."

"Me sir? Why me?" She asked defensively.

"That's something the new chief of security would do," he matter-of-factly replied.

"Head of security? ME! Why me?" She asked in disbelief.

"It seems that a certain officer seems to think you might do a good job of it. And I have looked into your file and you have the necessary background and requirements."

"But General!", the Air Force Lieutenant Colonel at the end of the table protested. "Security is an Air Force job."

The General spoke up to put the fire out. "The only reason you're here at all is because the Fifth is so under strength after its fight with the aliens. But don't worry, the Air Force will still be providing security at

Ground Zero. We don't have the manpower for that. She will be in charge of security here at HERO HQ and over Marshal wherever he is."

"I wonder who that certain officer was?" Heather whispered to Major Otis as she leaned back in her seat. Then she perked up, sat up and asked the general, "does that mean I can order the Major around?"

"If it pertains to security, Major Otis is under you," was the quick reply.

"Did you hear that? You're under me," she leaned back and slyly whispered to the Major next to her. He flexed his eyebrows like Groucho Marx and they both smirked.

The general pointed at Heather and Colonel Newcommb saying, "security is becoming a bigger issue every day. They found a dozen bugs after the UN visit and there have been four arrests at Ground Zero and three more here at HERO, and there have been thousands of cyber attacks, all kinds of people are trying to hack in and find out what we know. And not all of them are harmless hackers."

Major Otis offered his idea. "Maybe we should give them a site where they can see... whatever it is we want them to see. We could provide them with links to links to links that lead them nowhere, in that way we could disseminate misinformation. It would be cheaper than trying to chase them all down."

Heather slid back in her chair smiling. "Look at you, Major Henry Otis, cyber warrior."

"Not me, I've been talking with MIB," he explained.

Quick to latch on to a good idea, General Solo spoke. "We'll do what he said. Captain Seagle, get your men on it."

"Yes sir."

"I guess that leaves us with just two more issues for now." The general turned to the Top Sergeant saying "Top."

The old soldier jumped up to attention and read from a sheet of paper. Attention to orders! Effective this date Major Henry Otis is herby promoted to the rank of Lieutenant Colonel by order of the commanding General. You are hereby directed to assume command of the Fifth Special Security Group, pursuant to... you know the rest of it sir. Good luck."

After a round of congratulations the general resumes the meeting. "The last item is, Lt. Holmes, Dr. Cooly, pack your bags. You're taking a trip to Dreamland."

"To Dreamland sir?" They both said in unison.

"That's right, Dreamland. Area 51. Doctor Brewville has some new equipment I want Dauntless to check out and familiarize herself with. He may be able to help you with the alien technology," he explained.

Dr. Cooly asked, "how long will we be gone?"

"Not more than a week."

"Will Marshal be going?" Heather asked hopefully.

The general put Heather's hopes out with his answer. "No, just the girls. You'll be staying here with Marshal."

"But I don't understand." Brandy was confused by Heather's apparent enthusiasm about going to Dreamland. "Where is Dreamland?"

"Baby, you're going to Vegas.", Heather gushed.

Later that day, the new Ltc. (Lieutenant Colonel) and chief of security find themselves walking down the hall. He sports his new silver oak leaves on his class A's and she has commmpletely changed her outfit. Gone is the silk shirt and dress. Heather now wears black biker leathers. She playfully dusts off his new rank insignia and with a giggle says, "silver looks good. Congrats, you deserve it."

"Thanks," he eyes her up and down. "That's a new look for you."

"Not really," she objected as they walked.

"Why the leathers?" He asked.

"What else am I supposed to wear? My bike's parked outside."

"That's yours?" He inquired, not quite believing his ears.

"Yep, it's mine," she insisted.

"I thought you had a Charger," he countered.

"I do, but this is more fun," she smiled.

When they reached the intersection of the halls, she stopped and asked, "why did you recommend me to General Solo?"

He folded his arms across his chest. "I felt you could do the job. You did notice Lee dropping those bugs. It never occurred to me that he would put you in charge over me."

"Kind of a slip up for a military man, isn't it?" She snorted.

"Slip up?" He shifted his weight. "No, I don't think so. I wasn't aiming to get promoted or for your job either. We were just talking about the personnel shortage and how we needed someone to be specifically in charge, and your name just came up. I mean, after reading your file and all."

She stoped him in the hall. "You read my file?" She was a little alarmed with the news. *What does he know about me,* she wondered?

With his hand to his chin he continued. "Yes, and I'm impressed. I'd like to know how you did that business with the pirates in Hafun."

She cocked her head. "You know about that?"

"I know it happened, not the details," he reassured her.

Then it came to her, and she leaned into him a little. "Why were you reading my file?"

"Just part of the job at the time," he said nonchalantly.

"I guess, seeing that I'm in charge now I'll be reading your file. Is there anything juicy in there?" She playfully asked.

"Maybe, if your clearance is high enough," he said with a smirk.

"If my clearance is … Oh stop fooling around!" She slapped his shoulder.

"I was going to suggest you come down and meet the men while I break the news to em. But I guess it can wait until Monday." He started to go.

"No, why wait, I can meet them now." She changed course and followed him.

"I don't know," he said with a little apprehension. "One look at you in that outfit and they just might eat you up."

"Oh I think I can handle em," she said with playful confidence.

"Really?" He asked.

"Really!" She insisted. "I'm in charge and I can handle them."

"Okay, it's your funeral," he resigned as he opened the door to the day room. There were a dozen soldiers goofing off after the long day's duty. The room contained a pool table, pop machine, TV and some institutional furniture.

As the door swung open, "TEN HUT!" rang out and a dozen soldiers in class A uniforms snapped to attention.

He looked them over, most had their uniform coats off. Many had either loosened or taken their ties off. It was their day room after hours. He chose to overlook it. He commanded, "as you were!" And magically, the soldiers relaxed

"Men, gather around." And of course they did. "I've got some news for you. From now on, you're going to be taking orders from the little lady here." He motioned to Heather. She smiled broadly.

"AW! Come-on Colonel, stop kidding," someone said.

"He's just trying to get out of buying tonight!" Someone else heckled.

"No, it's true. She's in charge of security, here at HQ and with Marshal," he countered.

"That's right, but I'm not going to be telling the soldiers what to do. I'm going to be telling the new Colonel here what to do," Heather said as she stepped up trying to be heard over the good-natured heckling.

"That's good because you couldn't keep up with us!" A private with no tie and his coat unbuttoned said.

"Oh, you don't think I can keep up?" She said bobbing her head in exaggerated disbelief.

A voice in the crowd cried out, "that's right blondy! You might be dressed for it now, but one day with us and you'd be crying about your broken fingernails."

"You see, we aren't out there play acting. We're the real deal! The Private insisted.

"You ain't so tough," Heather said in a low tone.

"What's that you say?" Pvt. Holster said loudly.

She stepped up and got in his face with her head bobing up and down. "I said you aren't so tough, I can take you," she said trying to egg him on.

"What's that you say princess? You think you can take me? Take me where?" Hollister called out sarcastically, cupping his hand to his ear to aid his hearing.

"In a fight, I can take you, I can take you all," she said as she shifted her weight and put her hands on her hips, ready for action.

He stepped back. "Oh them's big words from a little girl!"

"Especially with the Colonel standing right there," someone else pointed out.

She turns to the Colonel and asks, "Henry, is it okay if I show them?"

He looked around and shrugged his shoulders. "You called them out. It's okay with me, just don't break anything. But I must be going. Let me know how things work out." As he turned to go, he ran into Lt. Holmes and Marshal coming in. "Come with me Lieutenant."

"But Marshal," Brandy started to protest, but stopped as he passed her in the doorway.

"He will be okay, he's with the chief of security. We can't be here for this," he said as he prompted her into motion. She went along but she was confused about what was going on.

"The door closed and she turned to face them. She unzipped her jacket and took it off and handed it to Marshal, who took it with a little confusion but said nothing. Next, she unbuttoned her white silk blouse, and removed it, exposing a black bra containing her ample breast. She smiled flirtatiously and handed the blouse to Marshal. The flash of her perfect skin was met with the unbridled approval of the soldiers who voiced their approval in the usual way. She kept her driving gloves on.

She turned to face the mob. Their mood had changed. Hollister was standing there all wide-eyed with his mouth open. "What? The blouse is silk! I don't want anything to happen to it," she explained.

Standing with Marshal at her back and the crowd all around, she pointed out Holster and said, "okay big boy, you're first!"

"But, but!" was all he could say before she had him. She was quick. She took his arm and wrenched it around his back and kicked out his feet. Down he went. She had his arm pinned behind him and was applying pressure.

"I can break it off if you want?" She threatened from on top of his back. She started to use her body weight to increase the pressure on his arm.

"NO! I GIVE!" He cried out. She let go and he sprang up to his feet rubbing his arm. "That don't prove nothing! I wasn't ready!" He protested.

She reached over and plucked the distinctive unit badge that was on his uniform epaulet. "I'll take that as a souvenir if you don't mind," she said as she pinned it to her bra.

"You can't!" Despite his protest, Holster was shuffled out of the way by another soldier.

"Holster you're a wuss!" He turned his attention to Heather. "Just because you know a little judo doesn't mean you can run with us. He reached out and started to play with her hair. Big mistake. She grabbed his fingers and gave them a twist and forced him down to his knees. But he caught himself on the way down and wound up with his face planted squarely between her breasts. This brought on a series of cat calls, whooping and hollering.

Marshal was even more confused by this, but remained neutral. Morison reached around Heather's waist and spun her around. Now he had her back but not for long. She reached up behind her and flipped him over winding up behind him. She slipped her right arm under his chin around his neck and squeezed for all she as worth. He started to get up but collapsed, out cold. Kneeling over him, she collected her second badge. She stopped to admire it and noticed that it was different from the first.

The fifth Special Security Detachment was a commposite unit. All of the soldiers wore different badges from their previous units to avoid being identified. She thought it was pretty and pinned it on her bra.

"I want me some of that action!" A large black soldier ventured out of the crowd.

"That's the only way you're ever going to get a pretty girl, with a mug like yours," someone heckled.

And the heckling only got worse. "Man! You're so ugly your mother had to hang a pork chop around your neck just to get the family dog to play with you!"

"Johnson, you're so ugly when your mother gave birth to you the doctor didn't know which end to spank!" The catcalls and taunting just continued.

Johnson can't help it! He takes after his mother. His mother's so ugly that…"

This enraged the soldier. "You leave my mother out of this!

"Don't mess her face up!"

"I'll show you! He rushed her, head down like a football tackler. She jumped aside and he slammed into the pop machine cracking the glass. He fell back with a trickle of blood coming from his scalp.

She took his badge saying," that was too easy." She pinned her third badge on.

"That was luck!" Yet another challenger came forward.

"So, you think that was luck," she challenged him as she straightened up. They locked hands and a shoving match ensued, with Heather having her hands pinned behind her, and her challenger pressing up against her.

He looked her in the eye as she struggled in vain to free herself. "I'll give you one thing, you're spirited." He didn't get to enjoy having Heather pressed up against his body for long. She stomped on his toe with her two-inch heel. This broke his hold and she quickly elbowed him alongside his head, which put him down on one knee.

From his lowered position, he punched her in her flat stomach, which caused her to back away and double over with the wind knocked out of her. As he started to get up, she grabbed hold of both of his shoulders and kneed him in the groin, doubling him and sending him to his knees.

Another soldier came out with his hands up but before he could do anything, she spun around doing a spinning back kick, which landed in his unprotected stomach causing him to double over holding his mid section. She instinctively followed up with a kick to the family jewels, putting him down on his knees next to the other challenger. She walked up to both of them and plucked their badges off and pinned them on her bra with her other trophies.

She spun around thinking someone else was challenging her but there were no more takers. Unsure, she backed into someone. She spun and chopped Marshal right in the stomach having no effect at all. They looked at each other for a couple of seconds.

She reached out one hand. Marshal looked at her puzzled. Then he reached over and removed the medal the VP had pinned on him at the ceremony and started to pin it on her bra. She was breathing heavily, her breasts were heaving up and falling with each breath, quite distracting, really. He was having some trouble, not wanting to stick her with the pin, he stopped. She looked up at him and nodded saying, "its okay big guy you won't hurt me." He managed to slide one large finger under the strap and he pinned her. They both smiled.

She took her jacket and put it on without the blouse. Turning to face the remaining soldiers, she tucked her thumb in her belt and said, "well I guess that shows I can run with you." They accepted her.

"Come-on! Colonel Otis is buying!" One of the soldiers shouted. The big blue alien and feisty blond were hustled down the hallway by the torrent of high-spirited soldiers.

Near the front doors, they caught up to Colonel Otis and Lt. Holmes. Heather guided Marshal into Brandy and hooked the Colonels arm in one motion, carrying him along with the crowd. Lt. Holmes and the big blue alien looked on in confusion as Heather called out to them. "You watch him! I've got to see what kind of man I have under me!" She started to laugh as they headed out the door.

This brought a round of catcalls from the soldiers. Colonel Otis called out as he was carried out the door, "she didn't mean it like that!"

Are you sure about that Colonel? And, oh yes she did, were only a couple of the calls heard as the party made its way out the door.

CHAPTER FIVE

BRANDY DOES VEGAS, THE MISADVENTURES OF ROCKET GIRL

Saturday morning there was a knock at the door. Brandy, in a T-shirt and jeans, tossed an armload of clothes down on her bed and answered the door. She had to look twice before she recognized who it was. "Beverly? Is that you?"

"Of course it's me. Do I really look that different?" She asked as she moved in.

"Well, DUH! Look at you," Brandy implored. And indeed she did look different. Her auburn hair was down around her shoulders instead of its customary bun. Her lab coat, suit jacket and dress had also gone the way of the dodo, replaced with slacks and a V-neck exposing just a little of her ample cleavage.

She was definitely a sweater girl. She still wore her glasses and oversized belt buckle that made her waist look positively tiny. "Aren't you done packing yet?"

"No, I'm not!" Brandy snapped back in frustration.

Beverly scanned the room. Brandy had suitcases sitting open everywhere, all open and half full of clothing, just crammed in. "What's all this? We're only going for a few days."

"I've never been there, what do I need?" Brandy said as she plopped down on the bed among the piles of clothing.

"We have a two day layover in Vegas before taking the shuttle to Dreamland. You'll need clothes to travel in, two or three days for fun, your Dauntless uniform and some of your soldier's kit," Beverly answered with one hand on her hip.

Beverly helped Brandy pack. While they worked, Brandy asked, "what are you going to do with your two days in Vegas?"

"The shows baby! And you?"

"You are getting into this aren't you? Oh, I don't know, maybe some serious partying," Brandy giggled as she packed.

Captain Reynolds, a short Army officer with thinning hair was the DO (Duty Officer) that morning. He met them at the front door foyer. He instructed two passing soldiers to take their luggage up to the north heli pad.

"I thought we were taking a cab," Brandy questioned.

"No, you're too well known around here. The paparazzi would mob you at the airport. You'll be flying out of the military terminal," he said as he handed them their travel vouchers and necessary papers.

"Some vacation," Brandy spouted, sounding disappointed. "What are we going in? Please, not a 130," she added.

"It's not a vacation, you're going out there to work, but no, you're not going on a C130. I think you'll be surprised." As they headed for the elevators he added, "have fun."

"Yeah right," Lt. Holmes sighed as she left.

"What's that?" The Captain caught her.

"Yeah, right sir!" She corrected. She hadn't been an officer and a gentleman all that long and was still a citizen soldier at heart. Then her curiosity kicked in, causing her to ask, "how come Colonel Otis or Heather aren't here to send us off?

"It's Saturday, they're off duty and I haven't heard from either of them. Brandy and Beverly shot glances at each other and got in the elevator.

An hour later they were in a Gulf stream 50 streaking over Illinois headed west. "Cool!" The in flight movie was Gone With The Wind. They were informed that it was General Solo's favorite. They had seen it.

The Gulf Stream jet rolled to a stop on the tarmac in Las Vegas. The engines whined as they spun down. The door to the cabin cracked and swung open stairs at the ready, but no one deplaned.

Inside, Beverly Cooly was knocking on the door to the little girl's room; Brandy was locked inside. Finally, the door opened and the good doctor was shocked and then amused by what she saw.

"What!" Brandy demanded.

"It's just… that you're so different," she explained.

"I'm supposed to look different, remember?" Brandy emphasized as she came out. She was no longer a blond. Now she had jet-black hair down to her shoulder blades and bangs. A fake beauty mark on her right cheek and dark sunglasses commpleted her transformation. "How do I look?"

Beverly stepped back with her hand to her mouth studying Brandy. "You remind me of someone. But who?" She thought for a few more seconds "I know, you remind me of Betty Page," she announced.

They started to make their way out of the plane. "Betty who?" Brandy asked not having a clue.

"You know, Betty Page, you look just like her, only you have a way better figure," Beverly repeated.

Brandy gave it some thought before responding,"naw, Veronica was the black haired one. Betty was the blond with a ponytail."Now Beverly was the one who had to think about it. Then it came to her. "Not that Betty!" Beverly exclaimed as they entered the terminal. "Oh, never mind."

They collected their bags and had an uneventful cab ride to their hotel where they checked in. The desk clerk eyed Brandy with suspicion when she saw the name on the registration. They make their way to their adjacent rooms. "Are you sure you don't want to see the show with me?" Beverly asked as they opened their doors.

"Naw, I don't care for his singing. I think I'll just go and see what action I can find," Brandy said as she stepped aside for the bellhop with her luggage.

"The next show isn't for another three hours. We could have dinner together."

"Okay Bev, lets get all dressed up and do dinner, who knows, you might even get lucky," Brandy said with a glint in her eye and a smirk on her face.

"Me, get lucky! I'm not the one who'd be the lucky one!" She chimed back as she disappeared into her room.

As Brandy entered her room she wondered, *is Beverly going to go wild on me? She leads a pretty dull life and she's not used to all this partying. Maybe I'd better watch out for her. Naw, she's a big girl. Let's see what happens.* Opening her bag she pulled out a black sequined number. Looking pleased with it she thought, *this'll knock em out.* She started to change.

Not exactly a short time later, Brandy knocked at Beverly's door. She is all decked out in a slinky strapless black sequined gown and her black wig.

The door opens "Come on in. I'm having trouble with my hair," Beverly said from the other side of the door.

Brandy took one step and froze in place. "Wooo," was all she could say at first. "Holy shit! Look at you girl!" Beverly was walking back to the mirror working on her hair. She had on an equally slinky dress with no back and one bare shoulder. It was white but it shimmered. She has having trouble putting her auburn hair up over her head. Normally she wore it in a bun behind her head, but for some reason she couldn't coax it to stay up long enough to pin it.

Brandy helped her, and after applying face paint and donning earrings and bracelets, they deemed themselves ready. "We're going to drive em mad," Brandy said with a tone of optimism in her voice.

"Bran, we're too good for em," was the doctor's confident assessment. They playfully locked arms and made their way to the elevator. "Where should we go?"

"Dressed like this, only the best will do," was Brandy's reply.

"This could get expensive," Beverly sighed.

"You don't date much do you?" Brandy quipped back at her companion.

At the elevator, a man in a black suit and tie, white shirt and no distinguishing marks of any kind walked up to them. He flashed them his ID. "Lt. Holmes, Dr. Cooly, I'm R from MIB. I've been detailed to watch over you while you're here."

"Oh great, a chaperone, and one that looks like one of the Blues Brothers!" Brandy was beside herself.

"No, not a chaperone, I'm here to make sure nothing happens to alien technology, namely your Dauntless uniform," he said trying to defuse the situation.

"Oh, right, it's in my room," Brandy said deflated by the news. "I could lock it up in the hotel safe," she offered hopefully after a few seconds thought.

"No, that won't do. But don't worry; I'll watch your room. In that way we won't call any undue attention to it or yourself," was his thoughtful response.

"Then you're not going to be following us around all night?" Beverly asked.

"No, but I can give you this." He handed her a small electronic device.

"What is this, a phone?" She asked after examining it.

"Think of it as a panic button. Push it if you need help."

She took the button, and the girls got on the elevator determined not to let this run in with MIB security ruin their night. "That guy was a little creepy," Brandy retorted.

"A little creepy?" Beverly questioned her dinner date.

As they made their way through the crowded casino the two stunning ladies were the center of attention. "You know, looking as good as we do, if we play this right we won't have to pay for anything. But first, we should stop at the bar for some drinks.

Beverly, at first, wasn't so sure about all of this, but Brandy managed to talk her into it. And, sure enough, as soon as the unescorted beauties hit the bar, they were descended upon by all manner of men.

They finally hooked up with a pair of high rollers from Frisco and they joined them for dinner. Champagne and lobster tail followed by brandy and lots of small talk. Like, where are you girls from? Chicago. How long will you be in town? Just the weekend. What do you girls do? We work for the Department of Homeland Security. And you? I'm a dentist and Phil here owns a restaurant. Blah Blah Blah.

Time flies and the liquor flows. Suddenly, Beverly realizes it is time for her show. Ted assures her that he has connections and can take care of things, but they have to go now. Brandy and Phil don't want to go to the show but agree to meet them later at the Luxor.

Phil decides that Brandy must be his lady luck and he wants to test this theory in the casino. On the way, Brandy who has had a few too many, is feeling no pain. Phil has to help keep her steady as they make their way past the Elvis impersonator performing in the alcove.

Further down the hall she sees a karaoke bar over in the corner. She announces that she loves karaoke and wants to give it a try. What inhibition she would normally have has flown out the window.

Now Brandy is a lovely and athletic woman, but a singer she isn't. Not even a karaoke one. With Phil looking on somewhat bemused, Brandy climbs up on the small stage and starts to accommpany the recorded music to Viva Las Vegas commmplete with choreography.

To say Brandy was curvaceous wouldn't quite cover it. True, she had luscious full round breasts, but she had more. Her waist was small and her hips were well rounded with great legs. She had muscular arms for a girl and a wicked little smile with downright inviting eyes, if she wanted. A small button nose and pretty face; she had the full package.

She was quite a sight to see, with all those gyrations in that slinky sequined dress sparkling in the lights. Then the unthinkable happened.

Her black Betty Page wig slipped and fell off, exposing her short platinum, blond hair. This didn't stop her performance. She was a trooper. But someone in the audience recognized her as the superhero Dauntless!

Phil and the rest of the audience looked on in confusion and then disbelief but yes, it was true. The young lady dancing on the stage before them was none other than Dauntless, the superhero from Chicago.

Suddenly it all came to Phil, what she had said earlier about coming from Chicago and working for the Department Of Homeland Security. She really was Dauntless!

She went into the song from Ghost Busters, "Who you goinacall?" with some more creative dance moves. She was trying to put her wig back on while performing but even her wig couldn't stand her off key, offbeat singing, or so it seemed. She was having no luck putting it back on.

Finally, she gave up and tossed it out into the crowd, which brought a cheer. The toss nearly brought on a Janet Jackson like wardrobe malfunction, but she took the necessary corrective action before thing got out of hand. But not before the paparazzi showed up and started taking pictures.

The flash of flashbulbs didn't bother Brandy in the least. She was having a good time and so was everyone else who wasn't a music lover. Phil, on the other hand, didn't want his face to appear in the scandal sheets and decided to fade away.

After finishing her second number, the tipsy superhero was inundated by the crowd of well-wishers, autograph hounds, and, of course, the ever-present paparazzi. She was unable to move without the sea of humanity pressing all around and against her.

Her movements were further impaired when she broke the heel on her shoe. She almost fell which excited the crowd even more. It was like a school of sharks going into a feeding frenzy, only there was no blood in the water. The crowd was stating to get loud, things were definitely getting out of control.

Hotel and casino security moved in trying to calm things down. Brandy, half in a daze holding one of her shoes and pushing her hair out of her eyes suddenly noticed that someone had a firm hold on her arm.

She turned to see Elvis standing there. Or, at least he looked look Elvis. He had the white suit with high collar and sequins and a scarf. He even sounded like Elvis.

"Come with me little lady, I know a way out of here." It seemed like a good idea, being rescued from the mob by the King. So, she went along. Back across the stage and through a slit in the curtains. They were backstage.

They quickly made their way past some startled hotel employees, Brandy hobbling all the way, out the back door into the night. She stopped and took her other shoe off and tossed them both away.

Still holding her by the arm, he tried to get her to go, but she was an unmovable object. "Look, we don't have much time before they come around. Where are you staying?" He implored trying to get her to respond.

She hesitated, trying to think, but she couldn't remember. A crowd of people came running around the corner of the building. "Oh never mind. Let's get out of here!" He exclaimed as he took her hand and took off running.

"Where are we going? She asked as they ran.

"My bike is parked over there by the telephone pole. They'll never catch us if we can get there!" He gestured to the parking lot.

She swept the King off of his feet and carried him away in her arms. As she ran, she veered to the left and right a little, but she still hit a speed of nearly 30 miles an hour.

A few seconds later they arrived at the telephone pole. There was a gigantic white and chrome Harley Davidson Electra Glide motorcycle chained to it. He unlocked it, hopped on, and gave it a kick. The bike roared to life. "Get on!" He commanded.

She started to, but stopped to rip a gap in the side of her dress, enabling her to swing her leg over. With Brandy hanging on, the King gunned it and they roared down the road followed by the crowd.

Even in Vegas the sight of the King and a beautiful girl in an evening dress on a massive Harley is going to be noticed. They stopped at the red light at the corner intersection. The pedestrians crossing the street immediately noticed them.

Perhaps it was the sight of Elvis on this massive hog or maybe it was the gorgeous superhero in a torn evening dress hanging on to his waist that got their attention, but whatever it was, the crowd just sort of started to form around them, right there in the street.

The friendly inquisitive crowd slowed their departure from the intersection allowing the paparazzi on a motor scooter to catch up and start taking pictures. "Let's blow this clambake!" Elvis gunned it and left them standing at the intersection.

Elvis and friend roared down the crowded Las Vegas streets weaving their way through traffic, with the scooter buzzing along in pursuit. I don't think you could call it hot pursuit. The scooter sounded more like a castrated lawnmower than anything and the King's Harley, well... let's just say it was a mismatch.

Two blocks further along and they came to another red light. "Having fun?" He asked.

"YAHOO! Loads," was her enthusiastic answer. As they waited for the light to change, a car pulled up along side of them. There was another flash. The paparazzi had caught up to them again.

"They don't give up easy, do they?" He asked his passenger.

"No, they don't."

"Shall I show'em just what this thing can do?" He asked, hoping for an affirmative answer.

He wasn't disappointed. "Let's lose em," was her encouraging reply. The light changed and the Harley thundered off. The bike pulled away from the car as they raced down the side streets of Vegas.

As they rode he asked his eager passenger, "does this sort of thing happen to you often?"

"It was hard for her to hear but she got the drift of his question. "What sort of thing? Being rescued by the King, or chased on a motorcycle by the paparazzi?" Was her playful response.

"Either!" He said as he gunned it through a changing traffic light and took a turn a little on the fast side. A Las Vegas police car that had been in the oncoming lane hit his lights and made a hard turn going after them.

Elvis poured on the speed and pulled away making for parts unknown. The LVPD car in pursuit put out a call and the paparazzi in the car overheard it with their police band radio and continued with their chase.

A few miles outside of town, the white Harley pulled off of the road at a roadside bar. There were fifty bikes parked around the little building. "What's this? A biker bar?" She asked as she stumbled her way off of the back of the bike.

"Looks that way,' he answered as he got off and set the kickstand. "You're a little overdressed and I'm..." He motioned to his Elvis outfit. "Are you game?"

"Am I game?" She snickered, reached over and slid the scarf from around his neck and wrapped it around hers saying, "are you up to it?"

"Baby, I'm the King! I was born up to it." He straightened his collar to its upright position, pulled a commb out, and ran it through his shiny black hair. They went in. It was dark and the music loud. Their entrance didn't go unnoticed.

Inside, he stopped and she bumped into him and parked her head on his shoulder. She started to nod off. As the patrons of the bar gathered around he came to the conclusion, "maybe this wasn't such a good idea."

She started to wake up. "What's the matter? Don't they want to play nice?"

"Honey, we always play nice," was the reply from the biggest of the patrons.

"Mister Presley, is it?"

"Please, call me Elvis."

"Elvis, mind if I dance with your date?"

Under the circumstances, he couldn't refuse. Something by Alabama was playing on the jukebox. The tall ruffian took the semiconscious Brandy Holmes and pulled her close against his body and started slow dancing with her.

His hands started to wander and Brandy awoke and realized what was going on. She pushed him away sending him flying into the bar knocking down four other patrons and sending stools flying.

Elvis struck a fighting stance. "I must warn you, my hands are deadly weapons. I have a black belt in karate." A beer bottle broke over his head and he slumped to the floor. Another of the bar goers said, "I crown you King of beers!" They all started to laugh.

Meanwhile, tall, tanned and not too bright came charging after the lady in the torn sequined evening dress. A split second later he found himself flying through the air bouncing off of the pool table.

Brandy stooped over and helped up the now semiconscious Elvis back to his feet. "Did they hurt you Elvis baby?" He wasn't able to answer.

Big tall and stupid came back for some more. This time Brandy caught hold of him before he could do anything. Holding him with one hand around his neck and Elvis on her hip, she lifted the man clean off the floor. He flailed about to no effect. After a few seconds of studying him, she decided to just toss him away. He sailed over the bar and crashed into the bottles behind it smashing the mirror. "Let's go sweet cheeks."

Outside, Brandy stopped and looked at the row of parked motorcycles and said, "we can't have them chasing us." Still holding Elvis around his waist, she kicked the first bike over, sending it into the next and the next, knocking all of them over, just like a row of chrome and steel dominoes.

She made her uneven way over to his bike. Looking at him still woozy she said, "you're in no condition to drive. Better let me." She tossed her shapely leg over and got on, with him on back with his hands wrapped around her waist, she asked, "Uh, how do you start this thing?"

He motioned and she got the Harley started. The bikers poured out of the bar and started to untangle their bikes. The Harley and its riders thundered off into the darkness.

"Where's the lights?"

As they entered the city limits they were pulled over by a patrol car. The officer got out and approached the dual on the bike. "What's the problem officer?" Brandy said, trying to act innocent.

"There was a report of a disturbance and a couple meeting your description fleeing the scene. Let's see your license and registration."

Elvis on the back, now revived by the night air tried to intervene. "Officer, this is my bike. The registration is here in the saddle bag." He started to get off to get it for him.

This startled the officer and he backed away. "Stay right where you are!" A second officer joined them.

Brandy fumbled around for a few seconds before realizing, "I don't seem to have my license with me. But I do have one! I promise!" She didn't think it would make a difference. It didn't, and even in her impaired state she could tell. "But I'm Lieutenant Brandy Holmes."

"Lieutenant, Lieutenant of what? The first officer asked.

"The Army! Don't you know who I am?" She implored.

"No, should I? Just who are you?" He asked again.

"I'm Lt Brandy Holmes, I'm also known as Dauntless!" She explained.

"Yeah, sure you are, and he's really the King," he motioned tipping his head.

This supprised her. "You mean he isn't?"

"But she really is," Elvis chimed in. He didn't get to finish.

"Right, and I know who you are Joe." The second officer spoke up.

"Joe?" Brandy turned to her riding companion all confused.

"Joe Ferguson," he explained. Elvis then turned his attention back to the officer. "But, she really is Dauntless. You must be the only one in Vegas who doesn't know it."

"Look, I can prove I'm Dauntless," Brandy offered.

A car pulled up and parked on the other side of the street as Brandy managed to get off of the bike. The officer announced, "You're intoxicated and operating a vehicle without a license. I'm afraid I'm going to have to take you in."

Brandy's head was spinning. "Don't be cruel. We were only trying to get away from those people."

"Don't be cruel, that's one of mine."

"Sure it is, but we need to see some ID."

"But I really am Dauntless," she protested. "If I really wasn't Dauntless, could I do this?" She picked up the Harley and lifted it up with both hands holding it up over her head.

The three men backed away as cameras flashed in the car. She put the bike down. "It's all their fault!" She said, pointing at the paparazzi filled car.

"Okay, calm down Miss Dauntless, I believe you," the second policeman said as he approached her. "But, we really can't let you drive in your present condition. And Joe here has a cut on the back of his head, he needs medical attention."

"And there's the little matter of the disturbance outside of town," the first officer brought up.

"That's not our concern."

"Listen, I don't want any medical treatment and, I can drive. It really wasn't our fault. It was the paparazzi that caused all the trouble," Elvis explained

The two cops got together for a powwow. "She's a government agent or something. We can't go arresting her," said the second officer."

Yeah, but we can't let her go like this. She's a menace," his partner protested.

The second officer offered, "I know Joe, he's not a trouble maker. Let me handle it." His partner saw no reason not to.

He walked over to the two offenders, "Joe, can you keep her out of trouble?"

"Martin! We can't just let them go! What about them?" The first cop gestured to the carload of paparazzi across the street.

The older office thought about it for a few seconds and then went over to the paparazzi and spoke with them for a minute and then returned. "There'll be no more chasing you around tonight if you'll agree to speak with them tomorrow."

"I'm okay with that as long as they play nice," Brandy replied.

"They said she's at the MGM Grand," he told them.

"I'll take her straight home," Elvis said as he shot Brandy a glance. She looked at him and seemed agreeable.

With a wave of his arm the cop commanded, "get out of here, before I change my mind."

"Thank you, thank you very much," he said as he got on his bike.

"You just had to say it didn't you?" The officer said shaking his head in amusement.

"Hey baby, it's what I do." Brandy got on the bike behind him and they were off.

"How did you get them to agree to that?" The first officer asked as they made their way back to the car.

"I just appealed to their better judgment and sense of fair play. I explained that they already had their pictures for the night and there was little more for them."

"Ah, and then you threatened to run them in for interfering with a police officer," the first officer said, having seen the light.

Sunday afternoon there is a knocking at Brandy's hotel room door. It's Beverly, "Are you alright? I heard from Captain creepy in the black suit that an Elvis impersonator commplete with outfit and everything brought you in this morning. What happened?"

From behind the door came Brandy's voice. "Go away! And let me die in peace. He voice faded off. Beverly looked over at the man in black and he shook his head. Later that day the two girls got together, this time more casually dressed. "What happed to you last night?" Beverly asked. "You never showed up."

"I'm not sure of all the details but I seem to remember being in an Elvis Presley movie. Or something. Is there one where he rides a motorcycle?' I may have been spotted by the paparazzi. They even left notes at the desk for me to meet with them."

"You're not going to meet with them are you?" Beverly asked.

'I don't know. It might be fun. Who knows, it might even help things. It's not like I have a secret identity to keep or anything like that. It's just a secret address I have to worry about. If they get to know me they'll figure out that I'm just like everybody else and not very interesting and leave me alone," Brandy said rubbing her head.

"But that's just it, you're not like everybody else. You can lift a car with your bare hands and keep up with traffic on foot." Maybe you should check with the Major before you do anything," Beverly advised.

"Okay."

"Let's go get something to eat." Beverly was ready to go.

"I can't," Brandy sighed half pouting.

"Why not?" Beverly demanded.

"I can't until you go and bring me a wig. I seem to have lost mine last night," Brandy explained.

"Oh, that can't be good," Beverly said as she left the room.

With the help of MIB, they remained undetected for the remainder of the day and the next morning, Brandy and Dr. Cooly, back in their normal work clothes, make their way through McCarran airport and wait for their flight in the private section of the airport. They board the unmarked 727 with 145 other people and make the hop to Dreamland; a runway in the middle of the desert surrounded by barren hills and various nondescript building and hangars.

Brandy stops at the head of the stairs and looks around. The ground crew is working on the Janice plane. The heat of the day is already starting to radiate off of the tarmac. As she exits the plane she wonders, *why do they call this Dreamland, it's a dump!*

At the bottom of the steps they see a thin man in an ill fitting suit nervously fidgeting. As the girls reach the bottom of the stair he steps forward. "You must be Dr. Cooly," he said shaking her hand with both of his. Turning to Brandy, "and you must be Dauntless! I've heard so much about you, it's a real honor to get to meet you." He similarly shook her hand.

"Down boy! Just who are you?" Beverly asked.

"Oh, I didn't introduce myself did I? I'm sorry," he gushed.

After a few seconds pause, "and you still haven't," Brandy spoke up.

"Oh I'm doing it again… Sorry… I'm Doctor Brewville's assistant, Dr. Parker."

"And just where is Dr. Brewville?" Dr. Cooly asked, as they walked to the small terminal building.

"He's at the Nellis range. He's expecting you there," Parker answered.

"But what?..." Brandy started to ask, but before she could finish he answered.

"Don't worry about your bags, they will be taken to the VIP quarters. That's where you'll be staying while you're here."

"But what about my Dauntless uniform?" Brandy asked.

"You're right! You should probably change before going out there." He nervously answered as he ushered them along. He took them past several buses that were loading and directed Brandy to a place where she could change.

While they waited for Brandy to change, Dr. Cooly asked, "what's the deal here?"

"Oh, they all work in different areas, they are quartered here during the week and go home for the weekend. One word of advice, don't ask them about their work." He looked over and there was Brandy in her Dauntless uniform. "My, that didn't take long."

"There were spiders," Dauntless sheepishly explained. And with that they made their way to a waiting UH1 helicopter for the ride to the range.

The Nellis range, a broad expanse of nothing but Yucca scrub, rock and sand. The chopper drops down and flies by Mt. Helen. Near the base of the moutain is a concrete wall with a target painted on it. A mile down range from the rocky outcropping is a small commmplex, nothing more than a portable building, some gear, and a concrete slab with a strange looking big gun mounted on it. The chopper touches down kicking up a little dust storm.

The girls and Parker get out and dash away from the bird. They were met by a man in a lab coat. Dr. Brewville, another thin unkept man with a crumpled lab coat, scraggly beard, glasses and a ponytail. As he shook hands with Beverly, she noticed that he wore canvas top tennis shoes with his dress pants. *What an odd couple Parker and Brewville are,* she thought. "Hello, you must be Dr, Brewville, pleased to meet you," she said trying to be polite.

"Hello, I'm Dr. Brewville, and I bet you're wondering why you're here," he said looking over his glasses.

"That's right," Dr. Cooly said pushing her glasses back up.

"I'm about to test fire this alien gun that was recovered from Ground Zero and my superiors felt it would be a good idea for you and Marshal to look it over before I did," he explained with his arms folded across his chest.

"But Marshal isn't here?" Beverly exclaimed.

"We have a video feed set up," he said as he walked them over to the gun.

"Why am I here? Dauntless asked, as she looked at the video display. "I don't know anything about alien guns and technology."

"That is about to change. I have some, uh, special equipment that needs to be tested, and you, with your unique physiology are the right man ... uh, person to do it. Also, you might find it useful in your role of superhero."

"Sounds spooky."

"Is that the real uniform?" Brewville asked as he leaned over to more closely examine her uniform.

"It is. Why does everybody think I have on a copy? She said as she looked over to Beverly for guidance.

"May I feel it?" He asked. This sort of put Brandy off for a second but then she extended her right arm.

He fingered the material. "Amazing! Is it identical to Marshals?"

"No, well yes, now. His cape was destroyed before we had a chance to make a copy of it. But the coat is the same," she explained.

"Pity, that must have been an interesting experience leaping from buildings and suddenly finding yourself sailing along, hanging from a paraglider," he said, pondering the endless possibilities.

"Yes, that was quite an experience. The badges are different also. He didn't have a star. The star functions as a comm link as his did, sort of. The wings are just decorative like the ones on his uniform to make him feel more commfortable. And, of course, I have no translator."

"And you say there are nanobots on the inside that will repair any damage to it and the wearer?" He said as she withdrew her arm.

"Pretty much, but the nanos are also in my blood," she ventured to explain.

"I'd love to get a sample of that," he murmured to himself.

"We might be able to accommodate you there," Dr. Cooly piped in as she examined the equipment closest to her.

"Right this way." He smiled like the cat that had just eaten the canary as he ushered them along.

As Dr. Cooly examined the gun, a technician worked the video camera. Brandy had nothing to do. General Solo, Colonel Otis and Heather were on the plasma screen ready for the conference. She noticed that Colonel Otis looked a little under the weather and asked, "how you doin' Maj, … Colonel, you look a little out of it."

"Just a long weekend, that's all," he sighed.

"Colonel, I think one of your doodads is missing."

"He leaned back away from the video camera at his end, looked at the general and Heather and said. "It must have popped off during the promotion ceremony." Heather, in the background, looked amused.

He went on to say, "I hear you had quite a time in Vegas."

"Oh, you heard that did you?" She started to squirm. "Where did you hear that from?" She asked, suspecting Beverly had told him. His answer surprised her.

"It's in all of the tabloids."

The paparazzi! She thought. "It is? What do they say?" She asked not wanting to hear it.

General Solo interrupted, "we'll get into that when you return Lt. Holmes." She knew she was in trouble.

Dr. Cooly comes over to Brewville saying, "Everything seems to be in order, but it's really not my field. Why am I here? The guys in the tech lab should be here."

"Because Dr. Brewville requested you," Colonel Otis reported.

She shot a look at him and he turned away. She went on to ask, "I was wondering, where did you get the ammunition for it?"

"It basically fires a larger version of the ammo for Marshal's sidearm. As it turned out, we had some recovered from a previous crash. We didn't know what it was until we had Marshal's to study." We only have the one round but we know how to make it. We only need to see if it works as we think," Brewville said as he sipped lemonade.

Turning to the video, Dr. Brewville asked, "well, you heard her. Do we have your permission to fire?"

"We were hoping to have Marshal here, but he is still weak from his regeneration and we are still having trouble with his translator, so we'll forgo that," General Solo explained.

Heather leaned in adding, "we showed him pictures and the schematic you sent us and as far as we could tell he identified them as for use in space on ships."

"Well, if there are no further objections? Dr. Brewville turned to a row of techs each working a different screen in the control building. They answered in order.

"Satellite check. No Russian birds in sight range."

"T lem go!"

"High speed check!"

The next tech turned to report. "The range is clear."

"Weapon is hot."

"Fire on my mark. Three, two, one FIRE!" Dr. Brewville commanded with gusto.

The gun fired an orange blast. A streak could be seen going down range. Three seconds later, the concrete wall at the moutains base exploded, sending fragments in every direction, but the wall stayed upright. Then the sound of the round slicing its way through the air was heard.

A second later there was another explosion even further down range at the base of the rocky outcropping called Mount Helen. There was a rumbling sound that persisted for four or five seconds, followed by more muffled booms. As the dust started to settle, there was yet another muffled boom. Dr. Brewville was beside himself. He was giddy with excitement and anticipation. "Come on! Let's go see if we hit anything!"

As they left the control building, they noticed that parts of the gun where either red-hot or had commmpletely melted and fallen off. They all stopped and looked to Dr. Brewville for an explanation. "Well, it wasn't commmpletely 100 percent alien." He shrugged it off.

Dr. Brewville, his staff and the girls piled into three jeeps and headed down range. It took them a couple minutes to make the trip by jeep down range to where the two-foot thick concrete wall stood. There was a neat four-inch hole through it. The concrete was cracked and burned but intact. "Just look at that!" Brewville exclaimed.

Just behind the target wall was a four-inch thick wall of steel to act as a backstop. It to had a neat four-inch hole through it. Dr. Brewville just stood there saying, "Would you look at that?"

Soon, the jeep driver called to everyone's attention, "look over here!" He was pointing to the chain link fence that surrounded the base of the mountain. There was a hole in the fence, and the rocks behind had definitely been hit. Upon closer examination, there was a tunnel going clean through the moutain where none had been before. Daylight could be seen coming from the other end. The walls of the tunnel glowed a dull orange color. There was the hissing sound of rocks cooling.

"Oh my God!" Was all he could say.

"It went through a mile of rock." Even Brandy was in shock.

"And it kept on going. Maybe that's why it's for use in space," Dr. Cooly speculated out loud.

Dr. Brewville turned to the man with the video camera. After getting his attention he reported, "well, uh, I'll get back to you when I know the extent, uh no, when I have some results to report." He motioned to the man to cut.

Dr. Brewville turned around to his assistant. "Parker, will you take the ladies back to their quarters. I've got to see how far this went." It was getting hot. They were happy to go.

Back in Chicago, General Solo announced that he was thinking of having a guard escort Lt. Holmes around. Colonel Otis offered his thoughts saying, "they're in Dreamland in the middle of the desert. What more could happen out there?"

"Perhaps you're right," the senior soldier agreed. As the trio was breaking up, Heather commmplained, "that was all very interesting, but I don't understand why you wanted us to watch it. It had nothing to do with us or Marshal."

"Or our people either, that man is a security risk," the newly promoted Colonel added as he eased himself out of his chair.

"Chairman's orders," General Solo explained. Eyeing the Colonel he asked, "Henry, are you alright?"

"Yes sir, just a long weekend, that's all sir," he answered.

"I see, work hard, play harder. Agent Carter, may I have a word with you? Colonel Otis, you may go."

Henry and Heather exchanged glances as he left. "You wanted to talk to me General?" She sheepishly asked.

"Colonel Otis would never say anything but is there a problem with him being under you?" Before she could answer, the general continued, "Because if there is, you had better work it out. Got it?"

"There's no problem with him being under me, General sir. I got it!" She replied and quickly left the room relieved.

In the next room, Colonel Otis is speaking with Top as she comes up. "What did he want?" Colonel Otis asked.

"He just wanted to know if I had any problems with you being under me." She slid in closer. "There aren't any problems with you being under me are there?" She asked with a sly little smile and slight giggle.

"No, there isn't," he quipped.

"Good," and she turned and left them. The two soldiers just enjoyed the view as she happily sashayed her way down the hall. "Let me know if you need help finding your missing doodad."

"Poetry in motion," Otis sighed. "Oh to be young again,"

"Colonel, that's one dangerous young lady," the old NCO said.

"Top, you have no idea." He reached into his pocket and handed three distinctive unit badges to the old soldier saying, "these must have popped off of some of the men's uniforms. See that these get back to their rightful owners."

"There's a lot of that going around." Top looked at the badges in his hand and wondered how the Colonel had come to have them.

After a jeep, helicopter and another jeep ride, they were finally back at what passed for civilization in the middle of the desert, an underground housing commmplex more like a hotel than anything else. There was a central foyer with shops and a food court. Even here, Dauntless drew attention. But unlike the rest of the world they didn't come running over to her. In fact, they tried not to impose upon her. She kind of liked it.

Before going to her room she asked, "Dr. Parker, is there anyplace I can get a copy of this week's tabloids?"

"Sure, they fly them in every three or four days. The newsstand should have them." He pointed the stand out to them. The girls went over to see what they had.

"OHMYGOD! What have you done?" Was Beverly's first response upon seeing the headlines. Some of them read, "Elvis to the rescue." "The King and the Superhero." "The King rides again." Brandy just buried her face in her hands.

"OH, this one is my favorite, Dauntless does Vegas," Beverly laughed as she held up the papers.

"I'm as good as dead. General Solo is going to kill me and they will never find my body out here in the desert."

"Oh, I doubt that very much. If he turned you into food for the worms he'd wind up with a bunch of mutant superworms." Beverly was trying to cheer Brandy up. "And you know how he feels about that!"

They laughed, "OH, this is going to be bad," Brandy moaned as they looked at the papers.

Beverly added, "good picture."

The next day the girls find themselves outside in the bright desert sunlight by the door to AT5 lab, Dr. Cooly is invited to go along with Dr. Parker while Dauntless stays with Dr. Brewville. "Why am I here?" Brandy in her Dauntless uniform asks.

"There's some equipment that I need your help to check out," Dr. Brewville answered as he used the palm reader to unlock the door.

"You need me to check out?" Dauntless was puzzled. They went in and he turned on the lights. As the lights flickered they could see a myriad of strange looking devices and things scattered all about.

He leads Dauntless over to a table with a strange looking backpack on it. You could tell it was a backpack because it had shoulder straps. There were two metallic canisters that resembled giant lipstick tubes. There was a hand control attached to it by some wires.

Brandy playfully picked up the controller and joked, "What's this?"

He snatched it out of her hand. "Careful with that, you cow! That's the controller to the rocket pack."

"The what?' She ignored the cow comment.

"That's right. It's a rocket pack and that's the control for it. It's not the original controller for it. We never found it, but I rigged that up and it should work just fine for you," he said in his condescending way.

"I'm not flying that thing," she protested, with one hand on her hip and the other waving about in the air.

"Sure you are. It'll be fun!" He smiled a big toothy smile.

"If it's so much fun, why don't you fly it?"

"I just might. After you do," he said scratching his beard.

"That thing isn't safe! How do we know it will even work?" He could hear the concern in Brandy's voice.

"It works all right. I've tested it on a stand. But I need someone like you to test fly it," he implored.

"But there isn't anyone like me!" She cried defensively.

"That's why I need you. You're the only super strong, super tough human on the planet. You're the only one who can test it without worrying about getting hurt. You're the perfect test pilot," he pleaded. After 15 more minutes pleading, Dauntless found herself wearing a leather jacket over her Dauntless uniform and the rocket pack on her back.

"Why do I have to wear the leather coat?" She asked.

He motioned with his hand to her backside saying, "the rocket will get hot. It won't damage your uniform but your..."

His hand was getting too close. "Touch my butt and I'll break your hand."

He backs off and explains the controller in her hand. "The little dial on the controller is your speed control. Push the dial up to go faster, down to slow down or turn off the rockets."

"I can't believe I'm going along with this." She was shaking her head.

"It'll be fun," he cajoled her.

"You keep saying that, but somehow I'm not convinced. How do I steer?" She asked.

"Good question," he said as he walked over to the table. He returned carrying a gold helmet saying, "That's where this helmet comes in."

"Oh you've got to be kidding? That thing looks like something a space cadet would wear!"

"They probably would if they existed and if they had rocket packs. The dorsal fin is there to act like a rudder on a boat. You steer with your head and body. You'll get the feel of it once you're in the air." He handed her the helmet that covered her full face. It had a fin, but no eye openings.

"Getting in the air. That's what bothers me," Dauntless said mindlessly to herself as she examined the helmet.

"Just be sure to get plenty of altitude before you try anything. That way, if you have a problem you'll have plenty of time to correct it," he advised her.

She asked about the helmet before his last statement had sunk in. "How do I see with this thing on? Huh, make corrections?"

"You know, like learning how to turn and go up and down, things like that. That's how they train pilots, they take them up and let them learn where it's safe with nothing for them to run into," he explained.

"OH, ... But what about seeing?" She asked again.

"It's transparent. You can see through it from the inside. And I have put a voice activated mic inside so all you have to do is talk and we'll hear you on the ground," he pointed out to her.

A few minutes later Dauntless was standing on the tarmac in front of AT5 with the helmet and rocket pack on ready to go. Dr. Brewville is walking up to her saying, "one last thing...' He didn't get to finish. FOOOSH ! There was a bright flash and a cloud of brown smoke. Dauntless was streaking skyward at over 600 MPH!

"WOOOOO!" was the only thing they could hear on the radio.

Looking up, the brown smoke turned to white and she zigzagged across the sky. "She's out of sight!" was the second thing he said.

Doctors Cooly and Parker came running. He turned to them trying to reassure them saying, "don't worry, she'll be fine."

"But, ... how?" Beverly was speechless.

"Like I said, she will be fine. She has enough fuel for 20 minutes at 600 MPH."

Rocket girl twisted and turned violently through the sky for several minutes. She zoomed straight up and plunged back down, headlong, narrowly avoiding crashing into the Earth. She leveled off four feet off of the deck and found herself racing along at 600 MPH, kicking up stones and a cloud of dust in her wake. She weaved her way around rocks and cacti. Small desert animals scurried away as she thundered by. Her heart was racing almost as fast as she was going.

Finally, she gained control and slowed it down. By then she was nowhere near anywhere. She was lost! She climbed up for a better view but she was truly in the middle of nowhere. She flew over desolate deserts, cactus flats and dry lakes. With the Toquima Mountain range to her right, she eventually spotted a highway down below and followed it to the sleepy desert town of Tonopah.

It was at this time she realized she didn't know how to land. She tried to hover but, only found herself falling! She shot into the sky like a human skyrocket before falling back and hitting terra firma. After several more attempts, which drew the attention of the entire town, she tried coming in like a plane. She was a little high and snagged the banner strung across the street proclaiming Jim Butler Days. She crashed (which wasn't pretty), and went skidding along Highway 6 nearly taking out the gas station before the rockets stopped roaring.

Top knocked on Colonel Otis' office and went in saying, "Sir, we just received a phone call from the Sheriff of Tonopah."

"Ton oh where?" He said looking up at the top Sergeant.

"It must be a small town in Nevada. Anyway, sir, he says he has Dauntless and her rocket pack in the hospital and wants to know what to do about it."

He looked up with a blank expression, and after a few seconds he replied. "I'll have to get back to you on that."

A few minuts later, General Solo exploded. "She stole an experimental rocket pack and broke her leg crash-landing in some town in the middle of the desert?!"

"Not exactly sir. She didn't steal the rocket pack. She was test flying it and sort of got lost."

"Is that all?'

"No sir. Apparently she caused quite a stir upsetting their local festival. There was a fire and some property damage. I have sent Captain Reynolds and a team with some MIB to get her and bring her back."

General Solo just shook his head in disbelief.

CHAPTER SIX

THE WILD, WILD WEST

In the next week, General Solo is called back to Washington DC to try and explain why the funding for the HERO Organization shouldn't be cut. While he was out of town, the others were all busy with their own assignments, Dr. Brewville had to make repairs to the rocket pack and work on other bits of alien technology. MaCos Ex, the pig faced alien with extra joints, worked on the universal translator and the visored memory helmet, as they were starting to call it.

Brandy convalesced with her broken leg. She was milking it for everything it was worth, and Colonel Otis suspected as much. *After all, she had those alien nano whatever's in her blood. She was supposed to heal faster and be tougher in the first place, but he couldn't prove it and saw no reason to push it.* He felt sorry for his newest reluctant Lieutenant. But orders were orders. He gave her a crash course on how to be an officer. "I know just a few weeks ago you were a Spec. 4 in the National Guard struggling to make ends meet and now, you're a world wide celebrity, the Earth's only superhero able to pick up a car, ten times faster than any man and able to withstand … whatever it is you can withstand." This brought a smile to her pretty face. He paused before continuing. "I also know you never intended to join the military and that it was only a means to pay for college for you, and that you intended to become a law enforcement officer. And now, through no choice of your own, you find yourself an officer and a gentleman in the regular Army. I also know you didn't want any of this. But, since it has happened, let's try and make the best of it. Your actions not only reflect on you, but upon the Army and the HERO organization. Everything you do is being watched."

"Don't you think I know it?" That's why I have to live in this building, hidden away from the outside world," Brandy answered with her leg propped up.

"It takes most people four years to become an officer. I have some books for you to read that will help you with the transition from citizen soldier to officer. And no, there're not some boring book of regulations. They're self help books for new officers. Kind of a how to be an officer for dummies if you will. It won't take you four years to read them." He gave her copies of the Officer's Guide and the Officer's Handbook. After he hands her the books he leaves. Just as soon as he is gone, Brandy jumps up and puts on her headphones and starts sipping on a Coke.

One floor up in the HERO building, Heather and Dr. Cooly are working with Marshal trying to teach him English. Heather would work with him in the morning and Beverly in the afternoons. Heather stands before the seated Marshal with her arms folded. "How do I get into these messes? Okay, lets see how this works." She indicates with her hands on her chest that, "My name is Heather." She then reaches over to his chest and says, "your name is Marshal."

After pausing and not receiving a response, she repeated it adding, "And now you try." Marshal reaches over to Heather's chest, she jumps back.

He looks confused and says, "my name is Feather." She shakes her head, greatly exaggerating her movements saying, "no, no. My name is Heather! Yours is Marshal!"

This was met by more confused looks. "Look, it's easy." She tapped herself on the chest saying, "my name is Heather." She then took his big blue hand and he allowed her to tap him with it. "Marshal."

He thumped his solid chest and said, "Marshal." He then pointed to her saying, "my name is Feather."

"Close, big guy." She thought to herself, *They're not paying me enough for this.*

The HERO building wasn't the only place in Chicago with activity. In his cluttered basement apartment, Pete, the HVAC workman, comes up with a plan to make a million dollars. All he needs is a lunchbox and some home made sandwiches. The next Monday he sets his plan into motion.

At Ground Zero, the workers are checked by the Air Force guards before they can enter or exit the work area. Anything they bring in, like lunch boxes, are checked. Pete stands in line to have his brand new aluminum lunch box checked by security. The guard asked, "since when do you bring your lunch?" As he checked the contents of Petes box.

"Since Mom started making lunch," he joked with him. That got him in. During lunch, when no one was around, Pete took his lunchbox and snuck around to the restricted section where the alien cryo beds were. He made his way down and double checked that no one was there. Satisfied that he was alone he quickly worked the PC hooked to the core and one of the sarcophagi slid out and opened its outer door. This was a different one from before. He had gotten something wrong but still, there it was. He went over to it and looked in. *There was something inside. But, what?* He couldn't tell, the gasses inside had fogged the glass. He tried the controls on the bed and the inner lid opened.

He was repulsed at what he saw. Some kind of alien bug, it was ugly! What he was looking at would soon be known as the Harbinger Queen. It was a man sized insect, all black and tan, with a segmented body. The carapaces was all mottled with tan growth rings.

The face was like a cross between a praying mantis and a human vampire, with a pointy chin, small mouth and sunken cheeks. The black quasi-human eyes were deep set and disturbing to look at.

She had two sets of arms. The top set had a giant lobster like claw while the lower arms were more human-like, with bony fingers that ended in great, three inch, cat-like claws.

Two sets of spider-like legs, all covered with bristles, supported the Queen. The Queen's long prehensile tail ended in a foot-long stinger with three barbs that was hidden from his view.

This was no good. He couldn't take it with him. He was hoping for some nice little piece of alien technology to take with him, not this. Then he noticed there was something else in the sarcophagus with her.

There were about half a dozen, eight-inch long bugs, all drawn up dead at the foot of the bed. They were all black and brown and wicked looking. Kind of a cross between an ant and a scorpion with claws. These were perfect. *He could take two and nobody would suspect a thing. The Chinese would pay big bucks for anything alien, and these were definitely alien. He could take two and leave the rest. No harm done and no one the wiser.* Or so he thought.

He quickly took two of the bugs and crammed them into his lunchbox. Closing the lid, he next looked around and closed the lid to the cryo bed and used the PC to close up everything. He made it over to the edge of the work area and slid his lunch box into the ducts leading out.

He then resumed his normal routine and passed through security without his lunchbox. He ducked around the corner outside of the Air

Force security perimeter and went for his lunchbox in the ductwork. On the way out, he was stopped by a roving security patrol. He explained that he had just gone back for his lunchbox. They let him go. He was outside the secure zone. He was pumped with adrenalin, but he got it!

Dr. Cooly was working with Marshal in one of the upstairs labs. She hangs up her lab coat and takes off her glasses, putting them in the pocket of the lab coat. "Okay, let's see what you remember." She walks up to him. "What is it called?" Standing before him she put her hands on her cheeks.

"Face"

"Good," she pointed to her eye.

"Eyes"

"Very good." Next she held out her hands.

"Fands."

"That's hands." Next, her ear.

"Fipps!'

"No Marshal, these are my ears" He was having trouble saying the H sound.

"Fipps no?" He pointed to her ears.

She took his hands and placed them on her ears saying, "ears"

"Ears!"

"That's right! Show me your hips."

He took his hands from her ears and moved them down to her hips. As soon as she did it she realized that it was an ill-advised move. They were in very close proximity and she could feel his pheromones starting to affect her. All of the girls had built up a resistance to his pheromones, but being in close like this with the added stimulus of rubbing up against him was another thing. Her resistance was melting and it felt good.

At that moment, Nurse Chapel and Heather came busting in through the door carrying a pizza box. Heather said, "I got your pizza! OHMY!"

"I hear you can use them as a weapon if you're not going to eat it. Or should we just get the fire hose, to cool you two down?" Heather wisecracked.

Beverly jumped back from Marshal. "I was teaching him his body parts," she quickly explained.

"Looks like he's learning your body parts if you ask me," Heather joked. "Is that the Braille system you're using?"

"Could be fun. That's one class, I wouldn't mind auditing," Linda quipped. They laughed.

Heather kept the ball rolling. "Tell me doctor, is there any scientific reason to justify the three of us jumping his bones?" The joke flopped.

Beverly shook her head. "No, and I can't believe you even asked!"

"Just kidding!" Then she got serious. "It's happened to all of us, don't sweat it, just be more careful," she cautioned."

Linda asked, "who wants pizza?" They all dived in.

"Where is everyone?" Beverly asked.

Heather answered, "Dr. Brewville, Colonel O and Dauntless are on a boat on Lake Michigan. She has to learn how to work that rocket pack."

Beverly exclaimed, "that repulsive little man is back!"

"If you mean Dr. Brewville, the answer is yes. He flew in this morning," Heather replied. "I haven't met the man, what's your problem with him?"

"I think they have kept him in the desert too long. I mean, sure he must be smart or they wouldn't have him, but his attitude. UGH! He looks like a hermit in a lab coat. He smells and don't get to close to him while he eats is all I can say."

"Note to self. Stay clear of Brewville," Heather said.

At that time, 20 miles off the coast in Lake Michigan, Heather's boat, is actually a 60 footer bobbing up and down in the waves. FOOSH! Kerplunk! There's a splash and a smoke trail leading into the water. Seconds later Dauntless is bobbing in the water.

"NO! NO, try it again!" Dr. Brewville shouted from the railing with a cold drink in his hand.

Colonel Otis came forward. "It's a good thing she's a good swimmer." He then shouted to Dauntless, "come in and take a break!" He gave her a hand climbing aboard.

She swims in and they help her up into the boat. She dried herself off a little and asked, "why are we out here?"

"You need the practice and there's nothing for you to hit out here," Brewville answered.

"Seriously, when am I or anyone else for that matter ever going to use this thing?" She had a valid point.

"Going 600 miles an hour for 20 minutes or 300 for 80 minutes might just come in handy some time," was Brewville's answer. He then turns to Colonel Otis saying, "I was hoping to be working with Dr. Cooly. Why isn't she here with us?'

"This is a tech question. She studies alien life forms, not technology. You won't be working with her much," the Colonel said as he helped Brandy take her backpack off.

"Pity."

"But you will be working with MaCos Ex," the Colonel added.

"The alien engineer!" Brewville exclaimed. "I thought you had him in deep sleep."

"No, we have him working on some projects for us. We just haven't informed the rest of the world yet," the Colonel Said.

Later that night in the basement apartment of the Lewis brothers, Pete comes in clutching his lunchbox. "Roy, I did it!"

Roy came in putting on his last mostly clean shirt. "Did what?"

"I got some of the alien bugs to sell to the Chinese," Pete said as he flopped down on the couch putting his lunchbox down on the rickety coffee table.

No way!"

"Yes way! Wanta see em?" Pete exclaimed.

"Sure!" Roy said, as he plopped down next to his elder Brother.

Pete opened the box and reached in putting the bugs on the table in front of them. It looked like a cross between an ant and a scorpion. It had four hind legs, two pinchers, and two forearms with a segmented body and a prehensile tail with a hooked stinger. "That's some nasty looking bugs!" Roy exclaimed.

Pete poked it a little. "YEOW! One of the bugs sprang to life and had hold of his thumb. As Pete pulled it off he got bit again. "Yeoow!" He shook it off but his hand kept throbbing and then he just slowed down and froze in place. As Roy freaked out, the bug came back and crawled up his back and stung him on the back of his neck. Pete's expression was one of shock in the extreme. After a few seconds, he started to move again. Roy, rolled up a magazine and used it to try to knock the bug off of his brothers neck, but wound up beating his brother with the rolled up magazine.

After a few seconds of being flailed upon, Pete started to defend himself and shoved his brother down with him landing on the other bug. "YEOW!" Well, you know what happened. He rolled over and stiffened up. The second bug scurried over to him and stung him in the back of his neck.

A few seconds later Roy sat up and Pete fell back onto the couch. They both started to convulse. After a few seconds they stopped and looked at each other.

"AMALGAMATION COMMPLETE!" Pete hollered with a blank expression on his face.

Roy looked at him with an equally blank look, saying, "why are you yelling?"

"I didn't mean to. Is this better?" He responded.

They both just sat there looking around at their hands and feeling their bodies. "We were very fortunate," Pete says.

"So, this is what it is like to possess a higher intellect. Fascinating. Before I had nothing, just The Hive and now," Roy paused to think, a new experience for him. "And now, I realize I wasn't even aware of it before. I LOVE THIS!"

"Love? Yes, these hosts have a higher intelligence. I can think and express my thoughts! I can use tools and technology! The Queen will be most pleased," Pete said as he rose to his feet and took a couple of uneasy steps. "These hosts are bipedal. It will take just a few minutes to adjust. We must free the Queen!"

"No, not now. We must first access our host memories and determine how best this may be done," Roy objected.

A sun beat down from the deep blue azure sky, baking everything below. A hot dry wind blew, kicking up dust, blurring your vision. While you couldn't see, you noticed a sound somewhere off in the distance. The plinking of a player piano or was it a harpsichord? *What was the tune it was playing?' It was strangely familiar and yet, unknown.*

With the return of your vision you could see down the empty street of what looked like a Wild West ghost town, commmplete with animals tied to the hitching post and covered boardwalks.

You were standing in the intersection of two streets, if you could call them streets; they were nothing more than dust covered dirt roads with buildings on either side. Before you was the source of the music, a saloon with swinging doors. Looking north past the saloon was an animal pen and what looked like a livery stable, and a few scattered shacks. The street led down to a sparkling stream surrounded with desert flowers and plants.

Something flew over you casting a shadow on you as it passed. Looking up you have to shield your eyes from the sun's glare. You catch a glimpse of a winged lizard lazily soaring in circles over head. You look again and it's not a lizard, it's a turkey vulture.

Looking west past the saloon were some shops and stores. The Grand Hotel dominated the other side of the street, all two stories of it. The only other two story building in town lies to the east, Madam Cluso's palace, the only ornate building in town. Outside of town there wasn't much. Just scrub and rolling hills. Purple mountains lying to the east were visible. Hot air rising off the floor of the desert distorted the view.

Looking south behind you were some more nondescript buildings. At the end of the street is a domed temple with a minaret. *The heat off the dusty street is playing tricks with your eyes,* for when you look again, you see a simple white board church with a steeple and bell. On the other side of the street, among some more businesses is the Sheriff's office and jail. The sound of running feet from behind you catches your attention and you turn to see two barefoot young boys running towards two cowboys carrying small packages. They had just come out of the emporium building. The boys rush up to them saying, "do you know who's in the saloon?"

"No Jacko. Who's in the saloon?" The taller Cowboy asked.

"Lacota! That's who! And he's ridden Lubbock's animal!" The boy exclaimed excitedly.

"Lacota, on Lubbock's animal? Are you sure boy?" He doubted the veracity of the young one's report. He walked over to his animal and placed the package in the saddlebag.

"Yep, it's him alright, that's his animal tied to the post." The boy offered his observation as proof.

The cowboy's companion put his package away in the saddlebag of his mount next to the other animal and said, "maybe we should check it out?"

"He'd have to have a lot of nerve to come back here after what happened. But still, I could use a drink." He fastened his saddlebag closed and the two cowboys made their way down the street. They stopped to examine the animals tied to the post.

The pack mule had bags of dried beans and canned goods. There was a slab of smoked meat in a cheesecloth. Tied next to it was an Ostrosloth, a type of large flightless bird used for riding. It was unencumbered except for the saddle and empty rifle scabbard. "Looks like Lubbock's bird," Scorro the taller one said.

Turning to the young boys Scorro said, "Jacko, you did good. Now go fetch the Sheriff while Mordo and me watch him and make sure he doesn't get away."

The boy just stood there. "Now GO! I said!" Scorro hastened the boy along with a slap to his backside.

Mordo walked away saying, "I'll get my iron."

"Bring mine back with you," Scorro commanded. Mordo quickly went to his mount and recovered his sidearm and put on his gun belt. He got Scorro's disrupter and brought it back. Scorro strapped on his .45 Colt Peace Maker and they eased up to the door of the saloon. Looking in over the top of the swinging doors they could see Lacota drinking at the bar with his back to them.

Lacota was a large, make that a very large, broad shouldered man in buckskins. He had a dirty red sash around his waist with a huge knife in a beaded sheath tucked in the small of his back. He had no gun belt on. He was drinking a red fizzy drink through a straw. He was the only one at the bar. Four other men, townsfolk, sat at a table playing dominos.

Lacota's gunbelt hung on a peg on the wall by the end of the bar. His rifle was there too, leaning against the wall. The player piano played in the corner. The only other person in the saloon was the bartender. Scorro sized up the situation and said to his partner, "he's got his back to us and he's unarmed, we can take him.

"I don't know, I think we should wait for the Sheriff." Mordo wasn't so eager.

Jacko came running back, calling out, "The Sheriff's not there!" Lacota heard this and straightened up at the bar.

Mordo left saying, "I bet I know where he is. I'll be right back."

Hell, he ain't so tough. I can take him, Scorro thought as he eased into the bar. Reaching over, he took Lacota's rifle, a Norton particle accelerator with auto load. It looked like a big bore Sharps single shot buffalo gun with a fancy trigger guard. Lacota just chugged the shot of whisky he was drinking, watching Scorro all the time in the mirror behind the bar. A slight smile came to his lips and he shook his head.

He pulled the big hammer back cocking the rifle as he brought it up waist high. "Locota, I've got you now." The anger in his voice was evident, as was his intent.

The grizzled old Locota turned to face down the cowboy. "I don't know you boy! What's your problem?"

This flustered the cowboy. He hadn't thought this out, he was expecting Locota to try for the gun and he'd blow him away. But now he was talking to him. He had to explain. "You killed my friend Lubbock and stole his bird."

"Huh? Just what are you talking about boy?" He didn't want to get thrown out of another town for killing another son of Mexzona.

"Trying to talk your way out of it won't work. You're going to die. Scorro was excited and barely in control.

"Hell boy! We're all going to die. Just who is it I'm supposed to have killed anyway?" He said easing his hand behind his back as he inched his way closer to Scorro.

"You've killed so many men you can't even remember who you've killed! Just how many have you killed anyway?" Scorro was losing it and Locota had heard enough.

"It's hard to say, it's still early today."

Scorro squeezed the trigger and the hammer fell, CLACK! He looked down at the rifle in disbelief. Locota snatched hold of the muzzle end of the barrel and yanked it away from the tall cowboy, all in one motion. "It wasn't loaded," he explained.

Scorro went for his gun. As he drew, Locota knocked the gun from his hand with the rifle, using it like a war club. The gun went sailing across the room. There was a flash, the glint of sunlight on polished metal. All eyes in the saloon where fixed on it. The largest knife anyone had ever seen. It was long and broad, with a clipped point. The razor sharp edge bore the scour marks of hours of sharpening and grinding. The sunlight danced on its razor sharp edge.

He slowly waved it back and forth in a hypnotic motion. "Boy, you're getting into something you don't want no part of."

Scorro wasn't none too smart. He lunged for the knife and got it! Zit, Zit! Locota had carved his initial into the tall cowboy. As they drew closer together, he plunged the point of the knife deep into the cowboy. He drove it home with such force that the clipped point pierced him clean through and exited out his back a good three inches.

The cowboy started to tremble and Locota removed the blade, not by pulling it out mind you, but by slicing his way out the side of his victim, nearly cutting him in two. The blade easily knifed its was through the cowboy, slicing him just above the hip. As the knife exited his body, blood and guts came gushing out in a torrent. All the air left him and he collapsed to the floor. He was destined to ride the purple range never more.

The foul smell of rent entrails filled the saloon. He wipped off his knife on his victim's shirt and put the man killer away. The townsfolk took it as their cue to leave. Locota returned to the bar and poured another drink. "How much do I owe you?"

"Nothin', nothin' at all. In fact, why don't you keep the bottle," the bartender stammered as he backed away.

"Very neighborly of you. Just be sure to tell your Sheriff that it was self-defense." He slapped down a couple hard coins and turned to go, picking up his rifle, heading for the door. He walked around the growing pool of blood and stopped at the door to put his gun belt on. Outside, there was a bunch of townsfolk gathering. The crowd was starting to get ugly. Better get out of here before they get organized and turn nasty.

As he started out the door, someone in the crowd spotted him and took a shot, missing by inches, hitting the doorsill behind him. He ducked back in the saloon.

Mordo and the Sheriff came from the east. The crowd informed them the Locota had killed Scorro in the saloon, and that he was still holed up in there. The townsfolk, who didn't have their guns with them, went to get their guns and returned.

Locota turned to the bartender asking, "is there a back way out?"

"Just the side door. To Maws," he said pointing around to the other side of the bar. "Maws got sort of a restaurant back there. Nothin fancy, just good food." Locota went around and started to go and ran into Maw coming out.

"What's all the commotion about?" She asked. She stopped when her eyes fell on Locota.

"Sorry Mama. Just passin through," he said as he passed her. There were two men with scatterguns outside the door. "I'm not going out that way."

"MERCY!" Maw had discovered the pool of blood and lifeless body on the saloon floor. She was visibly shaken. The bartender had to steady her.

"Why don't you take her out of here. This could turn nasty," Locota advised them.

"LOCOTA! THIS IS SHERIFF ELWOOD! I'M COMING IN." The Sheriff was standing in front of the growing crowd. He handed his shotgun to Mordo.

"COME ON IN SHERIFF! Locota called out to him staying clear of the doorway. The Sheriff headed in.

The Sheriff went into the saloon and saw the dead body on the floor. "What a bloody mess."

"It was self-defense," Locota said as he motioned with his rifle in hand to the corpus.

"That's what they all say," the Sheriff said as he studied the body.

"But it was. He came at me with my own rifle and then his gun. They saw what happened. They'll back me up."Locota implored him as he backed away from the doorway.

"If that's true, then you have nothing to worry about."

"It's the truth," Locota assures him.

"Care to explain how you came to have that bird?" The Sheriff casually asked.

"I got it from another son of Mexzona."

"This son of Mexzona have a name?" The Sheriff asked hopefully.

"Didn't get it." Locota's reply didn't satisfy the Sheriff.

"I don't suppose you got a receipt?"

"We didn't have any paper and he couldn't write," Locota explained.

"Come with me. We'll have to sort this all out." The Sheriff motioned for them to leave. He met resistance to this idea.

"Go with you? For how long?" Locota asked.

The Sheriff scratched his head before answering. "The circuit judge won't be around for another month."

Locota started shaking his head. "I can't stay here for a month waiting for your judge to mosey by. I've got animals to feed and trap lines that need tending. I've got to see a man about a dog."

"And here I thought you were supposed to be some kind of hired gunman."

"That was a long time ago. Just look at me, do I look like a hired killer?" Locota said drawing attention to his buckskins.

"No, I have to admit, you don't, but that doesn't mean you're not dangerous, the Sheriff countered.

"By reputation only, I can assure you. But I can't go with you. That would ruin me," Locota said as he passed his rifle to his hand.

"I can't jest let you go," the Sheriff said trying to avoid more bloodshed.

"Sheriff, you do what you have to do and I'll do what I have to do. Just remember, a lot of townsfolk are going to die if you try to take me. Why not just let me go? I'll come back next month and clear this up. I'll even have a receipt for the bird," Locota said trying to win the Sheriff over.

"I thought you said you didn't have one?"

"That doesn't mean I can't get one." He wasn't above manufacturing one, and the Sheriff knew it.

The Sheriff started shaking his head. "Sorry, I can't do it."

The Sheriff leaves the saloon and rejoins the crowd. They have started building barricades across the street around the saloon. Mordo asks, "what are we going to do Sheriff?

"He's loaded for bear so we can't go in there and get him. So I guess we have to smoke him out," Sheriff Elwood said.

"But Sheriff! That will burn down the saloon," the bartender protested.

"MYGOD! WHAT WAS I THINKING?" The Sheriff answered sarcastically. "There's a man's life at stake here!"

"A durty murders life!" Someone in the crowd chimed in.

"We don't know that for sure. It's up to the court to decide." The Sheriff called out, trying to maintain control over the crowd. The crowd grew uglier and uglier. Sheriff Elwood was forced to concede to the will of the mob. "I guess we could just blast him out."

"That's what we'll do! We'll blast him out of there!"

Sheriff Elwood commanded, "EVERYBODY start firing on my command. And be sure to aim high! We'll pump the saloon full of lead. When he surrenders and comes out we'll take him alive! GOT IT?" He looked around to see if they had.

Inside the saloon, Locota was busy setting up a little fort of his own, using the tables and the music machine. Then he got an idea. He set up all of the bottles on the bar and set a lantern on the bar with them. He went around the saloon collecting all of the lanterns and set them up on the bar. He placed a few cartridges on the bar with them. He lit the lanterns and pulled out his man killer knife and checked the edge with his thumb.

Thirty rifles, pistols and shotguns started firing at once. The air was thick with smoke in a few seconds. No one could see what they were shooting at, but they kept on firing. They would pop up shoot and duck back down again. The firing reverberated down the street, rattling the shop windows.

Every window in the saloon was shattered and blown away in the first few seconds. The swinging doors were shot off their hinges and the doors and windowsills were chewed up. The animale that had been tied to the front hitching post broke free and headed for quieter pastures.

After about 30 seconds everyone was out of ammunition and had to stop to reload. Sheriff Elwood called out to Locota, "had enough? Come out with your hands up!"

"Come and get me Sheriff!" Was the reply from inside. This inspired a second round of fire from the crowd. Inside the saloon, as the hail of lead slammed into the building, splinters of wood flew everywhere. The fancy felt covered gaming table was ventilated, even the music machine suffered. Strings and machinery gave off a most unusual sound when hit by a bullet. The mirror behind the bar was one of the first causalities. Occasionally, one of the bottles on the bar would explode, spilling its contents everywhere. One of the lanterns was hit and suffered a similar fate.

The 30 second hailstorm of lead stopped and once again the Sheriff called out. The reply was the same. The air was thick with the pungent smell of rotten eggs, the smell of old time black powder gunpowder. They could hardly see. *What's he up to?* Sheriff Elwood wondered, and then it came to him. As they reloaded he called out to them, "he has to be on the floor!"

The third barrage went off on cue. Several rounds hit the street kicking up dust, and ricocheting to God only knows where. The water trough was hit sending water spewing out. The wooden wall of the saloon was riddled with bullet holes. Inside, one of the tables was hit, causing it to jump up and spin around. There was a fire spreading over the top of the bar.

After the customary 30 second firestorm, once again, Sheriff Elwood tried to talk Locota into surrendering. But this time there was no answer. "Did we get him? Or is he playing possum?" Someone called out. The Sheriff called out again and again, receiving no reply.

"We got him! Let's go get him!" The townsfolk cried out.

"Are you sure? Do you want to be the first one to go in and find out?" Sheriff Elwood asked knowing the answer before he asked.

"That's your job Sheriff!"

"We'll wait a little," was his reply.

"I think I see something moving in there," one of the crowd reported. BANG!

"He's shooting back!" They all dived for cover. There were a couple more shots fired from inside. The crowd responded in the predictable way, another 30 seconds of hell.

There was no response of any kind to their next offer to surrender. They reloaded and emptied their guns into the saloon again, just to make sure. By now, the saloon was scarcely recognizable, and it was apparent that there was a fire inside.

The Sheriff and four deputies went in. The saloon was full of shattered furniture, broken glass and the bar was on fire filling the room with smoke. But there was only one body, the cleaved cowboy.

They retreated out the front door, "he's not in there!"

"Come-on, help us put the fire out!" The crowd jumped into action forming a bucket brigade with buckets from one of the nearby shops. After the smoke had cleared, Sheriff Elwood discovered a large hole had been chopped through the back wall.

Outside there was the sound of a bird running and a shotgun blast. "There he goes! He's getting away!"

Elwood quickly formed a posse and road after Locota. Your vision gets blurry and suddenly, everything goes black and there is a large headed Gray alien in fancy robes talking to you." The proceeding, as I stated at the beginning was a single source reconstruction of the events leading up to the formation of the board of inquiry investigating the conduct of Federation Marshal shield number 8181, and the events leading to the deaths of 157 beings and the destruction of commerce station 17. These images may not be accurate and will self adjust as directed by your perception and cognition centers of your brain. They are only intended to serve as background information, explaining the formation of the board of inquiry, and how and why Sheriff Ken Elwood came to be part of the board.

"These images are not intended to be used as evidence in any tribunals, trials or prosecutions, in accordance with Federation law, cited earlier." A field of alien text appears behind the judge as he continues to speak.

"The next record is made from mutable registered sources and has been rectified, and is admissible in any proceeding. ZZZzz" The Gray man becomes blurry. Everything goes black.

Colonel Otis removes the memory helmet and looks over to Dr. Cooly. "This is not good. We have to know what happened at this Commerce Station 17 before we can let Marshal use the helmet to recover his memory. Get MaCos on it. Let me know if you have any luck or need anything."

.

CHAPTER SEVEN

IT WAS ONE OF THOSE DAYS

In the conference room, Colonel Otis is seated at the head of the table at General Solo's usual place. Doctors Brewville and Cooly are there, as are Dauntless and Heather with Marshal, and two army captains in BDUs. Heather asks, "Where is General Solo?"

"You're in charge of Marshal's security and nothing more. In the general's absence I'm in charge, and in my absence, it's the DO. Do I make myself understood?"

"He's in Washington, I called this meeting," the Colonel reported.

"You called the meeting? I'm in charge of…," Heather didn't get to finish.

"You're in charge of Marshal's security and nothing more. In the General's absence, I'm in command, and in my absence the DO is in charge. That is the chain of command. Do I make myself clear?"

"Commpletely," she said leaning back in her seat.

"Here's your duty assignments for today. Dr. Cooly, you're working with MaCos trying to get that helmet working. We need to know about the charges brought against him and about that trial, if we can rely on him and if we can use it to help Marshal recover his missing memories. He said something about a neural interphase. It sounded like something straight up your alley. I'll talk to you later if you have any questions. Beverly pushed her glasses back up her nose and nodded to indicate she understood.

Turning his attention to Dauntless, "you're going hang gliding. That should help you with controlling the rocket pack. See Top for all the details. Work on your landings and don't come back until you've mastered it. Take the rocket pack and by all means be careful, you won't be wearing your Dauntless uniform," he said with genuine concern for her well being. Brandy wasn't sure how to respond to this, and he picked up on this and advised her, "think of this as a new challenge for you or maybe adventure training."

She responded, "Got it, see Top." He moved on to the next point of interest on his agenda.

"Heather, will you please teach Marshal as much English as he can learn?" He said with a smile. Then he reminded her. "Be careful around those pheromones."

"Oh, very funny." She was all flustered.

"Dr. Brewville, you're in the lab working on ammo for Marshal's sidearm. And doctor, this isn't Dreamland, so please keep the explosions down to the minimum."

Brewville banged his paper cup down on the table in annoyance at Otis's comments. *The nerve of the oaf,* he thought to himself.

The Colonel continued. "A company has the duty this week. B is on standby, weapons inspection, 1500 today. Charley is standing down." He flipped through some papers saying, "nothing new from MIB. No new threats to report. Unless any of you have anything?" He looked around at them.

They all looked around. "Nothing. Good. Ladies and gentlemen, you have your instructions. Have a good day. Dismissed."

He hooked Beverly's arm before she could get out of the room. "We have to know about his background before we can let him have access to the helmet. He doesn't get to use it until we know what's in it, and that it's safe. Are we clear on this?" He asked sternly.

The redheaded buxom beauty removed his hand from her arm and looked him in the eye nose to nose. "When I know you'll know."

"Excellent."

Dr. Brewville came over to the Colonel asking, "who will be assisting me in the lab?"

"You will be your own assistant doctor. Sorry, we don't have the manpower Dreamland does. But, I can give you the lower level lab to use."

A short time later in the upper level lab, Dr. Cooly goes past the guard at the door and joins MaCos Ex, who is already working on the helmet. "MaCos, we have got to get that thing working 100 percent. I need to know about Marshal's background."

"I can tell you some of it," the pig faced alien reported, "but it'll cost you."

"How much this time?" She took off her glasses. She had heard this routine before.

I would like some more of those pretzels and the garlic bread and much more cabbage," he said rubbing his multi-jointed hands together in anticipation.

"Fine, done. What can you tell me?" She leaned back with one elbow on the worktable behind her.

"He's Aurorian, he's part of the Ohmahaw Exchange."

This meant nothing to her, only names. "You'll have to do better than that. Those are just meaningless names to me," she explained.

"Oh, very well, think big picture." He paused, gathering his thoughts before continuing. "There are 56 starfaring species in the known universe. With another 200 or more lesser or subservient intelligent species that have not yet attained star travel by themselves, but have access to the stars through contact and usually servitude to higher technologies, with more out there not yet contacted."

"Forty of these species have joined together for mutual protection and trade. This alliance is called the Gateway Federation. Marshal comes from a primitive planet called Aurora. It is subservient to the Andorian Star Emirate.

The Aurorians are an intelligent species, the dominant specie on their planet. But being so incredibly strong and tough they never had to evolve any higher technology. They can be trained if taken at an early age. And that is what has happened to our Marshal here.

The Ohmahaw Exchanges allow for small numbers of low-tech species to be brought into higher tech worlds for research and development. After they reach full development, they must be released into society and allowed a normal life. You must understand, a normal life is a relative concept."

"The Andorians and the Federation have an exchange program where they each send some of their citizens to live and work in the other's world. Every species is represented. Think of it as a cultural exchange."

"This Marshal is very unusual. He is the first one I have actually seen. Does that help you?" MaCos sat down twirling a tool around in his fingers.

Dr. Cooly leaned forward on her elbow, intrigued by his story and asked, "What makes him so strong? And so tough? It can't be his muscles."

MaCos scratched his neck as he answered. "That's biology, if I had to guess. I would say it has something to do with atmospheric pressure or the conversion of sunlight into energy." Or maybe, he just took his vitamins."

"MaCos Ex! Did you just make a joke?" She came to life.

"One tries," he quipped. "Do I get the food?"

"That was more than we knew, but it's not enough. However, I'll tell them." She spun around on her stool and undid the bun her hair was in. Her silky auburn hair flowed down around her neck and shoulders. Shaking it out she asked, "is the helmet ready for use?"

"I was working on it and I think you will be able to access some of the earlier records. Just give me a few minutes."

A black SUV going south on LSD (Lake Shore Drive) was passing the new Soldier's Field. Brandy is riding shotgun with three other soldiers, all in civvies. Brandy asks, "just where are we going?"

Sergeant Lopez in back answered, "we're going to an abandoned quarry. You'll be able to practice there all day without anyone bothering you, Sir."

"Sir?" She started to comment but stopped. She tended to forget she's an officer.

"Can we stop and get some drinks?" She asked without thinking.

"I don't see why not. We got-a-eat and you're the officer, Sir," he answered.

"Cool!" She started to settle down in her seat. "Since we're in our civvies and undercover and all, you can call me Brandy."

The NCO introduced the others to the LT. "I'm Carlos and this is Dave next to me and the wheel man is Tex.

"Tex huh? Where you from?" She asked.

"Albuquerque."

"This left her confused. Before she could follow up, her phone rang. She scooched around and answered it. Dr. Cooly's voice came out, loud and clear. "MARSHAL'S DYING, I NEED YOU FAST!"

"He's dying!? But? ...What can I do?"

"CPR!"

They all could hear. Tex offered, "I can turn around but it will take us an hour or more to get back there with this traffic."

"####(expletive deleted) Pull it over!" She commanded.

On the side of the road she got out and went to the back of the SUV. Pounding on the roof she demanded, "open it up!"

The rear hatch opened as the soldiers got out and joined her. As school busses, trucks and cars whizzed by, she put on the brown leather jacket that went with the backpack. Sergeant Lopez tried to reason with her. "Lieutenant! Think what you're doing!"

As she zipped up the front she answered, "he's dying and this is the only way! Come on and help with this thing."

Tex and Dave helped her with the straps of the rocket backpack. They hooked up the control wires that ran from the jacket to the pack as she donned the golden flight helmet. "Get back!" Was all she said.

There was a flash, a puff of smoke and, FOOOSH! She zipped up and out of sight, leaving a plume of smoke trailing after her. The three soldiers just watched her disappear and then looked back and forth at each other. "Well, I guess that's the end of this road trip," Lopez said.

She zoomed past the lakefront stadiums, museums and the giant ferriswheel on Navy Pier. She swooped over the harbors filled with docked sailboats, past the row of tall high-rise buildings, until she neared the northern end where she veered inland, rocketing between apartment buildings on the edge of the park towards the Truman University campus.

She cut the power and pancacked (a type of bad landing.) trying to lose speed and set up to land on top the HERO Building, but she carried a little too much speed and started her landing flair too late. As a result, she slammed into the top floor of the building. "OHHH NOOO!"

As luck would have it, she didn't splatter her guts all over the side of the building. She hit a window and careened on in, landing on a hospital cart with wheels and went careening out of the examination room, across the central main room and crashed into the cabinets of the C locker on the other side of the room. The glass doors exploded and medical supplies went flying as she came to a rest in a crumpled heap.

Seconds later she came to life! The back of her blue jean legs was on fire! She franticly kicked them off. "HOT HOT!" There she stood, ankle deep in the debris and smoke, barelegged wearing the heavy leather coat, gold helmet and rocket pack. MaCos Ex and his guard were the only ones up there and they were speechless.

She pulled the helmet off and tossed it with the jacket to the stupefied soldier saying as she ran by, "Where is he?"

"Uh, Dr. Cooly rushed out and went to the main floor," the trooper stammered as she hopped in the elevator.

MaCos turned to him saying, "this is a very strange planet you have here."

The elevator door opened revealing Marshal lying on the floor with his uniform jacket thrown open and a Bic pen sticking out his throat! As Brandy hesitantly walked forward in not much more than a plaid shirt and running shoes, Dr. Cooly ran in carrying a small defibilator. "You got here fast!" She said eyeing Brandy's lack of attire.

"What happened?" Brandy asked.

"He's had a reaction to something he ate. His tongue, mouth and neck have swollen shut! I had to do a trach on him. Then his heart stopped. He's too strong for me to do CPR!" She said as she opened the case the device came in.

Both girls knelt on either side of the fallen blue giant. "Give him some air while I set this up!" Dr. Cooly commanded.

Brandy looked down at him in confusion "HUH?"

"Blow some air in the pen!" She explained, as she got the patches out.

"Oh." Brandy knelt down over him, took a deep breath and blew on the end of the pen sticking out of his neck. She saw his chest rise and fall. She blew again. The same.

"Defibilator charging," the device said in a cold mechanical voice. "Ready!"

Beverly shouted, "Clear!" and he was shocked with no effect. Beverly tried blowing on the pen but her lungs weren't strong enough to inflate his. "You'll have to do it," she said, and turned her attention back to the defib device. Brandy started doing chest commpressions as the device charged again.

At that time in the lower level lab, Dr. Brewville is explaining things to the Colonel. "Do you see why I need the gun?" Only the material the gun is made from will cut the material the bullets are made from, and I can't make the material the gun is made from so I need to use the actual gun parts to work with the material."

"Sounds dangerous," he responded to his companion.

"The material is in a metastable state all the time so yes, it could be dangerous, that's why I need the gun to work with," Brewville implored him, adding, I never had these problems with the Air Force."

Otis, smelling BS, tersely replied. "this ain't Dreamland." As he left he added, "you'll get access to the gun." The Colonel headed for the elevator. The doors opened and he ran into Heather, all flustered. "Fancy meeting you here," he said joking with her. He looked around and didn't see Marshal anywhere. This prompted him to ask, "where's your student?"

She gave him a blank stare, not knowing what to say.

"You know, the big guy. He comes from outer space. You remember don't you?"

Exasperated she replied, "It was lunch time and you know how he loves Chicago style pizza." She was flustered about something but so far she was making sense.

Yeah? He nodded his head. "

She shifted her weight to one hip and with her hands waving, continued. "Well, he was doing so well and all so I thought I'd reward him with a pizza, but seeing how we just had pizza I decided to try something different

Yeah?" He was starting to get concerned.

"Who would have thought?" She said with hands flailing.

He caught her hands asking, "Who would have thought what?"

Startled by this, she jerked her hands free. "Who would have thought that a big guy like Marshal couldn't eat pepperoni?" She explained.

"What?" He exclaimed.

"He can't eat pepperoni! His tongue swelled up and everything. I had to rush him to the Med. Section. But we didn't make it," she explained looking frightened.

"Did you call Dr. Cooly?" Now he was alarmed.

"DUH!" She sighed with an exaggerated swinging of her head. "She's with him now, COME ON!" She commanded and they turned back to the elevator.

"It's always somethin'!" He said as the elevator door closed. Now he was starting to *wonder if his recommendation of Heather to the general was a good idea.*

They exited the elevator and the first thing he saw was Brandy's rounded buttocks sticking up in the air with her bent down over Marshal. The sight of those white panties straining to cover her was burned into his memory.

She gave another puff on the pen and started another chest commpression when Beverly said, "CHARGED, STAND CLEAR!" Brandy straightened up clear of Marshal and the Doctor shocked him again. His body strained and relaxed. Checking for a pulse, Dr. Cooly reported, "we have a pulse!"

Marshal came to and after a few seconds tried to speak but was unable to make a sound. He reached for the pen stuck in his throat and Brandy had to stop him. Brandy has the strength of ten men but even she's no match for Marshal. A brief wrestling match erupted which resulted in Brandy being pulled on top of Marshal. He tossed her aside and started to pull the pen out when she leapt back on him landing nose to nose. She cried out, "NO, DON'T!"

He stopped, it hurt, and he was terrified, she could tell. She went on to say in a calmer tone, "I know it hurts but you have to leave it in for now. You can trust me."

Nurse Chapel came running in with a syringe and Dr. Coolly used it to give him a shot in the back of his hand. Looking up she explained, "that should take care of the swelling."

Heather, standing in back, tilted her head and asked, "I thought he was bullet proof. How can you give him a shot?"

"He's not bullet proof, only very tough. We had some special very strong and sharp needles prepared just for use on him," Beverly explained.

"Wouldn't he heal faster if you closed his jacket?" Colonel Otis asked, motioning to Brandy to get up.

"I had to open it to do the trach. It doesn't protect his head but now, I suppose it's a good idea."

"Lt. Holmes, get up," he commanded.

"Sir, I can't. He's got hold of me," she reported. She turned to Marshal and lowered herself close to him and whispered in his ear, "I don't know if you can understand me or not but, you have to let go of me. I promise I won't go anywhere." A couple of intense seconds passed and then she gave him a peck on the cheek. He nodded and released her.

She sat on the floor next to him and they closed the flap on his jacket. He clasped the collar around the pen. She studied his hand. He didn't try to remove the pen. After a minute there was a gurgling sound. Dr. Cooly pronounced, "it's working."

The pen came squirting out in another minute and he was sitting up with Brandy holding him. With the situation apparently in hand, the Colonel turned to Heather and asked, "I don't suppose you can tell me what happened to Lt. Holme's pants?"

"Not a clue," she said shaking her head.

Brandy turned away from Marshal for a second to answer. "I kicked them off because they were on fire."

He started to question her, "Ho, .. Bu, ..What? ,.. Oh never mind." He turned and left.

A few minutes later, with the disaster averted, Dr. Cooly and Heather exit the elevator at the upper level lab. Heather was trying to explain that she wasn't trying to poison him; she was trying to be nice to him. But as soon as her attention shifted to the room they just entered, her mouth drooped open. "Holy ####! What happened here!"?

Dr. Cooly was speechless. Her normally perfectly orderly lab was a shambles.

There was smoke in the air and broken glass and medical supplies all over the floor. MaCos Ex spun around to face them and held up a still smoldering pair of blue jeans.

Heather spotted the visored helmet and asked, "Is that the memory helmet?"

Dr. Cooly just walked over in a daze murmuring to herself.

MaCos joined Heather explaining that, "Yes, you call it that, but that's not it's intended purpose."

"What was its intended purpose?" He had piqued her curiosity.

"It was meant to document the day to day events, sort of a daily log book," he explained as he handed the helmet to her.

"I thought it played movies or something." She was puzzled as she looked at the helmet.

"It would seem like that to you. It takes any and all files that relate to any given event or time and commbines them in your head. The end result is somewhat like being in a movie only it's a recreation of history as seen from every perspective. You truly experience being there, without being there, of course."

"We can see anything in the universes?" She asked hopefully.

"No, only things related to Marshal," and only things up to the last uploading."

"I've got to try this!" She proclaimed.

"I just made some repairs to it, you can access some older files," MaCos offered.

"Is it safe? How does it work?" She asked as she studied the inside of the helmet.

"Just put it on, close the visor to activate it and think." She took the helmet and plopped down in the big chair in Dr. Cooly's office, as the others picked up the pieces of Beverly's lab, she watched the movie.

The hatch of the shuttle slid open and eight recruits exited carrying their gear. There were seven of them, human-like except for red skin, which made them look a little devilish. They all wore green and brown uniforms with different insignias on them. The eighth had blue skin and was slightly taller then the rest, and he wore the all black jumpsuit uniform of fleet service.

The recruits form up in two ranks of four. They are in a sheltered courtyard with flowering vines growing on the stonewalls. Music is playing somewhere in the distance. The sky is a greenish blue with white clouds. This is the old quarter of Shambailla.

The group is called to attention as a man wearing a highly engraved gold breastplate and flowing robes comes in. "I am Rizone Lex, I will be your instructor."

He turns and points to the open gate behind him. "Through these portals pass some of the finest warriors in the universe. All of you have qualified to be in the Imperial Guard. But I demand more, much more. Most of you will not make the grade. You will wind up in the Imperial Guard forces acting as umpires on War World. Or perhaps near one of the Emeers commpounds. But perhaps one or two of you will be good enough to become Sea Ay Knights.

Everything goes blurry for a second and then refocuses. The location has changed. The tall blue fellow and one of his fellow recruits are now wearing a silver breastplate and flowing red robes of an Sea Ay Knight. They are walking down a broad and busy street. People coming and going in all directions, no vehicles or animals, just foot traffic.

The buildings on either side sport flying buttresses, minarets and domes of every size and shape. All are pastel colored with balconies on the second or third level. An euphony of music is provided by the live bands or orchestras playing from some of these balconies, each spaced so as to not conflict with the other. Street vendors rub shoulders with politicians. This is Shambailla, the capital of the Emirate, the grandest city in the universe. There are no Grays here except for visiting diplomats and businessmen. Even the air is scented so to increase your pleasure.

Overhead, is the silvery moon, celestial home of the Emeer of Andora, Shambailla Primus. Normally you would be up there, that is where the Sea Ay and Ess Sea Ay Knights serve and protect the Emeer and his family, but today is different. You are assigned to the Trihendron.

You and your companion walk on making simple small talk. You enter the Grand Plaza. A five sided stone plaza is flanked by the five Houses of State. In front of each are statues of heroes such as Felspar The Magnificent, Jordan of the Air, Alberta the Truculent, Crocket of Tenn and, of course, the Red Barron. "I don't believe you have been cleared for that yet!" It was Colonel Otis's voice.

Heather removed the helmet. Before her stood the Colonel asking, "how is Marshal?"

She put the helmet down on the desk and jumped up to her feet. "He's alright!"

"Good," he replied. "Seeing that you're the new head of Marshal security, I suppose it will be okay for you to use the helmet. But not until you give yourself clearance." He paused to laugh. "General Solo should be back tomorrow. See you in the AM," he said with a sly smile as he turned to go.

She jumped up after him saying, "Just a minute Colonel! I'm not done with you."

He stopped and turned to face her. "What is it?"

She got right up nearly bumping into him and got in his face. "That's twice you've told me what to do. And I let you get away with it just to let you save face in front of the others. But just you remember, you're not the boss of me. I'm in charge!

She was really leaning into him now and her closeness made him uncommfortable and he backed off a little, but she just kept on coming. "And I can handle myself. I think I already proved that when..."

He had regrouped and he didn't let her finish. "We will never speak of that again. It was very unprofessional of us and it'll never happen again."

Heather took a step back, hands on hips, and tossed her hair back. "Don't flatter yourself!"

Now he advanced on her. "Listen to me little lady. As I said before, you're in charge of Marshal's security. I, on the other hand, am the Commanding officer of the 5th. We are both part of HERO. My unit will support you and Marshal. When General Solo isn't here I'm in charge of HERO so, you do your job and I'll do mine. Got it?" He turned and left shaking his head. "Civilians!" *Was she testing me or is she really like that?*

This got her thinking, *if I'm here and Dr. Cooly is here and Nurse Chapel is here,* she could see Chapel helping Beverly finishing up in the lab. *Who, if anyone, was with Marshal?* She dashed out of the office looking around; there was no sign of him.

Better go find him. Who knows what trouble he could get into by himself. She darted into the elevator. He wasn't in the Med Section. Dr. Brewville was the only one in the lower labs, and he claimed that he hadn't seen anyone for hours. He wasn't in the mess hall or day rooms. Mr. T on the front desk said he hadn't left the building and he would know. That only left the living quarters. *Of course! That's where he is. He's probably gone to bed. After all that's happened to him he's probably asleep.*

Heather snuck into Marshal's room, She didn't want to disturb him but she felt a little guilty about doing it. After all, the last time she had been in there they... well that was then. She wondered if he wore pajamas or slept in the natural. The thought excited her. He wasn't there either!

That only left one possibility. She went down the hall to Brandy's room and listened to the door. She could hear movement and heavy breathing! She tried the door; it wasn't locked. Heather was conflicted. She didn't want to intrude, but then again, it was her job. She eased in and closed the door behind her.

She was in the living room, not much to talk about, hotel furniture. The action was taking place in the next room. She eased up to the doorway to get a better look and she got an eyeful.

Brandy, in all her glory au natural on top of Marshal, gyrating and grinding away, with their hands interlocked. Heather at first didn't know what to do. She hadn't thought it through. The more she watched the more she was drawn in. She bit her finger but couldn't pull herself away. *Those damned pheromones!*

Brandy was putting on quite a show, rocking back and forth, stretching and swaying as if to some unheard music. Her sexy sculpted stomach undulated like the ocean. She arched her back, heaving her full breasts up towards the ceiling. They magically hung there for a few seconds and then came crashing down against his blue chest like a wave breaking on the beach.

Heather was getting the urge and she was trying to resist it. Marshal was the first to notice her when he rose up into a seated position with Brandy still going strong. He was only briefly distracted when he saw her standing there. There was nothing he could do or say. He was in Brandy's grip, and there was no getting out of it, not that he wanted to in the slightest.

His eyes started to flutter and roll up in their sockets. His head snapped back and he arched his back. He soon found himself once again on the bottom, with the sea that was Brandy crashing over him. Then, Brandy became aware of Heathers prescence. Brandy, in her state of near ecstasy, kept up with her motion and simply beckoned to Heather to join them with her hand. The aroused Heather was overpowered by those damned pheromones.

Now Heather and Brandy would be too much for any one man to handle, downright lethal, even if Brandy wasn't superhuman. But Marshal isn't exactly human either, and that's the only thing that saved him that night.

CHAPTER EIGHT

AMALGAMATION

The next morning, General Solo conducted his usual daily briefing with everyone present. He reported, "the Congress isn't to happy about funding a super hero organization with only one or two superheroes. They say that's not much of an organization." He paused and looked at the girls. "And then there was this, uh, what should we call it, this thing, this event, mishap or escapade in Las Vegas."

No one offered an answer. After an uncommfortable silence he continued. "We need to be seen doing more good things! Like that fire rescue you did the other day. Good work Dauntless."

"Just what are we supposed to do? They can't just go out on patrol can they? The Colonel asked.

"I don't know, it might come down to that but I doubt it. This alien technology is too valuable to be putting on the streets. If it does happen, it will only be after all of the technology has been transferred to the Air Force's custody." Dr. Brewville was full of mixed emotions upon hearing the general's answer. He liked being in Chicago and being surrounded by beautiful women.

"Have you made any progress with the translator?" Solo asked Dr. Cooly.

"No General, we've hit a brick wall there, and we've pretty much given up on it. Heather has been concentrating on teaching him English. I've been concentrating on the visored memory helmet. We think, if we can help him recover his lost memory, his translator might start to work."

"Have you been able to view all of the files and determine if it's safe for us to let him have access to them?" She shook her head. "Then keep after it," he added.

"How is your student doing?" He asked turning to Heather.

"Uh, it's not going very well. We've had some, uh difficulties. But I'm willing to work with him all day and night if I have to," Heather offered.

"What about getting him an English teacher?" He leaned back in his overstuffed chair.

"I've been working on it General. There just aren't any English teachers with high security clearances," she defensively replied.

"Then you should look into finding a teacher you can get a high clearance for." He then changed the subject. "I understand that Marshal's pheromones are starting to cause problems again."

Heather and Brandy shot each other looks as Beverly answered, "no General, I don't think so, nothing major anyway. We are developing resistance. It's only an issue when we're in close quarters for a prolonged period of time."

Doctor Brewville offered his solution to the problem. "If we had an all male crew working with Marshal that would eliminate the problem altogether."

"You're just trying to take over,' Dr. Cooly snapped back at him.

"We're not going to change personnel, that would only worsen security. If anything, we need fewer people, but you can't unlearn something so I guess for now, everyone is in."

"There is one last thing," the General paused before asking, "just what the hell went on here yesterday?"

They all froze up and tried to look innocent. Then the Colonel had to speak up. "Uh, sir, it was just one of those days when everything went wrong, sir. Just what are you referring to in particular. "

"How about Dauntless buzzing the lakefront with the rocket pack or the head of security poisoning the person she is supposed to be guarding!"

"Uh, when you put it that way it sounds much worse than it really was. The poisoning brought on the buzzing sir. The poisoning was accidental and the buzzing, though unfortunate, was necessary to save Marshal's life." As the Colonel answered, he could see his pension disappearing before his eyes.

"Colonel Otis, we will speak of this later."

Pete pokes his head out of the end of the duct over the cryo beds. Seeing the coast is clear, he tosses his lunchbox out, and eases himself out of the duct and over to the PC used to access the core. He starts to work the commputer, but before he can do much, an Air Force guard discovers him. "Hey! What you doin' there!"

"Just accessing the core," Pete said as the guard approached.

"You're not supposed to be here," the guard added as he raised his M16.

"Sure I am, just look here, it's got my name on it," Pete protested and motioned to the PC screen for the airman to look.

As he glanced down, Pete struck him over the head with his lunchbox knocking the guard down to his knees. Pete opened the lunchbox as the guard started to recover. The alien bug that had been controlling Roy scurried out and onto the downed airman. It was all over in a matter of seconds.

The stricken airman straightens and looks around in a daze for a few seconds before saying, "I am of The Hive. This host is smarter and more developed than the other host. But he also is unable to make contact with his hive."

"The humans do not have a hive. They are all alone, a single entity," Pete explained.

"Good, this makes them more vunerable, less likely to cooperate and coordinate their attacks. We shail prevail," the new drone said.

Pete now had an air force airman to guard his back as he accessed the cryo bed.

A cryo bed slid out of the core. The wrong one! "This isn't the Queen!"

The guard urged him to put it back and try again. After some manipulation of the PC Pete got the bed to return to the core and another one, the right one, to slide out. He dashed over to the bed and worked the controls to open the inner lid.

The lid popped open and he lifted it revealing the Queen and remaining bugs. The Queen was man sized with a vaguely female face, and an armored segmented body of an ant. Her spider like lower legs were all drawn up with her forearms and claws folded across her thorax. Neither the Queen nor the bugs moved or displayed any sign of life.

The airman came over to the bed and looked in. "They're not moving, are they dead?"

"I don't know, I don't think so," Pete replied. They both jumped at the sound of someone working nearby. "I'll tend to the Queen. You see that we are not interfered with," Pete instructed his fellow drone.

As the guard left, with M16 at the ready, the bugs started to stir. Four bugs scurry out of the bed and are about to attack Pete when he holds out his hand and snaps his fingers four times. They stop dead in their tracks. Pete starts to speak to them. "Stop and understand what I am saying. I am of The Hive."

The quasi-human black eyes of the Queen opened and fixed upon them. "I am yours," Pete said to the Queen. She looked around.

"I only sense two drones, I must have more," she said as she started to rise out of the cryo bed. "Are there no more workers?" She asked as she affixed her attention on Pete.

"These are all that I know of, but perhaps there are more in one of the other cabinets," Pete said as he returned to the PC. Pete could not read the alien marking in the commputer, but there was another one with the same markings as the Queen's chamber had had. He quickly worked the commputer and the adjacent Cryo bed slid out and he opened the outer hatch. Advancing over to the cabinet he looked through the glass lid and saw hundreds more worker bugs. He worked the controls on the bed slide and the lid popped open. "They are here and I have just freed them. They will revive shortly," Pete reported to his Queen.

As the Queen got out of the cryo bed, she revealed her whip like barbed tail. She was as tall as he was. "I need to feed and I need a source of silicone and host bodies for the amalgamation to begin."

The Air Force guard brings two of the workmen from the site in saying to them, "You have really got to see this." They stopped when they first laid eyes on the alien Queen. Before they could turn to run, they were lost to the swarm of worker bugs. One of the workmen cried out and whimpered a little but it was over quickly.

"Time to swarm! Fan out and add to The Hive!" She motioned to them snapping her claws together. There was a buzzing sound and the bugs fanned out covering the ground in every direction.

"And now I must feed," the Queen said as she fixed her gaze on Pete. He staggered back.

"No my Queen! Not me! I am the one who freed you!" Pete pleaded with her.

"Then it ssshould be your honor to sssustain your Queen." She hissed at him as she moved closer and wrapped her tail around him.

"I am useful, I know where you can find silicone on this planet!" He pleaded once again.

She released him. "Sssilicone for the grafting, yesss, bring me another one to feed on!" She commanded.

"Where can I find the sssilicone I need for the grafting to proceed?" The Queen leered at him.

Pete retreated saying, "they use it for sealing leaks and to augment the breasts of their women."

"Bring me sssome ssso I may start with the grafting. I must prepare an army, these humans are going to put up resistance," the Queen stated as Pete left on his quest.

Moments later there was a scream and the bugs carried a carpenter (judging by his tool belt) to the Queen. He had been bitten but not stung. He had not been taken over by the bugs and could only look on in horror as the Queen eased over to him baring her needle-like teeth. She grasped him in her hands and claws. There was a low crunching sound when she bit into his skull. His eyes popped out of his head and just dangled from their sockets as the Queen fed on his brains.

She used one of her claws to snip off one of his arms and continued to feed on it, dropping the rest of the bloody corpse on the ground. After she was finished eating his arm, bones and all! She turned her attention to his tool belt. Rifling through the contents she declared, "primitive but ussseful. But I must have a sssource of sssilicone before I can ssstart the grafting. If that one fails me I will have his head!"

Outside at the Ground Zero work site, the bugs are attacking anything that moves. Some of the workers try to fight the bugs by stomping on them while others use whatever is at hand as a weapon. Some are successful to some extent but eventually, all are swarmed over. The smart ones try running. Some make it, some don't.

The Air Force guards spray the ground with lead from their M16 in a pointless exercise of resistance. The report of automatic weapon fire draws the attention of the nearby police and they come to investigate and are also swarmed over by the relentless bugs.

One of the possessed guards stands before the Queen as she studies his M16. "Yesss! Thisss will do much better than thossse primitive toolsss. But where isss my sssilicone?" Just as she finishes speaking, Pete returns to his Queen with tubes of silicone used to seal leaks. She takes the tube and bites the end off and squirts it into her mouth like toothpaste.

The bug drops off of the neck of the now paralyzed airman, and scurries off in search of another victim. The Queen bites his arms and hands, whips her tail around and rips open the bitten area with her barbed tail. Placing the M16 in his injured hand, the Queen stabs him with her stinger pumping him full of silicone and other chemicals causing the M16 and flesh to meld and heal. She then rips open his chest and puts a piece of corrugated steel on it and once again stings him to amalgamate the metal into his body.

"The first of my warriors is done! Bring me another!" She demands. Panic and terror quickly spread across Ground Zero.

At HERO HQ Colonel Otis is having a conference with his staff. "People! We have got to do a better job! If these shenanigans continue, we are all going to be in a world of hurt. The only ones who haven't caused any trouble are Dr. Brewville and MaCos Ex, and he's an alien we don't admit to having working for us."

He continued, "If something is classified top secret eyes only, that means no one else is supposed to know anything about it. That means no buzzing the lakefront in top secret rocket packs, and no accessing top secret alien technology without the proper clearances and even then, only when you have a need to know."

He threw his hands up to quiet all of the coming defensive remarks. "Yes, I know there were extenuating circumstances every time and nobody is in any trouble. This time."

He then turned his attention to Marshal, seated in his specially reinforced chair at the end of the table between Heather and Dauntless. "Marshal, can you understand me?" He obviously had his attention, so he continued. "Heather, please make sure he understands this, go over it with him later. I know he cannot control the effect his pheromones have on the female staff. But, if he finds himself getting into close proximity to any of the ladies, I want him to do his best to keep his distance."

He paused and continued, "and I want you ladies to try to do the same." The three of them traded glances and nodded indicating commpliance.

Satisfied with this, the Colonel continued, "Dr. Brewville, your assignments are to continue working on ammo for Marshal's sidearm and to make repairs to the rocket pack." Doctor Brewville just sat there shaking his head. This caught the Colonel's attention prompting him to follow up asking, "is there a problem?"

"No, I was just thinking of my poor rocket pack," the Doctor replied.

"Dauntless, there will be no further flight training at this time. I was considering having you train at night but the glow off of the rocket would only attract more viewers. You're grounded until further notice." She had no problem with that. She was starting to like the flying but she didn't think she would ever be using it.

"Dr. Cooly, please continue working with MaCos Ex on the helmet. We will assume you are correct about his memory loss affecting the translator." He glanced down at his notes before continuing.

"Heather, one more thing, the general wants me to encourage you to find an English teacher for Marshal."

Dr. Cooly interrupted. "I know someone at the university who might work out. I could give you her number if you want," she said turning to Heather.

"Good, look into it. There are no other changes to assignments so, are there any issues?" He said trying to wrap things up.

Captain Anderson, the CO of A Commpany spoke up. "Sergeant Dickerson's wife just gave birth to a son, his first, and he's gone home on leave. That leaves A Commpany short another NCO."

"Bravo Commpany is on standby, Captain Walker, see if you can loan Captain Anderson an NCO for a couple days." The two Captains looked at each other and nodded.

There was a knock at the door and a clerk came in and handed Top a note. The old soldier looked at it and stood up as he announced, "Sir, there's a report of shots fired at Ground Zero and something about a giant bug infestation with swarms of bugs carrying away people."

"Who sent this message?" the Colonel asked suspecting a hoax.

"It's from the Chicago PD sir."

"See if you can raise the Air Force. Anderson, get Alpha Commpany ready to move. Walker, consider this your alert order. Get Bravo ready just in case." Let's do it people!"

As the soldiers jumped up and left the room, the Colonel stopped and turned to Dauntless, "I guess you're in this too."

Marshal put his hand on the Colonel's chest as he went by stopping him abruptly. Marshal stood up towering over the Colonel. "Okay, very well, you can go too. Heather you had better come along to watch over him."

Captain Anderson came over to the Colonel saying, "It will take over an hour for use to get there over land with all the traffic."

"There are three birds on the roof, tell them to get ready. You take two of them and go. I'll take team Hero in the third. The rest of your people can stand ready here and go if needed on the next stick."

Back at Ground Zero, more and more police are being drawn in and overwhelmed by the swarming bugs. Sergeant Banks of the Chicago police is in his patrol car on the radio trying to explain to his higher ups what is going on. As he talks, he holds up the remains of a battered and twisted worker bug. "That's right! I said giant space bugs! I'm looking at one now I killed with the shotgun. It's almost a foot long!"

A voice comes in over the radio. "What's it look like November 3,4?"

"It's nasty I tell you! It's got a tail and claws and it's attacking people and taking them over!"

"Say again November 3,4. It sounded like you said they were attacking people and taking them over?"

"That's right! They're everywhere and they're attacking everybody. We need help! Send the Army. Send the Orkin man, just send somebody!" Just then, one of the bugs climbed up on his car and stood on the driver side review mirror. Banks saw it and went for his gun.

As he tried to get his gun out, the bug turned around on the mirror and jumped in through the open window, landing on Bank's stomach. He slapped wildly at it as it darted about on him. Finally, it found his neck and bit him. After he slowed down and stopped, it got on the back of his neck and stung him with its tail.

Three Army Black Hawk helicopters race along over the city headed for Ground Zero, headed for trouble. In the back of the lead ship are Colonel Otis, Dauntless, Marshal and Heather along with half a dozen combat loaded troops.

Heather had changed into her leather biker outfit and she noticed Colonel Otis eyeing her. She wasn't sure *if it was because he liked what he saw. Why shouldn't he?* She thought, *or was it because he remembered the last time he saw her in them.* Then it came to her. "I had to change into these. It's all I had to wear, I couldn't wear my office clothes to, ... God knows what we'll find!" She explained.

"Good thinking!" He responded.

The crew chief tapped the Colonel on the shoulder to get his attention. "Sir, we're listening in on the police band and there is definitely something going on down there."

"What's our ETA?" He asked.

"Five minutes if we don't have any problems with traffic from Midway."

Five minutes later, the three Army choppers are circling Ground Zero, doing a quick recon of the situation before going in. There is construction equipment scattered everywhere, but no work is going on. There is a small fire burning near a stack of sheet metal. At the center of the construction sight is the skeleton of a building going up; three stories so far. The center of the building, the part containing the UFO and the core with the cryo beds, cannot be seen. There are tarps strung up blocking the view. "I don't see anything," the Colonel said. "Put her down on the helio pad. Get out quick and bring back a second load. There's definitely something wrong here."

Inside the building, the Queen is surrounded by 100 human drones. Some of them, the warriors, have armor and weapons grafted directly onto their bodies. The vibration and the WHOP WHOP WHOP of the choppers alert her. "The humansss are coming, go meet them my children. Bring me more host bodiesss I can amalgamate into warriorsss!

She then turned looking for the drone known as Pete, finding him, she commands, "Bring me more sssilicone." Pete turns and goes with the rest of the human drones and warriors. Some of the bugs drop off of their hosts as they go.

The choppers set down. The troopers jump out and dash away from the birds, fanning out, weapons ready. No one fires. The two birds in trail lift off and go to pick up more troops. The troops form five elements, one on each corner of a diamond formation with the fifth in the center with team Hero. (Marshal, Dauntless, Heather and Colonel Otis.)

Using hand signals, the diamond formation starts to move across the construction site towards the partially finished building. Marshal, Dauntless and Heather venture over to investigate the fire by the metal sheeting. A torch had started a small, smoky, but harmless fire. They left it to burn for now.

People started coming out of the building, mostly construction workers but some police officers and Air Force personnel were among them. The soldier on point called to them to "HALT!" But they just kept coming.

Some one fired and both sides opened up on the other with M16s and shotguns. The drone police used their service sidearms. Soldiers and drone alike dove for cover. One drone warrior that didn't dive was seen to be hit several times as each round that hit him gave off a spark as it hit his armored body. He crumpled to his knees and fell over face first.

The warrior drones had numbers on their sides. They were tougher to bring down than the troopers and had better coordination between drones but, they lacked the weapon skills and tactics of the soldiers. The soldiers had left in such a hurry that they didn't have all of their combat gear, no grenades or body armor.

Team Hero, minus Colonel Otis, was over by the fire when the firefight broke out. "SWEET JESUS! WHAT'S THAT?" Heather shouted, as they took cover. The sound of the firefight was growing in intensity as they started moving towards the sounds of the guns. "This is crazy! We're not even armed," Heather exclaimed.

"Who's not armed?" Dauntless said, turning back to face Heather, pulling out her 9mm. Marshal went to draw his sidearm and found his holster empty. He checked the contents of the pouches on his belt. They were all empty. He looked at them with an incredulous look on his face.

As the firefight raged on, bugs started crossing nomansland rushing the soldiers. The first few were handled easily enough with automatic fire or but-strokes with rifle butt stocks, but the bugs kept coming.

Four bugs rushed Colonel Otis. He rapidly dispatched three of them with three aimed shots with his .45, but the last shot took his last round and the fourth one jumped on his leg and started to climb up. He swatted it off with the empty .45 and crushed the bug under foot, grinding it into the glassy soil. The army position was becoming desperate.

Some of the fallen drone warriors with their bugs still attached to them started to get up again. They were hit again and fell, but got back up! One of the soldiers yelled over to the Colonel, "we're in deep doo doo! It's like fighting zombies!"

"Soldier, there are no such things as zombies. You've been watching too many movies," he said as he reloaded his .45

The Queen and several warriors came around the flank and observed Marshal and the two girls making their way toward the fight. "Large breasted women! I must have their sssilicone," the Queen said to her drones. With two snaps of her claws they fanned out and started moving in on them.

Marshal was the first one to make contact with the enemy. Three men, one of them a cop, rushed out from behind a stack of steel followed by some bugs. The cop shot Marshal three times at close range, doubling him over, but he remained on his feet.

Marshal hit the first one to reach him with the back of his left hand sending him flying into the stack of steel. He crumpled to the ground like a marionette with its strings cut. The next one was caught by his right and sent flying backwards past the Queen. "I must have that blue one!" The Queen commanded.

The cop, the third on rusher, was disarmed when Marshal grabbed hold of his sidearm and ripped the gun and fingers off of his hand! This startled Marshal who stopped and studied the bloody weapon he was holding for a few seconds before tossing it away. The cop was still flailing about as Marshal tossed him up and over the stack of steel. He landed with a crash. He didn't return.

A bug climbed up Marshal's back and tried to sting him in the back of his neck but couldn't because of Marshal's high collar. As Marshal flailed about trying to remove the bug, Dauntless was jumped by two men and Heather by another one.

These new attackers were workmen drones. They had no weapons other than what they could carry and no armor at all.

Dauntless traded punches with them, knocking them out with one punch each. Well, to be truthful, she pistol-whipped the first one. She broke his jaw. The second attacker landed a right cross on Dauntless' chin. She returned the favor with her left and the fight was over. She turned to see Heather flip her assailant over her back. He landed at Brandy's feet. She bonked him on the head with her 9mm and he was out cold. Heather protested, "I could have finished him."

Looking up at Heather, Dauntless joked, "what took you so long?"

The bug on Marshal moved to his cheek and bit him. The blue giant started to slow down and became unsteady on his feet and then snapped out of it! He crushed the bug against his face. In obvious disgust he grabbed the remains of the bug and threw it down on the ground and stomped on it forcefully. He said something in unintelligible alien gibberish.

Dauntless decided that they should rejoin the unit and using sign language, gets Marshal to follow her as they head for the sound of gun fire once again. Heather, the last one in line, is jumped by another unseen warrior, and is wrestled to the ground where a bug jumps on her and bites her, paralyzing her in seconds.

The Queen rushes up to her. "Sssome of my drones find you very attractive and you may be ussseful to me later, ssso I will not kill you." She bites Heather in the neck!

"You will ssserve The Hive as one of my droness in waiting." The eager drones gather around their Queen as she takes a deep breath. "But

I must have your sssilicone." The Queen sinks her needle like teeth deep into Heathers breast! There is a flash of blood and nothing.

The Queen reels back from Heather throwing her to the ground. "Ssshe has no sssilicone!" And the drones start to gather around her.

Dauntless and Marshal realize that Heather isn't with them and they return for her. Retracing their steps, Dauntless climbs up on top of a pile of steel I beams. Peeking over the edge, she sees Heather lying on the ground, paralyzed with the Queen and about 30 of her drones and countless bugs. "Not good. We need a plan," Dauntless said not, expecting Marshal to understand. But he did.

He motioned to Brandy to get down from the stack of I-beams. He taps his chest with his thumb and says, "Heather." He then points to Dauntless, patted her hip holster and pointed at a gas tank over by the stack of metal, and made a jester with his hands rapidly opening up.

"Oh, I think I got you! She said as she drew her 9mm.

The Queen has her tail wrapped around Pete with her claw around his neck. "You provided me with bad information, that large breasted female had no sssilicone and your host is inferior and of little use to The Hive. I will use you to inspire the remainder to do better for their Queen." The bug jumped off and the Queen snipped Pete's head off with her great lobster like claw. Blood sprayed as his head thumped down onto the ground and rolled around with the shocked expression frozen on Pete's dismembered head. The headless body stood there for several seconds before crumpling down next to Heather's body.

The bug, scampered over to her body and stung her in the back of her neck. Heather was a bloody mess when she came too with the bug in control. "Amalgamation commpleted. Peter was an inferior host. This one is much smarter. She will serve you well," Heather said.

Marshal landed next to them with a loud THUD! He tossed the gas tank onto the ground in front of the Queen, grabbed Heather with his right arm, pulled her close to him and leapt back over the stack of I-beams clearing Dauntless' head by a good foot.

She drew careful aim on the tank with her 9mm. "I wish I could think of something snappy to say, but I can't, what can I say? I got nothing." She squeezed off a shot and hit the tip end of the tank. FFFFF! The tank shot across the ground like a rocket propelled torpedo. Dauntless was just as suprised as everyone else.

They all watched in amazement as the tank slid right into the fire, collided with some more tanks, and exploded. Bits of tank and metal sheeting went all over. There was a copious amount of smoke. Dauntless looked at her pistol in amazement and holstered it saying, "I'll take it!" Dauntless slids down and joined Marshal.

Heather is trying to resist Marshal, her arms and legs are kicking and flailing about furiously to no avail. Heather was a skilled martial artist but he could, and had, survived being hit by a train. No blow from a mere human stood much of a chance of hurting him in the least. Crushing her against his body with one hand, he ripped the bug off of her neck with the other. Heather immediately collapsed in his arm. He crushed the bug under his foot.

Dauntless slids down joining them saying, "we need to get out of here!"

Marshal pulls the girls close to his body, one in each arm, and squats down and gives a mighty leap. They sailed over the stacks of sheet metal and steel I-beams. The army has fallen back to a perimeter just around the helipad. Dauntless came running up first. "It's about time you showed up," Colonel Otis said.

"Heather's been bitten!" She said, as Marshal came up carrying Heather's limp body. The hundreds of pinprick wounds had broken open all around her right breast. She was bleeding profusely and she was out cold. Reaching the helipad, Marshal removed her shredded leather jacket and blood soaked blouse and tossed her black bra away. He removed his uniform jacket. Dauntless helps hold Heather up as he places his jacket on her. He repositions her nearly severed right breast and closes the flap, securing the high neck collar around her, being careful to keep her hair out of the jacket collar.

One of the soldiers picked up the tattered and blood soaked bra, and ponders what he found. Three unit badges, one of which was the Colonel's and Marshal's blood splattered Presidential Medal of Freedom, were still pinned to it. "Here comes the cavalry!" Another soldier shouted as two choppers came in.

One of the soldiers cried out, "Colonel! It looks like they're bugging out!"

Another soldier added, "it looks like the zombies are running away!"

The older soldier turned to this man saying, "trooper, what did I tell you about zombies?" The soldier started to answer but the Colonel added, "don't bother, I know what you meant."

Indeed, some of the workmen, warriors and even some of the fallen soldiers were running away. *But why?* The Colonel wondered to himself. As he watched, it took a couple of seconds for him to realize what was going on. The bugs were flying off! No one had noticed that some of the bugs had wings and they were taking off and picking up the wingless bugs and swarming about and heading off to the south.

The flutter of a hundred bug wings ebbs as they fade away and is drowned out by the sound of the two choppers coming in. Dauntless said, "Colonel! We can't let them get away like this!"

"I know," he announced in a low determined voice. As the two big Sikorsky Black Hawks landed and disgorged their troops. The Colonel's face lit up, and he turned to Captain Anderson. "Captain, have you your compass?" He did, and the Colonel commanded, "shoot a bearing on the swarm before it gets out of sight. Maybe we can't chase them but that doesn't mean I'm letting them get away."

The sound of distant gunfire rang out. "The fleeing zombies! AFTER THEM!" He turned to the soldier and admitted, "we have to call them something. NOW GET GOING!" The Colonel commanded and every soldier jumped into action.

Lt. Hunter ran over to the Colonel saying, "we could follow the bugs with one of the Black Hawks, sir."

"Good idea, you go. Take this bird, but don't engage, just follow them." As he commmpleted his instructions to the Lieutenant an Air Force helicopter passed overhead and circled about. The Colonel noticed it and pointed it out to the Lieutenant. "Be sure to tell him what you're doing."

Turning to Dauntless, "I want you with me. Marshal, get her back to HQ."

Marshal looked up at him cradling Heather in his arms. Henry motioned for him to pick her up and go to the other helicopter on the ground behind him. "Get all the wounded on the bird!" Marshal and Heather were joined by four walking wounded and one more seriously wounded soldier carried over by two of his brothers-in-arms.

The two choppers took off and headed in opposite directions. Colonel Otis turned his face out of the prop wash and found he was alone on the helipad, except for one lone soldier, and Dauntless. "Sergeant Lopez! Which way did they go?"

"They went this way Colonel!" He pointed off to the south and they were on their way. Three blocks ahead at the edge of the ring of devastation surrounding the Ground Zero crater, the fleeing worker and warrior drones had run into Chicago's finest and a gun battle ensued.

The police, though thoroughly confused and bewildered, put up a valiant but ultimately futile resistance. Their police 9mm and .40 caliber handguns were no match for the armored warriors or the captured M16s.

One officer managed to retrieve the 12 gauge pump gun from his cruiser and used it with some success, dropping the first workman that came after him. While he pumped two more rounds of buckshot into an oncoming armored warrior, the bug from the downed workman jumped on the slain host body and scurried over to the police officer and bit him on the ankle.

The officer reacted as anyone would; he kicked the bug away. He turned to face the warrior and just slowly fell into a heap. As the police fought the drones, the bugs controlling them would jump off and leave their old host and seek out another host to amalgamate with. The old host drone, if unhurt, would continue on as if controlled by The Hive. As police resistance waned, the drones started to commandeer cars and vans; any vehicle available as they made their getaway.

The troopers of the 5th Special Security Unit made their way cautiously and arrived too late to help the police. "They got away, sir," Captain Anderson reported as the Colonel came up.

"Let's hope Lt. Hunter has better luck," Colonel Otis said under his breath.

Chicago's southwestern suburbs echoed with the beating of helicopter blades and the fluttering sound of 100 insect wings. The alien swarm swayed back and forth at little more than tree top level. The persuing choppers had to stay higher to avoid power transmission lines and water towers. The Air Force chopper raced ahead of the Black Hawk "This is Air Force 3,2,3,4. We are pursuing the alien insects. We are bearing 178 passing Oak Park, headed towards Alsip. Requesting instructions, over."

Soon the reply came. "Air Force 3,2,3,4, this is Dream Catcher 7, maintain visual contact. We are unable to track them at their present altitude. They're hidden in the ground clutter.

Nearing the small town of Alsip, the swarm suddenly changes directions turning east, but several went unnoticed and turned back and headed for the first chopper. As the bugs neared the helicopter, they were sucked into the engine. The eight-inch long armored bugs were ingested into the engines, causing the engines to spit fire and turban blades.

The chopper was too low to autogyro down so it fell like a rock. Coming down in the parking lot of a large flea market, the chopper crumbled like a crushed Dixie cup.

There was a poof and the sickly sweet smell of JP4 (jet fuel).

The Black Hawk circled the site calling in the emergency. They watched for a few seconds before having to continue after the alien flyers. The crew chief in back was able to watch out the side as they left the scene. There was no fire, but no one walked away.

The swarm continued on and dissipated over a large junkyard. "We've lost them," the pilot reported to Lt. Hunter.

"Circle around, maybe we flew past them. We can't afford to lose them," Lt. Hunter told the pilot.

"I don't see'em anywhere, maybe they landed," the co-pilot reported.

"There's lots of places for them to hide down there. We'll never find them like this. We'll need boots on the ground," the pilot said but the Lieutenant insisted they keep looking. They circled for 15 minutes without finding anything. They got a fix on their location and called it in and retraced their path, just in case. As they over flew the Alsip crash site, they could see fire and emergency vehicles on the scene.

"This is one bad day," Lt. Hunter said, as he was about to call in.

CHAPTER NINE

THE HARBINGER

A Black Hawk helicopter landed on the HERO building. Marshal gets out carrying Heather who is wearing his uniform coat. Dr. Cooly comes out on the roof to meet them and is startled by the amount of blood on Heather and the coat. "Is this all her blood?" She asked before realizing he probably couldn't understand what she was saying.

They go immediately to the Med. Center where Marshal places her on a cart. Dr. Cooly and Nurse Chapel start working on her. "What happened to her?" Beverly asked.

Marshal gave her that blank look. She gestured to the wound on Heathers breasts and looked at him as to ask what happened. He understood and gestured, biting the air.

"This is a bite?" She turned to Chapel who was cleaning the area. "Oh my God! This could be bad."

Heather came to and grabbed Dr. Cooley's lab coat. "Beverly, it hurts. Don't let me die."

"I won't," Beverly said trying to sound reassuring. In truth, she didn't have a clue but it didn't seem to be life threatening.

Nurse Chapel escorted Marshal out of the Med. Center while they worked on Heather. MaCos Ex came over to keep him commpany.

Chapel started an IV in Heathers hand. "OW! That hurts." Dr. Cooly came over and injected a clear liquid into the IV, and she was out cold in seconds.

"Time to see what we're working on," the good doctor said to Nurse Chapel as they opened Marshal's jacket exposing Heather's chest. Her right breast was swollen and discolored commpared to her left.

At first she couldn't believe her eyes, so she had Nurse Chapel look at the wounds. There were hundreds of them, all closing up and healing themselves as they watched. It was *amazing. Marshal's coat never worked that fast before, did it?* They closed the coat up around her to let it work at its fullest.

"Quick, get a chest x-ray. We might be missing something."

As they struggled to figure out the X-Ray machine, MaCos Ex tried to speak with Marshal. Even with his universal translator working, MaCos was only able to understand part of what Marshal was saying.

The first X-ray attempt was overexposed and useless so they had to try it again. The second one was negative, nothing for them to worry about. "No internal injuries." Dr. Cooly came out and gave Marshal the thumbs up sign. She only hoped it meant the same thing to him. He seemed to be relieved.

He motioned to his chest, and she nodded yes. "She's going to be fine." Then he motioned to the back of his neck. This confused the Doctor for a few seconds. "Are you injured?" She asked as she started to move over to him to look at his neck.

He stopped her and shook his head, pointed at his neck and then pointed at Heather. Then the light came on. "OH! You mean she has a neck injury also! We didn't know!" She ran back into the Med. Center.

She ran up to Nurse Chapel. "Linda, she has a neck injury!" They both did their best to immobilize Heather as they rolled her body and head as one. Dr. Cooly brushed Heather's beautiful wavy golden blond hair out of the way. There was a nasty scar just above the top of the jacket's collar in the shape of a snowflake. "What's that?"

She got a magnifier and looked through it. There was something in the center of the snowflake. It looked like a stinger. Beverly turned away to get something to remove the stinger. Heather jumped up and elbowed Linda knocking her down.

Beverly turned around in time to get kicked in the face. She collapsed like a house of cards. The noise alerted Marshal that something was amiss. He got up and headed for the door to the Med. Center.

Heather came running out and attacked him. She landed three punches to his midsection in rapid succession. Each blow was like a sledgehammer crashing down on rock. Marshal flinched, and grabbed for her, but she only ducked down and avoided him. She now did a spinning back kick, which also landed in his rock hard midsection. This backed him up a step. *She shouldn't be this strong,* he thought.

She started to go around him but he had the size advantage and was able to block her move. His open hand caught her in the mid section but she bounced off. She hit him twice on the chin hurting her fist. She tried going the other way and again he had her blocked. Holding both arms out wide he could cover a large area. She decided to try going up the middle on him.

She kicked him in the family jewels and hurt her fist on his chin twice more. He more or less staggered into her from the effects of the kick and grabbed her in a bearhug. Fight over. "I must get you for the Queen," was the only thing she said.

He just held her as she squirmed about vainly trying to free herself. Eventually she stopped and buried her face in his bare chest. She was breathing heavily from all of the exertion of trying to escape, and now she took an extra hard hit from his pheromones. Seconds ago she was franticly struggling to get away from this blue giant and now, quite the opposite, She couldn't get close enough to this blue image of masculine perfection.

Sex was the furthest thing from Marshal's mind when he grabbed hold of Heather. But now with Heather kissing his chest and rubbing her luscious body up against his, he was becoming aroused. He sighed something in alien gibberish and his eyes rolled up. He picked her up gently and, carried her back into the Med. Center he found Nurse Chapel helping Dr. Cooly up from the floor.

Beverly rubbed the side of her face and put her glasses back on. As Marshal held Heather against his body they were able to access the snowflake-like scab that was on the back of her neck where she had been stung. As she scraped it off, Heather collapsed in Marshal's arms. The skin underneath was intact. No stinger sticking out, no entrance wound. Marshal laid her down on the cart and pushed her head down and pushed the collar up so her neck was covered by the collar.

In a dark angular place the Queen rose up over her growing Hive and proclaimed, "I must have the blue one!"

Colonel Otis and Dauntless arrived with several other soldiers and are met by Top. "How is Agent Carter?"

Top answered, "she kicked Dr. Cooly in the face but from what I hear, they both are expected to make a full and commplete recovery. Any orders Sir?" He knew there would be.

"Call everyone back. The entire 5th is going on full alert. Have full combat loads issued now!

"What happened out there sir? I know a bird went down," the old soldier asked as he turned to make the call.

"Not one of ours, it was Air Force. We ran into an ambush. We lost a lot of good men today because we weren't ready. That won't happen again. Call the SAL, get us every bird you can. Alien bug things have escaped and are taking over people. And now they're on the loose and we've got to find them."

He turned to Dauntless asking, "Do you still have that bug?" She held up a partially squashed bug and showed it to Top and the Colonel. "Take that bug and show it to MaCos Ex or Dr. Cooly or Marshal. I don't care who you show it to, just find out what it is and how to kill it," he commanded.

She left and ran into one of the MIB. She showed it to him, and he never saw anything like it before. He takes a picture of it with his phone and sends it to his HQ; perhaps they can help.

Brandy takes the bug upstairs and shows it to Marshal. It is not known to him, or at least he doesn't seem to know anything about it. Catching up to Dr. Cooly whose face is swollen on one side, she looks at it and speculates that's one nasty bug. And she adds, "that can't be an intelligent criminal, I wonder why it was in the cryo beds?"

Beverly looks at Brandy and follows up with another question. "This did come from the cryo beds, didn't it?"

"We're not sure, we think so. Something was freed from two of the beds," Dauntless said. "The area is a mess. The Air Force hasn't shared with us yet just what was freed," she confided in the Doctor.

"Maybe it's a parasite," Beverly speculated.

Dauntless comes across MaCos Ex and asks him if he knows what it is. He does, he's seen them before, not in real life but he has heard of them. "That's a Harbinger. They were the scourges of the universe. But I thought they were extinct, wiped out."

"Apparently not, what can you tell me about them?" She asked, hoping for an easy fix to a bad situation.

MaCos sat down and started to talk. "The Harbinger are a kind of super parasite, slash predator. A parasite simply lives off of its host. The Harbinger take over the host, and the host is changed and made part of The Hive."

"The Hive?" Brandy asked sounding concerned.

"They have a hive mentality, I think they are all linked mentally, but I'm not sure. There are two, no three, types of Harbingers. This one is a scout, or worker bug. They go out and find hosts and convert them into drones. The drones mindlessly serve The Hive and the Harbinger Queen.

The Queen can convert drones into warriors by grafting weapons directly into their bodies. She can make other types of special purpose drones. When a host is captured its knowledge is accessible to the bug and then The Hive."

"That is bad news. How many of these bugs were there?" She asked

"I have no idea, but each scout can convert many hosts into drones. It doesn't have to be on the drone to control it. I think they have better control when they are on the drone, but even if they are not actually on the drone, the drone is still under the influence of The Hive," he explained.

"How can we fight these things?" She asked hoping for some useful news.

MaCos Ex shook his head. "You have to kill them. Once a host is converted you have to kill them, or surgically remove the stinger."

"How much time does it take?" She was grasping for straws.

"The scouts bite first to immobilize the victim and then sting with their tails and hang on or drop off as they wish. You are now part of The Hive, a drone. It doesn't take long, not long at all. It's different with the Queen. If she has decided to convert you, let's say into a warrior, she will take you, the drone, and sting you first, injecting you with some kind of, oh I don't know, some sort of hormone I guess. This hormone speeds up the victim's metabolism and speeds healing."

"Speeds up healing?" This piqued her curiosity.

He went on to explain. "After stinging you, she will graft the weapon onto your body. It's all very crude and you would bleed to death if you didn't heal first. And there you have it! A new warrior for The Hive," he said as he studied the bug's remains.

"So, all we have to do is kill them!" She summed it up, speaking more to herself than anyone else. Then it came to her to ask, 'how?"

"You can kill them anyway you like, but you must realize that the scout bugs will, if not killed, will jump to a new host and make another drone," he explained.

She shook her head. "No, not the drones, we already know how to kill them I think? What about the Queen?"

"I'm not sure," he replied apologetically.

"She got up to go. "If that's it, I'll be going."

"Wait, there's more." He stopped her.

"More?" She asked, dreading what he might say next.

"They can make things."

"Make things? Like what? This puzzled her.

"That depends on what's available and how intelligent the hosts are," he said as he pondered the endless possibilities.

She turned to go, took a few steps and stopped to ask. "Is there anything about these Harbingers in the helmet memory?"

"I don't know. I can look," MaCos Ex replied, as she left.

A short time later, Dauntless ran into Nurse Chapel who is carrying the blood soaked Marshal uniform jacket. Dauntless stops her. "How is she?"

Linda looked concerned. "Her injuries have healed, but she is having some kind of reaction. Her heart and respiration are all over the place. And her temperature is up. Dr. Cooly thinks it's an infection or allergic reaction to something."

Brandy thought for a few seconds. "Tell her to look for alien hormones."

"She has already, Heather's full of them but we're having trouble identifying them. Why? What do you know about it?"

"It's just something MaCos said. They may be healing her super fast, I think." She took the elevator down to the main floor and found Colonel Otis busy with some other officers. "Colonel, I think I may have found something," she interrupted.

Colonel Otis and a full Air Force Colonel turned to face her. They both answered saying, "what is it?"

This startled her, she stuttered before answering. "Uh, oh sorry sir. All we have to do is kill them sir."

"Kill them who?" The full Colonel asked. "The zombies?"

"Yes, and no sir. The bugs make and control the uh, zombies. The zombies are just drones made to serve The Hive. They all know what each other are thinking. MaCos is using the helmet to find a way to kill them."

Colonel Otis caught her attention. "I want you to go back up there and use the helmet to find out how to stop these ..."

She informed her CO, "They're called Harbingers sir. They're alien bugs and they get smarter as they take over more people and they make things."

"Make things?" The full Colonel asked, "just what does that mean?"

"I'm not exactly sure sir."

On Chicago's southeast side are several steel mills, many of which have been closed and abandoned for decades due to changes in the economy.

Some have been torn down and the land reclaimed, but not all. The seines of old heavy industry are everywhere.

The area is laced with railroad tracks, highways and shipping canals and old abandoned and dilapidated buildings. Trains and barges still haul ore and coke to the great smelters still in operation. The air is heavy with the stench of 150 years of steel making. The predominate colors are black, rusty orange and the gray of concrete.

One of the long dead mills is no longer dormant. There is a buzz of activity coming from within. It is to this area that the Harbinger Queen has directed her new Hive. The Queen surrounded by her subjects proclaims, "Thisss isss a sssutable placess to build The Hive home. We can fortify the wallss and there are ample raw materialsss for the construction of our war machinesess.'

One of the drones, an X construction worker, approaches her saying, "My Queen, there is one among us with knowledge of a far superior type of war machine. One vastly superior to these guns and knives."

"Good, bring him forward ssso I may know him better." She leers at the drone.

Another drone steps forward, this one had been a cop in his previous life. "Your majesty, we have suffered the loss of many of our nobles. If we are to start on such an enterprise we are in need of more."

"I can't lay a clutch of eggs without the use of a connsssort," the Queen replied.

"There are many fine males among the host drones, perhaps one of us may serve as your consort?" The police officer said.

The Queen shook her head no. "No, I have ssseen the one I want. Bring me the big blue one or one like him."

The cop spoke up. "My Queen, I think he may be unique to this planet, he may be the only one like him."

"Then you had better start looking. Noblesss, go forth and bring me more drones. You workmen drones bring me more materialsss and more silicone to be used in the amalgamation of a thousand more drone workersss and warriorsss.

"Do you know where we can find him for you?" The workman drone asked.

"He was with those large breasted femalesss. Find them and you will find him," she explained.

"I know of the females you speak. They are with the Army to the north," the cop spoke up.

"The Army, I'll make more warriorsss."

A short time later, on the opposite side of the city, Dauntless has returned upstairs and is seated in Dr. Cooly's big chair. She has with her the gold visored memory helmet. She puts the helmet on and settles into the chair as if she was going to be watching a movie. "Damn! I forgot the popcorn. MaCos leaves her alone.

In the lab, Dr. Brewville joins MaCos. The Doctor shows the alien engineer some chemical formulas on a sheet of paper saying; "I think I have the formula for the ammunition in Marshal's gun. Could you check these?"

MaCos looks at him declining to take the paper out of his hand. "My translator does not allow me to read your language, just speak and understand the spoken word."

This put the Doctor off for a couple seconds as he studied his notes. "I'm sure they're right."

"Perhaps if we went down to your lab I could see what you have," MaCos offered. This was better than he had hoped for. And they both went enthusiastically down to his lab.

Dauntless removed the helmet and looked around. She is alone. She can see Dr. Cooly and Nurse Chapel with Heather in the Med. Center exam room. She puts the helmet down and goes to see how she is doing.

Heather is sitting up in bed with a hospital gown and her black leather biker pants on. She has a wide-eyed expression on her face. She keeps moving her head rapidly about, briefly fixing her attention on one thing and then another. "OHGOD! OhGod, why won't you people help me?"

She jumped up. "What is it with you people?" She looked about and started to go. "I can't stay here, I've got things to do."

Nurse Chapel and Dr. Cooly try to stop her but she just pushes her way past them. Dauntless stepped up and caught hold of Heather and lifted her up back on to the bed. The enraged Heather started to get back up and Dauntless went to pin her to the bed. After a few seconds she was able to pin Heather down but it wasn't easy. "She's strong!" Dauntless exclaimed.

"It's Marshal's coat! It's made her super strong just like you!" Beverly explained.

Dauntless struggled to hold down Heather as she jerked around trying to free herself from the vice like grip of Dauntless. "I can't hold her much longer! Give her something!"

Chapel tried to give her an injection but the needle bent! Heather finally broke free from Dauntless and shoved her back. She bolted off of the bed before anyone could react and darted out the door and smack into Marshal. "Not this time big boy!" She mocked him as she darted around and under his arms.

The three girls came rushing out of the Med center and ran up to Marshal. "Where is she?" Beverly asked.

Marshal pointed at the door to the stairway as it closed. He explained, "Feather's my name, fast!"

Dr. Cooly went over to the phone on the wall. "Lock down the building. Heather's running loose and she's super strong and super fast." She then turned to Marshal and Dauntless. "Go get her and bring her back before she hurts someone or herself."

Two soldiers and a Man In Black lay unconscious on the floor of the main foyer. Heather kicks another soldier in the stomach. He goes flying back through the doors. The last soldier tries to grab her, but she hits him in the chest with her open palm and he is knocked down on his butt. She turns to go out the doors and she is hit in the head from behind.

Heather goes down on one knee and grabs her head. After a few seconds, she's up again confronting her assailant, Colonel Otis. She grabs hold of both of his arms and pins him against the wall and presses up against him. "You want to play rough? I like it rough," she said with a wide smile on her face. "But you already know that. Don't you?" She gazed into his eyes nose to nose with a crazy smile on her face. She planted a great big sloppy kiss on his mouth and left him speechless saying, "see yah around suckers!" And she was out the door.

He tried to stop her by grabing her shoulder. She quickly spun around and backhanded him, sending him flying back into the foyer.

The sound of Heather's bike firing up and roaring off down the street could be heard as Dauntless arrived in the foyer. "She got away," was all she said.

"We've got to get her back," he said as he straightened his uniform and looked out the door.

"But how? Sir," she asked as she joined him. They traded glances and turned to help the downed soldiers up.

Dr. Cooly and Marshal arrive moments later and the Colonel wants to know "Just what happened up there? Why is Heather super?"

"It's Marshal's coat, Colonel, I think," Dr. Cooly explained, as Marshal put his coat on.

"That much is obvious! We've used it on people before without turning them into super... whatever! Lt. Holmes is the only one who got the super treatment. Or did we miss something?" He asked and folded his arm across his chest waiting for an explanation.

"We didn't miss anything," Dr. Cooly replied defensively.'

Dauntless interrupted saying, "I think I can explain."

The Colonel turned his head in her direction. "You can explain? Please do."

"I only just now learned this while working with MaCos and the memory helmet," Brandy explained defensively. As she continued, she shifted her weight to one hip and used her hands to explain, "Heather was bitten by the Harbinger Queen. That's what they're called, The Harbingers. The Queen converts drones into something more, like warriors."

"The ones we encountered with the guns grafted into their bodies," the Colonel stated.

Brandy nodded her head as she spoke. "Exactly. But that's not all. You see, before the Queen does this, she injects her victims with something that makes them heal super fast, so they won't bleed to death while she is converting them."

"Very thoughtful of her," he said sarcastically adding, "go on."

"We interrupted her before she could finish," Dauntless explained.

Doctor Cooly's face lights up. "Now I've got it. She had this alien enzyme in her blood stream when Marshal put his jacket on her to stop the bleeding and save her life. But what Marshal didn't know, couldn't know, was that she already saved by the injection in her blood stream."

She went on, "We overexposed her to X-rays whiles this was going on causing the new cells to mutate and Marshal's jacket detected this change and the speeding up of her metabolism and made it even more." She paused to let it all sink in. He still had that look on his face. So she tried to explain again. "The nanos in Marshal's jacket are activated when the jacket gets wet."

"I thought it had something to do with kinetic energy," he said.

"No, the nanos are powered by kinetic energy, but they are activated by moisture. Like blood, When they get wet they turn on and go looking for things to fix. The nanos read the cell structure and make repairs accordingly. Heather's cell structure was being rewritten. Part of the healing process involves growing new cells. The newly grown cells were being mutated by the radiation we exposed her to at the time, and her metabolism was being accelerated by the Harbinger's sting. The nanos in the jacket read this and made all of her cells heal faster and stronger. Apparently, she not only heals fast, but she is just plain fast."

He took it all in. "Okay, that's what happened. How do we get her back?"

Marshal said, "activate tracking device."

"Your translator is working!" Colonel Otis said.

"Occasionally zzz"

"We may not have to do anything. She may just come to her senses and return on her own," Dr. Cooly said hopefully.

"Is that your advice Doctor, that we do nothing and hope for the best?" The Colonel asked redirecting his attention to her.

"No. I was just saying, you know, sometimes people just get better on their own. It happens all the time," she replied.

Dauntless suddenly perked up. "That reminds me, Colonel, that's why I was looking for you when all this happened. I found something in the memory helmet's record about the Harbingers."

""Hope it's something good," he dryly said.

She smiled. "Besides the fact that they are referred to as the scourge on the universe, there is a way to kill them without killing the host."

"Don't keep us in suspense, what is it?" He inquired.

"If we can kill or put the Queen to sleep that will cause The Hive to lose its cohesion. Or we can use a chemical on them. It kills the Harbingers, but not the host."

"Don't tell me you forgot what it was."

"No, I remember what it was, it was sodium crystals. Or something like that." She said not sure of its meaning.

"Lieutenant, uh Dauntless, are you telling me rock salt will kill the scourge of the universe?" He couldn't believe what he was hearing.

"Actually, they use particle accelerators to launch the crystals and imbed them into the bodies of the Harbingers," Dauntless reported

"Hmm, sounds like old fashioned shotguns loaded with rock salt to me." The Colonel scratched his chin.

"There was something else I wanted to check out in the helmet if you don't mind?" Dauntless asked.

At that moment downstairs in the lower lab Dr. Brewville and MaCos Ex are having a discussion. "I don't know about this. It doesn't smell right to me," the pig faced alien said as he handled a block of waxy looking material.

"It should work just fine. I had to substitute some materials because we just don't have them here on Earth, but it should work," Dr. Brewville insisted as he took the block of plasma back from his alien adviser.

"It may work. I just don't think it's stable enough. Look, I made some for Adack before we got captured. I could cook some up in the lab if you like. It won't be full strength but it will work," MaCos offered.

"No, that won't be necessary," Dr. Brewville insisted.

"The only way to tell for sure if it works is to test it in the gun," MaCos summed it up as he left. Dr. Brewville followed him into the elevator. It stopped at the first floor and Dr. Cooly was helping some soldiers get in. He saw Marshal standing there in the foyer and went over to him with the block of plasma.

Dr. Brewville handed the block over to Marshal saying, "try the fit, we need to go to the range and test fire it."

Marshal took the block of ammo, drew his sidearm and slapped the ammo in and returned the gun to its holster. "Finally ZZZ other equipmentZZZZ." His translator was only partially working but partially was better than not at all.

Dr. Cooly helped the last of the soldiers into the elevator on their way to the Med. Center. Marshal turned to join them and then something caught his attention. It was the rumble of Heather's motorcycle coming back.

Heather road her bike right up to the front steps, killed the engine, hit the kick stand and swung her long leg off. She took her black riding helmet off and tossed it over to the grass, tossed her long golden hair back and gave it a shake. She was still wearing the hospital gown and black leather pants.

A carload of paparazzi pulled up and their cameras went into overdrive. Marshal, who normally never comes out the front, came out to meet Heather on the steps. She ripped open her gown exposing her full round breasts, supporting them in each hand she asked, "do you want some more of these?" *The unveiling of her stunning double D's should have been accompanied with a TAA DAA!* She had healed commpletely, and a more tempting invitation would be hard to find.

Dr. Brewville, who was still in the foyer, stumbled back and sat on the desk and adjusted his glasses. Things like this never happened in Dreamland.

Marshal was unsure of her words but was certain of her meaning. *She could not be under the influence of his pheromones, this must be something else,* he thought.

He didn't have long to think about it. She walked right up to him and threw her arms around him. "Come with me big boy, I'll show you a real good time," she said with an evil smile on her pretty face.

Her very close proximity and physical contact made the translator work better. "Heather, you should come with me and see Dr. Cooly."

"I came back for you," she cooed.

"You are not yourself,"

"I'm super strong now, you don't have to worry about hurting me."

"This is not right, let's go inside." He tried to convince her to cooperate.

"You really should come with me. The Hive is calling you." She was using all of her charms on him. He was weakening.

The Hive! He thought, *she must be under the control of the Queen. If I go along I will be able to find The Hive and destroy it. If not, they can track me through the tracker in my badge.* He wrapped his huge arms around her and kissed her passionately. It was easy to lose yourself while in her embrace. Each of his arms was nearly as big as her waist was. She nearly disappeared when he hugged her like that.

She covered up as they went to her bike. She got on and he got on behind her. The weight was too much for the bike. They went over to the paparazzi car and evicted the occupants forcibly. They got in with Heather driving and took off, leaving the paparazzi standing in the street of the traffic circle.

Colonel Otis took a phone call. "Colonel this is the front desk calling. It seems we have had an incident down her involving the gentlemen of the press. It seems, Marshal and a virtually nude blond girl fitting Heathers description have stolen a car."

The Colonel took in a deep breath and let it out. "I'll be right down. Don't let them go anywhere. Get some of your friends in MIB down there right away." He hung up and just shook his head.

A light blue garbage truck belonging to the City of Chicago slows to a stop along a chain link fence enclosing a play lot, adjacent to a three story brown brick school building. The students are inside, the streets are empty. The passenger, a large white workman with a partially armored body turns to the driver who is also armored and asks, "What now?"

"The drone driver points to the school and says, "see that?"

"The school? What about it?"

"It may be a school for them, but for us, it's one stop shopping. We can get everything we need in there. Teachers to make smart drones, athletes to make into warriors and we can even take some of the small ones for snacking on."

"And no weapons to defend themselves with." The passenger was catching on, as were the drones on the back of the truck. One cracked a whip to get their attention. "I'll drive em up to you with the whip while you use the cargo net to catch em!"

"I'll feed em to our friends," the other drone added, clanging the giant vice like claw that was on his right hand. As he spoke, several of the alien bugs scurried about the back of the garbage truck in anxious anticipation of adding to The Hive.

The truck engine roared as the blue monster crashed through the fence. "Remember, we need them alive!" The driver called out to his fellow Harbingers.

Princess Kara strolls down the stone pathway in the formal garden. The palace of the Emeer towers high above the trees that ring the garden. The planet of Shambailla fills a quarter of the sky. She leaves the path and the formal garden to take a shortcut across a meadow filled with clover to a shallow pond with lilies growing around and in it.

The water birds, with their long graceful necks, glide along on the surface of the water displaying their brilliant plumage unafraid. There is a white marble bench that would normally be at the edge of the pond, but the water is up a bit and the bench is actually in the water by a foot.

The princess reaches the edge of the water and lifts the hem of her long dress to keep it out of the water as she tiptoes in bare feet to the bench. The birds come over expecting to be fed but she has nothing to give them. The birds make a nuisance of themselves and she resorts to kicking water on them. The birds beat a noisy retreat.

The ruckus brings one of the Palace's Sea Ay knights charged with the protection of the royal family. It is Marshal, he is much younger but it is definitely him. No white jacket and utility belt, that lies in the future. Now he wears the flowing robes and silver breastplate of a Sea Ay knight.

The Princess sees him running towards her and she jumps off the bench splashing in the pond getting her dress wet. Seeing the princess is not in any mortal danger, he turns to go. But she calls him over. They are joined by one of her maids in waiting.

"You are not one of my usual guards. What is the meaning of all this running about?" The Princess inquired.

The young knight bowed slightly before addressing her. "Sorry to disturb you my lady, I was alarmed by the birds. Sir Barns, your usual guardian, was in an accident earlier today and was unable to fulfill his duties. Normally I am assigned to Prince Herc, but seeing he is off world today there wasn't much for me to guard so here I am, his replacement."

He takes her outstretched hand to steady her as she slips her shoes back on. "Is there anything else you required my lady?"

"I am bored, there is no one to talk to. Kindly speak with me," she commanded as she took her hand back.

"Gladly. Do you have a subject in mind?" He asked as they strolled back to the path with his hands behind his back.

"No, tell me about yourself Where do you come from?" She flashed a winning smile.

He spoke as they slowly walked down the flower-lined path. "I come from Aurora Prim, but I do not remember it, I was harvested at an early age and raised in the Chytown colony. I served with the ground forces on Senn and later with the fleet during the Nam war. Then I was selected for knight selection and I won my spurs just a few months ago." His sleeve bore the two golden chevrons and crossed sabers of a Sea Ay Knight.

She stopped to play with a vine that hung down from a trellis along the side of the path. "That's all very impressive I'm sure, but I didn't ask for your resume. Tell me something about you."

He looked around and down at the flagstone beneath his feet. "Uh, in Chytown I was trained in the arts before I started to grow."

"You're an artist? A big fellow like you!" She almost started to laugh.

"I was trained," he apologized, "in art and Music."

"What instrument do you play?" She asked with a smile on her face. She was clearly amused by this. Marshal only looked to be about 300 Lb. by then, big, but not like now.

"Several actually, but I am most proud of my mastery of the Quaddratar, he chimed.

"A big fellow like you plays the Quad!" She was incredulous about his statements. *Could he be lying about his achievements to impress a Princess?*

"I play base usually. I've attained the 4th degree of mastery."

"Now look who's showing off." She was certain of it now.

"No my lady, it's true," he tried to reassure her.

Turning to her maid in waiting she commanded, "Gwen, go bring us some cold beverages and a Quaddratar for my guardian to serenade me with." She motioned for her to go with her hand.

Gwen left them immediately. He protested. "Please my lady, it's been some time since I last played."

She was enjoying this. "But a 4th level master of the Quad should never be out of practice."

Back in the kitchen, Gwen poured two drinks and placed them on a silver serving tray, but something was missing. She went to get something and while she was gone, a man came by and secretly dropped small white pills in each drink. Gwen returned with napkins with the royal crest on them.

After a few minutes of his trying to talk her out of it and her insisting that he play, Gwen came back carrying a silver tray with two crystal goblets filled with an amber liquid that fizzed. Behind her came the man carrying a massive stringed instrument.

The Quaddratar is a large four-sided stringed instrument with silver keys on top. It stands five foot tall and is played somewhat like a base fiddle. You can pluck or strum the strings like a guitar or use a bow. With a simple touch of one of the silver keys you can cause several different sets of strings to reverberate at the same time, giving you the ability to accommpany yourself. The strings on the front and back sound much like an acoustic guitar would. The strings on one side are metallic and sound more organic, while the other side sounds like brass. A full orchestra all in one instrument. Very difficult to play, let alone to master.

"Very well, if you insist. Is there something in particular you would like to hear?" He asked as he prepared to play rolling up the sleeves of his robes.

"Being a 4th level master you must have commpleted your Metron," she stated, still amused with the whole thing.

"Of course," he mater-of-factly replied, with the Quad leaning against his chest.

"Then play me your song," she commanded as she sat down on the low stonewall that ran along the pathway at this part of the walk. She sipped her drink.

"But it's silly," he protested.

"I command it," she pouted and drank some more.

He took a drink to clear his throat. "Very well. As you command. It is a love song, a song of sorrow and devotion. It is called, My Darling Beverlee." He simply started picking the strings, playing slowly and softly, playing rythmically, adding accommpaniment in the second movement and full orchestral to finish off.

(Sung and played to the tune of Canta Libre, by Neil Diamond.)

"My darling Beverlee--,   I still love you so—much.   And I always have--. And I always will--."

"You are the sunshine that fills my day. Makes me feel like a young bird fly---ing. Now that you're gone all I know is pain. Makes me feel like an old man die---ing."

"My darling Beverlee---, I still love you so—much, And I always have, and I always will. My darling Beverlee---." He had a clear crisp bass voice, He could not hit the high notes and didn't even try, He used the Quad to play them, his fingers sliding up and down the neck of the quad producing a magical, almost mesmerizing tone. He played with great emotion and she was moved by it. He stopped playing and the notes faded away. His mood was somber; the song obviously was more than just a song to him. She was impressed.

After a few seconds of reflection, he toasted her and had another drink and then started playing something more lively. The Princess suddenly got dizzy and fell over.

Gwen was the first to get to her. Marshal stopped playing and rushed over to her. As Marshal knelt over the Princess trying to figure out what to do, the servant that had brought the quad struck Gwen over the head with the serving tray knocking her out.

Marshal stood up and the servant also hit him with the serving tray, bending it around Marshal's head. Marshal staggered back and cleared his head. The man pulled out a club and rushed at Marshal. Big mistake. Marshal hit him with enough force to send him flying 15 feet. He came down like a rag doll.

Marshal turned to the Princess. He started to pick her up when he realized he wasn't alone. A dark figure came out of the flowers and threw down her cloak, revealing it to be a purple skinned female of substantial proportions and stature. She had glowing green eyes and fiery red hair and a strange suit of armor, if you could call, a few pieces of metal stuck together a suit.

She was a Thugee. A race noted for their strength and toughness. Their warriors had an unusual code of honor. They only protected their heads, arms and legs. A wound to those locations was deemed unhonorable and thus unjust so, they tried to protect those areas. Wounds to more vital parts of the body were deemed to be honorable and thus acceptable. If you could hit them, they figured they deserved the consequences.

Her massive bust and hips were barely covered and certainly not armored. Her navel was exposed. Her physical appearance was at the least distracting and quite possibly intimidating. She held a two-foot long cleaver like blade with a sharpened point in her gloved hand.

She was as tall as Marshal. She silently moved closer. Marshal put the Princess down and drew his saber from behind his back. The four-foot long thin razor sharp Vorpal blade made a zinging sound when it was drawn.

They circled each other, looking for an opening. She spoke, "it's a pity you've seen my face."

"That's not all I've seen," he answered referring to her lack of costume.

"Now you'll have to die. You weren't supposed to be here. We were expecting Sir Barnes. You're the blue one they're all talking about, aren't you?"

"That's me," he said as he parried her thrust.

"This would have been an interesting challenge," she said as she similarly parried his counterthrust.

"Would have been?" His head started to spin.

"Yes, you see, your drink was drugged. You'll be out soon. Pity, I would have liked to test my blade against you," she said with a smile of confidence on her face.

ZING, ZANG! Their blades rang out as they CLANGED against each other. He staggered back; the exertion was hastening the effects of the drug. His head was spinning once again. He pulled a signaling device from out of his pocket, but before he could use it, she flicked it out of his unsteady hand with the point of her blade. She cooed, "we don't want to be interrupted by any uninvited guest do we?"

He lunged at her with his saber. She parried his lunge with her blade and caught hold of his wrist with her free hand. He stumbled as she pulled him forward. He fell, planting his face in her stomach, almost knocking her over.

As he started to recover, the hilt of her bald came crashing down on his head. He collapsed, falling forward, pinning her to the ground with him on top. The weight of his body pinned her lower body down. His face was lying on her stomach. She sat up, stabbed him in his right arm, causing him to drop his saber. She flipped her blade around and drove it into Marshal's back penetrating two inches. He gave out a grunt as it hit, and started to move.

She struggled to pull the blade out. Using both hands she drove it in deeper this time. SKUCH! He jerked with the impact. She worked her blade free and rolled him over using her long powerful legs to kick him off of her.

His right hand caught hold of her shoulder pad and held on. She was about to cut his throat when his left fist crashed into her head. The palace guard found both of them lying there with him still holding on to her shoulder pad. The attempted kidnapping of Princess Kara had been foiled.

Not many people can claim to have defeated a Thugee thief and assassin, but Marshal could. He was placed in the military hospital where the Princess visited him daily. Upon his commmplete recovery, he was commissioned a Knight of the Ess Sea Ay order, despite the objections of some of the nobility. Probably because of the insistence of the Princess.

The Order of Ess Sea Ay Knights is one of the highest orders of knighthood. It is usually reserved for the sons of nobility who will not be inheriting the family title and have distinguished themselves in the various military orders. Their duties usually involved safeguarding state secrets and holy relics and powerful artifacts.

Even though he now had the third golden chevron and crossed sabers of an Ess SEA Ay knight, his duties remained the same, protecting the royal family, Princess Kara in particular.

The family of the Emeer, and Princess Kara in particular, remained safe under his watchful eye for the next two years until the Princess was married off to the Prince of Riticqulong. Her safety and welfare then became the Prince's concern.

The nobles, still not happy having a commoner and a giant blue freak at that, holding such a high position moved to have him transferred out. There was talk of using him as an instructor of knights, but again, he was of common birth. Extraordinary yes, but not nobility.

When the Federation Ambassador expressed an interest in an exchange of citizens under the Ohmahaw accord, the nobles found their answer. Marshal was commissioned to serve the Federation. Being a commissioned Knight of the Ess Sea Ay, he could not refuse to go.

Marshal was formally adopted by the Federation, making him a ward of the state, and eligible for citizenship. This was done even though he was an adult, to facilitate the training and reeducation he would need in a total alien environment. He was then taken to his new home to begin his new life. Interestingly enough, his commission as an Ess SEA AY knight and his warrant to protect the royal family were never withdrawn.

Dr. Cooly's voice chimed in. "How are you doing?" Dauntless took off the helmet and straightened her short blond hair. "That wasn't what I was looking for."

"Did you find anything useful?" The Doctor asked.

"No, nothing useful, unless you were looking for a fairy tail with a modern day ending," Brandy said as she got up. "Why did you call me anyway? How long was I in there?"

"I don't know. The Colonel is looking for you."

Dauntless finds the Colonel and several soldiers getting ready for action. "What's up?" She asks without thinking. The Colonel shoots her a look. She catches on and adds, "Sir."

"Marshal is not in the building and the locator beacon in his badge has been activated," the Colonel said, as he readied his pistol belt, replacing the magazines in the ammo pouches with fresh ones. "We're going wheels up in five! Be upstairs on the main helipad."

Heather is driving fast down the expressway with Marshal riding shotgun in the commandeered car. They have his windows down and the wind is blowing her hair around, She looks over at him and asks, "I don't suppose you have any money on you do you?" He looked at her blankly. "Of course not! That's the problem with you. No money." She sighed as she blew through the tollbooth.

The trooper standing by the car he had just pulled over watched her go by as he wrote a ticket. "Maybe next time." She looks over and notices Marshal watching the police car as they pass. Fearful of losing her influence over him she unties her hospital gown and flips it open exposing her perky breast and navel. The sunlight danced on her perfect skin. *That'll hold his attention.* But to seal the deal she reaches over and strokes him with her free hand.

They raced along the Chicago Skyway, an elevated expressway passing over old neighborhoods and older industrial areas. The air turns foul as they cross over the Calumet. Exiting the Skyway, she took him down some old streets that had seen better days with lots of potholes. The streets were strangely empty of traffic.

She drove past empty storefronts and bars. An eight-inch long bug landed on their windshield and started to scurry around on its way inside the car. Marshal caught it and was about to crush it when Heather called out, "STOP! DON'T KILL IT! It's part of The Hive." Marshal pretended to just toss it out the window, but he actually threw it down with enough force to splatter it on the pavement.

Several humans with armor and nasty looking cutting tools grafted into their bodies are discussing what to do with four Mini Cooper cars. "They are inferior and of little use to us."

"I thought we could use them as ammunition," the drone said, as he thumped his one human hand down on top of the tiny auto. He thought for a few seconds and added, "perhaps if we attached some chains." An approaching car diverted their attention.

Heather crossed railroad tracks and drove along a fenced-in building that had been a steel mill. She stopped at the gate of the old abandoned Republic Steel South Chicago Works and two warriors came over and let the car in. She pulls up the main entrance and is met by several more warriors armed with oversized cleavers and guns.

Heather slides over to Marshal, reaches around his head, and gives him a long, slow, wet kiss. "Before we uh.. I want you to meet the Queen."

Marshal was thinking, *I'm not sure just what she is planning or how long I can resist her advances, but if it gives me a chance to get the Queen it's worth it.*

One of the warriors came over to Heather stating, "he is not of The Hive."

Heather explained as she stopped rubbing up against Marshal and got out of the car, "I can control him. He desires my body, all men desire this body, see?" She opened her hospital gown for the warrior to see her exposed breasts for a second or two, before closing it again. He could not argue with her. They instructed Marshal to get out of the car. He does.

There was all manner of heavy equipment and machinery scattered about. Most of it heavily rusted. They were accumulating raw materials by the freight carload. Scrap metal and iron ore and tanker cars of chemicals and acids.

An Army Black Hawk flying low southbound over the Museum of Science and Industry nears the city's lakefront. In the back are Colonel Otis, Dauntless and half a dozen combat ready soldiers. The Colonel is talking on a handset. "Give the pilot a vector and let us know if he starts moving. And tell Charley Commpany where we are going and get them moving!" He hands the handset back to the crew chief. He sat down next to Dauntless and uses his COMM link to speak to her. "He's in South Chicago."

"South Chicago! What's there that he could be interested in?" She asked.

"According to the map, it's close to where the Air Force bird went down and where they lost track of the bugs."

"She looked at him asking, "you don't suppose?"

"I don't suppose anything Dauntless. We're just going where his locator says he is."

Inside the mill, great hooks bigger than a man hang from the ceiling. Humongous foundry buckets are scattered here and there, each with a capacity big enough to hold several cars. There are roller tables and machinery all over the place. They are trying to light the great furnaces in the foundry. Sparks are flying and bouncing off the floor and everything else in the way.

Marshal holds on to Heather as they are escorted by 30 warriors, all having different types of weaponry grafted into them. *Marshal is not afraid, nor is he lost to Heather's considerable charms. The closer he stays to her, the better his translator works and he needs to know what's going on. And if it appears he's under her dominance they might not be expecting anything. At least, that was his hope.*

One of the ceiling cranes rolls overhead and lowers a platform supported by four massive chains, one on each corner. On the platform is the Harbinger Queen and two servants. The Queen speaks. "Bring me more sssilicone." She turns her attention to Heather and Marshal "Yesss, that's the one. Heather you have done well."

One of the drones comes forward and informs the Queen that, "The nest is not yet ready."

She turns to him. "THEN MAKE IT READY!" She angrily commands.

"Your majesty, he has not been prepared for you. He is still not part of The Hive. Shall I prepare him for you?" One of the Servant Drones asks.

"No, his offspring will be that much ssstronger if he is not controlled when I harvest him," she says. Turning back to Heather she continues, "Heather you have done a good job. Keep him quiet and under your influence but don't get him over ssstimulated. I need all he hasss to offer for my next clutch of eggsss.

Marshal had heard enough. He drew his side arm and aimed it at the Queen. The warriors all jumped into action around him but froze in place when the Queen commanded them to "HOLD!" She was looking down the muzzle of a .75 caliber plasma pistol. It was bigger and nastier than anything they had.

Marshal commanded, "ZZZTt, HIVE no! ZZzzt" his translator wasn't up to it without someone being in direct contact with it.

Heather stepped forward with her arms held out to calm the warriors. "Fear not! He has no ammunition in his weapon. It is harmless."

I wouldn't be so sure if I were you, he thought. He said something, probably meaning the same thing in his native alien gibberish. He reestablishes his aim as the warriors gather closer around him. He pulls the trigger. And they all brace themselves expecting some sort of explosion of unpredicted magnitude. And? He pulls it again and? … Nothing?! A glob of glowing goop resembling striped toothpaste oozed from the muzzle and dripped down onto the floor, sending up a small puff of smoke and a sizzling sound as it hit.

He pistol-whips the three closest to him, sending them crashing into the drones behind them. Her loyal subjects rapidly whisk the Queen on her platform away from danger.

Heather jumps on his back and starts to flail on him, having no effect. Marshal grabs a chain off a cart and starts twirling it about keeping the drones off. Heather shouts, "DON'T SHOOT! The Queen wants him as he is! I'll bring him under my control! Just stay back!"

Marshal continued to swing the chain around keeping the drones at bay. With Heather still on his back, he started for the exit. But by now she was trying a different tactic. She eased her head down against his, cheek to cheek. "Come on big boy. You know you can't get out of here. And I know you want me. You don't have to mate with the Queen, she is incommpatible with you anyway. You can mate with me and I'll transfer your seed to the Queen's royal jelly. It will be glorious."

A couple of drones got too close and were eviscerated by the swinging chain. He continued toward the doors. She slid around on his body and buried his face in-between her breasts. "MUPH!"

"You cannot resist me!" She announced as his forward progress stopped. "SEE! HE IS MINE!" She proclaimed. He faltered and weakened and rallied his resistance and grabbed hold of Heather by her sharply curved hips and lifted her out of his face and chucked her over his left shoulder. He held her on his shoulder with his hand on her butt as she kicked and screamed. He ran for the door, swinging the chain overhead as he went.

The Army Black Hawk passed over the elevated expressway and dropped down closer to the empty warehouse and factory building. It banked as it flew over a barge in the Calumet and skimmed along at just under 100 mph. "He is down there somewhere! We can't get a good fix. There's too much interference. All this steel!" The pilot reported to Colonel Otis.

He turned and commanded, "KEEP LOOKING!"

Four drone bodies went flying backwards out the door, followed shortly by Marshal and Heather still kicking and screaming on his shoulder. Out in the open, Marshal heard a familiar sound. The sound of a Black Hawk flying nearby. The WHOOP WHOOP WHOOP, reverberated in the large empty buildings. He saw them going by. They didn't see him. He needed to signal them some way.

He put the chain and Heather down and picked up the car. He tossed it in front of the helicopter's path. Heather jumped up on Marshal's back again this time, putting a choke hold around his neck and wrapped her legs around his midsection. "Okay! We tried to be nice and look where it got us. I'm super strong now. I can put you down the old fashioned way!" And she squeezed with all her might.

"Look!" The co-pilot spotted it first. "There's something you don't see every day, a flying car," the pilot added as he banked in the direction the car came from, "It must be one of the new Toyotas. He must be over there."

At first, Marshal just kept swatting drones away as they came forward with Heather still on his back. She kept applying the pressure. He started to stagger a little and he grabbed Heather's arm and removed her from around his neck.

The infuriated Heather hung on with her legs around his waist and pounded his back with her fist. More drones approached, some with nasty looking edged weapons more than four feet long. Marshal picked up the chain and started to swing it again.

Heather, who was still on his back, was not going to give up, but she could see she needed to change here tactics. She used her newly acquired super speed to catch the chain as Marshal was starting to swing it and wrapped it around his neck. One of the nearby drones tossed her a crowbar and she quickly slipped it between the chain and Marshal's neck and used it to twist and tighten the chain around his neck!

Marshal struggled to grab hold of her or the chain, but he couldn't get his fingers under it. It doesn't matter how strong you are, if your brain doesn't get its supply of blood carrying oxygen, nothing is going to work for very long. He stumbled and went down on one knee. Heather was now standing on the ground behind him. She had let go with her legs as he started down. She was still giving it everything she had, squeezing his neck. "I said you're going down!" She gritted her teeth and gave the crowbar another half twist tightening the chain even more. The crowbar started to bend, just as Marshal went limp and was hanging by his neck in her grip.

Loads of dust are kicked up as the chopper comes in for a landing. "Look! She's dragging him out of the steel mill!" The crew chief called out. Hundreds of angry worker and warrior drones appeared from every nook and cranny rushing towards the chopper on the ground.

Dauntless, two soldiers and Colonel Otis rushed out of the chopper to help Heather get in the bird with Marshal. They were in for a surprise. Heather dropped Marshal face down and backhanded both of the soldiers in rapid secession. WHAP WHAP! They were down and out for the count.

Dauntless and Heather got into a pushing match. Colonel Otis, seeing the crowbar used to tighten the chain around Marshal's neck, put two and two together and cracked Heather in the back of her head with the butt of his .45. She went down on one knee and holding her head, turned back to face Colonel Otis. "That's twice you've hit me from behind today! Time for payback!"

Dauntless tapped Heather on the shoulder from behind. She turned to see WHAM! Dauntless knocked her out with a roundhouse punch. With the chain loosened, Marshal started to come to. "Come-on big blue! We've got to get out of here!" Dauntless said as she picked up Heather and one of the KO'd soldiers. Marshal stumbled along as he and Otis helped the other soldier up and into the waiting chopper. The chopper took fire from the ground as it lifted out but they made it.

As they road back home Dauntless asked, "what happened back there, what's with Heather?"

Marshal was sitting on the floor of the bird holding Heather on top of him. "She is under the influence of The Hive."

"You can talk! Can you understand us! We can understand you. Is your translator working?" The Colonel asked hopefully.

"No Colonel, she is in extremely close proximity to me and the translator, that is why it's working."

Heather came to on the way back to HERO but this time Marshal held on. By the time they were coming in for a landing, Heather was once again under the influence of Marshal's pheromones, and trying to seduce him with her body. Dauntless took over for Marshal and they got home without any further incident.

Heather was carried kicking and screaming into the Med. Center where they gave her a sedative, which didn't work as long as it took to battle her down and give it to her. Marshal managed to forcibly hold her still for another X-ray, this time of the head and neck. That's when they found it.

Dr. Cooly explained the situation to Colonel Otis while showing him the X-rays. "There is a stinger under her skin and it is still pumping its venom into her system. We didn't find it because her skin had healed over it hiding it from detection. It has to be removed. I can do the surgery but it is dangerous. I'll be cutting on her neck while she's fighting back all the time."

"Can't you knock her out?" He asked.

"Not with drugs. She's resistant, super resistant."

Dauntless and Marshal are given the difficult job of restraining Heather. It fell to Marshal to hold her in place while Dauntless fastened the restraints. Soon she was immobilized on a board but she could still squirm about.

Dr. Cooly handed an old-fashioned police billy club to Colonel Otis. He took it. "I wonder how you come to have this." He turned and stepped up to Heather ready to strike, and turned away "I have, as she pointed out earlier, hit her twice and it didn't get the job done." He handed the club to Marshal.

He took the club and looked at it for a few seconds. He handed it back to the Colonel shaking his head no. It fell to Dauntless to do the deed. WACK! And it was over. They placed her on the table face down and Dr. Cooly brushed her hair back to expose her neck.

The operation should have been straightforward, one quick incision and remove the stinger. But no! She kept healing up before Beverly could do anything. Finally she had to cut extra deep and forcibly hold the incision open with retractors.

Removing the stinger wasn't straightforward either. There were tendrils growing out of the stinger and into her spinal cord. They had to be stripped away one by one and kept out of the way or they would reattach.

She started to come to and fight back. Marshal stepped up and knocked her out with a solid blow that cracked her skull! Later he explained that he realized, "That she would heal back fast with out any ill affects." His logic could not be disproved.

Dr. Cooly, realizing he was probably right, used a similar theory to remove the stinger and tendrils. She was closed up in record time. Not a half-hour later Heather was her normal self.

Captain Reynolds came by saying, "Dauntless, Marshal, you can stand down. The Air Force has taken over and relieved us."

CHAPTER TEN

CALL ME SUPERSTAR

Two F16 Falcons loaded with napalm roared by as two A10s and several Air Force helicopters circled overhead. Dozens of heavily armed air police move in on the old Republic Steel South Chicago Works. A Bradley armored fighting vehicle crashed through the gate, and a dozen airmen poured out and moved in on the main entrance.

They were using shoot and scoot tactics, but no one was shooting. They moved from behind piles of steel to parked heavy equipment, never exposing themselves for more than a few seconds while they moved. After a few minutes, it became apparent that they were the only ones there. The Harbingers had moved. They found a few dead bodies and nothing more.

Dr. Cooly finished examining Heather who is sitting on the table in the exam room as Dauntless comes in carrying some clothes. "We can't have you going around dressed like that. Here are some of my clothes, they should fit."

Heather takes the sweatshirt and eyes it suspiciously. She pulls it on and hands Brandy back her jeans. "I'll keep these on," referring to her black leather pants.

Colonel Otis and Marshal drop by to check up on her, and in a split second, she leaps off the table and into Marshal's startled arms. "OHMYGOD! OHMYGOD! I could have killed you! Can you ever forgive me?" She cried out with her hands wrapped around his neck.

Marshal didn't know what to say as she hugged him. She stopped to examine his neck, satisfied he was not injured she returned to using his pecs as a pillow. He smelled good, and she was relieved. But the Colonel picked up on something. "Do you remember what happened?"

She pulled her head away from his chest. "Yes! I remember it all! It wasn't me! I mean it was, but it wasn't." She sounded like herself.

"Heather, I am content to visualize that you have recovered from the ordeal of subjugation to the ruler of the Harbingers, but you may relinquish me now," Marshal said as he looked down at her with his translator working, sort of.

She looked up at him and hesitantly backed away. "Huh? Oh! Sorry!"

"What was it like?" Dr. Cooly asked as she took her glasses off.

"I could here people's voices in my head. The Queen spoke with a lisp. Some were talking to me, some weren't. It was like being in a room full of people all talking at the same time. The Hive knows what you know, but only if they look and you know what they know if you look. It's like being in a library. All of the answers are there if you look. Some of the people were smart, some were like, I don't know, zombies?"

"There's that word again." Colonel Otis sighed.

Heather went on saying, "The ones with the bugs still attached were the smart ones."

"Can you hear them now?" He asked with some enthusiasm.

"No, it's all quiet," she quipped.

"What about the Queen?" He persisted, thinking *there must be something we can use.*

Heather approached him. "She could control you, tell you what to do. She wants to mate with Marshal, sort of, she thinks he'll produce stronger offspring. Oh my! I just realized! She's building a nest to lay more eggs," she said as she looked around at Marshal.

"Lay more eggs?" This puzzled him.

"That's right, to make more of the bugs," she explained

Dr. Cooly took it from there. "The Queen must lay eggs that hatch into the bugs. The bugs take over the people making them drones and the Queen converts the drones into warrior or workers, whatever The Hive needs."

"That's right, and she wanted Marshal to fertilize the eggs. She wanted him pure and uncontaminated," Heather chimed in.

"EUUU!" Brandy was revolted at the thought.

Marshal said something in alien gibberish. He grabbed Brandy and pulled her close against his body. "I desire to vocalize with Lord Brewville."

"Who?" Brandy asked.

Heather giggled with delight, and hid her mouth with her hand. "Oh, I bet you do! This is going to be good." They all head for the elevator.

As Marshal and the two girls head for the elevator, Colonel Otis takes Beverly's arm and stops her and asks, "what's the scoop on Heather?"

She looks at him as she puts her glasses back on to examine Heather's chart. "I'm not sure I should be telling you this. Patient confidentiality and all that."

"It's for the General," he countered.

"She's strong, super strong, not as strong as Brandy, but if I had to say how strong she is," she paused, eyeing the Colonel, "and I guess I do have to say how strong she is, I'd say she has the strength of four or five men. Her metabolism has settled down, but it can speed up to incredible levels. Any wound or injury will heal in less than a minute. And she's fast. Her reflexes are off the board. She can move, oh I don't know, maybe 200 times faster than any human."

"Okay, she's strong and fast, but how was she able to do that to Marshal?" He asked.

She scratched her neck and put her chin in her hand. "She's not that strong, I'll have to get back to you on that."

"Sounds like we have another superhero, better make a report to the General," he said as he turned to go. He races and catches the elevator with the rest of them, and they all get on. He turns to Marshal and asks, "just what happened?"

Marshal's answer was unintelligible. "Oh for pete's sake!" Brandy reached up and adjusted his translator on his collar. "Try, again," she commanded.

"Heather was obviously under the influence of ZZtttz. When she tried to seduce me. I decided to ZZTZTZ. It was a chance to get to the Harbinger Queen."

"Oh, I was just wondering because it looked like she was trying to rip your head off to me." He smiled to himself.

Heather tapped Marshal on the chest to get his attention. He turned and looked down at her standing close to him. "You know it wasn't my idea to seduce you. It was something I had to do for the Queen. I really didn't mean any of it." They all shot her glances. Defensively she continued, "but if it had been my idea and I really wanted to seduce you, you would have stayed seduced." She paused again and finished up by punctuating her last statement with her finger on his chest. "And don't you forget it!"

He wanted to grab hold of her and kiss her until her teeth rattled. He could tell there was more to it than just obeying the Queen's command. But he didn't. *Maybe it was just his pheromones working on her. These human females are commplicated.*

The elevator stopped at the main floor and Colonel Otis gets out and meets General Solo coming in. "The Air Force let them get away! What's our status?" He asked as he stormed by. The Colonel chased after him.

"I have the entire 5th called in but standing down. Alpha and Bravo are down to less then 30% each. Charlie is about 80% strength. We have full air and ground and full combat loads. Are we going in?'

"Not at this time."

Colonel Otis adds to his report. "And we have a situation with Agent Carter." They stop walking and the Colonel fills the General in on the recent events.

They go their separate ways with the General saying, "monitor the police frequencies. I'll make the call to the Secretary."

In the lower lab, Dr. Brewville and MaCos Ex are working on some small equipment when Marshal and the others come in. Marshal does not look happy. He goes up to the doctor and starts to talk in his alien gibberish as the others form around them. "I'm sorry. I can't understand a thing you're saying,' Dr. Brewville said as he started to turn away from Marshal.

Dr. Brewville kept his hair pulled back in a ponytail and Marshal used it as a handle to redirect his attention. Marshal drew his sidearm, which caused everyone to gasp. Dauntless reached to grab his arm saying, "don't do it!"

He pointed his gun at the opposite concrete wall and pulled the trigger. After a few seconds, the toothpaste like substance oozed out and plopped on the linoleum floor raising a small puff of smoke and a fizzing sound.

"Dr. Brewville looked both relieved and puzzled. "It shouldn't do that."

"No shit Sherlock," Brandy answered sarcastically.

With the threat of imminent death passed, the mood lightened up. MaCos Ex reminded Dr. Brewville that he had told him that the ammo wasn't going to work. It wasn't stable at room temperature. But this was having no effect on him. He wasn't even paying any attention to him. Having spent most of his time cooped up in area 51, he was unaccustomed to being in the commpany of women, let alone three attractive ones. Brandy was young, pretty and a comic book goddess come to life. Heather was the proverbial blond bombshell, large breasted with the body of an aerobics instructor, and then there was Dr. Cooly. Beverly was a mature beauty, behind those glasses were bright green eyes and red hair. She had a sharp mind, that much was obvious as was her body that her lab coat couldn't contain without the help of the oversized belt that only enhanced her hourglass figure.

While Brewville was taking all this in, Marshal kept on speaking in his native gibberish and was getting closer and closer to the doctor. Suddenly, his attention was back on Marshal. He reached up and removed the broken translator from Marshal's collar and started to examine it. This startled Marshal, and he backed away. Brandy assured the big blue alien that it was okay.

He put on a magnifier to see the translator better. There were three thin wires coming out of it. He shook his head and tsk, tsked. He did something to one of the wires and then hit the whole thing with the butt end of a screwdriver handle. WHAP! All of the little things on the worktable bounced around. Everyone jumped back and looked back and forth at each other. He then used the screwdriver like a chisel and hit it three times with his hand and examined his work. Satisfied, a smile came to his face and he turned back to Marshal and jabbed the translator back into his collar and neck!

"OW! That is sharp," Marshal said, as he felt his neck.

"It works! You fixed it. That's amazing!" Heather announced.

He turned to her, "That's right, didn't they tell you I'm a genius." He started to say something else to her but she sighed and turned and walked away.

Brandy challenged him. "Okay, genius, explain the ammo."

"It wasn't ready for field use, but I think I've got it licked." Brandy nodded and left.

He turned his attention on Dr. Cooly, looking her up and down. He took a drink of ice tea from the oversized mug he had. He smacked his lips loudly and said, "Not bad."

She threw her hands on her hips, and turned to the Colonel saying, "I have to be going, the General wanted some additional tests run on Heather and Brandy." She shot a look of utter distaste at Dr. Brewville and in a huff stormed off calling out to Heather, "Wait up! I have some more tests to run."

"They're gone! Was it something I said?" He paused and thought for a second. "I meant the tea!" He said as he looked to Colonel Otis for answers.

"They're way out of your league," was all he said as he too turned to go.

Marshal standing there offered his take on it. "Sergeant Block told me it had something to do with being in a club."

This confused the doctor even more.

A short time later, Dauntless shows up in the Med. Center, where Nurse Chapel meets her. Brandy explains that she is supposed to use the helmet and find out about the charges against Marshal. MaCos Ex was supposed to work on it. Linda doesn't know anything about the charges but he did work on it for a while, "The helmet is in Dr. Coolie's office. You're welcome to use it there."

"I wouldn't want to interrupt the doctor," Brandy replied.

"You won't be interrupting anything, she's testing Heather out back," Nurse Chapel reassured her.

Dauntless went in and got commfortable; She took her utility belt off and laid it on the desk. She loosened her collar and flap and opened her jacket, she had a tank top tee shirt on over a bra under the jacket. Parking herself in the doctor's big easy chair, she put the helmet on.

A series of disconnected images come rushing into her head. She sees a space station explode and shower sparks and debris rain down onto a tan colored planet. She sees Marshal standing by a gazebo in a formal garden, he's watching a young girl off in the distance. She sees the long legged, purple Thugee assassin stalking up behind him. She slides a knife out of her boot top and lunges at him. Next she sees Marshal standing in a walled open expanse. He has no uniform, no weapons. A half man, half goat with three curved horns comes rushing at him with a five-foot long scimitar. The crowd off in the darkness goes wild. The image blurs.

Next, she sees a small gray alien sitting behind a desk, he's wearing a uniform like Marshal's. He says, "I think we have found the perfect partner for you." He pushes a button on his desk and commands, "send her in." He motions to the door behind them; it opens and in walks a giant blue female in the same uniform. "Meet Officer Dru."

A bird's eye view of, two large flightless birds are racing along on the wide-open planes, with its rolling hills and purple sage. The birds are bigger than an ostrich and are running as fast as they can, kicking up a small trail of dust as they go.

Zooming in closer, a man in buckskins is hunched down, riding one of the birds. As the birds reach the top of a hill overlooking an arroyo, he stops and looks back across the rolling hills and purple sagebrush. There is a dust cloud low on the horizon.

He changes birds and takes off on his fresh mount with the other bird running alongside. A disembodied voice chimes in, "Are you sure about this? Do we really need to do this?"

Two small gray aliens with large heads are standing before a viewscreen in their flying saucer. One had great dark almond shaped eyes. They both wear the flowing robes of Federation Judges. The one with almond eyes answers. "Yes, I have consulted with the Federation consul, and a board of inquiry must be convened,"

"But we already know what happened," the Judge Advocate stated.

"Do we? You have the word of one Federation Marshal and nothing else to go on," the Judge inquirer replied.

"That would normally be good enough," the Advocate coolly replied.

"Yes, but due to the extraordinary nature of this affair, a board of inquiry must be called. A fair and thorough investigation must be held," the Inquirer reassured his taller companion.

"Is it that this particular Marshal comes from outside the Federation?" The Advocate asked.

"That may play a part in it. But I personally doubt it," the Inquirer shook his head as he answered.

"Then if it's not political, it must be the insurance commmpanies trying to find a excuse to avoid payment on the claims," the Advocate reasoned.

"That may be what's driving the push for the Board of Inquiry. If we find that the Marshal's actions played a role causing the destruction of the station and the loss of 157 lives, that could mitigate their responsibility and transfer it onto the Federation."

They watched the rider go for a bit and then the Advocate spoke up. "That's why we're doing this, but do we have to include the primitives? Just look at that one. He's wearing animal skins and riding on one as well."

"The station was in orbit around their planet, clearly within their jurisdiction if they wish to prosecute," the Judge Inquirer shrugged his tiny bony shoulders.

"But they didn't even know of the station's existence!" The Advocate protested knowing the response before it was made.

"But it was there. And the charter clearly states that they must be included in the proceedings," the shorter judge responded.

"But involving them in the proceeding violates the none interaction clause of the charter, and are they even capable of making such commplicated decisions?" The Advocate asked.

The judge's almond shaped eyes got brighter as he answered. "They are. We must find a duly appointed representative of theirs and put it to him."

"But this is a protected primitive planet. We cannot establish contact with them," the Advocate said defensively.

The Judge Inquirer knew he had the answer to that as he spoke. "That is why we are here over their desert. We should be able to keep our contact to a minimum," he aid reassuringly.

"But how do you intend to find a duly appointed representative of these primitive people without making contact?" The Advocate was stumped.

"Simple, we abduct one." He smiled.

"How do we find this representative?" The puzzled Advocate inquired.

The Judge Inquirer's smile got bigger as he directed his companion's attention back to the viewscreen. "Observe. That primitive is obviously a felon fleeing from authority. All we have to do is wait and see who comes after him."

The Advocate saw the light. "And that man must be one of their law enforcement officials and thus a duly appointed representative of the people! Brilliant."

Sheriff Ken Elwood and his posse of ten are pushing their animals hard trying to catch Locota. They reach the same hilltop and stop; their animals are played out.

The large dogs they had been riding start to whimper and whine, some start barking. Two of the posse are thrown from their mounts. A dust clod is kicked up and then they see it. But they just don't know what it is. "What in tarn-nation is that?"

"Never seen nothing like it!" A silver flying saucer 100 feet across is hovering just in front of them. "What the HELL is it?" Silently it moves over them and hovers.

Inside the vessel, a tall, thin, greenish gray man in a black jump suit comes over to the Judges. The shorter Judge points out the Sheriff on the viewscreen. "See the one with the stat insignia on his chest. He is the leader; he must be the chief law enforcement official. Bring him aboard."

"Shall we land your honor?" The black suited officer asked.

"NO! That would be too dangerous. He's armed. Use the tractor beam and have him disarmed before he is brought before us."

A hatch opened on the lower surface of the disk and a beam of the most intense light ever seen on this or any other planet strikes the Sheriff and his mount. The beam focuses on the Sheriff only and he is levitated up off of his mount, up into the air and into the open hatch.

The posse is dumbstruck by watching all of this. They see two of the strangest looking little fellers come up to the Sheriff. He gives them his guns. The hatch closes up, and the saucer effortlessly sails off, making a grand sweep of the area. In just a matter of seconds it is clean out of sight. "Did you see that?"

"No! And neither did you!" The Deputy answered as he tried to keep his hat on.

The cowboy got on his mount and settled down enough to ask, "but what about the Sheriff?"

The Deputy had an answer ready for him. "The folks back in town will never believe any of this. Hell, I saw it and I don't believe it. They're all going to say we rode out here and got drunk. And that's just what I'm going to do!"

"But what about Locota?" Another posse member called out.

"Haven't you noticed, he got clean away."

The view turns dark. A thin spindly light gray alien is seated at a desk. He begins to speak. "I am Zorgth, the court reporter. The following is a multi source reconstruction of the conduct of the Board of Inquiries and the events leading up to its formation. As such these records are admissible in any court within the Jurisdiction of the Gate Way Federation. Due to the classified and potentially sensitive nature of the testimony given, the record has been sealed. A judiciary clearance of four or higher is required to open and view the record." The reporter disappears and the great seal of the Federation appears before your eyes, and nothing more.

Brandy removes the helmet and straightens her hair. "Is that it?" She puts herself back together and leaves the office and heads down to the lower lab where MaCos Ex is working. She gives him the helmet telling him about the sealed records. He tells her that he will do what he can.

In the hallway, Dauntless runs into Capt. Reynolds, who tells her that, "I've got two things for you, Dr. Cooly and Agent Carter are looking for you."

"I was just up there, what is it now?" She asked.

"The General has ordered some additional tests."

"She started to go but he stopped her, prompting her to ask, "oh yes, sorry, you said you had two things. What's the other thing?" She had meant no disrespect, Captain Reynolds had always treated her fairly, and he was a professional soldier, and a true officer and gentleman. She was just distracted.

He looked up at her studying her face. She was a good six inches taller than he was. "The rocket pack has been repaired and refueled. It should be safe for you to use."

"Captain, that thing will never be safe to use."

Her answer caused him to chuckle to himself. "Lt. Holmes, you may be right about that." He went on his way to operations. Captain Siegel needed something.

Three black men are talking smack outside of a convenience store. A light blue city garbage truck rumbles down the street and pulls up in front of them. A large white man jumps out of the passenger side. He has a metal shirt and machanical claw. Two more men jump off of the back of the truck and come around. One is carrying a whip. "Take the two big ones!" And they moved in on the black men.

"You ain't takin nobody!" He pulled a small caliber automatic from his jacket pocket. The smallest of them took the cue and left the scene in the most expeditious way. "Man! You don't know who you are messin' with!"

The large white worker came at him and the black man emptied his gun into him. The bullets just bounced off harmlessly and he kept on coming. There was a loud CRACK! His companion's arm was entangled by the whip. A brief tug of war erupted over the whip before an electrical discharge ended it, putting the large black man to sleep.

The mechanical claw came crashing down on the head of the other man and he joined his friends on the pavement. Their bodies were quickly picked up and tossed into the back of the garbage truck.

There were four other bodies lying in the back and two bugs waiting for them. They quickly scurried on to the new additions and stung them in the back of their necks.

The three drones hopped back on the truck and they were off looking for more victims to be converted into drones.

The next day, the General is conducting his normal morning meeting. Colonel Otis, the two Doctors and Heather are in attendance along with several other officers. He starts by addressing Heather, "Agent Carter, I have some news for you. I have here in my hand your release from the Agency and transfer to HERO, effective immediately. You are now directly under my command. Welcome aboard."

"But, but." She was not expecting to hear anything like that.

"You are now in the superhero business. Go and draw your uniform and equipment. I'm sure you know the drill," he said.

"Uniform!"

"That's right, uniform. You won't be wearing the same thing Dauntless and Marshal do. I'm told that you won't be needing it."

"If I'm going to be a superhero, I want more money!"

"We can talk about that," he replied

"And I'm not going to move into the building. I want a penthouse."

"We'll see about that." He was trying to be reasonable.

"And I want…"

She didn't get to finish. The old soldier was losing his patience with her.

"Let's see how you do before we start negotiating. Shall we? Now GO! And get started on that uniform. And come up with a superhero name. Something for the press to use." He dismissed her and continued with the briefing.

The General turns to Dr. Cooly. "Good, now that's she's gone we can hear your test results doctor."

She looked around and was a little hesitant about reporting. "Well uh, I wasn't expecting so many people. I'm not sure I should reveal them. Doctor patient confidentiality and all that."

"Doctor, you work for us. These offices need to know the results of your test. Anything said in this room remains a secret," he reassured her.

"It's really quite amazing, really. I think I know why Marshal is so strong. I didn't find it at first because it's hidden when not active, but I found it while testing Heather and rechecked the test results on Dauntless and Marshal." She was starting to ramble with excitement.

"What did you find doctor?" Dr. Brewville interrupted.

"Marshal's body produces a fast acting muscle amplifying enzyme. But here's the kicker! He only produces it when his muscles are being taxed. When he's relaxed his muscles are only 40 times denser, or more powerful, than normal human muscle fibers, but when he starts to use his muscles the enzyme kicks in and starts to amplify his muscle's strength. The more her tries to lift something the more enzymes he produces and the stronger he becomes. And just as soon as he stops the enzymes are used up and go away."

"So, just how strong is he?" She had piqued the General's curiosity.

She hesitated to answer. "Uh, he can easily lift 7,000 pounds or more, with one arm, but if he keeps trying he could lift, … oh I don't know, … 35 tons."

"35 tons!"

"Yes, that is about right, with one hand," she explained.

"Impossible!" The General snorted.

"How is it that Heather was able to knock him out?" Doctor Brewville asked not believing what he was hearing.

She offered her explanation. "I guess he wasn't straining his neck muscles when she started to strangle him. And she was strong too, don't forget."

"And she was using leverage to tighten the chain around his neck," the Colonel added.

"Okay, what about Dauntless and Carter?" The General sat back and asked.

"Dauntless also has the enzyme. But her body isn't able to use it as much as his. And before you ask," she said looking at Dr. Brewville, she added, "she can lift about 300 pounds with one hand before she has to start straining at it, but then she can lift about 7,500 pounds. With one hand."

Dr. Brewville sank back in his seat and rose to the occasion asking, "What about Agent Carter, does she have the same enzymes?"

"Yes and no. She has the muscle amplifying enzyme in her system now but she can't produce any. She's super strong now, but that won't last. She also has a fast activating enzyme that promotes rapid healing and unbelievably fast muscle response. That's why she's so fast. Her body is producing that enzyme so she'll be super fast from now on. But her super strength is limited for the time being."

"Why are they different?" the General asked.

She paused and thought how to best explain this so he'd understand. "Brandy's cells were in a state of flux when Marshal's coat was used on her. Her DNA was falling apart due to the radiation exposure. The nanos had to follow something and the only commmplete, working DNA they had to follow was Marshals. They copied part of his DNA into her cells when they repaired her body. She's mostly human but she's also part alien. That's why she has some of Marshal's physical traits like his strength and toughness."

She paused to see that everyone was following her so far, and continued. But with Heather it was different. She was only injured so Marshal's coat could read and copy her DNA. But she also had the alien venom in her system, the venom that promotes accelerated healing. The nanos must have read that as part of her system and copied it into her DNA. That's why she's heals super fast. It's also why she can move so fast. Her entire system is capable of super fast speeds. But not super strength, like I said earlier, that's only temporary."

"Just how fast is she?" Brewville asked.

She thought about it before answering. "Given the right circumstances, supersonic. But it would have to be perfect running conditions, smoothe flat, and clear. But I don't think she could keep it up for long."

"Why is that?" Brewville was chewing on his pencil.

"It would take an enormous amount of energy for her to keep it up for any amount of time. She would just plain get tired."

"Hmmm, we could come up with a super high protein bar or maybe a dietary supplement for her to eat." Dr. Brewville was thinking about the possible options but, he had missed the biggest one. General Solo didn't.

"Dr. Cooly, do you think you could isolate and reproduce this enzyme of Marshal's, this, whatchamacallit?" The General was tongue-tied.

"The FAMAE? I have already isolated it but I don't know about reproducing it. There are some strange organic chemicals in it that I have not been able to identify. It's part of his alien make up."

Dr. Brewville was becoming animated. "Do you realize what this could mean?'

She answered him saying, "We could use it to heal almost any injury, cure any disease."

The General added to the possibilities, "make a whole battalion of super soldiers." He had the look of wonderment on his face, not unlike the look of a child on Christmas morn.

"I don't think we could, or even should, consider making super soldiers. Just think of the possible problems keeping them in line. What about when they're enlistments run out and they're no longer soldiers?"

The General was nodding his head in approval. "Good thinking Doctor. Perhaps a super serum with a short half-life would be the better way to go. The troops could be made super just before going into combat, and return to normal later."

He held up his hand to stop the objections of Dr. Cooly before they got started saying, "we should also look into Heather's fast enzyme. But neither of these questions are for us to answer. Not now anyway. I'll have to kick them upstairs for authorization. The Air Force will probably try and commandeer the whole thing and we'll never hear about it. They can't get enough of alien technology. They've got area 51 filled up with it."

The rest of the meeting dealt with day-to-day housekeeping matters and duty assignments. After the meeting is adjourned, Captain Reynolds joins Captain Siegel in the Comm. Shack, a room on the second floor filled with commputers and all manner of radio and satellite links. The three enlisted men make room for the officer. "Okay Manny, what do you have for me?" Captain Reynolds asked as he came up behind his fellow officer.

Manny Siegel, a signal corps captain of Jewish-Greek descent, had a broad smile and a nose you could park a tank under. "Todd, I think you're going to like what we found. We've been listening to the police band for any strange reports. There are a large number of abductions and missing persons reported in this area." He motions to a map of the southern suburbs.

"Then we got access to one of the Air Force Comm Starbirds and used it to look over the area a bit more. Look what we found." He directed Todd's attention to a commputer screen with a satellite image on it. Looking down at an abandoned steel mill, alien bugs and Harbinger drones can be seen coming and going. "Look, they keep checking to make sure no one sees them."

Captain Reynolds looked at the screen with a look of wonder and ah ha! We've got you now. "Where is that?"

Manny swung around in his chair and leaned back. "You won't believe it, but that's the Republic Steel South Chicago Works."

Captain Reynolds replied in disbelief, "but the Air Force went in after them there and they said they were gone."

Manny explained, "either they missed them or they came back thinking we wouldn't search there again."

"Those sneaky little bugs! Good work. I'll pass it along."

A light blue city of Chicago garbage truck rumbles down the street, the air brakes hiss and the truck comes to a stop in front of the First Baptist Church of Christ The Redeemer of South Chicago. The drone in the passenger seat asks, "Why are we stopping here?"

The drone driver motions to the full parking lot next to the church. "A flock awaiting us." Two more armored drones get off of the back of the truck and walk around to the front as the passengers jump out. One of the drones has a massive claw that looks as if it had come off a forklift.

"How are we going to do this?" The other drone with the whip asks.

The driver answers, "I'll pull the back of the truck up to the front door. You just funnel them into the back and let our little brothers take their pick."

"But how will we get them out?"

The passenger has the answer. "I'll light up the roof with this!" He reaches back behind the seat in the cab and pulls out a gas tank for a grill and some hose. He opens that valve and lights his Zippo. FUSH! A blue, orange fireball bursts forth and dissipates in the air. "Flamethrower!"

As the congregation sang a hymn inside the church, the warning alarm beep beep beeped as the blue garbage truck backed up to the steps. A spray of flames shot out and landed on the roof. "It won't be long now."

Doctor Brewville, carrying a crumpled shopping bag, finds Dauntless in the hallway with Marshal. He takes a medium sized gift box out of the bag and hands it to her saying, "Here, I want you to wear this today while you're testing the rocket pack."

Puzzled by his statement, she pauses before taking the box from him. "I'm not testing the rocket pack today."

"Yes you are, if you don't believe me, just ask Heather," he countered.

"Ask Heather? Why?"

"Because I asked her about it and she said she didn't see why not," he explained.

"She didn't see why not what?" Brandy asked.

"I figured that since this is the public HQ for the HERO organization, we could test the rocket pack from the roof. It's not like the public doesn't already know we are here. And after your little adventure with the pack on the lakefront, it's not exactly top secret any more."

Brandy looked back over her shoulder at Marshal and back to Brewville asking, "but why did you ask Heather about that in the first place?"

"Because she's the one in charge of security," he answered as he wrung his hands in anticipation.

Brandy corrected him telling him that, "she's not in charge of security, just Marshal's security." She motioned to the big guy behind her.

"Oh," he was put off. But then he rallied his enthusiasm. "Don't you want to see what's in the box?"

She turns her attention to the box in her hands and opens it. "Why, what's in it?" She pulls out a blue jacket made of something very much like vinyl or leather, only much thinner. Suspiciously eyeing the obviously too small jacket, she asked, "What's this for?"

"It's your new flight jacket. And before you say anything, it stretches. I had it made for you, so you won't have to put on that heavy old leather jacket. It's made from the same material your first Dauntless uniform was. Heather is having her uniform made out of it too."

"Good, then she can fly the rocket pack. Heather is having a uniform made?"

"Of course she is, she's a superhero like you now," he said defensively.

Dr. Cooly came walking down the hall and he stopped her by grabbing her arm as she passed. "Beverly, I have something for you also."

She stopped abruptly and looked sharply at his hand on her arm which he quickly withdrew. "What is it Doctor, I was on my way to the roof."

He pulled a four inch wide brown leather belt with an oversized rectangular silver buckle on it out of the shopping bag. He fumbles with it for a few seconds and then tries to put it around her waist. She stops him and takes the belt from him. "What's this?" She demanded to know, before she had taken the time to examine and admire the silver buckle with a Navaho pattern inscribed in the buckle with inlaid turquoise. "It's very nice, but I can't."

She didn't get to finish before he replied, "that's for you, it's a hidden utility belt like the others have, only yours has a micro ER and science lab in it."

A few minutes later they are all on the roof. Brandy has peeled off her utility belt and uniform jacket and stripped down from the waist up revealing a tank top tee shirt. She is struggling to pull the flight jacket on. The Velcro flap is straining to stay closed. She turns to Dr. Brewville who is obviously enjoying the show. "Did it have to be so small?"

"The tighter it is the better aerodynamics and more speed you'll get, but perhaps you're right. It may be a tad too tight." he agreed with her.

"A tad too tight! I'm afraid to take a deep breath."

"Then don't," he cautioned.

"Okay Doc, what's the plane?" She asked as she walked over to him holding the space cadet helmet.

"You need to learn how to land safely. And we can't have you crashing into the building or through the roof either for that matter so, I have come up with a plan," he said with a smile on his face that didn't instill confidence in Brandy or Beverly either.

He walked over to the edge of the roof where a small platform was and he directed their attention to it. "If we have Marshal hold the platform out over the edge you can practice landing on it. If you miss, you will pass harmlessly by the building without all that nasty crashing and burning."

"Hmm, why didn't you just have the platform built to stick out over the edge, instead of depending on Marshal to hold it?" Dr. Cooly asked.

"Good question! The presence of a permanent platform would give the paparazzi and foreign intelligence agencies a place to concentrate on. This way, we can move the landing sight to avoid being observed, and at the same time, adjust for the direction of the wind."

"I get the moving the platform part, but they know we are here. We're surrounded by tall buildings," Brandy protested.

"They do, but we don't have to make it too easy for them," he said with a wink.

As Dauntless and Marshal made their preparations, the two Doctors spoke. "I guess Heather wanted me to be up here for medical support, but it's funny she's not here."

"Oh, she may not know we're up here," he said mater-of-factly.

"May not even know? But I thought she authorized the test?"

"She said she saw no reason why not to test. I just…" He didn't finish before Dauntless took off, leaving a trail of smoke. FFFOSH!

Doctor Cooly rushed over to Marshal's side. "We've got to bring her back!"

Marshal looked at her with a puzzled look. "She just go." The HERO building is the tallest building situated in the center of the Truman University Campus. Dauntless was zipping in and out, darting between the other tall buildings on the campus. The students ten stories below were being treated to an unscheduled air show.

The sound of her rocket engines echoed and the windows reverberated when she swooped down between them. The noise lessoned considerably when she was flying over the lower buildings surrounding the university.

On her first couple of landing attempts, she carried too much momentum and it caused her to overshoot the platform and go harmlessly sailing past the side of the building. After she missed, she simply opened the throttle on the rocket and zoomed up again. Dr. Brewville was pleased with himself. "See, I told you. She missed and she's safe to try again."

She went around a few more times, each time getting closer, but not yet sticking it. "Your fuel should be getting low. Let's try just one more, and if you don't make it, we'll have Marshal catch you," Brewville instructed her over the comm. link.

It was during this last go-around that Heather made her appearance on the roof. She was dressed in her new superhero uniform. She wore black boots under black pants that resembled her biker outfit, but were made of the aforementioned material. It was a short, shiny white jacket that barely covered her butt that zipped up the front with a black hidden utility belt like Dauntless had, with a silver star shaped buckle with an

"S" in the star and another star in the middle of the "S". Add to this a gold Marshal's star on her chest and topped off with black sunglasses and you've got it.

"HEY EVERYBODY! What do you think?" She called out as she twirled about to give everyone the full view. Her zipper was only two thirds of the way up and some of her ample cleavage was exposed. The men were definitely distracted by the sight.

"Very nice," Beverly said.

"Wha… what's the S stand for?" Stammering, Brewville managed to inquire.

"Heather swayed back and forth acting shy, loving all of the attention. "At first, I was thinking Supergirl or maybe Superwoman, but Colonel Otis said no, they were taken. Then I thought I'm fast, how about The Speedster or Dash, and then I thought I'm more than just fast so I thought Speed Star. It was kind of a play on words, get it, Speedster, Speed Star, but then it came to me. Star, but not just Star but Superstar! Call me, Heather Carter, Superstar."

Dr. Brewville asked, pointing to the sunglasses stuck in her hair, "are those the new personal heads up display?"

"The sunglasses? No, they're just cool." She demonstrated by sliding them down over her eyes.

The sound of Dauntless' rocket motors roaring back caught everyone's attention. She was coming in to land on the platform being held out by Marshal. She came in slowly, adjusting the thrust from her backpack. She killed the power just as her toes touched the platform. Her feet skidded across the small landing pad and she came to rest half on and half off, swinging her arms around trying to catch her balance. She spun around and fell of backwards head over heels. "WOOO!"

Heather, the new self proclaimed Superstar, anxious to prove herself worthy of the title superhero and the million dollars she was asking for, saw a chance to prove her point. In a split second she was racing down the stairs, faster than the human eye could see. There was only a black blur with a trace of golden hair and the rush of air.

Two seconds later she was standing on the grass that surrounded the building. She scanned the sky looking for her falling friend, but there was none to be seen. Her sudden arrival didn't go unnoticed; one of the passing students was nearly knocked over by her sudden appearance. "WOOO where'd she come from?"

She took off her sunglasses and searched the sky again. The student took the two steps necessary to approach her and started to ask, but "do" was all he got out.

"I'm on the wrong side of the building!" Superstar exclaimed, and just as suddenly as she had arrived she disappeared with a gust of wind in her wake.

"Dude! There was a girl just standing there?" He exclaimed to his friend.

"There's no one there."

"But she was just there!"

"What'd she look like?"

"She was an angel in leather, a vision, like something out of Heavy Metal."

"Dude, you're seein' things."

On the other side of the building, there was a sudden gust of wind and Superstar was standing there looking into the sky. There was a smoke trail, and she could see Marshal and Dr. Cooly looking down over the edge of the building. There was a FOOSHing sound up in the air behind her. She turned to find Dauntless hovering in air about 30 feet up. "Looking for something?" She asked.

Heather stood there trying to think of something to say to save face when the rocket pack sputtered and quit! Dauntless plummeted down. Superstar raced to catch her. Dauntless crashed down on the ground landing on her backside. "OWWW!"

The flight jacket had put up a noble effort in an ultimately unwinable battle. Something as small as that flight jacket was never intended to contain anything as big and powerful as Brandy's breasts. It was too much to ask of a mere strip of Velcro. The strain was beyond its endurance, her breasts too big, too resilient, she burst forth!

"AWSOME!" The closeby student was obviously impressed.

She just sat there on the ground in a daze for a second or two before she tried to close the wayward flap. Discovering that she was still covered by her T-shirt, she thought better of it and left the flap open. "Lucky I landed on something soft," she said to the gathering crowd.

A few seconds later, the soft land zone that was Heather started to stir. "Oohh, my face hurts." The voice coming from under her startled Dauntless at first.

"Get your butt out of my face!" Dauntless scrambled to her feet revealing the crumpled mass of Heather Carter, Superstar. A crowd of students formed around the two fledgling superheroes sitting on the ground. "I don't get it! I just don't get it." Heather said in disbelief. Brandy helped Heather up.

"Oh you're going to get it all right! WHAT THE HELL IS GOING ON HERE? I didn't authorize any rocket pack flights! I want the two of you in my office NOW!" The Colonel, standing among the students, wasn't the least bit amused.

CHAPTER ELEVEN

HARBINGERS OF WAR

There is a small gathering of all of the key personnel of the HERO organization in Colonels Otis' office. "I didn't authorize anything! I just said I thought it would be okay," Heather said defensively, still wearing her new Superstar uniform.

"And I took it to mean it was okay to test," Dr. Brewville added to the testimony.

Dauntless looked back and forth and shrugged her shoulders before answering. "I thought it was an authorized test."

They all turned their attention on Dr. Cooly. "I didn't know anything about the test. I was there to see Heather's new uniform."

"I was with them." Marshal commpleted the commentary.

The Colonel sat there shaking his head. Marshal, Dr. Cooly you're free to go."

Outside in the hall as they closed the door, Marshal asked Beverly, "What is the nature of the problem?"

"I think someone's goose is cooked," she replied.

"Are we having prepared bird carcass to consume?"

"Huh" No, nothing like that. Well, maybe we are, now that you mention it. Are you hungry?" She asked as she took his arm and guided him down the hall.

That evening, General Solo is on the phone in his office. "No General! That's a terrible idea." He paused to listen. "Do you know what they call Chicago?" He turned in his chair. "They call it the windy city for a reason." He turned back to his deck pushing back his thinning hair with his free hand. "In the morning?"

On the other end of the conversation was an Air Force three star General. "That's right, we're going to hit them in the morning before the winds pick up and the bugs become active."

"But General Cook, they're not just bugs." General Solo was becoming agitated with his senior officer from a sister branch.

"We know that General, and we've made allowances for it. This will be over by zero six thirty hours tomorrow."

A short time later, Colonel Otis is called into General Solo's office. "Come in Henry, take a seat, we've got a problem."

Colonel Otis took the seat with a small degree of trepidation. "What seems to be the problem sir?"

"The Air Force is going to hit the steel mill where the aliens have set up their Hive."

"And just how is that a problem sir?"

"They're going to hit it from the air using gas and pesticide. They plan on killing the bugs and putting the humans to sleep. After the smoke clears they intend to go in on foot and mop up." The General leaned back in his chair.

"But General, it's not just a bunch of bugs, they can control humans and they know what they know, if they have any Air Force personnel they'll know."

"I tried to tell them that. But they preferred the opinion of their expert over ours."

"What is our part in this mission?" The Colonel asked as he leaned forward.

"We don't have one. This is an Air Force operation. But I want team Hero ready for anything by zero six hundred. If they get it wrong, there's going to be hell to pay."

"Using gas in an urban environment," he shook his head in disbelief. "How do they expect to hit the target with the precision required?"

"They've got one of their ground controllers down there to do close air support. I guess they're going to paint the target so they can hit it with smart ordnance." (When a target is painted, a man on the ground will shine a laser beam on the target, the smart bombs will lock in on this and guide themselves into the target. Hopefully.)

"Sir, I served as operations officer for the 21st SAL (Special Air Liaison) before joining 5th group. I can't see F16s swooping in and hitting the target with smart bombs. I don't think they can put Pave Tack on gas munitions."

"They must have something in mind. I want your team to be ready to provide the heroics if this goes badly."

"I'll have everyone check their gasmasks."

05:00, it's dark, the sun hasn't made it up yet. The roof of the HERO building is awash with activity and blinking lights. Three Black Hawks are ready to go, one on each of the three helipads. Colonel Otis is in full battle dress and is giving his final briefing to about 150 soldiers and Team Hero.

Dauntless is helping Superstar strap her gas mask case to her leg. Marshal already has his on and is examining it closely.

Colonel Otis is standing before a large map. "I don't suppose any of you brought a pointer with you?" They laughed. He takes the M16 from a nearby soldier and pulls the magazine out, pops the pin and breaks the rifle open, slides the bolt and charging handle out, hits the other pin and breaks the rifle in two. He uses the upper receiver as a pointer. (The part with the barrel)

"The wind, if there is any, will be out of the northwest blowing to the south east. We will deploy to the north of the target and be ready to lend assistance to any civilians who may stray into the affected areas.

Captain Anderson and Alpha Commpany will be with Team Hero, with me in position before the strike. Captain Reynolds will come in next with Charley Commpany after the strike. Captain Walker will bring in the reserves with Bravo if needed.

We aren't expected to engage the aliens. We are only there just in case. Remember your training, and put those masks on fast if you hear the word." After he finished, he returned the weapon in pieces back to its owner.

Dawn, two men in BDUs are on top of an abandoned building overlooking the Republic Steel South Chicago Works. One is watching the steel mill while the other watches a flight of three Black Hawk helicopters going away at low levels. He makes a call on the radio. "This is ground control one to the Orkin man, The Army birds have left the area. You are clear to make your run.

Colonel Otis is trying to see what's going on. "This is no good, I can't see a thing! I'm looking into the sun. He turns to his RTO (Radiotelephone Operator) and tells him to "tell the General we are in position and there's no wind.

"This thing makes me look fat," Superstar commmplained about her gas mask case on her hip.

"It's not meant to be a fashion statement," Dauntless snapped back to her.

"But it's green, it doesn't go with my uniform."

"Like I said," Dauntless paused before adding, "the mask is black and maybe we can have the case dyed for you when we get back." Brandy had been in the NG (National Guard) before all this superhero business started; she was familiar with gasmasks and other operational considerations. This was all new to Heather. Brandy took a small amount of amusement out of Heather's discommfort.

"Let's just hope we don't have to use them," Lt. Hunter chimed in.

"Do we have to use them much in this line of work?" Heather asked sounding concerned.

"No, I've never used mine," Lt. Hunter replied.

"I've used mine once, when I found Marshal," Dauntless added.

Hearing the sound of choppers approaching, Colonel Otis turns around saying, that was fast." He was wrong.

The sound of two Air Force Sikorsky helicopters rushing by had caught the attention of the Colonel. "Those aren't our birds! That's how they're going to do it. They're going to spray the building from a chopper."

"Ground Control to the Orkin man, we are designating the target building now."

"Roger that! I have your target designation in sight. We're going in."

A spray bar was extended out the side of the big chopper and it started to swoop in. Billowing clouds of a reddish brown mist swirled about behind them as they came in. The second chopper followed at a safe distance spraying a white cloud behind it.

A black shape sailed up past the first chopper. The crew of the second chopper got a better view of the object as it plunged back to Earth. It was a small toy like car with chains dragging along behind it. "Did you see that?"

"I heard the Army reported seeing flying cars out here yesterday. Was that one of them?" Both choppers make their first pass and turn to make another pass, when the pilot in the lead bird sees something on the ground. "What's that?"

A dozen or so warrior drones are manning a catapult, cranking back the spring-loaded arm while others are preparing to load another Mini Cooper. With the throwing arm in the full back position, four drones pick up the minuscule auto and place it on the throwing end of the arm.

The lead bird tries to make a run directly on them, but just as they near the target, the catapult springs into life hurling its projectile directly into the windshield of the giant Sikorsky. The bird flips over and falls straight down, it's rotor blades beating the ground like a giant lawn mower sending up a cloud of dust and debris and red brown smoke. The fuel tanks rupture and explode with an angry yellow and black ball of flame. The site is instantly engulfed in smoke and flame.

The catapult and crew are engulfed in smoke. The crew continues working the winch to recock the arm. They start to cough. The Harbinger bug on the back of one of the drones drops off and flees. Two of the men stop working and are slain by the others. They resume their tasks.

The second bird circles around trying to see what happened. "Did you see it? What did they have? Was it some kind of missile?" The pilot frantically looks around trying to see through the smoke.

"Whatever it was, if we can put 'em to sleep, they won't be using it again," the crew chief chimed in. They swooped in even lower and faster than before and turned around for another pass, one to many as it turned out.

The downblast of the chopper's rotors blew the smoke away allowing the catapult crew on the ground to see the chopper overhead. They let the catapult go. The Mini passed harmlessly behind the chopper but the chain trailing behind it caught in the chopper's rotors, and as the chain wound around the chopper, the Mini cooper was flung around as if it were some demented child's toy.

Around and around the diminutive car sailed until the chopper reeled it in like a small fish on the line. The car slammed into the chopper's tail. The bird disintegrated in midair and the big bits fell to the ground and burst into flames. Smoke and dust obscured the view of what was going on at the crash sight.

Neither the ground controller a half-mile away or Colonel Otis, who was even further away, could see or do anything. Lieutenant Hunter wanted to go in. "And do what?" The Colonel asked.

"They went down! There could be survivors sir," the junior officer protested.

Otis looked through his field glasses. "I can't see shit! If there are any survivors, the bugs will have 'em long before we get there."

Superstar said as she stepped forward and took hold of the Colonel's arm, "Not me Colonel. I could zoom on down there and back before they even heard me coming."

"Trying to earn that superhero pay? Just hold on a second," he cautioned, as he watched the events unfolding before them. After a minute, the smoke started to clear some and he could make out movement. There was a survivor from the second bird. He must have been thrown free. The bugs hadn't got to him yet.

"Carter, uh sorry, Superstar, there's one survivor down there over by that pile of tires. Go get him." There was a sudden gust of wind and she was gone. In a matter of seconds, she had raced the three quarters of a mile to the steel mill through the main gate, and made her way around the two crashed choppers through the smoke and to the lone survivor.

His leg was all bloody and he could hardly stand, but he had a gasmask on and she hadn't bothered to put hers on. She struggled to lift him over her shoulder. "I used to be stronger." She carried the injured airman through the smoke and out the gate. She nearly fell inside the fence; she tripped on some steel mesh that was on the ground. She stumbled and regained her balance and sped off, only to slow down, stumble and fall, sending both of them tumbling down the street outside the chain link fence that surrounded the property.

"She's down!" The Colonel announced, turning to Dauntless. "How fast are you?"

"I can do maybe 35," she said trying to sound upbeat.

"And you Marshal?" He asked.

"Maximum velocity less than Dauntless," the large blue alien replied.

"Huh?"

"Not that fast," she interpreted for him.

"Then I guess it's on you Dauntless. Go get them out of there and put your gasmask on first!" He commanded as he rolled over to see what was going on down there. He watched for what seemed an eternity, but it was actually less then two minutes.

A pickup truck came racing out of the steel mill towards Dauntless who had just arrived on the scene. She drew her sidearm and emptied the magazine at the oncoming truck. The truck screeched to a halt and two armored drones jumped out and rushed at Dauntless whose pistol was out of ammo.

Marshal grabbed a steel girder and threw it like a spear. The first drone to reach her had a chainsaw on his left arm. He tried to use it on Dauntless but she dropped her gun and caught his arm as it came in. The chain saw revved as it cut into the empty air just inches from her face.

The driver of the truck came up with a whip as they were struggling and let Brandy have it, cutting deep into her side, with a CRACK! "OWWW!"

Dauntless recoiled in pain tossing the chainsaw wielding drone off to the side.

Voosh voosh voosh, CHUNG SKRUNNCH! Something unseen passed overhead and a steel girder came crashing down out of nowhere on the street behind them. The girder careened on down the street, finally crashing into a small bar and grill commpletely demolishing the front window.

The alarmed driver took one look at the girder and back at Dauntless. She grabbed hold of the whip and jerked it out of his hand. This was enough for him and he took off running past the truck headed for the safety of the main gate.

The remaining drone came at Brandy swinging the chainsaw frantically back and forth. She jumped back avoiding the saw blade. Next, she ducked down and jumped over the saw as it hit the ground where she had been standing. As she jumped, she kicked the drone in the face, sending him falling backwards. She came down in a fighting stance, ready for him but he didn't come up for more. She had knocked him out.

She rushed over to the pickup truck and started to pick it up with the intention of throwing it at the fleeing driver, but as she struggled to lift it over her head, she thought better of it and put the truck down, and loaded the survivor and Superstar in the back of the truck. She stood over the KO'd Drone with the chain saw on his arm, She rolled him over face down and took out her grappling hook and line. She used the line to tie him up before unceremoniously dumping him in the back with the others. She hopped in the cab and floored it, sending dust and gravel flying.

As she drove off, she passed Air Force ground security troops rushing the mill with their gasmasks on and weapons ready. They blew a hole in the fence and rushed in.

"What's going on down there Colonel?" Lt. Hunter asked.

"She's got them and is on the way out. The Air Force is moving in!" He answered his junior officer as he watched the Air Force troops deploy and fan out across the yard of the mill. The crackle of small arms fire rang out as they moved in. "Get going, they're going to need our help," He commanded.

As the soldiers got up and started to move out he added to his instructions. Go in through the hole in the fence and flank right to the railroad tracks and engulf the main building. I'll have Charley and Bravo Commpanies land in the rail yard and move in to support you." Turning to his RTO he commanded, "Get me Captain Reynolds."

As the soldiers of Alpha Commpany moved out, he looked through his field glasses again, an expression of horror washed over him. The sound of battle ceased. He called his troops back. Down in the yard of the abandoned steel mill the Air Force troopers had advanced near the main building using fire and movement. There was a shower of sparks from an electrical transformer and all of the troopers that were kneeling or in a prone position jumped and jerked and slumped over dead, electrocuted! Then the other airmen who came to the aid of their fallen commrade also started to jerk and convulse and fall over dead. Soon they all were fried. The steel mesh that lay on the ground all around the mill was electrified.

The pickup truck driven by Dauntless pulled up to the abandoned silo being used as an OP by Colonel Otis. Several troopers surrounded the truck with weapons ready. "Wooo there! Calm down, he's out cold and I got him tied up. He aint going anywhere. Four soldiers lift him out of the truck and carry him away.

Sgt. Lopez sees the injured airman and calls for a medic. They rig a poncho into a stretcher and carry him off. Colonel Otis comes down to see what's going on. He sees Superstar asleep in the back of the truck. At first he thinks she's dead or hurt. His fears are relieved when she curls up and starts to snore.

Dauntless rips off her gasmask and shakes out her short blond hair. Before explaining, "she's not hurt Sir, the gas got her, she didn't have her mask on."

"Are you sure? Have the medic look at her." Just as soon as he finished saying that, a medic magically appeared. It's not often that they get a chance to work on anyone that looks like Heather.

"She just needs a stimulus to bring her out of it sir, I'll..." The Medic explained but didn't get to finish.

"Go take care of the injured," he commanded. He raised his hand as if he was going to slap Heather's face but Dauntless stopped him.

"I wouldn't do that sir," she cautioned.

"Very well." He reached for his canteen.

"I wouldn't do that either Colonel." Again, she cautioned him.

"And why not Lieutenant?" The annoyed officer asked.

"Well sir, she spends a lot of time in the morning putting on her make up. Maybe we could make a lot of noise to awaken her."

Marshal stepped up saying, "If it is stimulation that she requires, I could massage her breasts."

This was met by silence and an exchange of glances. Dauntless, embarrassed, reached over to Marshal's collar and tried to adjust his translator. "He doesn't mean breast! His translator is on the fritz again. He probably meant lungs, you know, as in give her some air."

This explanation was accepted by the Colonel until Marshal spoke up to clarify. Having additional air to breathe would be valuable to her, but I was referring to stimulating her by massaging her mammary glands. She became very stimulated the other night…" He stopped seeing the look of distress on Brandy's face. She was shaking her head faster and faster. "But you both were very stimulated by, Oh." He glanced at Brandy and the Colonel and finally caught on. "Never mind."

The Colonel looked to his newest Lieutenant for an explanation. "It was after hours sir," was all she could say.

Marshal interceded at this point. "Do not punish my friends for recreating with me. They were under the influence of my pheromones at the time. It will not happen again."

The Colonel said nothing and just shook his head with a funny smile, and then he was back to the matter at hand, "Oh for Petes sake!" Was his reply. SLAP!

"OWW! You slapped me!" she replied feeling her cheek.

"We can't have you sleeping on the job on your first day," he said and started to chuckle to himself. He wanted to say more but he didn't.

"What?" She was confused, then it ocurred to her, "You came and got me."

"Not me, Dauntless. Besides, now that I've got you under me, I want another chance to see what you can do."

She was up leaning back on her elbows by now, "That's what I like. A man with ambition." He started to go and she grabbed his arm. "What happened out there? I could hardly lift him. What happened to my super strength?"

"Didn't they tell you?" He asked.

"Tell me what?" Now she was sitting up and taking things seriously.

"Your super strength was only temporary."

"But what about my other …"She was at a loss for words.

"You're still super fast and will heal almost instantly." He filled her in.

"So, I'm not super strong but I am super fast and can't be hurt." She summed it up. The Colonel left and the soldiers crowded around the two girls and Marshal.

A few minutes later Colonel Otis is on the horn to the General. "That's right sir. The entire Air Force mission is a failure. Their birds are down and the ground troops have been wiped out."

He shook his head as he listened to his superior. "No sir. There's no way we can go in there. I recommend that we get more troops down here and set up a perimeter with armed troops around the steel mill to prevent them from spreading and taking any more people."

"My people have no vehicles sir, but we can set up road blocks." There was a slight pause in the conversation, "Very well sir, will do. Sierra Gulf one out." The Colonel calls his officers together. "Gentlemen, we have our orders, we are to set up a series of road blocks surrounding the steel mill and keep everybody out."

Pulling out a map, he points to places as he talks. "We don't have enough men to sweep the building to get any remaining people out, they'll be on their own. All we can do is set up roadblocks along this major street and keep everybody else out. By staying on this main street we should be able to see each other and support each other if needed."

"Sir, that's nearly two miles, with 150 men? How long will we be holding the line?" Captain Reynolds asked.

"Not too long, I hope, Todd. There's an armored infantry unit in the National Guard armory not far from here. They're being called up as we speak."

He turns to Dauntless. "You did good out there. I have been told to turn over the captured drone to the Air Force for interrogation. They just didn't say when. I want you to take one of the choppers and the prisoner back to HERO HQ. Get Dr. Cooly working on it. Send the chopper back with Dr. Brewville's special munitions. You stay and provide security for Dr. Cooly. Don't let anything happen to her."

"Yes sir, Uh sir, what about Marshal?" She asked.

"I may need some muscle here if they try to move. I'm keeping him and Superstar here with me for now," he explained and motioned for her to get going.

As she heads for the waiting chopper, Sgt. Lopez says to her, "I saw you pick up that pickup truck and hold it up over your head! That was awesome. But I gottaknow why did you do it?"

She stopped and smiled before answering. "I was thinking of buying it and wanted to check it for leaks." They both laughed and she moved on with the prisoner, his arms bound behind his back with the chain removed from the chain saw that was part of his body.

Some of the soldiers were talking as she went by. "Marshal and those two girls! Can you imagine it! Some guys have all the luck!"

She stopped to address them. "And some guys have all the pheromones. That's the last I want to hear about this. Do you understand soldier?"

"Yes sir! Sorry sir!"

She made her way to the waiting chopper and left. "Is that you Buster? Take me home."

A short time later, Colonel Otis has set up a CP (Command Post) in an abandoned furniture store and is organizing the roadblocks. Heather comes in and plops down on the counter near the Colonel and sighs, "It's too bad that Marshal's plan didn't work."

"Yes, it would have saved a lot of lives." But you know, it should have worked, it was only bad luck that it didn't."

"Really?"

"Yes, he had the Harbinger Queen in his sights but his gun didn't work."

"So I heard."

"We, uh, I could make the plan work."

"You, how?"

"You see, the Queen has the hots for Marshal, She thinks he will give her super bugs. She'll do anything to get at him. I could.."

"No you couldn't. It would never work. They would be all over the both of you in a minute, and then what?"

"That's where you're wrong. She doesn't want Marshal taken over. She wants him pure and unpolluted so he'll make the strongest offspring for her. And they think I'm part of The Hive."

"Let me get this straight, you and Marshal just waltz in there and shoot the Queen?"

"That's about it."

"It'll never work, they might want Marshal unpolluted but they'll jump you for sure."

"No, they'll want me to control him for the Queen."

"Control him? How?'

"I have this power over men."

"No you don't."

"Yes I do."

"No you don't. What is this power you claim to have?"

"Just look at me! Men can't resist me."

"You're delusional, yes they can."

"Well maybe I can't exactly control them, but I can definitely influence them."

"Maybe the bugs believe that, but if you believe it, you should have Doc Cooly check you out when we get back. Maybe you suffered a head injury or something."

She was taken back by his rejection. She hopped off of the counter and eased over to him and started to ease the zipper on her top down slowly. As she pulled the zipper down, the opening expanded, exposing more and more of her generous cleavage and black lacy bra.

He noticed this right away and couldn't help but watch until the bra was exposed. The bra reminded him of something and it made him uncommfortable. He started to ease away from her. She just slid along with him. "Agent Carter! What are you trying to do?" he demanded to know.

"Just demonstrating that I can influence you," she slyly said as she zipped up her top. "What have you got to lose? We can't be hurt. I can't be caught, and he can't be stopped. We can't fail." He gave her a stern look. He knew better. She was smiling broadly.

A shot time later, Superstar is in the driver's seat of the pickup truck and Marshal is riding shotgun. Colonel Otis is standing beside the driver's side door asking, "Are you sure you want to do this?"

"Nothing to it," was her confident reply.

She turned to Marshal and scooted over closer to him on the bench seat so the translator would work better. "Just remember, you're supposed to be under my control, so do everything I tell you to. You're my sex slave."

"I'm subservient to you?"

"Just pretend."

A soldier came up with two 12-gauge pump guns. The Colonel takes them and passes them in through the window. "Here, take these shotguns, they're loaded with rock salt."

"Rock salt?" Heather was puzzled.

"It's lethal to the bugs but won't kill the humans," he explained. "Okay, what are you going to do?" He wanted to double check the operation plan.

"Go in, kill the Queen and get out in time for dinner and you're buying," She answered as she slid her sunglasses down over her eyes.

"Got it! Good." He thumped the roof of the truck and she pulled away.

As she started to roll a voice came from nowhere. "Commo check!"

"We're on channel two, you're coming in loud and clear," Heather said as she tapped her ear piece.

"When we get back we'll have to see about getting you a small video camera."

The truck rolled the two blocks to the steel mill's main gate. Several armed warrior drones met them.

The head guard and armored warrior with parts of an Air Force uniform and an SAW (Squad Automatic Weapon, a type of machine gun.) on his arm walked up to the stopped truck and recognized her. "You have returned!"

Another warrior exclaimed, "she is not of The Hive!"

Superstar called out to them waving her hand out of the window. "STOP brothers! I was captured and my connection with The Hive was forcibly severed. But I remember how wonderful it was to be part of The Hive and I have returned to serve the Queen."

"She has the blue one with her," one of the warriors noticed and called out.

"Yes! I have brought him with me for the Queen."

One of the Harbinger bugs disconnects itself from a warrior and leaps through the open window at Marshal. Superstar instantly catches it and tosses it back. "No! He is not to be amalgamated into The Hive. The Queen wants him unpolluted as he is so he will make super strong offspring."

"That is true, but how can he serve the Queen if he is not part of The Hive?" The X airman asked.

"I am in commmplete control of him. He is my sex slave. He will do anything I command. He cannot resist."

The warriors exchange glances. After some sort of agreement was struck, the X airman directed her to, "pull it in over there." He motioned to a spot near the main entrance to the foundry building. She did, and a dozen warriors surrounded the truck. "Surrender your weapons before seeing the Queen," they commanded in unison.

This startled Superstar, but she commmplied. As she took the shotgun from Marshal he whispered to her, "they conspire to ambush us." They passed their shotguns out the window to the warriors and remained in the truck.

"There, we have commmplied with all of your instructions. Take us to the Queen," Heather demanded.

"Not all of our instructions. You are to collect his uh, essence and bring it to the rookery.

A thousand thoughts raced through Heather's mind, none of them particularly pleasant. "As you ask." She leaned over to Marshal and commanded him to kiss her.

He embraced her and kissed her passionately. As they kissed he asked, "Now what?"

Her reply was, "I know how much you're looking forward to me collecting your essence, but that's not going to happen. This isn't working."

"Do not egress from the vehicle, the ground is electrified," he whispered back to her.

"Time for plan B!" The voice from the radio chimed in.

"What is plan B?" Marshal asked, as Heather pulled away from him.

Again, from the disembodied voice came, "BEAT FEET OUT OF THERE!"

"HUH?" He didn't understand.

She explained as she floored it. "It means to leave town." The engine revved and the tires spun out kicking up a cloud of dust. She ran over two warriors who weren't fast enough to get out of her way.

The truck fishtailed, sending warriors scrambling in all directions. Marshal drew his sidearm and fired at a passing warrior FOOOP! A glowing ball of goo flew out and landed on the warrior's chest armor and basically made a mess but did no harm.

Marshal muttered something about Brewville and an intellectually challenged storage vessel of excrement, and put his pistol away.

The X airman with the machine gun opened up on them as they passed by, riddling the side and door with bullet holes. Both Marshal and Superstar where hit. "UGHT!" Heather slumped over losing control of the truck which slammed into a pile of steel bits and pieces which included a forklift.

Marshal was thrown out of the truck and bounced off and careened over the pile. A warrior came running up to him as he started to get to his feet and tried to wrap a chain around his neck in the same way Heather had before. Marshal wasn't having any of it, not this time. He broke the chain with his hands and slammed the warrior down. Next, he picked up the rag-doll-like remains of the warrior and flung him into another oncoming warrior.

In the cab of the truck, Superstar was still behind the wheel. "Ohh. That hurt, a lot! She felt her side and she felt her ribs and leg were wet. She was bleeding. She'd been shot! Twice in the left rib cage and two more in her upper thigh. This wasn't right! Then she saw the bullets back themselves out of her wounds and she stopped bleeding. She was a little sore but otherwise, okay!" She looked around and found that she was alone.

The pile of steel part started to move! It rumbled and clambered about, and finally rose up. It was some kind of demented robotic machine built out of junk parts. It resembled a rhinoceros with a forklift for a horn. It grabbed hold of the truck and started to crush it! "Time to go!"

She leapt from the truck and did a flying karate kick landing on the nearest warrior's chin. WHAP! He went down like a sack of potatoes. They may be nasty, but there're still basically human. Two more warriors with edged weapons rushed at her and she dodged the first one's attack, grabbing hold of his arm and using it to propel her self high into the second oncoming attacker, landing on his face with both of her feet. She spun and landed three punches in rapid succession on the first man, knocking him down. She finished him off with a kick like a football player kicking off.

A burst of machine gun fire slammed into her knocking her down. She had multiple hits again on the same leg and side. It really hurt! The roar of an engine caught her attention. The mechanical rhino was about to run her over. She couldn't move her leg. She ducked, and the monster stopped just inches short of crushing her.

It's engine revved but it gained no ground. The bullets popped out as before and she looked up to see that Marshal had hold of the back end of the mechanical robot. He picked up the mechanical rhino and slammed it down on its back, SMASH! And then on its feet, SMASH! And then on its back again, SMASH DING! Each time parts went flying off.

Finally, all he had was a twisted mangled heap of disassociated parts with a human in the central roll cage. He tossed it away.

By this time, Superstar had defeated three more of the warriors in hand to hand fighting. Yet another burst of machine gun fire and again she was hit! Twice in the back. She turned to deal with this guy once and for all and he hit her with another burst. This time one in the stomach. It was hard to breathe. She was coughing up foamy blood. He stopped shooting to reload. He pulled the spent magazine off and started to put another magazine on the gun. *She had to take him out before he could shoot again.* Just as she started to regain some strength, a man's hand came down on her head from behind and pulled her head up with her hair. A knife blade was thrust up against her neck ready to slice off her head!

The bolt of the machine gun slammed forward and it barked. Just as it did, she reached up and grabbed the knife and ducked down. The machine gun rounds passed over her and ripped into her unseen attacker. More blood sprayed everywhere.

She took a step forward and stumbled to the ground She had been cut by the knife as she ducked and hit yet again by the machine gun. She was wheezing and bleeding badly. Her pretty uniform was a shredded bloody mess. She looked up to the gunner ready to finish her off. When, WHAM! A large diesel engine came crashing down on him from above. He was squashed like a bug. Marshal was throwing things again.

She zipped over to him saying, "It's time for us to leave." She grabbed his arm but she could not move him.

"We can still get the Queen, she must be in the rookery. Find it and we find her," he said as he turned back to the main entrance of the nearby foundry building.

A warrior with one of their shotguns came up and opened fire on them. BLAM! The rock salt bounced off of Marshal but it imbedded itself into Heather's softer flesh. "OWWW! It stings!"

The warrior was having trouble sliding the pump back, his left hand had been replaced with a pitchfork like prosthesis. Marshal charged him, grabbed the muzzle of the shotgun, and jerked it away from the warrior who, upon losing the gun, went for the ax he had tucked in his belt. Marshal backhanded him with the shotgun, breaking the butt stock off. The swatted warrior sailed twenty feet through the air and came down on the other side of another pile of bits and pieces of unrelated steel.

They both looked around, and only a couple of warriors could be seen fleeing from the scene. Heather shook the blood and loose fabric off her Superstar uniform. Most of her left side is shredded and bare flesh is exposed. "This really sucks!"

"What is creating a vacuum?" He asked confused by her statement.

"Huh? No it's great that I heal so fast, but does it have to hurt?" She didn't give him a chance to answer. "Listen, you stay here and I'll go search for the Queen in that building, it should take only a few seconds. If she's in there we can go get her. If she's not, we're out of here."

Marshal reached down to her and scooped her up in one arm, lifting her up to be eye to eye, he planted a kiss on her. "We have a plan." She was breathless and speechless. This seldom happened to Heather. He explained, "That was for good luck. I saw it on one of your TV programs the other night." He returned her to the ground.

She bit her lip as she slid down his chest. "Well, I had better be going. I'll be right back!" And with that said, she zipped into the foundry building. As she turned away from Marshal and put on the speed, the electrical transformer off in the background gave off a shower of sparks.

Inside the massive building were all manner of tools and equipment scattered about. Giant hooks hung from the ceiling, suspended from rails that spanned the length of the building. Piles of coal ten feet high were being fed into giant furnaces by worker drones. Humans in a trancelike state stood in rows waiting to be amalgamated into The Hive by the Queen.

Worker drones were busy placing and welding great sheets of steel armor plate onto strange machines that had no apparent purpose. A small army of warriors surrounded a raised platform that was well lit and had a dome over it.

She hit a slippery patch of silicone on the floor and nearly fell, catching herself on a steel girder supporting work platform. Her misstep caught the attention of the nearby warriors. One turned and saw her. He was heavily armored like a medieval knight, and had a great pole arm with a four-foot blade. Much to her relief and suspicion, he did nothing but watch her.

The Queen appeared on the edge of the platform looking down at her. She was eight feet tall, had a slightly female looking face on an ant like body, two human like arms, and two arms with crab claws. She had four insect legs and a long whip tail with a large barbed stinger. There was movement behind her, but Superstar could not see what it was. She looked for a way up to her but there was none. The platform was suspended from the roof.

"Zzo, my dear Heather, you have returned to me. But have you brought me what I dezzire," the Queen asked.

Here's my chance! Heather thought, but she had no weapon! She looked around trying to find something, anything; she could use against the Harbinger Queen but nothing presented itself. *If I can get closer, maybe I can steal one of the guard's weapons and use it on her.* "Yes, my Queen! I have it here with me."

"If you have it, why do you rezzist my droneszz? Where iszz it?"

Heather was unable to come up with an answer for her. "I left it in the car. I'll go and get it for you. I'll be right back." No one believed her.

The Queen commanded, "CATCH HER!" Superstar easily dodged the warrior's pole arm as it clanged into the steel girder. She was darting about still trying to find a way to get to the Queen when the work platform she was standing under started to move. It was like a ten-foot tall bug made of steel girders. It had one of those pneumatic chisels used to break up the highways on it. BAMM! It slammed down imbedding itself into the floor where Superstar had been standing just a half second before. She ducked and dodged slicing and stabbing blades.

Two warriors wheeled up a pneumatic spear gun with eight tubes on it and started firing at her. Each shot made the same distinctive sound of a pneumatic gun firing PFFTUU! She slid on the floor under the hail of spears and got to her feet in time to kick one of them where it counted most. She headed for the exit, pouring on the speed. Several gunshots were heard, but her speed prevented any of them from finding home.

Outside, the blond speedster found Marshal on the ground with smoke wafting up from him. He smelt like bacon frying. He was still quivering and convulsing. She saw an electric spark arching from the ground to his body. She managed to stop before setting foot on the steel mesh that covered that part of the ground. Warriors were coming from both sides. *What could she do?*

The sound of heavy engines revving and the sudden burst of a heavy machine gun caught her attention. The area erupted and a bunch of small explosions and the ground shook! What now? Then she saw it.

The Illinois National Guard still had some old M113s APCs (Old tracked armored personnel carriers with a .50 caliber machine gun on top. Very old school, Colonel Otis would approve.) As the 50 hammered away, a two and a half ton truck being driven by Tex, bounced up and turned around, backing up to where Marshal lay.

In the back of the deuce and a half were Colonel Otis and three soldiers. "DON'T TOUCH THE MAT! Don't touch anything touching the mat. It's electrified, don't touch him, you'll get shocked," he said as he jumped down from the truck.

"But you're standing on the mat?" She asked.

"Our boots will protect us from the electricity, rubber soles. Just don't touch anything else," he explained as he walked up to her. Looking her over he had to ask, "are you alright?"

She looked down at herself and back to him explaining, "me, I'm fine."

"You look like.. well you look like you've had it. You're a bloody mess," he said hesitatingly.

"I got better. How do we get him out of here if we can't touch him?" She asked.

"Watch!" He turned and waved to someone unseen in the distance. A few seconds later, a soldier pops up with a small green tube on his shoulder. A sudden blast of smoke and fire and a LAW rocket goes streaking at the sparking transformer. There's a flash and a BANG BOOM! The transformer jumps into the air and the sparks stop. (A LAW is a type of Light Antitank Weapon. It's a small disposable single shot rocket launcher.)

With the power to the mat turned off, Marshal's body stopped twitching and he just lay there. The two soldiers in the back of the truck jumped down and joined the Colonel in trying to pick up Marshal. "He smells like bacon!"

"Doesn't mean a thing soldier," the Colonel explained as they struggled with him and finally got him up. The Colonel hops up back in the truck and they are trying to pull him up into the back of the truck without much luck. "He weighs a ton"

"And it's all dead weight," Sgt. Block commmplained.

"Maybe if you helped," the Colonel said to Heather.

Superstar stopped looking around and stepped forward saying, "here, let me help you." She volunteered putting Marshal's arm over her shoulder. "The trick is to use your legs when lifting," she informed them. They all heaved and he slowly started to go up then Superstar started to gain strength and before long, she was holding Marshal up in her arms, virtually by herself. The two soldiers with her on the ground were amazed. She heaved and he landed in the back bed of the deuce and a half, with a thud. "Wow, I did it! I thought you said I wasn't super strong any more."

Just as she spoke, the 10-foot tall, bug like work platform with the pneumatic chisel walked out of the building and impaled the APC on its chisel. KERPLUNK!

"WHAT THE HELL IS THAT?" The Colonel demanded to know.

"They're making things in there," she answered as the two soldiers climbed onboard the truck. The mechanical bug lifted the APC, stuck on its chisel and slammed it down on its side. SLAM! The back ramp popped off, and the soldiers inside came running out. They came running for the truck with the impaler coming after them.

"Shoot it with that rocket launcher!" Heather called out.

"Sorry, it's a single shot weapon and we only had one," the Colonel apologized as he motioned for her to get on the truck.

One by one, the National Guardsmen piled into the back of the truck as the walker came closer and closer. Soon, Superstar was the only one not in the truck.

The chisel of death and destruction came crashing down, barely missing Superstar, who was too fast to be hit. She darted back and forth, stopping every so often so the human drone operating the walker could see where she was and come after her. She was trying to lead the walker away from the truck, and it might have worked if the Colonel hadn't started shooting at the human drone inside with his .45.

BLAM, BLAM, BLAM, three shoots rang out, three slugs bounced off of the armored drone at the controls of the walker. The walker turned back to the truck and was about to plunge the chisel into the back of the truck when Superstar grabbed one of its legs and tried to stop it by pulling it back. "NOOO!"

She was unable to slow the machine but she did manage to distract the operator, who took a second to shake her off of the leg. He tried to stomp on her but once again she was too fast for it.

The Colonel extended his hand to Heather to help her up into the truck. She raced over to the truck. She took his hand, he pulled, and she jumped, knocking him down with her landing on top of him. "Oooph!"

"Well, look who's under who," she said smiling.

"TEX, GET US THE HELL OUT OF HERE!" The big army truck lurched forward and rumbled over the broken ground. They made it out the hole in the fence.

The Colonel and Heather bounced up and down still on the truck bed floor which was made of steel covered with hard wood flooring.

She was still laying on him cheek to cheek with her arms more or less around his neck. As they were jostled about on the floor he asked, "Heather, uh Superstar, are you alright?"

"Huh? Oh just let me lay here for a couple of seconds and bleed," she said half dazed.

One of the National Guardsmen said, "it's good to be a Colonel."

"Indeed it is soldier," the Colonel joked with him as he and Heather started to get up. Both of them were covered with blood.

One of the concerned troopers asked, "Colonel, are you alright?"

He looked down and took notice of the blood for the first time. "I'm okay, it's hers." This confused the NGs and they looked to Superstar for answers.

She explained, "I'm Superstar. I'm the newest hero on the team and I heal really really fast. In fact, I can do everything really fast."

"Everything?"

"Everything if I want." They all laughed.

Their attention turned to the big blue alien on the floor of the bed. "That's him isn't it? That's Marshal," one of the soldiers said. They all looked at him as if on cue, and the square-jawed Aurorian started to stir and mumbled to himself.

She sat down next to him and put his head on her lap. "There, there big guy, you just take it easy, we'll get you back home."

CHAPTER TWELVE

THE FURY OF SUPERSTAR

The deuce and a half made its way through the streets of the city until it reached the rendezvous point where they met a Black Hawk helicopter for the short cross-town flight back to the Hero building on the city's far north side.

The bird landed on the rooftop helipad. Colonel Otis, all bloodied up by Heather, and his soldiers got out. He sent them to go get cleaned up. Heather, in her torn and bloodied Superstar uniform and Marshal also got out.

The Colonel turned and directed them to, "take him to the Med. Center and then get washed up and change clothes."

She cornered him as they reached the stairway down to the elevator. "What other secrets are you keeping from me?" She angrily asked.

"What secrets?" He said defensively.

She got in his face gritting her teeth. "What about my super powers, what haven't you told me?" She demanded to know.

"I have no knowledge of anything being kept from you. Your powers are just as new to us as they are to you. Maybe Dr. Cooly can better explain what's going on with them."

Dauntless stands guard over the Harbinger drone she captured earlier. They are in the Med. Center and Doctors Cooly and Brewville are attending to the drone. Nurse Chapel is assisting. "The nerves and tendons are fused directly onto the chainsaw. We can remove it but he will have no hand," Beverly says.

She straightens up as she hears someone come in. She turns and adjusts her glasses to see Marshal and the bloody mess answering to the name of Superstar coming through the doors. "OHMYGOD!"

"Be cool Doc, he's fine, he only took 10,000 volts, and it's me we have to talk about," she angrily said.

"Are you alright?' She asked, not paying any attention to the tone of Heather's voice. She was concerned that half of her left leg was exposed, as was her stomach, side and back. She saw no wounds, but her uniform was blood soaked and torn. "What happened?"

"Looks like she walked in front of a machine gun to me," Dauntless ventured a guess.

"They can wait," Heather said as she took Beverly's arm and walked her into her nearby office and closed the door. Dauntless and Chapel looked back and forth exchanging puzzled looks. Dauntless directed Chapel, "you take care of the big guy, I'll watch this."

"You may have me now, but you will all become part of The Hive and serve the Harbinger Queen," the drone called out from the table.

"You shut up and be quiet or I'll put your lights out and it won't be with a anesthetic." Dauntless made a fist to emphasize her point. Dr. Brewville backed away and then proceeded to go to work on the drone's arm.

In the office, Heather is in Beverly's face. "Okay, what's going on with my powers? What haven't you told me?"

"Calm down, and tell me what happened out there." She was trying to make sense of Heather's ranting.

"I'm super fast alright, but it hurts like hell to get shot and I'm super strong part of the time. What else haven't you told me? Am I going to mutate into some kind of freak? And, why am I so hungry all of a sudden?"

"I didn't get to go over this with you. I didn't have all of the test results back yet. But of course it hurts to get shot. What did you expect? I said you would heal rapidly, not that you were indestructible. As for your super strength, you will always have the strength of four men; it's just the higher levels of strength will vary. Were you injured at the time?"

Heather nodded her head, Dr. Cooly continued, "That explains it. When you're hurt, you start to heal, but if you're bleeding that also activated the FAMAEs you received from Marshal and they will give you extra super strength for a limited time."

She sat back in her oversized chair and added, "and that's it. I'm not keeping any secrets from you. You're not going to mutate or anything." She got up and adjusted her glasses again. "And now, if you'll excuse me, if you don't have any medical problems, I'm needed elsewhere." She stopped at the door and turned to say, "Oh yes! You may experience an increase in your aggression and sex drive; the Harbinger injecton may also reduce your inhibitions. I haven't had a chance to study all of the results yet, but it's possible."

"Possible?" Heather said, "But why am I so hungry?"

"Oh." The good doctor paused in the door. "Look at all you've been through, it's only natural that you would be hungry." The redhaired doctor was playing it off as if it was nothing.

"But what do I do about it?" The blond superhero asked.

"We have this new treatment, it's call eating. You should try it." And she left.

A soldier sitting in front of a video screen turns around and calls his superior over. "Captain Siegel, you need to see this."

The officer comes over and leans down for a better look. "What is it you have there?"

"It's the security feed from the Med. Center sir."

"Is this the only view we have?"

"That's it, sir."

The Captain picks up the mic and calls Dauntless on her COMM link.

In the Med. Center, Dauntless taps her badge and then her earpiece and listens carefully. She glances over at the drone and Nurse Chapel, and backs away slowly, keeping both of them in view.

Colonel Otis walks in and the phone rings. He looks around and Dauntless tells him to, "Pick it up, it's for you." This puzzled him but he answered the phone. He turned his attention to the drone and Chapel as he listened. "Are you sure of this?"

"Yes sir, we can see the bug jump off of the drone and over towards Nurse Chapel, Captain Siegel answered on the phone.

"Send a team up."

"They're already in position outside the door."

"Good man." The Colonel hung up the phone and reached for his sidearm, He didn't have it on. He slid over to Dauntless while Chapel worked on the drone. He instructed Brandy to, "give me your side arm and watch the drone."

He walked over to Chapel with his hands behind his back. She stopped working and started to turn and face him. He quickly grabbed her and forced her to bend over the table with the drone on it. Dauntless rushed up and held the drone.

Holding a gun to her head he brushed her hair away from her neck. "Nothing!" He let go of the frightened nurse and she spun around and slapped him.

Holding his cheek he apologized to her. "Sorry, we thought…" he turned to Dauntless. "Check his neck!"

She reached up and forced his chin down into his chest to examine his neck. There was a red spot with the tip of the stinger sticking out. "He's got a stinger in him!"

He looked up at the surveillance camera and shouted. "Who else was in the room?"

Dauntless relays the answer, "The two doctors and Superstar."

"Where's Dr. Brewville?" He asked Chapel.

The flustered nurse took a second to gather her thoughts before answering, "He went downstair to get some tools, He's coming right back."

In the lower lever lab, MaCos Ex is working on some red fabric as Brewville comes in. "Doctor, I think I have the cape ready."

"Not now, later perhaps. I need the magnifier and micro tool set. Where is it?" Four heavily armed soldiers burst into the lab and force Dr. Brewville face down on the floor. One of them flicks the doctor's ponytail away with the toe of his boot to check his neck. "Nothing nada zip o."

Doctor Cooly came out of her office. "What's going on out here?" She stops abruptly when she became instantly aware of the muzzle of Brandy's 9mm under her nose. Her eyes expanded to twice their normal size and her glasses slid all the way down her nose.

Colonel Otis, holding the gun, explained in a stern voice, "hold it right there! I don't want to shoot you but I will if I have to. Show me your neck."

Alarmed and confused, she tilted her head back to the left and right. "No. The back of your neck," he corrected her.

She turned and tilted her head down. Her hair was up in its customary bun. Her neck was free of alien inhabitation. "You're clean!" He said.

To say she was set back by all of this would be an understatement, her heart was pounding. She regained her commposure in a few seconds and asked as she turned back to face him, "I hope you have a good explanation for all of this."

"There was a bug on his neck when he was brought in and now it's gone. We saw it jump off but not where it went to," he explained.

Dauntless stepped up still holding the drone down with one hand. "They're telling me on the comm link that Dr. Brewville is clean. That only leaves Heather."

"Why am I not surprised? Where is she?" He asked, sarcastically.

"She was going to wash up and change clothes," Dr. Cooly replied.

"She doesn't live here in the building. Where would she go to shower and change?" He asked.

"She has a locker on the ground floor, but she wouldn't use the showers down there with all the men. She's been using the shower in my apartment on ten," Dauntless chimed in."

He dashed off, pistol in hand. "Guard that prisoner!" He waved to the four soldiers waiting in the hall and they followed. They ran down the stairs and stopped at Brandy's door. The Colonel cautioned them, "be ready for anything, she can be quite strong. Have your handcuffs ready. Stay here, I'll call." He listened to the door and opened it. He could hear something inside. He eased his way in, with his trusty .45 in hand. The soldiers braced themselves on both sides of the doorway with their weapons ready.

With his pistol poised for action, Colonel Otis went in. He could hear the shower running and headed for it. As he made his way into the bedroom, the shower stopped and he could detect movement in the bathroom. The bedroom was a mess; the bed was broken down and collapsed on the floor. *It must have been some wild party.* He eased up to the bathroom door.

The door swung open and there was Heather all wet and glistening with a towel on her head and another just barely around her body. "Why Colonel, have you come to join me?" She grabbed him by his collar and swung him around pinning him against the bathroom wall. She grabbed both of his wrists and forced his hands up and pressed her body up against him holding him in place.

It's funny, the things that will pass through your mind while you are being pinned to the wall by an alien possessed, demented superhero. Things like, how hot her body looked and how good it feels pressed up against yours, not that it is preventing you from moving yours, or how you missed the smell of vanilla she usually wore. Then the thought that she just might put her fist through your face brings you out of it.

He struggled to resist her but she had four times his strength. She also had a wicked smile on her face. She was enjoying this. "My host body seemed to think this showering was necessary. And now you have joined us. My host would like to f### your brains out. I don't see any benefit in it. But, if I can dominate you with this body and can control you and your men; that would be most useful."

He tried to break free, but she just pressed against him harder. She kissed him long and forcefully. He kept turning his head trying to avoid her lips but she was most persistent. She let go of his left hand and used hers to hold his head still. She was all over his face and neck.

He tried to throw her off with his left, but her body was slick from the shower. The more he tried to throw her, the more he discovered her supple body under the towel. His resistance was waning. "I can influence you with this body," she said as she felt his body start to work with hers.

"I have a message for your Queen, influence is one thing, control is another, and we will never tolerate the presence of The Hive on Earth," he defiantly said.

BANG! The .45 in his right hand went off. This startled her. She smashed his hand against the wall and he dropped the gun. "It seems you have more resistance than she gives you credit for. Pity, you would have enjoyed it. I was going to jump, into your body, but this host body is far superior to yours."

He struggled to free himself, but she only reestablished her position of dominance. "You know what they say about Heather, she's the hostess with the mostess. If you take me over, my men will stop you."

"Since you'll only try to stop me, I'll have to settle for beating the crap out of you." She forcefully kissed him and then pulled him away from the wall and slammed him against it. The noise brought the other soldiers rushing in. She punched Henry twice so fast that you could hardly separate the cracking sounds. He started to crumple and she caught him and held him up with one hand on his throat.

She drove her fist deep into his stomach and kneed him in the stomach which doubled him over. He collapsed against her body, unable to defend himself. She finished him off with a hammer fist blow to the back of his head. He collapsed to the floor like a wet sack of (Expletive deleted)

She lost the towel from around her body and this caused the onrushing soldiers to hesitate. A flying karate kick to the chin KO'd the lead soldier. She landed among them and delivered a left cross that sent the last soldier toppling head over heels over the corner of the collapsed bed.

She grabbed the nearest one and ran around him with her feet on the wall. As she came around, she kicked the other soldier knocking him down. She landed in front of the soldier she had been running around, and threw him down to the floor and wailed on him. Two, three four times. He was out of the fight.

The toppled soldier started to get up, but she leapt upon him and knocked him down again and was sitting on his stomach. She ripped the M16 out of his hands and bashed him with it. CHUANK! She turned to the last remaining soldier, ready to fight.

Upstairs in the Med. Center, Marshal tells Dauntless, "you are faster than I am. I'll stay and guard the prisoner, you go help them find the drone." Nurse Chapel commented, "why don't all three of you go. I'll sedate the prisoner."

Doctor Cooly jumped at the chance to finally see some action. She grabbed her new utility belt and started to strap it on over her lab coat as they all headed for the door. "I've been dying to try this out ever since Dr. Brewville gave it to me."

Chapel readied the injections. The drone eased away from her in terror.

BAM! The other toppled soldier had brought his M16 into use. Heather's right shoulder was stinging like all get out. There was blood everywhere. She lunged at him grabbing hold of his M16. They wrestled for the weapon for several seconds before she gained the upper hand and wrenched it out of his grip and used it to bludgeon him repeatedly.

She got up and surveyed the destruction she had wrought. The bullet popped out of her shoulder and the wound closed itself. She recovered her wayward towel and used it to make a skirt, tucking it in around her flat stomach. She adjusted her boobs; *I might just need the distraction these will provide.*

She stepped out the door. The elevator came up and four soldiers got out and spotted her right away. "There she is!" They started to rush her with their weapons at the ready. She looked the other way to the stairs thinking it would be easier to outrun them. Just as she was about to take off, Dauntless came down the stairs and blocked her exit.

"Hold it there boys! She's all mine," Brandy called out to the onrushing soldiers.

Heather struck a fighting pose in her towel, "bring it on!"

Dauntless cautiously approached. "That looks like one of my towels."

"You can have it back!" She took it off and threw the balled up towel in Brandy's face. THUMP, THUMP, THUMP! Heather landed three punches into Brandy's unprotected midsection. Brandy fell back against the wall and threw off the towel.

Heather was just standing there, waiting to see what effect her attack had had. Brandy swung wildly and missed. They traded positions, and Brandy tried again, this time burying her fist into the wall.

As Brandy struggled to free her hand from the wall, Heather came up behind her and rammed her face into the wall. Brandy came out swinging, but Heather just ducked under. The only thing Brandy managed to do was knock Heather's turban off. From her lower position, Heather hit Brandy three more times in the stomach and came up with a right upper cut to her chin. CRACK!

Brandy collapsed against the wall holding her stomach. "How'd you get so strong?"

"They shot me," She replied as she grabbed hold of Brandy's shoulders and yanked her up. "And this is how I put Marshal down!" She spun Brandy around and got her right arm under Brandy's chin around her throat and began to squeeze!

Brandy struggled for a few seconds before going limp. Heather let her fall to the floor. The costumed superhero, with her boots and gun belt, lay defeated at the feet of her opponent, a nude girl. Heather, in commparison, had nothing on, not even a tan line, nothing. She was fair skinned and a true blond. She turned to the soldiers, smiling broadly, counting on her charms to distract them. Three out of four were.

BAP, BAP, BAP, BAP! The fourth soldier's M16 barked out on auto. Heather's stomach and right shoulder exploded with a flash of blood. She fell to the floor face down. "AUGH!"

The soldiers approached her. One of them asked, "Why'd you do that?"

Heather looked up with a crazy excited smile on her face. "My turn!" She suddenly sprinted forward and caught them commpletely off guard. She hit the shooter in his stomach with her shoulder driving him back like a football tackle.

She stopped, spun around, lifted him up over her head and threw him into one of his commrades, sending both of them sliding down the highly waxed floor. A roundhouse kick to the head finished off one of the two remaining standing soldiers.

She parried the other's M16 as it went off, and finished him off with a flurry of punches too fast and numerous to count. She dashed over to the two other soldiers. She grabbed the one on top, the shooter, and tossed him across the hall slamming him into the wall. A karate chop was used to dispatch the remaining trooper. She returned to the shooter and sat down on his chest with his head between her knees. She looked down at him and cupped her breast smiling. "There are millions of men who would pay to be in your position, but I bet you're not one of them." She snapped his neck!

She stood up and casually strolled over to Brandy's room. "I guess clothing would be a good idea." She rifled through Brandy's closet. First, she tried on a pair of Brandy's BDUs, but they were too baggy and made her look fat. Then she found a nice light blue satin top and a short black skirt to go with it and a fashionable belt, something like Dr. Cooly might wear. She was dressed in seconds, and tossed her hair back giving it a shake. She frantically looked thought the stuff on the dresser. "What, no sunglasses!"

She heard some movement out in the hall and decided it was time to go. She sped out the door and bounced off a wall called Marshal. "Lover boy! Just the man I wanted to see. Come with me."

She reached up around his neck with both hands and pulled herself up to him and kissed him passionately. He took her by her waist and started to remove her but she held on tight. He lifted her up to break her hold and she just shifted burying his face in her cleavage.

He lifted her higher, bumping her head on the ceiling, and he was free of her grasp. He eased her down to the floor and moved his hold to her forearms. She didn't quite know what to do. Looking down at her he said, "I have been informed that you are under the influence of the Harbingers. Please submit yourself for inspection."

The five bodies lying on the floor in the hallway were proof that the Harbinger had been here and it sure looked like her handywork, but he had to be sure.

She pressed up against him trying to distract him. "You want to check my neck, sure go right ahead." She started to turn to show him the back of her neck and slipped out of his grasp.

She elbowed Marshal in his stomach and took off running. For about two steps. He still had hold of her other arm and she suddenly whipped around and smacked into the wall knocking herself out.

He reached over as she slid down the wall, lifted her head, exposing the bug still on her back and in her neck. He once again grabbed the bug and ripped it off of her neck and crushed it in his hand as he pulled it out of her. SKRUNCH!

The elevator doors at the end of the hall open. Doctor Cooly comes running down the hall. There were bodies lying all over the place. She could see Marshal was holding Heather. She ran up to him. Seeing the situation she knew exactly what to do, having gone through it not so long ago. She took the necessary tools out of her new utility belt and as Marshal held Heather's head still, she performed the surgery to remove the stinger. It didn't take long, in just a minute she had the stinger removed. Seconds later the bleeding stopped.

Marshal scooped Heather up in his powerful arms and carried her off to the Med. Center. Dauntless started to come to and Dr. Cooly started to examine the other bodies.

The elevator door opened and Marshal stepped out carrying Heather. The Med. Center is in a mess. The exam table is overturned and there is no sign of the drone prisoner or Nurse Chapel. The sound of a scuffle and a muffled scream catches his attention. He puts Heather down and goes to investigate.

In the doorway leading to the stairs to the roof, he finds the drone holding Chapel at knifepoint. The drone is behind her using her as a shield with the blade of a scalpel at her throat. "STAY BACK! Or she dies!"

"Help me!" She was nearly hysterical in tears.

"What has transpired? Are your biometrics stable?" Marshal asked, as he eased forward. She was terrified and unable to answer.

"STAY BACK!" The drone commanded, as they stumbled their way up the steps backward.

"I am retaining my distance." They continued inching up the stairs. "I am the one that your Queen desires to mate with. Acquire me as your hostage and relinquish the one addressed as Chapel the Nurse."

"I can't use you as a hostage, you're too strong."

Finally, they arrived at the small landing to the door to the roof. "Take your weapon off and drop it down the stairwell or I kill her right here right now!" Marshal undid his utility belt and held it out and let it fall.

They all made their way out the door. The drone was just looking around at the city as he made his way to the edge. "If you anticipate me trying to overpower you there is cable, you could bind my extremity"

"Yeah right, you'd hit me just as soon as I got close enough to tie you up. No deal!"

"You could allow Chapel to perform the binding action, and relinquish control over her after establishing control over me."

The drone did not answer. He just kept going around the edge of the building and kept glancing off to the skyline as if he was trying to figure out just where he was. "You are unable to extricate yourself from this location. The structure is full of armed personnel. They will prevent your egress."

"Huh? Why are you talking so funny?"

"It is the functioning of my translator. If we were in closer proximity to each other it would function at a higher degree." Armed soldiers poured out onto the other two wings of the roof and took up positions ready to fire. Looking at them and turning back to the drone he added, "they are resolute in preventing your departure."

""Who said anything about leaving? The Queen can see what is going on and where we are. The Hive will come to my rescue. And you won't do anything about it as long as the life of this woman is in my hands."

"The Hive will not come, they will not jeopardize many warriors to reclaim one lowly drone. The humans will endeavor to do everything within their power to reclaim one of their own. Their medical personnel are able to assist you."

"I don't want any help! Being part of The Hive is everything to me. I am so much more than I ever was as a mere human."

"It is regrettable that it will only end undesirably for you. For both of you, both harbinger and human, that is." He was closer, but still not close enough to affect her rescue or his capture.

"If I were your hostage, they would come for me and you," Marshal put it to him.

"Go, bring the cable over here," the drone commanded, still holding tightly onto Chapel's waist, scalpel poised at her jugular. Marshal picked up the spool of cable used to lash down helicopters in bad weather and carried it over to him. "Put it down and lay down face down, with your hands behind your back."

With Marshal laying face down on the roof, the drone released Nurse Chapel telling her to, "tie him up good." He stayed with her holding the knife at her ribs. She took a hesitant step toward Marshal and there was a gust of wind and the drone was gone! WOOSH!

Chapel fell to her knees and looked around as Marshal got up confused as to what had just happened. The answer was waiting for him. Heather stood several feet away wearing a hospital gown, with one foot on the back of the drone who was now face down on the tarmac.

"I'm back!" She said with a smile.

General Solo and Colonel Otis are walking down the hall. "Damn, you look like a raccoon Henry, what did she hit you with?" The junior officer had two black eyes and his cheeks were swollen.

"Just her fist sir, I didn't know she was that strong. I should have realized it, but I didn't. I had heard that she was going to lose her super strength, and now I hear that she will retain the strength of four men."

"Can you see okay? Does it hurt?" General Solo asked, concerned that his key man might not be fit for duty.

"I can see alright, and it only hurts when I see something," he joked.

The General stopped in the hall and looked both ways. "I heard she was naked when she did this!"

"Not when I ran into her sir, almost, but not quite," the Colonel grimaced in pain as he answered.

They started walking again. "Don't let the Air Force hear about that. What's the situation now?"

"Superstar has made a commplete recovery, she is no longer under the control of the Harbinger Queen. She helped to recapture the drone after he escaped. The captured drone is being held in detention and he is still part of The Hive."

"Just how did he escape in the first place?" The General wanted to know.

"It seems the sedative that was given to him didn't work, and when the nurse's back was turned he made his move."

The Colonel went on to explain. "Our manpower is way down sir. She killed two of the soldiers and put a couple more in the hospital. But she was under the control of The Hive so it's not her fault. No charges will be filed. She remembers doing it, and it bothers her but she wasn't in control at the time."

The General nodded sadly, as he continued, "we have got to do something, sir. The Air Force just wants to bomb the whole place back to the Stone Age."

"And just what's so wrong with that?" The older soldier asked.

"It's an American city sir, and we'll never know if they got them all or even if it will work. Superstar knows where the Queen is and how to get to her. We almost got her the last two times."

They stopped walking. "Then why didn't you get her?" The General asked.

The Colonel, with the two black eyes hesitated to answer, "Uh, we've had equipment problems, but those problems have been addressed and are being taken care of even as we speak. They're at the Broadway Avenue armory using the range to test some new weapons."

"Why not the lakefront range?"

"Too public sir."

"Good, If Dr. Cooly is finished with the drone, send him along. The Air Force is raising cane about not receiving the prisoner. Seeing that he is still part of The Hive, they may know where our HQ is. We don't want them coming after us, do we?"

"That brings up another thing, sir," the Colonel said hesitantly.

"Another thing?" The General's curiosity was piqued.

"I have heard from Dr. Brewville that we have some of Marshal's equipment working, and with it we may be able to enter The Hive undetected and take down the Queen. Without the Queen, the Harbinger bugs will stop working. It's the best way to handle this. I have a plan that requires the use of the Harbinger drone we have in custody. I would like to run my plan past you."

"Let's hear it."

Later in the hall, Dr. Cooly stops Colonel Otis. "What are you doing up! You're in no condition to be up and about," she said concerned for his welfare.

"A couple black eyes won't interfere with my duty," he replied.

"What about the nausea and vomiting? You've got internal injuries and a concussion. I want you in bed!"

"That's very nice of you and the best offer I've had all day, but no, I have some things to take care of that can't wait. I promise I won't be going out on any missions."

She was standing in front of him blocking his way with her hands on her hips. Everyone who knew her knew that this was a sign meaning she meant business. "As medical officer, I could order you to bed, and no jokes!"

"Don't," he tried to sidestep her, but she shifted over blocking his way again. "Listen, if things works out at the range today, this will all be taken care of and then it's bed time for Henry."

She took his arm. "What's going on? I overheard some of the soldiers saying that they were going in the day after tomorrow. If we're going in, I want a uniform like the other, they may need medical attention on the scene and I'll need the extra protection one of those super uniforms provide."

"It seems they don't provide all that much protection after all judging by what happened to Superstar's uniform."

"I still want one." She folded her arms over her chest.

"Okay, you can have one, but you won't need it. We can't have you going out on missions. If something happened to you, what would we do?' If we don't come back we need you here to carry on. You're the only one that could do it. You're too important to us. We can be replaced but not you."

"But the others, Dauntless and Marshal and Superstar? You can't have a Hero organization without them." She wasn't buying his argument.

"They have to go, that's what they do. That's the only reason for the organization in the first place. But, we need you here to figure out things and keep everybody in one piece."

"You know, the soldiers talking about going on a mission like that is ..."

"Bad for security?" He helped her find the words. "Did the drone hear them?" He asked.

"I don't see how he didn't, he was right there in the room with them." You know, that's not very smart..."

He interrupted her, "It's very smart. It's not true, and we're counting on the Queen overhearing them, and not being ready for us tonight."

"Tonight? You can't go anywhere tonight," she stopped him.

"I'm not going anywhere, it all depends on if the weapons and equipment are ready. Dr. Brewville has made some new ammo for Marshal's gun. The last two batches didn't work and this time we are going to test it before we go out with it.

The Broadway Illinois National Guard Armory is a long brick building with a drill hall big enough to hold a track and field event. There's a small pistol range in back. Dauntless, Marshal, Dr. Brewville and Superstar, in a replacement uniform, along with some of the soldiers of the 5th are there.

Superstar is demonstrating that when it comes to shooting, she's no superstar. Brandy is razzing her about the other day. "I can't believe you got all the way to the Queen's chamber and didn't know you had no gun! That's so... I don't know what it is! I can see Marshal with dud ammo, but going on a mission without a weapon!"

"Okay! Enough already! I think I like the Walthers better, I like the looks." Heather was starting to bob back and forth like a little girl will when she's caught doing something she shouldn't.

"That's as good a reason as any, you'll never hit anything with it anyway so you might as well look good!" The Range Safety Officer called out, "maybe I could give you some pointers," he offered.

She accepted and he eagerly came over to give her some personal and up close instruction. Brandy just shook her head and walked away. "Can you believe it?"

Meanwhile, in the back of the range, Marshal is having an intense conversation with Dr. Brewville and MaCos Ex. Marshal is holding the doctor's hand up to his neck so his translator will work better. "Your ammunition nearly got me killed and allowed the Harbinger Queen to escape. What do you have to say for yourself?"

I wish I hadn't fixed your translator. "Look, I know there was a problem with the first two batches, but I know what the problem was and this time we have fixed it," Dr. Brewville said with a smile on his face that reminded you of a used car dealer.

MaCos explained, "There was a problem with the stability of the plasma in solid form."

"But this time I did the chemistry," Brewville added.

Heather started shooting again. MaCos suggested that, "while she is trying to familiarize herself with the weapon, perhaps we could go to the main hall and test your new cape."

"My new cape?" Marshal said enthusiastically.

"It's not an exact copy, but it should work. All I had to work from was a few photographs the humans provided."

"Let us go."

A few minutes later, while Heather banged away at the paper targets, Marshal, MaCos Ex and Dr. Brewville were on the upper deck that went around the main hall. MaCos was showing Marshal his latest creation. "I didn't know how it was attached to your uniform until I got a look at your collar, under it actually."

"I seem to remember buttons," Marshal said.

"There is one button on the left corner of the cape. If you press and hold it, the cape will stiffen and form an airfoil. All you have to do is hold the leading edges out and jump off something, and there you are, gliding."

"I seem to remember it," he said. They quickly attached the cape under his uniform's high collar and he stepped over the railing that ran along the upper deck. He pressed the button and the cape stiffened and formed a set of wings extending beyond both of his hands.

He said something in his native alien gibberish and lept off of the upper deck, sailed about 30 feet, and belly flopped on the hard wood floor. THUMP!

Dauntless, who was at the other end of the armory by the front foyer, tossed her can of Coke and raced out to Marshal lying face down on the floor with his arms still spread wide open. As she arrived, he started to push himself up off the floor. "OH, the intense discommfort of it all."

She helped him up. "Are you alright?"

"No, I am partially left as well."

"Huh?" That one stumped her. "Oh, you're making a joke. You're all right! But what happened to you? You know how to fly one of these things."

"My memory is incommplete. I must relearn it."

After several more painful attempts, he finally got the hang of hang gliding and they deemed the cape test a success and went back to the range to find Heather was doing much better, she was even able to hit the target.

It was time for Marshal to test the new ammo in his sidearm. He slapped a block of solid plasma into the open magazine in the pistol grip of his gun, walked up the firing line and took careful aim. There was a flash and the entire room reverberated with the explosion, FABOOM! The lights down range went out and the air was filled with dust. The ventilators prevented the room from commpletely filling with dust. As the dust cloud began to clear, it became obvious that the bullet trap at the other end of the range had failed to contain the projectile. There was a small hole in the brick wall. "I'd say that worked!" Proclaimed Dr. Brewville.

CHAPTER THIRTEEN

THE FURY AND PASSION OF CONQUEST

Colonel Otis is in his office planning the imminent attack on the Harbingers when Heather burst through his door. She's wearing her black biker slacks and boots and her black bra with the badges of her defeated opponents on it. She closes the door behind her and eases up to the desk. "Heather! What are you here for?' Why are you dressed like that?"

She bends over seductively squeezing her breast between her arms, getting the maximum exposure of her cleavage, and looking him eye to eye. "Henry darling, we didn't get to finish and I was so looking forward to it."

She straightens up and twists back and forth to give him a view to remember. "Why do you ask? Don't you like it?" A sweet smile washes over her face and she starts to unfasten her bra." Oh I see, too much. I can take care of that," and she giggled.

Still seated, his empty hand shot up to stop her. "No! Wait! That's quite enough! What is it with you? What's the matter?"

She bends back over his desk nose to nose. "What's the matter with me? Why Henry, nothing's wrong? I'm perfect, unless you think there's something wrong." She leaned way forward and gave him a peck on the forehead. She was obviously under the control of the Harbingers. *The surgery must not have worked. And with her super speed and strength and his impaired condition, he was in trouble,* and he knew it. "Why there's nothing wrong with you. What could possibly be wrong with you? That wasn't what I meant."

"Good, I wouldn't want anything to be wrong, not this time." She studied his face closely, the black eyes seemed to fascinate her. "Do they hurt?" She asked, as she caressed his face. He winced at her touch. This surprised her. "Here, let me make it better." And she kissed one eye and then the other. He recoiled, grimacing in pain as she did. "Oh, that really doesn't work, does it?"

He backed even further away in his seat and pressed the intercomm button. She looked down at his hand on the button and shyly turned back to him cooing, "Oh, what's the matter? Am I interrupting something? The destruction of the Harbinger Hive perhaps. I'm afraid they won't be answering. There's no one to interrupt us this time."

He remembered his old trusty .45 in the desk drawer. She eased her hip on top of the desk and spun around. Before he could act, her long legs were blocking the drawers. "Now, where were we?" She slid off the desk and landed sideways across his lap. She wrapped her arm around his neck and kissed him. "No, that's not it," she said.

She sat there and bit her lip. "Something is wrong. I know! Too much clothes. Last time I had nothing on, well, almost, this time why don't we try it the other way first." He started to resist. She stood up facing him, grabbed his collar and ripped open his shirt. He'd grab one hand and she would simply bat it away. She ripped off his dogtags and tossed them, after giving them a quick examination. "Very unattractive. Stop squirming!"

She sat down on his legs facing him this time. He grabbed hold of her shoulders and pushed her back. She tore his T-shirt open as he did, exposing a large purple burise all over his stomach. "Did I do that?" She tweaked his cheek.

He pushed again and she wound up seated on the desk behind her. "GET AWAY FROM ME YOU CRAZY SADISTIC BITCH!"

"Oh, you shouldn't have called me that. You might hurt my feelings. Besides, it's not Heather who wants to see you suffer, it is The Hive." She leaned back and crossed her legs and folded her arms over her chest. She was in charge and she knew it.

He knew he couldn't resist her, she had beaten him and Dauntless to a pulp, he had to goad her into making a mistake. It was a dangerous game he had to play, and he knew it. "Just do whatever it was you came to do and be done with it!"

"That's exactly what I'm doing my dear Colonel. You see, the Harbinger have been hunted and exterminated across the galaxy. To have a truly superior body like this one is … refreshing, and I'm going to enjoy your destruction. I came here to finish what I had started. But where to start?"

She uncrossed her legs and leaned over grabbing both of his forearms and pinned them to the arms of his chair. Nose to nose she studied his face looking for the terror that was sure to be there. "Hmm, the last time we danced this dance, we tried nice first and I wound up beating the crap out of you as I remember. Let's try it the other way around this time. With me still doing the beating of course," she laughed.

He knocked her legs out from under her and she fell halfway to the floor before she caught herself. He lunged at her and landed on her stomach and started throwing punches. She managed to block every one. They locked hands with Henry on top. "Henry! You old dog you! I didn't think you had it in you."

She slowly started to push against him, he struggled mightily but was unable to stem the tide that was Heather. She rose up pushing him back until their positions had reversed with Heather on top. She savored her position for a few seconds as he struggled beneath her.

She got up and pulled him up with her. He bounced off of her body and winced in pain. "What a shame, to think that touching something as desirable as this body can cause you such pain." She knocked the breath out of him when she hit him in the stomach with her open hand, knocking him back against the filing cabinet.

He stayed there half doubled over breathing hard. She rubbed her tummy. "Oh, it's not that my body causes you pain, it's touching your body that causes the pain." An evil grin appeared on her face.

She started to caress is face and he fended her off, then she kneed him in the stomach. He doubled over holding his stomach and went down to his knees. She moved in and picked him up by his shoulders, pushing him up against the cabinet. "Too hard?"

Holding him up with her left hand she slapped his face and backhanded the other cheek. CRACK, CRACK! He was seeing stars. She released him to hit him with her other hand and he slumped over into her breast. She pushed him back up.

"We'll have none of that!" She detected some slight imperfection with her full alluring breast. She whipped something off her breast and smiled as she looked at her fingers. "Oh, you enjoyed that didn't you?" Then she noticed a trace of blood. There was a small cut on his right cheek, one of the badges on her bra had cut him. She grabbed hold of his head with both hands and jerked his face into her breasts and drug his face across her breasts back and forth as he tried to free himself. If this had been Brandy or Beverly he surely would have suffocated, but as it was he barely survived.

She slammed him back against the cabinet, both cheeks were badly cut and bleeding. She grabbed his right hand with her left and leaned into him putting her left elbow across his windpipe. As he struggled to push her off, she squeezed his cheek with her other hand causing the blood to gush out. He screamed in pain and she stopped. Leaning in, she opened her mouth and her long pointed tongue came out and playfully danced across his face. She licked up some of the blood as it flowed. "Umm, not bad, needs salt."

She punched him with her left and down he went. She grabbed his right arm and started to pull him back up when he punched her in the stomach. It had little effect, other then to inspire her next attack.

She lifted him up from the floor, and bent him face down over the desk and leaned down to whisper into his ear. "You still seek to resist. The Queen is loving this. Keep it up as long as you can and maybe, just maybe, the Queen will have pity on you and make you part of The Hive.

She stood up behind him and he started to get up but she forced him back down. Standing on one foot she put her right knee behind his left shoulder and with both hands pulled up on his arm dislocating his arm. POP! "AUGH!"

She whispers in his ear again, "You'll won't hit anyone else ever again with that arm."

She rose up to contemplate her next move. "What should I do next? Dislocate your other arm? Naw! Too easy and it's been done. Hmm, I could try breaking your legs, but no, that would make things too clumsy with you not being able to stand and all. You can still stand can't you?"

She backed up commanding him to, "stand up!" He pushed himself up with his one good arm and turned to face her. He had his .45 in his hand, she dodged as he brought it up. The old Colt went off, BLAM! The bullet tore through her and blew out her back with a spray of blood and tissue. She staggered back. There was a hole in her beautifully sculpted tummy. Blood was gushing out. She instinctively tried to stop the flow of blood with her hands.

He brought the old automatic up and fired again, putting one round square in her forehead. Her head snapped back and she fell back against the wall. Her eyes rolled up into her head and fluttered for a few seconds. He emptied the gun into her chest and abdomen. She slowly sank down out of sight behind the desk, with a shocked expression permanently frozen on her face. There was a splattered blood trail on the broken wall behind her.

He put the smoking gun down on the desk and supported himself on his one good arm inching over to examine his handiwork. He had never shot a girl before and certainly not someone he knew. She sat in a pool of her own blood and suddenly she started to convulse, her wounds closing. After a few seconds she opened her eyes and looked up at the Colonel.

She started to get to her feet and he tried to get out of the room. She grabbed him as he went by and threw him up and back against the wall. "You're not going anywhere. I'm not finished with you."

He scrambled to his feet and headed for the door again and she punched him, knocking him off of his feet. As he lay on the floor by her foot, she took notice of the blood covering her, took the T-shirt she had ripped off of him and used it to wipe off the blood. She tasted it. "Umm, I'm delicious. But then why wouldn't I be."

She shoved the desk out of her way with one hand as if it were nothing. She started to move in on him. "Do you know how much that hurts?" She got right up to his face. "It hurts a lot! I can't kill you. The Queen wants you alive. But when I'm done with you you're going to wish you were dead."

She pinned him back with her left and drew her right back and slammed it into his side, breaking some ribs. SKRACK! The pain raced through his body. She drew her fist back again and the door behind her burst open! Dauntless came rushing in. She grabbed Heather's outstretched arm and spun her around, only to receive the punch that was intended for the Colonel. WHAM! Right between the eyes.

Dauntless staggered back out the door she had just come in. Heather let go of Henry to pursue her new challenger. He sank to his knees as she did. A right upper cut sent Dauntless bouncing off the ceiling and crashing down on Tops desk. "You, I can kill!"

"You can try!" was Brandy's reply as she got up to meet her attacker. They grabbed hold of each other's shoulders and started scuffling around. "You may be faster that I am, but I'm stronger than you are," Dauntless said with confidence as she wrestled with Heather.

"Are you really?" Heather asked with a wicked grin on her face. She stepped back pulling Brandy along. She used the momentum to pick her up and swing her over her head and slammed her down on the floor behind her. FUMP!

She bent over grabbing Dauntless by her hair, just as a large book came flying through the air hitting her on the top of her head. She stopped and looked up to see Colonel Otis grabbing another book off the top of the cabinet.

She let Brandy go and stormed over to him swatting the book out of his hands and pinning him to the wall. She glared at him nose to nose. He coughed and stammered, "I, I never actually threw the book at anyone before."

"Well then, this is a day of firsts, and it might be the first time you die. Now be a good boy and wait your turn. I promise not to take long. She grabbed his head and kissed him hard, taking the wind right out of him. She backhanded him, knocking him back. He was seeing stars. She turned to face Brandy.

Dauntless was back on her feet in a fighting stance. "How'd you do that? Was that some sort of karate thing?"

Heather walked up to her not even bothering to take a defensive stance. "No, nothing so commmplicated as that. I'm stronger than you are."

"That can't be true!" Dauntless threw a punch with her right, which Heather caught in mid flight with her right hand.

Heather squeezed Brandy's fist, her hand started to tremble, there was a crunching sound. "AUGH! Dauntless called out. Heather forced her down on one knee. "Oh, it's true alright. He shot me and made me stronger." She laughed.

Still holding Dauntless' right hand, Heather slugged Brandy in the side of the head, with her left. BAM, BAM, BAM! Three times. Brandy was out on her feet, rather than her knees and started to slouch over, but Heather caught her and held her up with her right hand.

Heather took a position behind Dauntless and sort of stepped over her, winding up sitting on her shoulders with one leg on either side of her neck. Taking hold of her head with both hands she gave it a quick jerk to the side and SNAP! Dauntless fell to the floor dead.

Heather stood over her victim triumphantly with her hand on her hips. "Hmm, I heal because my body is superior to yours. You heal because of that jacket, we can't have that now, can we?"

She reached down and dragged Brandy's body over to the corner of the office. There was a fire station in the wall. She broke the glass with her elbow cutting herself. "OWW! Never mind, it will heal." She took the fire ax out of the station and with one swift swing, chopped her head off! Brandy's beautiful body jumped and laid there, spurting blood in torrents.

Heather held up the severed head of Dauntless and examined it for a few seconds. The color left her cheeks and her mouth dropped open, her eyes were closed. Heather thoughtlessly tossed it and the fire ax away. She walked over to a dead soldier lying on the floor, a victim of a previous encounter. She ripped a piece of his uniform off and used it to wipe her hands.

An *American soldier never gives up, never surrenders.* He went for the extra magazine for his gun in the desk drawer. He was having trouble getting it out with his one good arm. The desk was partially against the wall, preventing him from opening the drawer. Finally, he got the magazine out and was fumbling with exchanging it, when Heather returned to the office carrying Dauntless' uniform jacket.

She stopped and watched him. "You know, if I put this jacket on you I could beat the crap out of you every day."

She was a vision of beauty, with her golden locks and curvaceous body as she stood in the doorway. Seeing her in his doorway filled him with terror, for he knew she was the bringer of death.

The Harbinger of death wore black. Black heels and a black sports bra, with the badges of her fallen foes pinned onto it.

The Harbinger of death had a broad smile, pink lipstick and perfect skin.

The Harbinger of death didn't hide her head with a hooded robe, but allowed her golden locks to flow and preferred to allow her perfect skin and form to be seen.

The Harbinger of death was a vision of feminine beauty, with her button nose and sparkling eyes, her ample breasts and hips and shapely legs.

The Harbinger of death didn't ride a black steed or carry a scythe, she used wicked karate skills coupled with superhuman strength and speed to dispatch those who opposed her.

The Harbinger of death was a thing of beauty, in both form and motion.

The Harbinger of death stood six foot tall and was standing in his doorway. The Harbinger of death was Heather Carter and she had come for him. And Colonel Henry Otis knew it.

She saw that he still had use of his hand but couldn't move his arm. She shook her head. He got the magazine changed and spun to face her, as the slide snapped forward, only to have her slap the gun out of his hand using the jacket as a whip. The gun went flying across the room.

She rushed up and used her superior strength and speed to pin him against the wall, with him facing the wall. As he struggled to free himself, or turn around She used her body to hold him as she worked her left arm around and under his chin. She took hold of his right hand, with both of her hands and slowly, ever so slowly bent his fingers back one by one until they touched the back of his hand.

With each finger, a new wave of pain would ignite a frenzy of thrashing about with him trying to free himself. But she had superior strength and position and was able to subdue each episode of fury and keep him pinned against the wall. She didn't want him to pass out so she would pause between fingers. "That's the spirit! Only four fingers left." Pop! "Only three fingers left to go." And so on.

Once she had finished with the fingers of his right hand she spun him around again and pinched his cheeks causing the blood to gush again. He was a quivering mess, unable to control his left arm and his right hand made useless with his fingers dangling from it, tears streaming from his eyes.

She backed away to wipe the blood off of her shoulder. She reached over, pulled him away from the wall and propped him up on the desk. They stood nose-to-nose with him dead on his feet and virtually defenseless while she was smiling broadly and hadn't even broken a sweat. "Good try! The Queen is impressed, but let's see if you can withstand this." He closed his eyes and braced himself.

THUMP, THUMP! She drove her right knee deep into his stomach while holding him up with her left. He fell like a rag doll against her. She lifted his chin and held him up and delivered a haymaker to his nose. Blood gushed and he fell back on the desk. He was bleeding from his broken nose and cheeks and coughing up dark blood.

She unbuckled his belt buckle and jerked down his pants and underwear in one quick move. His cheek bones where broken and swollen, he could hardly see, but he could still hear her. "Time for part two, this is the part you're supposed to enjoy. Me too, but for some reason I don't think you're going to get as much out of it as you might like."

She lifted his body and repositioned him on the desk. "Since I haven't been able to deliver Marshal's seed to the Queen she has decided that she will make do with yours until his can be provided." There was a zipping sound and she was on top of him. His whole body was on fire. Just as the heavenly body known as Heather Carter started to rock back and forth above him, she started to fade away and everything went black.

After a few seconds she stopped and looked down at him, puzzled at first and then dejected. "He's passed out!" She angrily slammed her fist down on his bare chest, causing his entire body to flinch. He gasped and coughed up some blood and went limp.

Shock and fear were the expressions that swept across her face. "He's dying! OHMYGOD! OHMYGOD I've killed him." She commposed herself and checked his neck for a pulse. He had one.

She looked around the office not knowing what to do. The Queen spoke to her in her head. "sssave him by ussssing the jacket of regeneration that Dauntlesssss wore. But before you put it on him, make his body bleed, that will hassten the jackestss functioning."

Heather, still perched on top of him, looked around the room looking for anything sharp to cut him with. *Where was that ax again?* Then a devilish grin came over her.

She made a fist with her right hand, but left her index finger pointing out. Using her left hand, she felt his abdomen. Her fingers lightly danced along his muscles from just below his navel up to his ribcage, finding the right spot just below where his ribs come together.

He was thin, his abdomen and chest were lightly muscled, not fat or powerful either. There was a tattoo of a pair of jump wings on his left chest. His stomach was all mottled, black and blue and purple from the battering he had been subjected to recently. His muscles quivered at her touch.

She shifted her weight and put her left hand on his chest to brace him. And then, slowly, ever so slowly, she lowered her finger to the right spot and took in a deep breath.

Suddenly, she drove her finger deep into his flesh! PLUNK! Her finger goes in all the way to her knuckle! He jumps and gasps, coughing up more blood! She could feel the warm mushy guts inside of him.

She turned her hand around, turning it palm down and curled up her finger making it into a hook. She paused before giving three mighty jerks. There was a ghastly ripping sound with each jerk. Each jerk of her hand is accommpanied by more jumping, more convulsions, and more blood. Her finger broke free at his navel and the skin snapped back down. His arms and legs flailed about without effect or control. She had split him, or rather tore him wide open, from his navel to his ribcage. There was blood spraying everywhere.

As grizzly and bloody as this may have seemed, she had been careful not to puncture any organs, If he didn't bleed to death, and if infection didn't get him, he just might make it.

As the blood continued to spread from the nearly gutted Colonel, she leaned back and wiped the blood off her hands and body. He had stopped flinching and his breathing was labored and shallow.

Using her super speed, they were both dressed in a matter of seconds. He was wearing the Dauntless jacket of regeneration while she was in her black sports bra and biker pants.

She scooped him off the desk and held him in her unbelievably powerful arms. His head flopped against her shoulder and blood from his mouth and facial wounds got on her shoulder and trickled down and around her breast. She looked at him in resignation, she was going to get blood on her.

A constant blast of fresh air awoke him, she was carrying him as she ran at nearly supersonic speeds, on her way to The Hive. His body was no longer on fire, but he was in a world of hurt.

He had lost a lot of blood and was fighting to remain conscious but she was moving very fast and things kind of turned into a blur. He passed out in her arms as they neared The Hive. She zoomed through the National Guard roadblocks, unchallenged, leaving some confused guardsmen behind in her wake.

The Harbinger Queen, in her rookery, is exuberant. "Victory, sweet victory!" Before her is a giant honeycommb filled with the larva of hundreds of Harbinger bugs waiting to be fertilized and hatched.

When he came to, he couldn't see, or it was dark, or both. He wasn't in Heather's arms any more. He felt better, stronger. It still hurt but it was bearable, but he still couldn't move, something was holding his arms and legs down, but he was not alone, he could detect movement around him, and hear a chattering sound, like a giant cicada. *This must be The Hive.*

The light came up a little and he could just make out two full moons trimmed in black hovering over him. *There was something magical about those moons. Was this a vision of their home world,* he thought. These magical spheres of delight swayed about and were joined by a third moon that was capped in gold. He smelled vanilla! It was Heather standing over him.

He was on an elevated platform, being held down by drone attendants. The lights came up brighter and he could feel the heat coming off of them. There is a vast crowd of warrior drones all around them, hundreds, maybe thousands of them, all with armor and strange weapons grafted into their bodies. They were there to see some sort of spectacle. He dreaded to think what role he might be playing in it.

Suddenly, the Harbinger Queen was standing at his head, She towered high above him. She waved to the throng and The Hive became very noisy, and just as suddenly, there was quiet. "He will give usss a troop of the most determined dronesss ever! We can amalgamate him into The Hive without the use of venom." The Queen turned and looked down at Heather and commanded, "fulfill your mission."

Heather sat down next to him on the platform. She still had her black outfit on. She was smiling seductively. He struggled and nearly broke free. She had to push him back down and the attendants improved their grip on him.

She gave her hair a flick to the side and reached behind her head and pulled the Harbinger bug off of her neck and allowed it to scurry down her arm and onto his body. She pulled his head up with both of her hands and the bug went around to the back of his neck and lashed him with its stinger, attaching itself to his neck just below the base of the skull. He jumped and kicked with his arms flailing about. She had to jump on top of him to hold him down. After a few seconds he was tranquil.

She started to get off of him and he asked, "Before you go, could you restore the use of my arms?" She looked down at him and shook her hair out of her face. "Sure. But you won't be using them much longer." She knelt down on him placing one knee across his chest, and with both hands wrenched his left arm back into its socket. His shoulder felt as if it was on fire and then a wave of relief passed over him. He held up his useless right hand and she set his fingers one by one back into place.

She eased over to his side and crossed her legs forming a figure four and pulled off her boots. She stood up with her back turned to him. He heard a zipping sound and Heather started to shimmy side to side easing her pants down past her full voluptuous hips. She had black lacy panties on underneath that just barely covered her. The crowd wanted more. She would not disappoint them.

She slid her thumbs under the top of her panties and with another shimmy, they slid down to her ankles. She bent down and stepped out of her panties and twirled them around her finger before letting them fly onto him. She slowly twirled around to give everyone a look. Two moons rarely looked any better. She was a true blond.

She looked at him with a sultry look on here face telling him he was in for the ride of his life. She started to remove the bra of many pins, but the Queen stopped her saying, "It wasn't necessary for her to remove it to fulfill her mission. His enjoyment wasn't a consideration."

Her expression turned to one of a pouting child. "But my Queen, it will enhance his performance if I do."

"Very well, remove it."

She looked down at Henry smiling broadly and gave him a wink. She unfastened the bra and eased her breasts out. She shrugged her shoulders, causing her boobs to jiggle. The crowd roared. Playfully, she held out the bra and draped it across his face. It smelled like vanilla.

She undid the flap of the Dauntless jacket and exposed his chest and ran her fingers along the muscles of his abdomen and chest. Her touch was electric.

His body didn't hurt anymore. He started to lose consciousness but was revived by something. It was Heather. She had swung her long leg over him and was seated on his knees. She bent over him and her long tongue cavorted along the length of his body, from his navel to his chin. Her breasts dragged against his body.

She spent extra time on his chest kissing and nipping at him. He was nearing ecstasy and the main event hadn't even really gotten started yet. There were a hundred voices in his head egging him on. In the background, he knew what they knew and they had his knowledge. There really was no resisting them. He was one of them, they were him. He didn't want to resist.

Heather's golden mane fell around his face and draped them both. She passionately kissed him long and hard. She pulled herself past his face and playfully battered his face with her breasts. He kissed and licked her as she did. His hands were trembling but he did not have the use of them. She slowly dragged her breast across his cheeks and back down.

He could feel the warm softness that was Heather, smell her perfume. All he could see was her lovely oval face, pink lips and sparkling eyes. Her golden locks that were draped down along both sides of his and her head shut out the rest of the world.

They both were rocking up and down swaying about. Her expression ran the full gambit, from determination to ecstasy and fulfillment and back to one of determination. Her rhythmic grinding and gyrations brought him into a state of rapture, He pressed his stomach against her and collapsed under her weight, spent, and breathing heavily.

She pushed herself up and studied her partner. She had more in store for him, much more. He was in pain? In her enthusiasm, she was crushing him with her super strength. She realized that he needed the jacket to keep up with her. She sat up and closed the jacket's flap and patted him on the chest.

"Is that it?' The Queen asked."

"No, there will be more." She slid her breasts up and down along his body stopping at his face to smother him in kisses. Before remounting, he was reenergized and aroused. She rode him as before with her body undulating in all directions. He sat up to join her and she playfully threw him back down and continued her gyrations. He was in Heaven and she not far away judging by the way she smiled with the nail of her little pinky finger between her teeth.

She descended upon him, again burying him in her hair and breasts. She was driving her body against his. She bit her lower lip and he just tightened every muscle in his face and body.

She stopped and looked pleased, rose up, flicked her hair back, turned her back on him and began rocking like an oil well. His head was rocking from side to side as she gained speed, finally, super speed! "AHHGH!" She stopped and arched her back to look around at him.

She turned to face him again and her gyrations only became more creative. Not once, not twice but three more times, he visited the state of rapture. With each visit more severe than the previous, more draining, requiring more time to recover. Time, Heather was not allowing for.

The jacket of regeneration he wore had bestowed upon him super human strength and stamina, as it would to anyone who wore it and was wounded. But it only lasted for so long and Heather could just keep on going. And she did. He rose in pain. He begged her to stop, that she was crushing him, but Heather granted him no relief. He fell exhausted and spent.

Heather was proving insatiable even though he had risen to the challenge over and over again. She was still aroused and not fully satisfied. As for him, it was all the coat. Not only healing wounds and replenishing him, it was also keeping him alive. His body would have failed and his heart surely would have given out.

His head is spinning when she gently, almost whimsically, stops and lies down on top of him pressing her body against his. She has a big happy smile on her face. She kisses him tenderly. He melts into her and she leaves him speechless. All he can see is Heather's perfect face. All he can feel is the weight of her body and the heat of her full breasts pressing against his chest, and her thighs crushing the life out of him. He thinks she's finally going to quit. "It's about time you quit." But one look in her eyes tells him he is wrong.

"Who's quitting? I was just giving you your just rewards for a job well done. Your unbelievable endurance must be a byproduct of the jacket. That was commmpletely unforeseen, but a most welcome benefit, don't you think? Would you like to be on top?"

"Are you kidding me? I'm dying here. If you're not careful, you're going to kill me right here, even with the jacket on!"

She kissed him on the mouth. "Well, actually, that is what we had originally planned, but now after this, I think I'll keep you alive as a pet. The Queen says it's alright with her."

"Your pet?"

She snuggled up against him with a contented smile. "I can beat you into a bloody pulp or have sex all day long with you, whichever I choose." He was part of The Hive but he didn't want to be beaten again.

He wanted to change the topic. "I can go one more time if you take it slower."

She turned to look directly into his eyes and with a flirty smile and kissed him again. "Are you sure you wouldn't prefer fast and rough?"

"I'll be dead in a minute."

She shifted around and rose up. "Go for it big boy," she playfully said. He was barely able to move his left arm as he tried to sit up to join her. His right hand still throbbed and was useless. She helped him up, burying his face in her cleavage and holding his head there for a while. She let him fall back down under her. She was not done frolicking yet, but he had met his limits even with the Dauntless jacket recharging him endlessly.

She settled in for another round but he could not answer the call. "The spirit is willing, but the flesh is weak." From then on, it was all Heather, as it had mostly been all along. She looked down at him knowingly and shook her head.

She reached down and pulled him up into her waiting body. The crowd roared as she covered his face with kisses. He was revived by this briefly and joked softly in her ear. "And here I had you down as some kind of a tease or a show pony."

She pulled her face away from his. "Huh?" she furrowed her brow, "A tease! How can you say that after your promotion party, and now this?"

"Just a bit, at first, that's what I thought."

"Oh, I'm going to tease you now for that!" She said and nipped at the tip of his nose.

""No! Please don't, I can't take anymore." She steadied his head with her arms, his mouth dropped open and she gave him a little tongue. She stopped and looked deep into his eyes while she held his head up with her hands on both sides of his head. She opened her mouth wide and forcefully clamped her mouth over his. She took his breath away. His eyes were closed, his neck would not support his head.

She slapped his face and he came too. "What was that other thing you called me?'

His head rolled about as he answered. "A show pony, it means you're all good looks and no stamina. Boy did I ever get that one wrong."

"You sure did." And she was determined to prove it.

Holding his limp body against hers, she wrapped her long shapely legs around his battered and spent body. She rolled back on her back, dragging him along for the ride. He flopped down on top of her, and actually bounced a little, but her breasts acted as shock absorbers. She tucked her feet in behind his hips and, using her long powerful legs, began to grind his pelvis into hers.

The crowd loved it, but it was pointless. He was dead to the world with nothing left to contribute. Truly out cold. And though she tried to revive him, there was no response.

She rolled back over putting herself back on top and used his body as a platform for her gyrations to be played out upon. As time passed, her gyrations grew more creative and more aggressive, but ultimately pointless. He was just an unresponsive prop for her to play with. The jacket may be able to keep him alive, but not this. It was never intended for this. She continued on for God knows how long.

The Queen stepped in and stopped Heather's gyrations. "We have better things to do with our time."

Heather slowly eased down on top of him breathing heavily, with beads of sweat running down her forehead and dancing along her breasts, dropping off and landing on him. Pushing her hair out of her eyes she said, "speak for yourself."

This drew a scornful look from the Queen.

"Just kidding!"

"Perhaps it is time for you to receive your armor," the Queen said as she bent down to look Heather in the eye.

"I will gladly accept any armor you see fit to install. But that will end my ability to influence the human males."

The Queen stroked Heather's hair with her great claw. "Perhaps I will leave you as you are for now." She raised Heather's chin with her human like hand. "But your pet needs to be made more suitable."

He is awakened by Heather's big toe tickling him under his chin. She is standing over him eating a piece of cake. "It's about time you got up." He is all balled up on the floor with no shirt. He throws the blanket off and finds his right hand is now a weapon. There is a twin edged pointed fork with a slot cut out of the middle to allow the .45 grafted into his hand to fire between the blades of the fork. He looks at it in amazement. It doesn't hurt a bit.

He looks for his shirt but can't find it. She explains that, "we didn't want the humans to find out you were part of The Hive and change their plans, so we put your shirt on one of the dead soldiers and let the humans find it. They think you're dead.

"If you can run around dressed like that I can too," he said.

She looked down at her exposed body and bosom. "It's one hell of a distraction to the enemy."

"That it is," he agreed.

He knows what she wants before she says it. She is still wearing the black sports bra, black pants and boots. She has added a pair of sunglasses that she currently has stuck back in her hair. "Come on, we need a plan," she sighs.

They sit on the edge of a giant beehive, but these aren't for bees. They accommodate six foot tall Harbingers; humans that have been converted into drones. "First we need to plan for the troops," he said.

"We already know what their plan of attack is thanks to you, and preparations are under way using overlapping fields of fire and other suggestions you made. But what about Marshal?" She said as she finished her piece of cake.

"You can't fight Marshal in a stand up fight, you'll lose."

'I beat him before," she retorted.

"Yes, but you got lucky that time he didn't hit you. You can't expect that to happen twice."

Then what would you have me do? The Queen still wants him taken alive."

"That poses a problem, but not an unsolvable one. Just don't let him hit you."

"That's not much of a plan."

"You're right, I have more. We do have one big advantage. We know where he is going. He is coming after the Queen, which means he will be coming here and we can prepare the ground to meet him. First, when you see him, go after him with a chain like you did the first time. He'll be ready for that, but he won't be ready for this."

They walked over to the center of the great workroom. There were overhead cranes on tracks, giant hooks to hang things from and move about, and huge steel buckets for carrying molten steel. Many tools of various sizes and description are scattered about. The floor had several inches of dirt and coke ash covering it. He kneels down and starts to sketch something out in the dirt. "And if this doesn't work, we should have at least three more traps ready for him," he added.

She stands over him and licks the frosting off of her fingers with her long tongue. "When do I eat?" he asked.

She looked down at him and says, "when we have Marshal." She played with his hair and leaves.

That evening, the commpound of The Hive is illuminated by great torches and bonfires. The air is alive with anticipation, all the warriors stand ready at their posts. All are straining to be the first to see the human enemy coming. They don't have to wait long. Heather and Otis are waiting in the rookery in the center of The Hive.

Smoke rounds go off in the courtyard around The Hive, soon the area is filled with brown smoke. The smoke obscures the movement of troops, but movement is detected by the lookouts above in the minarets. Power to the mill is cut. The only light comes from the fires. The air is thick with the smell of diesel and smoke.

A backup generator is fired up but the lights are kept off, to invite the enemy into the kill zone. The generators are providing 20,000 volts to the metal mesh covering different parts of the grounds. The troops are moving as before. A couple are shocked by the electricity but most are not. Closer they come with their weapons ready. They are holding their fire. All is just as expected. Several catapults throw cars overhead. The cars are trailing wire nets and cables.

As the wire nets settle down, the troops below are netted and entangled. The power is turned on and hundreds of troopers are fried!

A second wave of APCs rushes in, and after passing the nets disgorge their troops. Hundreds more soldiers come running out of the troop carriers. A flaming torch is hurled out at the approaching troops but falls short, or so it would seem.

The torch lands on the ground in front of the oncoming soldiers and the ground erupts in a firestorm! The ground had been saturated with gas and diesel fuel and now the soldiers were trapped in an ever-expanding inferno. The soldiers screamed in pain and agony!

Helicopter gun ships raced in. Blinded by all of the smoke, they fired blindly at the dome of The Hive. Some of the rockets hit home doing damage to the dome while other rockets would simply glance off and sail off harmlessly or hit something else.

A hail of arrows launched by ballista like weapons answered their fire. Again, the arrows trailed thin electrical wires and they fouled the rotors of the bird. The cables would tangle around the rotor drive shafts and they would cut themselves apart, bringing them down one by one.

Small arms fire erupts from all directions. Rounds start zinging overhead and bouncing off the steel walls. In the rookery, Heather was ready. Henry was on the elevated platform. She goes past some steel mesh and a coiled chain on the floor, and grabs a remote control box hanging from the ceiling and takes it over to him and says, "it's about time. Do me for luck." He is laying on the platform and leans over the edge to her and is face to face with her. She flinches as he jabs her in the stomach with his new weaponized right hand, puncturing her twice. He gives the blade a little twist before pulling it out.

"OWW! Why did you do that?" She asks as her wounds close and stop bleeding.

He smiles, "The twist was payback. The stick was for luck."

She wipes the blood off of her abdomen and smears it all over his face. "If, by luck, you mean added super strength to start the fight with, I'll take it. But you knew that already. Just you remember what they say about payback." He was starting to regret it already.

Marshal's voice rang out loud and clear. "What do they say about the repayment of a debt?"

Heather turned and casually strolled over to face him. She stops at an X drawn in the dirt in the center of the rookery. She puts her hands on her hips and gives him her warmest smile. She is rocking back and forth like a little girl, with her shoulders thrown back, her breasts springing up and to the front. There is no way anyone seeing her would confuse her with a little girl. It was quite distracting.

"I have come for the Queen," he said as he came closer to her.

"I defend the Queen," she said as she drifted over to a large chain with a cable attached to it on the floor.

He notices the steel mesh net on the ground and avoids it. She smiles a little smile as if something had happened to amuse her. "Heather, I do not desire to injure you. Stand aside and you will not be injured. You are the enemy, and injure you I will if it becomes necessary. Do not resist. I have been authorized the use of force."

She flexes her muscles. "It will be necessary, but it is you who will be injured, my friend. But not killed, the Queen still has plans for you," she announces confidently.

"And I, for her. Let me pass, so that we may commmpare plans," Marshal replies. Henry, who is unseen by Marshal, is watching from the platform ready to push the button on the remote control box.

"Never, I'm looking forward to adding your badge to my collection." She brushes off her right breast, from which the Presidential Medal Of Freedom dangles.

"You already have my medal. I guess it is time for me to reclaim it."

"You're welcome to try," she says as she shifts her weight, and pounded her fist into her hand.

The main event was starting, Henry Otis thought to himself.

"Use the chain!" Henry calls out from the platform.

She ducks down and picks up a loop of chain and starts swinging it about like a cowgirl with her lariat. She races up to her intended victim and entangles him in the chain. She starts to tighten it around his neck as before.

Marshal grabs the chain with both hands. She races off just as he rips the chains apart. Henry pushes the button. KAZAP! 20,000 volts of electricity course through Marshal's body. If he hadn't broken the chain he would have been all right.

He goes down to his hands and knees and shorts out the circuit. He mumbles something with his head hanging down. "IT DIDN'T WORK! YOU HAVE TO FINISH HIM OFF!" Henry calls out to Heather.

She races back to him and kicks him in the chin like a football player. WHAM! His head jerks back. She follows up with a right upper cut to the jaw followed by another left. WHAP, WHAP! She wound up and landed another right uppercut, POW! That knocked him back up to his feet.

He swung and she ducked down beneath it, going down on one knee. From a crouching position, she drove her right and left into his stomach. It was like punching a rock wall. She wasn't sure if it hurt her more that it did him, but she kept punching even while she was kneeling on both knees.

His fist came whistling down and she was only just able to lean back to avoid being driven into the floor like a nail. His fist came crashing down landing between her knees, cracking the concrete floor. BAMM!

She fell back away from the blue giant. She landed on her back with him standing bent over her. She pulled her knees up to her chest and lashed out with her feet! They both smashed into his face. Blue blood squirted out from his nose.

He went down onto his knees. Her feet just kept on going past his head. Marshal found himself with his head between her long powerful legs. She locked her feet together and started to squeeze his neck. "Enjoying the view?" She taunted him.

"I have fond memories of it, but if you must know, I've seen better," was his reply as she started to straighten up.

This only enraged her. She allowed herself to lean all the way back, her head touched the floor. The muscles in her abdomen tensed and her torso snapped up and she slammed both of her fists down on top of his unprotected head like a pile driver.

He reached for her hands, but she fended them off and grabbed hold of his head with both hands and yanked! She slid up his body until her pelvis was jammed under his chin. She improved her leg lock and squeezed even tighter. "I've got you now!" She said through gritted teeth.

The muscles in her abdomen drew tighter and tighter forming small valleys on either side of her tummy. Her clench was like steel, it drew her up over his head. She wrapped both arms around his head for added leverage and put her all into it. "AHHH! Why won't you go down?"

"You lack the necessary strength to subdue me."

"Do I really?" She strained every muscle in her body. The longer she strained the stronger she got. You could hear the scrunching sound like old saddle leather cracking. With all that force, you would think his head would pop off of his shoulders. It didn't.

Now Heather was strong and she would only get stronger as this went on and that was what she was counting on. But Marshal is really, really strong and like Heather, he too will only get stronger with a prolonged struggle.

Marshal was, by now, back up on his feet with Heathers thighs tightly clamped around his neck. He reached up taking hold of her thighs and pulled them apart! As he started to lift her she rolled and slipped out of his grasp. As she rolled away she knead him in the side of his head.

"DON'T GET SO CLOSE TO HIM! USE PLAN B!" Henry yelled out to her from the platform.

She landed on her feet and ducked as he swung wildly. VOOSH! There was a lot of power in those swings. She moved in and landed a right cross to his ribs and was sideswiped by his backhand on the rebound.

She went tumbling down. It was like being hit by a bus. On her knees, she managed to avoid being hit two more times before her head cleared. She scrambled back to her feet and backed away as he came on, advancing past a large B scratched in the dirt. She turned to Henry and shouted out, "HE'S IN POSITION!"

BLAM! Henry fired his gun, not at Marshal or Heather for that matter, but at the giant hook with quick release that hung over their heads. Hanging from the hook was several tons of loose steel girders. The shot hit the quick release and it snapped! The girders tumbled down on the unsuspecting alien.

He was hit by one, and then another and another until the entire load was scattered all over him. He was laying face down with several I-beams piled on top of him. Heather came over after the dust cleared and kicked his outstretched hand. There was no response. "I think we killed him!"

"No way! It would take a lot more than that. Even if it did, his jacket would only bring him back! Better check to make sure!" Henry called out from the relative safety of the elevated platform, his weaponized hand still smoking.

She knelt down over him and felt his neck, he was bleeding badly from the scalp. "He's out cold! Not dead!"

"QUICK! PLACE A DRONE ON HIM! Bring him into The Hive," the Queen commanded as she oversaw the action from the fourth floor balcony. A bug flew down to her and landed on Marshal's arm and tried to get to his neck but couldn't, his high collar was in the way.

Heather tried to peel the collar back but it just wouldn't work. The bug climbed back up on Heather's arm and perched on her shoulder. She stopped to consider her options. The sound of gunfire and explosions from outside interrupted her thoughts.

She tried to move one of the beams but it wouldn't budge. Heather stood there looking at him, scratching her head. "How am I supposed to get him out of there?"

The bug flew off. "Put your back into it!" The Queen commanded.

"Try using leverage," he added.

"HUH?"

"Use one of the girders as a pry bar to move the others," he explained.

She tried to lift the beam but couldn't. Her extra super strength was spent.

A shot rang out and a bullet smashed into and through her abdomen exiting her stomach, sending a spray of blood and tissue all over Marshal's unconscious body. "AUGH!" She went down on all fours. "OW! That hurt!" She angrily looks Henry's way.

"It looked like you needed a recharge."

She got up and was able to use the girder to move the beams piled up on Marshal's bloody mess of a body. "EEUUEE." As she started to tug on Marshal's arm and free him from under the pile, he started to come to. He lunged at her and she darted back.

He catches himself and starts to straighten up when Heather moves in to finish him off. There was an ear splitting SLAP! His head was about chest high to her when her foot came slamming into his chin. His head snapped back, and he was knocked back into the pile of girders knocking the remaining girders off of his legs. He went down on all fours again. He was seeing stars.

Standing before him with her feet wide apart, she wound up and swung from way back, landing a haymaker of a right uppercut. WHAM! His head snapped back and he fell back against the pile and recoiled only to slam into her oncoming left. That came up from ankle high, catching him on the jaw. He fell back against the pile and stayed there.

While he was still a little groggy, she landed three punches to his stomach with his back against the pile. The end result of her attack was to knock him back up to his feet. He swung wildly, WOOSH! She straight kicked him in the stomach.

"Don't let him hit you! Get out of there! You can't trade punches with him!" Henry hollered out to her.

Marshal grabbed one of the girders with one hand and swung it like a club, forcing Heather to back up. "This is futile, surrender, you can't win," he advised her.

"This isn't over yet!" She retorted, as she dodged the swinging girder.

There was another gunshot and a PATWANG! The girder went flying out of Marshal's hand as he swung it. Marshal grabbed his hand and shook it off, the bullet had hit the girder and sent a stinger up his arm.

Marshal looked and saw, "Colonel Otis! I am of mixed emotions, it gladdens me to see you are not dead, but you are now one of the enemy."

"I am no longer Colonel Otis. Now, I am Henry of The Hive."

Heather threw her hands up. "Can we get on with this? I'm starting to get hungry again."

"Use your super speed and hit him with this," Henry of The Hive called out to his impatient master. He struggled to drag a very large monkey wrench with his one hand to the edge of the platform and let it fall.

Heather zipped over and caught it with one hand. She raced around at a great speed too fast to see; she was only a blur. She only became visible when she hit Marshal with the wrench and it slowed her down. WHACK! His head whipped around, blood flew. So did the wrench. It went flying end over end and came down forty feet way.

Marshal stood there shaking off the effects of her first attack, when she recovered the wrench and repeated it to the other side of his head. WHACK! His head whipped the other way and he dropped to his knees, hands by his sides. He was bleeding profusely. CLANG! The wrench came down forty feet away in the other direction.

She stood before him in a fighting stance as he shook the effects of her attacks off. He started to draw his sidearm. Heather dashed and recovered the wayward wrench and used it to chop the gun out of Marshal's hand. TWANG! She followed up with a quick swing that connected with his chin. "Home run!"

She managed to hold on to the oversized plumber's tool. Marshal slouched back on his heels with his arms by his sides breathing heavily. He wiped the blood out of his eyes to see Heather standing before him raising the wrench over her head, with both hands like you would with an ax.

THUNK! She darted at him and nearly buried the wrench in the middle of his head. It wasn't her super strength that was doing all the damage. She was strong but not that strong, but her super speed was multiplying the force of her attacks a hundred times, maybe more.

Marshal fell to all fours with his head hanging low below his shoulders. She walked around him, savoring every moment of this. She was about to bring the mighty Marshal down again! She walked up along side of him coming up from his rear, threw her right leg over him and mounted him like a horse.

Raising the wrench over her head, she proceeded to bludgeon him repeatedly on the neck and shoulders. He collapsed under her assault, landing face first into the dirt. She sat on top of the toppled alien and flexed her right arm, making a muscle. "Who's not strong enough?" She held the bloody wrench triumphantly over her head.

"He isss mine," sayeth the Queen.

Standing astride the beaten Aurorian, she dropped the wrench next to his body and rolled him over. She removed the wing shaped badge he wore on his right chest and pinned it to her bra. She then shifted her attention to his gun belt and the flap on his uniform jacket. She worked to peel him out of the offending garment.

She couldn't help but come into close contact with his bare chest as she removed his coat. His massive muscles lay exposed. Her hand danced along his chiseled abdomen and chest. Soon these massive heavy muscles would be hers for the taking and take them she would. It was her duty for the Queen.

With his coat removed, she could smell his pheromones. They were starting to work on her but she was already in an aroused state. Her adrenalin was pumping. He was a bloody mess with several head wounds. She, in contrast, was unharmed.

The bug came down but was unable to attach itself to him. His skin was too thick. The Queen commanded to "bring him to the platform, and I ssshall possessss him mysssself."

Heather took an oily rag from a nearby pile of machinery and used it to wrap up Marshal's bleeding head. It wasn't a first aid measure, she knew he wouldn't need it, it was just that she didn't like the thought of getting all that blood on her.

After she finished, she picked his massive body up and carried him up to the Queen. She laid him down on the elevated platform where she had dominated Henry the day before. She noticed that the sounds of battle had faded away. They had won. The humans were commmpletely defeated.

The Queen joined them. "I desire him to be conscious when I take him"

Heather looked at Henry who shrugged and backed off the platform. She stepped across his body and sat down on him. She pulled his unconscious body into her and started to lick the blood off of his face. She playfully dragged her long pointed tongue over his face, lapping up the blood. It had a different tangy taste.

This revived him, and his eyes fluttered open to see Heather's sweet face. The Queen, standing several feet in back of him lashed her long thin whip-like tail around his neck. Heather leaned into him hugging him forcefully with both arms around his.

The Queen started to work her three-barbed stinger deep into his neck at the base of his skull. It was not a fast process. He could feel her boring into his body and then into his very consiousness. He tried to resist, but Heather was hugging him with all of her might.

He stopped struggling and had a shocked expression frozen on his face. The Queen released her tail and commanded Heather to, "collect from him what you can and deliver it to the larvae in the tank." And with that, the Queen withdrew her stinger, turned and left.

Marshal regained consciousness in time to see Heather removing her boots. She realized that he was awake and watching her. She took her time and slowly shimmied out of her pants and panties, giving him a private show. The way her tight round rump caught the light was almost magical. Unknown to Heather, he was only vaguely aware of what was going on, it seemed like some sort of fantasy to him. His head wounds had not had enough time to heal.

She twirled her panties around her finger and left them drop to the floor. She looked as though she was pleased with herself. Her flirtatious smile was back on her face. She removed his remaining clothing and eased herself down upon her willing partner. She slowly shimmied back and forth to settle in and went about the business of fulfilling her mission for the Queen.

Marshal's superhuman strength was not called for. What he needed most was his endurance. He was battered, unable to concentrate for long, and without his jacket, his injuries would heal more slowly. He was at a disadvantage. Without the uniform to sustain him, his injuries brought a repeat of yesterday's orgy, with Heather providing all the heroics.

The Queen turned to her army, commanding them," they are defeated! Make the necesssary preparations. Go forth and bring me all of the humansss! I need them to add to our army."

Later that night, a milky fluid is added to the warm water bath of the larvae and thousands of humans of all shapes and sized are hauled in to be made part of The Hive.

The next day, in the new courtyard of the ten story steel domed hive, thousands of armored warriors stand ready to go forth. In the front rank of warriors stood Marshal, Henry of The Hive and Heather, all with armor and strange edged weapons grafted into their bodies. Many of the warriors have captured military weaponry and helmets. With the ringing of a gong, they all turn and head out in search of more humans for The Hive.

Across town at Hero HQ, Dr. Cooly is on the phone with the President. "That's right Mister President. They must be stopped before they can swarm and take over another city.

Forty thousand feet above The Hive, an old B52 lumbers along. "Major, we have a valid go code." The mammoth plane slowly banks and opens its bombay doors. After leveling out for forty seconds, an oversized bomb falls away from the old bird. The bombay doors are closed and the B52 banks and heads home. "And may God forgive us."

Sixty five seconds later a second sun erupts on the city of Chicago's south side. An angry orange black mushroom cloud blooms and boils the city away. The shockwave fans out and everything goes black.

The ground is charred and everything is covered in ash, the ever-present breeze kicks dust devils. There is movement in the dust. A large blue bug with claws and a whiptail stinger and human like hands, emerges from the ruins of humanity.

CHAPTER FOURTEEN

RISE OF THE HARBINGER EMPIRE

The world had turned sideways, or he was lying on the floor. Heather was asking him, Colonel are you alright?" His vision cleared a bit. He could see the highly polished floor of the main hallway. Next he noticed a pair of women's non-military black boots, very stylish boots, he had seen before. In the boots where a pair of very shapely long legs topped by a short black skirt and light blue satin blouse. Heather was towering over him looking concerned.

She knelt down over him and he tried to fend her off. She scooped him up off the floor and carried him to the elevator. Terrified, he started to fight back. Her head snapped back when he punched her in the nose. She instinctively head butted him back. His head was spinning and they both had bloody noses. She said something but he wasn't sure what. She still had hold of him when he realized that he had his hand and was wearing his uniform and she was dressed. "What happened to you?" She asked.

"YOU HAPPENED TO ME!" He tried to get free but failed.

"ME!" Don't be silly." She looked at him as the elevator door closed. "Stay still, I might drop you." She struggled to hit the button, "Could you do it?" She asked.

"Where to?" He wasn't sure if he was dreaming or what.

"The Med. center, where else?" She said sarcastically. She was strong, she just stood there holding him in her arms. He was confused, something was wrong. He knew he couldn't resist her but what else could he do?

His face and body hurt. Finally the doors opened and she carried him over to the exam table and Dr. Cooly came rushing over. "What happened?"

"I don't know, I just found him on the floor in the main hallway, and I brought him here. He didn't seem to know what was going on when I found him. He attacked me."

Heather stood next to the good doctor as she started to examine him saying, "It's probably his concussion." His nose was bleeding and his face was badly swollen with two black eyes.

"Am I responsible for this?" Heather asked as Beverly worked.

"Not you, your body definitely, but it wasn't you at the controls," Beverly explained. She pointed out the blood on Heather's face and she wiped it off.

He started to get up saying something about operations. Beverly stopped him and pushed him back down gently. "You're not going anywhere Colonel. You're confined to bed rest." She turned to Heather and asked her to, "call the General and let him know Colonel Otis is on bed rest."

"No! I have to…" He started to get up again.

Dr. Cooly held him down and turned to Heather for help. "Help me hold him down!" Nurse Chapel came running up to assist. Beverly called out to Chapel, "SEDATION!"

Heather held him down. He couldn't get up. This seemed all too familiar to him. Chapel gave him the shot and he became calmer. "Let's get his boots and pants off, and he won't go anywhere," Dr. Cooly instructed them.

He lost consciousness and had no memory of the indignity of it all.

A short time later in General Solos office, doctor Cooly was in her customary white lab coat and hair up in a bun is talking with General Solo who was dressed in his BDUs. "I'm sorry General, but he cannot leave bed. He's suffered a concussion and is having hallucinations. He's also suffered two broken cheek bones and internal injuries. He can barely see, his face is so swollen. He's just in no condition to go anywhere. Dauntless and Superstar are good to go."

"But we have an operation going on tonight." He leaned forward to her.

"You'll just have to run it without him. He's sedated and will be out for some time," she explained as she shifted around in her seat.

Captain Reynolds offered his opinion. "Sir, we have the plan and personnel in place. The equipment has been tested. I have every confidence in Lt. Holmes, uh I mean, Dauntless' ability to pull this off."

The General turned to Dauntless sitting quietly in the corner. "What do you say?"

He looked back and forth as she answered. "We can do this, sir." She thought for a second or two and added, "if we don't, who will?"

He rapped his knuckles down on the big desk. "Very well, you're a go. Go out there and save humanity."

Doctor Cooly interrupted as the others got up to go. "Uh General, sir, I'd like to go along with them. I have a special protective lab coat I can wear and I would really like a chance to get a look at these aliens in their normal habitat."

He shook his head no. "Out of the question. Your work is too valuable to us to risk losing you to a stray bullet."

"But they may need my special knowledge." She wasn't giving up that easily.

"I said no, end of discussion," the General firmly replied.

Captain Reynolds spoke up, "Sir, we could rig some small video cameras on their uniforms and she could watch the video feed."

He looked at him. "Do it."

That evening in the Med Center, Heather in her Superstar uniform came in carrying the memory helmet. She meets Nurse Chapel in the hallway. "I'm here to see the Colonel, is he awake?"

"He's awake but a little groggy. I'm sure it would be okay for you to go in and see him, Just don't get him excited. He's in seventeen, in the hospital wing."

"Seventeen?" Heather asked, puzzled by the high number.

"We've had a few cases to take care of," Chapel replied and went on with her business.

She walks past the rooms full of soldiers, some of which, she, or at least her body, was responsible for putting there. Some of the soldiers see her and recoil at the sight of her, something she wasn't accustomed to, not at all. Quite the contrary to the usual reaction she had come to expect. *It wasn't me it was my body,* she tells herself. Coming to the room, she gently knocks before entering.

He is in bed; he looks to see who knocked and jumps when he sees her. Seeing her rekindles the visions both real and imagined of her. He starts to kick off the covers. He is visibly frightened by her, but she stops him. "Easy Colonel, I bring gifts," she said as she approached his bed. "Ooo, you look," she paused searching for the right words. "Does it hurt much?"

He recoils away from her, looking for anything he might be able to use as a weapon should she attack. "Only when I look at something," he answered, trying to buy time. "They tell me I have been hallucinating. I'm not sure what did and didn't happen. But I remember you and me. Uh."

"That was a dream," she smiled.

"It seemed pretty real to me," he snapped back at her.

"Well, it would wouldn't it?" She sat next to him on his bed.

He winced with pain and she recoiled from him not knowing what to do. "Oh sorry, I wasn't thinking." She put her hand on his chest to steady him.

He was starting to relax. "It's Okay."

"When I found you, you said that I had happened to you. What did you mean by that?" She smiled and watched his face for his reaction.

"Huh? I was delirious or maybe hallucinating about you and me."

"I guess that makes me the woman of your dreams," she teased him.

"Could be, but it was more like a nightmare, and you put me in the hospital. And that was no dream."

"That wasn't me," she answered turning away.

"It sure looked like you."

"It wasn't me. The Harbingers were in control of my body. They did it by proxy. Uh, sorry."

Dauntless came in carrying a pizza. He is ecstatic to see her. "I knew you'd like some good food," she said as she blew in.

He reaches out frantically to her and hugs her. The pizza winds up in Superstar's hands. "I'm so glad you're alive!"

She hugs him back, half confused. They had never been that close before. "That makes two of us."

He continues to hold her and explains, "I'm so relieved to see you're still alive. I thought Heather had chopped off your head."

She broke the embrace but remained close and explained. "She kicked my butt pretty good, but she never cut off my head."

He sat back in bed and looked back and forth at the two of them. Finally deciding on Heather he asked, "could you stick out your tongue?"

Both girls were taken by surprise by his request. They traded glances and she shrugged her shoulders and said, "sure." She leaned towards him and stuck it out in a childish manner. It was pink and rounded and not very big. He leaned forward to inspect it, sighing a sigh of relief and fell back against the pillows. The girls traded confused looks again.

He was excited. "Is there an operation going on tonight?" He asked.

"Yes, in a few hours we will put your plan into action," Dauntless replied.

He turned to Heather saying, "I remember planning it and you coming in and…"

"That never happened," she was quick to point out

"Good." He was relieved.

"That must have been some hallucination. You'll have to tell me about it some time," Brandy chimed in.

"Not a chance. What did you bring me?"

"Your favorite, thin crust sausage and cheese with onions," Brandy answered, as she turned around opening the pizza box.

And Heather added, "I figured you would get bored just sitting here so I brought you the memory helmet. I figured you could use it to find out about our big blue friend while you were in here."

He took the helmet from her saying, "could be interesting."

Heather got up. "We have to be going. Why they want me there so early I'll never understand."

"It's a mission thing. When you're in the Army you learn about this stuff. Go, I'll be fine."

She bent over and gave him a peck on the forehead. This sent a cold shiver running down his spine. Brandy similarly kissed him and they left. As their footsteps faded down the hall, he pulled up his hospital gown and checked his stomach. It was badly bruised and all gnarl'y and purple but there were no scars. He was able to put his fears behind him.

As the girls walked down the hall, Superstar turned to Dauntless. "I think the Colonel may have a kinky side to him."

"No way! But there is something I've wanted to ask you. What really happened the night he got promoted?" They kept on walking to the elevator speaking in low tones. As they reached the elevator, they both broke out laughing and got on the elevator.

Doctor Cooly sees him checking his stomach and comes in to check on him.

"You look relieved."

He turns to face her. "I am. I'm still not sure what happened and what didn't, but seeing the two of them normal, well, that took a great load off my mind."

She sat down on the foot of his bed. "That must have been some hell of a hallucination you had. Why don't you tell me about it and I can tell you what really happened and what didn't."

As tempting a proposition as it was to be spending time with the lovely and talented Dr. Cooly, he wasn't too sure about telling her about his dream of domination and failure, especially being dominated by a girl under his command like that. They spoke of other things and ate some pizza, which he only briefly kept down spoiling their little party. After getting him cleaned up she had to go. She assured him that they would speak of this later when he was feeling better. She left him with Heather's gift.

He fiddled with the helmet for a few seconds before deciding to put it on.

Let's see if I can find out how that western ended. He pulls the helmet over his head and closes the visor. After several attempts, he realizes that *MaCos Ex hasn't had time to fix it. I wonder what else is on?* Hmm, he got to thinking about his being dominated by Heather. *Has Marshal ever been dominated by a beautiful girl like I was in my dream?*

The scene starts to change, "Hey, I'm picking up something!" A much younger looking Marshal was walking down a busy alien street. He is a good hundred pounds lighter and not in his customary uniform. Instead, he wears flowing red robes trimmed in gold, and a Roman like breastplate with some ornate carvings and reliefs on it. By his side hangs a long thin saber.

There is live music in the background and urns burning sweet incense. He towers above all of the other aliens on the street. The smaller aliens clear a path for him as he walks among them. He goes past the tempura vendor and enters a tavern in the middle of the block.

Inside there are about a dozen people, all human-like, more or less. He immediately notices a tall, very tall, female with four other lesser aliens seated at a table having drinks.

She is as tall as he is, and definitely female. Even three layers of clothing could not hide that fact. Drawn to her, he keeps watching her until he catches a glimpse of her veiled face. He recognizes her at once as the Thugee assassin he stopped from kidnapping the Princess Kara.

She sees the look of recognition in his eyes and comes over to him at the bar. She lets her hood and veil down to expose her face and flaming red hair and green eyes with no pupils. She parks it on a tall stool. "So, you have found me. Finding me is one thing, taking me in is another."

He put his golden fizzy drink down. "Found you? I didn't even know you were lost? But now that you bring it up, why aren't you in jail?"

She turned around on her stool to her friends and motioned for them to stay put. They remained at the table speaking among themselves, but he was keeping a watchful eye on her and the big blue Ess Sea Ay knight.

She turned back to face him and took a drink from his glass and asked, "Would you believe they let me go?"

He shook his head. "No, you were caught trying to kidnap the Princess. I'm surprised you're still alive. You must have escaped."

"There isn't a prison that can hold me," she boasted. She put his glass down on the bar, and looking him straight in the eye, asked, "what are we going to do?"

He tilted his head. "Do?" He asked with a puzzled look on his face.

She leaned back on one elbow on the bar and her robes fell open exposing her massive purple breast in a deep cut blouse underneath. She just paused there and let the image of her full voluptuous cleavage sear its image into his head. She was counting on it distracting him should it become necessary. "We can fight in here or go outside. Knives or fists, I have no sidearm. Makes no difference to me."

"No side arms, I left mine in the armory. I'm off duty."

"But you retain your saber," she gestured to the weapon on his side.

He looked to his hip, and back up at her. "I'm a Knight of the Ess Sea Ay, I am required to be armed," he explained.

"Well, if you're off duty, perhaps we can come to an understanding." She leaned forward on her elbow and gave him a sly smile.

He was having none of it. "An understanding? You tried to kill me and kidnap the Princess. And you nearly succeeded. I have no police powers but I must turn you in to the authorities." He started to reach for her arm, but she pulled it away before he could take it.

She stood up and breathed deeply, bringing her breast into play again. "I'll not go quietly. I'll kill you and anyone who tries to take me."

Still on the bar stool, he leaned back on the bar and retorted, "I would stop you."

"Perhaps, perhaps not. Look, we are obviously meant to fight; it is our fate. But we don't have to do it here and risk hurting innocent people." She motioned to all of the other people in the tavern as she spoke. And then back to him. "And since you are the challenged one, you get to pick the time, place and weapons."

He cocked his head to one side and straightened up on the stool. "Challenged one? What are you talking about?"

She explained, "You are the only man to have ever bested me in combat. You also caused my capture, and worse yet, it is your fault that I failed my mission. It is a matter of honor with us Thugee that we must reclaim our honor once it is lost. I must reclaim it by defeating you, or I can never work again as a Thugee assassin."

He stood up shaking his head. "This is nonsense, you're never going to work as an assassin again and you are going with me and that's it."

She shook her head and put her hands on her hips and got in his face. "You're not listening, I won't go quietly so you'll have to find a way to take me in. All I'm asking is that we do it honorably."

He paused to ponder her last statement. "Let me get this straight, you want me to pick the time and place we fight?'

"Yes, and the weapons to be used as well," she added, and sat back down on her stool. The rest of the people in the tavern were becoming aware of the pending altercation.

"What if I said here and now with our fists, no weapons?" He folded his arms across his chest.

"I would say, that's agreeable with me. I see no reason to kill you if I can reclaim my honor. Let's go out back to settle this, here and now." She slid off of her stool showing quite a bit of leg and a glint of metal as she did.

"That's good, because it really doesn't matter what you agree to, you're going with me. Right now." He took hold of her forearm

"That is, if you win. But if I win I go free." She tried to pull her arm back but he retained his hold.

"As I see it, the loser won't have a lot to say about it, either way."

"Very perceptive of you. Shall we have one more before we start?"

"No, I'm not going to give you a chance to drug me again." Holding her arm he moved her away from the bar.

"Shall we go?' She asked.

"Ladies first." He jerked her into motion and let go of her arm.

"But of course, we will observe all of the formalities," she said as she walked in front of him rubbing her forearm.

They left the tavern together and she guided him around to a little side alley to the back of the tavern, which was enclosed by brick walls on all sides with the alley being the only way in or out. She motioned to the walls. We can settle this here, without the chance of outside interference.

He took off his cloak and placed it on top of a barrel in the corner. She turned to face him. "Since you specified no weapons, care to remove your saber?"

He put his hand over the hilt of the sword and said, "No, it stays on, just in case. I can defeat you without the use of it," he said with confidence. He was expecting her friends to intervene at any time but he wasn't concerned. He felt certain that he could take them all. He had never been beaten fighting without weapons.

"Very well." She sighed as she took off her hooded cloak and outside robe revealing a deeply cut dress with slits up the sides and short sleeves with wide openings. There was a sash wound around her waist which she unwound, revealing a metal linked belt around her tiny waist. From the belt hung a short sword. She unbuckled her belt and leaned it against the doorframe of the tavern's back door. She returned to the center of the courtyard and threw her hand up.

She wore high boots, bracelets on both arms and a large silver ring. She sashayed about a bit to loosen her flowing dress which now fit her loosely. "Shall we begin?"

"Is that it?" He asked pointing to her hip.

"This is a duel of honor, you may frisk me if you wish." And she held her arms out to invite him to do so. She was supremely confident. She had never been beaten before and he wasn't going to be the first. He had only beaten her because she couldn't break his death grip he had gotten on her just as she killed, or rather, almost killed him.

The thought of frisking her had not ocured to him but the idea seem to appeal to him. *Was it possible that she too had pheromones that affected the opposite sex?* He steped up to her and placed his hands around her tiny waist. The first thing he noticed was the curve of her hip. "Nothing there."

His hands worked their way around her hips. They were full, round and firm to the touch. She smirked and asked, "find anything you like or are you trying to guess my weight?"

He glanced into her eyes and said nothing. He worked down her long powerful thighs. At the mid-thigh boot top he found a dagger tucked in her boot.

She reached down and took it out, flipped it over catching it in mid-air by its point and in a single motion tossed it into the tavern's doorframe. It landed with a, thwang! "Sorry, forgot." She smirked again and draped her arms across his shoulders, putting them nose-to-nose. She was relishing his discommfort at her closeness.

This startled him at first, but seeing she wasn't trying anything he tried to ignore her smiling face. "Any more?" He asked as he continued down her legs. This brought his face uncommfortably close to her breast. He straightened up not finding any more weapons. She was counting on her physicality putting him off his game. It was.

She was standing quite close to him. 'Better check them, you never know, I could hide a lot under there." She was counting on making him even more uncommfortable.

He took a long look at her bosom. It was massive and perfectly shaped and proportional. There was a five-inch overhang where she certainly could hide several weapons. Each breast was the size of the largest melon, full, ripe and sumptuous, but free of foreign objects.

As he was examining her breast for hidden weapons of mass destruction, she undid the straps on his breastplate and opened the secret commmpartment in her ring revealing a small pill inside. She took the pill in her hand and popped it in her mouth. This motion pulled him into her breast. He bounced off and looked around. Not seeing anything, he returned to the search.

He was unable to reach around her, her breasts were just too big to reach around. She was never going to die of drowning, that much was for sure. She had a built in flotation device.

She turned around to offer him her back. It was clean and bare. Turning back to him she asked, "what about your armor?"

"It stays on," he replied.

"That's not very fair. Here I am letting you feel me up and you're going to wear that impenetrable breastplate. It's not fair." She pouted, to no effect.

"That may be true, but it stays on until you can take it off." He was expecting to be jumped by her friends at any moment and he saw no use making things easier for them.

She took a step closer to him and tapped on his chest piece. "As you say." She grabbed the top edge of the piece of armor and gave it a quick yank. And off it came! She tore his shirt wide open at the same time, exposing his powerful chest. He stood there surprised, not quite knowing what was coming off. She just admired the view for a few seconds.

The breastplate fell to the ground. She recovered it and swatted Marshal across the face with it. WHAM! "Fight's on!" He staggered back and assumed a fighting stance. She tossed the breastplate over by the barrels.

She was dancing about on her toes while Marshal was more flatfooted. They danced around looking for an opening. Her bouncing breasts proved their worth. He couldn't help but admire her spunk. She saw the first opening and took it. She threw a left jab that connected with his chin doing no damage. Some more dancing ensued, BAP, BAP! Two more punches in rapid succession also without apparent effect. "You don't stand a chance," he said.

Then she noticed that he was bleeding from the cheek. Her ring had cut his cheek. Nothing serious but still, it was his blood! She threw a left which he blocked, and she followed up with a knee to his stomach, which knocked him back a little. As he fell back, he brushed against her breast with his bleeding cheek.

Still bouncing around on her toes she noticed his blood on her breast and stopped to wipe it off with her fingers. "If I can't win, how come you're the one bleeding? He had noticed his blood on her but hadn't felt the cut.

Using her long shapely leg, she swept his legs out from under him. He went down landing on his right side. He was starting to get up when she leapt on him and landed straddling his left side. She latched her powerful legs around his midsection and squeezed. She had used this move many times before and her victims usually didn't last long. The commbination of her punching and squeezing the fight right out of them was a potent one. She had a good hold on him. Like a constricter snake, every time he took a breath, she tightened her grip a little more. Her thighs were clamped tight against his stomach and back. She could feel the rippling muscles of his stomach working against her inner thigh. It felt good, but something was wrong. He wasn't weakening.

He was trying to defend himself with his left and get up with his right. She grabbed his left and held it out of the way more or less and pounded his head and face with her right.

He collapsed under the relentless attack and rolled over on his back. She landed a couple more good punches to his jaw, cutting his lip. He was unable to strike back, her breasts were in the way. He tried pushing them out of the way, but they just sprang back. She was dominating the fight, but wasn't doing much real damage. She needed to do something more. She raised both of her hands up over her head and slammed them down landing on his nose. Blue blood spurted out, and he reacted to that. "That one hurt didn't it?" She quipped, as she wiped the blood from her hands onto her dress top.

While she was readying to slam him again, he grabbed her by her waist and threw her off, sending her crashing into the barrels. This knocked the wind out of her. They both took their time getting up. He took his ripped shirt off and threw it to the ground. He was now bleeding from his lip, cheek and nose.

Her friends came running down the alley, but she told them to "stay out of this! I can take him." They backed up, and settled in to watch and place some bets on the outcome.

The two combatants circled one another with her still bouncing on her toes and him holding the middle ground. She leapt up and kicked straight through his guard. Her heel landed square on his face. The force of the kick knocked him back against the tavern wall.

With his back against the wall, she moved in driving her left into his stomach. Boom! She followed with a right uppercut that landed in his unprotected breadbasket. "Oomph!" His right came out of nowhere, WACK! And snapped her head around she went tumbling to the ground and rolled away from him. She was seeing stars.

He allowed her to get up, part out of chivalry, part out of the need to breathe. Now she was the one doing the bleeding from the corner of her mouth. She wiped the blood away with the back of her hand and said, "damn you're strong!" She started circling him again.

"Let's see just how strong you are," she said as she offered her hands to him to take. They interlocked fingers and started pushing against one another. The muscles in their arms, backs and legs strained with the effort. It was obvious he had much more strength than she did. This she found unnerving, especially seeing that he was about to force her down to her knees.

Suddenly, she stopped pushing against him, and pulled him over her as he pushed. She rolled back onto the ground, putting her foot in his stomach as he passed over her, to keep him going and not come crashing down on her. She kept rolling with the momentum and rolled over onto him, all in one move, "A classic reversal, and you fell for it!" She was now on top of him sitting on his stomach, clearly in the superior position. Only problem was, he still had hold of her hands and she could do nothing. "Let go of me!"

She tried to gain an advantage, but he was too strong. He pushed his arms straight out and started to sit up still holding on to her hands, their fingers intertwined. As he came up, he pushed her arms back and out and as a result wound up with his face buried in her cleavage. This caught both of them by surprise but it didn't stay that way long. He continued to push her back and up.

She was being pushed back and on to her feet before he was. While he was still on one knee, she drove her powerful leg into his chest as he was about to get up. This staggered him a little and caused him to fall back to both of his knees.

He rested his head against her tummy with her navel at his eye level. It made a wonderful pillow. With him on his knees pushing her back and still holding her hands, she backed as far away as she could and drove her knee up into his jaw catching him under the chin. His head snapped back and rested against her thigh for a few seconds, wondering, *what had happened to that wonderful pillow he had?* This gave her time to wind up and drive her knee into his jaw, again and again. He fell back letting go of her hands. He flopped on his back. "UGH!" He lay there exposed and vulnerable.

She took a couple steps back and taunted him. "Didn't like that! Did you?"

As he scrambled to his feet she rushed up, WOOMPH! and kicked him in the stomach, lifting him clean off the ground! He landed against the barrels. *Was she getting stronger or was he getting weaker?*

She knew the answer to the unasked question. She could feel the rush of adrenoloxlin coursing through her veins. The pill she secretly took while being searched was starting to take effect. The muscles in her arms started to budge. She had to slide her armbands down to her wrists. Her small tummy was now rippling with muscles, no longer a tempting pillow but a powerful six-pack. Her legs developed muscles on muscles. "Blue, you're in big trouble now!" One of the crowd members heckled.

He was using one of the barrels to lean against to get up as she wound up and threw a roundhouse punch that whipped his head around and sent him staggering back into the center of the courtyard. She picked up one of the barrels and hoisted it up over her head and slammed it down on him. CRASH! The barrel exploded as it hit Marshal, emptying its liquid contents all over the courtyard. "Careful! That's imported ale," one of the audience called out.

She reached down and picked up Marshal by his hair and held his head chest high readying to punch him with her other hand. He lunged at her and bounced off, as her punch landed home on the side of his head knocking him down. His hand caught her garment and ripped it clean open, exposing her abdomen and lower half of her breasts. Her breasts and muscular abdomen glistened with tiny beads of sweat

She put the boot to his stomach and he was in the fetal position on the ground. She grabbed a hand full of hair and lifted him up by it. Holding him up at full arms length, he dangled by his hair. She stopped to inspect her handiwork.

He flailed away at her but her arms were longer than his and he could only reach her breasts, which he wasn't interested in punching. She punched him twice in the face. BAP, BAP! He was bleeding more freely now. She stopped pounding him to wipe the beads of sweat off of her forehead. Big mistake. "You're going down Andorian!"

"FINISH HIM OFF CANDY!" One of her friends called out as he watched the fight unfolding.

He grabbed hold of her arm with a vice-like grip. She flinched in pain and grabbed his arm trying to do the same. She pushed him down to one knee and was going to kick him when he pushed back even stronger and regained his footing. They were locked in each other's arms. He pushed her back against the wall and jerked his right hand free.

She grabbed hold of his head and drove her knee into his face, SMACK! while she pushed his head down into the oncoming joint. Blood splattered in every direction. His left hand lost its hold on her arm, but she was not able to escape as his hand had only slid over and was now trapped between her breasts, caught in her cleavage. This distracted her and prevented her from taking the evasive action she should have.

His right fist came sailing in, impacting on the left side of her jaw, BABAM! driving her head through the brick wall. Fight over.

She crumpled to her knees and fell against his body, with her bloody face landing against his stomach. He took a step back and she slumped over onto the ground. He stood over her soaking wet and bleeding from the nose mouth and cheek. He looked over to the men in the crowd. "Why did you call her Candy? Her name is Shelk."

"We call her that because of her sweet and sunny disposition."

Marshal turned to pick her up and there was a stinging pain in his neck. He pulled out a dart, and slumped over and fell on top of her. He had his wonderful pillow back.

A short time later, she was standing over his body, talking with her four friends from the bar. "Maybe I can reclaim my honor by kidnapping the Princess now that he's out of the picture."

"She's married and off world, on her honeymoon."

"What are we going to do with him?" One of the other men asked.

"I say kill him." Yet another voice from the peanut gallery threw it's two cents worth in.

"We're not killing anyone, He's one tough customer, and that makes him valuable. I think we can make some money out of this," she advised them as she leaned on top of one of her friend's heads. Everything gets fuzzy and goes black.

Colonel Otis pulls the helmet off, and looks around. He is in his hospital bed. "Where is everybody?"

Dr. Cooly comes in carrying a tray with some hospital food and drink. She puts it down next to the bed. "Do you know what time it is? I have to be going! Where are my clothes?"

She takes a styrofoam cup of water and gives it to him with some pills. "Here, take these."

He suspiciously eyeballs the pills. "What's this for?" He asked.

"It'll calm your stomach and help your headache."

He took the pills and gulped the water and suddenly sat up in bed at attention and slumped over in his bed. "And knock you out so we don't have to worry about you during the mission," she added as she dusted off her hands and turned to leave, smiling a cute little smile of satisfaction.

At that time downstairs, the scene is one of organized chaos, with soldiers standing in rows checking their equipment and making final preparations. Everyone is armed with a shotgun of some kind. Dauntless runs into Dr. Cooly, "what are you doing here Dr. Cooly?"

"I'm going on the mission with you. They decided that having a forward area science and Med. center was a good idea. I won't actually be going in with you but, I'll be nearby if I'm needed."

"Good for you! Have you seen Sergeant Lopez? He has my rocket pack." The Doctor shakes her head no and Brandy goes off in search of her rocket pack. Beverly turns and sees Dr. Brewville in a mechanical armored suit carrying a street sweeper shotgun.

"What are you doing in that get up?" She asked. He clanks over to her and points to his back.

"Excuse me, would you be so kind as to connect my power relay in back. I don't seem to be able to reach it." He turns and she finds the wayward connectors and snaps them together.

"Don't tell me you're going in this getup."

"It should provide more than adequate protection. Colonel Otis has a brilliant plan, but I was thinking if the first two diversions didn't work they would never be expecting a third attack. I'll just walk in and take the Queen down with my trusty shotgun."

She looks at his weapon. It looks like an old time Tommy gun on steroids. "That's a shotgun?"

"It's basically a light machine gun made to fire 12 gauge shot. There are 40 rounds in the drum magazine and I have an extra one if I need it. He sees some soldier waving to him and he takes off, leaving her standing among all the commotion. "That's my ride!"

Captain Reynolds finds her and directs her to the roof. You're flying out on Hero One. After the drop, they'll take you to the RP. You can set up your gear there. Gottago! He dashed off.

She was standing there befuddled. "What gear?" She pulls her lab coat closed and heads for the elevator.

Shortly after sunset, three Army Black Hawk helicopters take off from the HERO building and head south. They are quickly overtaken and escorted by three Apache gun ships.

In the back of one of the choppers, Beverly is seated with Marshal and Superstar. She is speaking with General Solo through a headset. "General, why did we wait until sundown to go. It's going to be hard to see anything by the time we get there.

The General's voice came in loud and clear. "You're responsible for deciding when we go in doctor."

"Me responsible, how?"

"It's the time the bugs would be less active and their human drones will be less effective. We thought about going at dawn but decided against it."

"But won't they hear the choppers coming?"

"They would if the choppers were going in."

"IP two minutes," the pilot announced, and they went to red light.

The crew chief opens the door and there is a gust of fresh air. The noise level goes way up. They are flying along the south side's lakeshore at an altitude of 1000 feet. He goes over to Superstar and yells into her ear, "remember, steer 210.

Heather takes the harness she is wearing and hooks it up to another harness on Marshal. She gives him a peck on the cheek, "For good luck," she explains and he looks at her. She steps in front of him and he moves up close to her. She turns and faces him and hugs him. He wraps his arms around her holding the edges of his cape.

A small light by the door turns green and Marshal jumps out carrying Superstar with him. They fall clear of the chopper in a second. The rush of cold air hits them, it feels good. He unfurls his arms and with the push of a button, his cape magically turns into a pair of wings. They are gliding over lake Calumet. Superstar checks the commpass and points off in the direction of 210 degrees. In the distance a great onion shaped dome of steel and concrete stands out. There are bonfires all around it.

Superstar, hanging underneath Marshal, decides to improve her position by wrapping her long legs around his body. She accidentally kicks the wing and they are knocked for a loop before Marshal can take corrective measures. "Please Heather, now is not the time."

"OHMYGOD, OHMYGOD! I thought we were going to die. Do it again!"

Several miles to the north, over 100 stories up on the observation platform on top of the Hancock building, there is a bright orange flash and a yellow streak flies off headed south. It's Dauntless with her rocket pack.

She effortlessly zipped along at over 400 mph. She could see the chopper up ahead and she was closing in on them fast. Besides her rocket pack and usual utility belt full of gadgets, she had a bandolier of 12 gauge shot gun shells for her autoloader she had been supplied with. With a simple turn of her head she could weave her way across the sky. As she started to get close, she eased off the power making less noise.

No need to be too obvious about this.

Marshal and Superstar sailed effortlessly, and, more importantly, silently, over the fence that surrounded the old steel mill. There was no movement as they came in for landing. Heather's foot was caught in the fabric of the wing and it caused their landing to be less than what they had hoped for.

They came tumbling in end over end and crashed into a pile of car parts. He instinctively did his best to shield her from injury, something he didn't have to do. She would heal much quicker than he would and she would benefit from the added boost in her super strength.

They came to a stop with her lying on top of him with his arms wrapped around her. This seemed strangely familiar to both of them. "Was it good for you?" She asked.

He didn't get her little joke and they got up and looked around. No one saw them. She used her comm link to report, "Hero One down, no contact. Superstar pulled her shotgun off of her back and told Marshal, "I'll go see if the Queen is in the rookery. If she is, I'll take her down. You follow as best you can."

They started to go but had to duck behind some sheet metal as four guards ran by. She turned back to him, looks like Dauntless is on the job."

On the other side of The Hive commmpound, Dauntless was having landing problems of her own. On final approach, she killed her power and flared to land and flew right smack dab into some high-tension wires. The wires wrapped around her feet and halted her landing. She didn't actually crash; you have to actually to hit the surface to have a crash. She was just sort of dangling head down three feet off the ground.

The noise of the wires pulling out had alerted the guards who were rushing in from all corners of the commmpound. It was basically her mission to draw off the guards. She just wasn't supposed to get caught in the first ten seconds.

Inside the darkened Hive there was a gust of wind and a blur by the bonfires. Superstar was racing about looking for the Queen and not having any luck. She stopped to report, "The Queen has moved, start search and destroy."

Marshal moves into the building. As he goes in, a giant steel skeleton comes to life and grabs the sheet metal they had just been using for cover and started slapping it onto the sides of the mechanical skeleton, transforming it into a thirty foot tall warbot.

With a mechanical whirring sound, it started to stomp its way in the building but suddenly stopped and turned back to the perimeter. The outside fence exploded with demolition charges and several armored fighting vehicles came roaring in. The heavy weapons mounted on top of the vehicles opened up on anything that moved. It sounded like a war zone. It was.

The warbot walked over to the first Bradley, picked it up with its huge mechanical forklift and slammed it down, while the Bradley's gunner poured hot 20mm into it. Parts went flying off but nothing vital had been hit. The warbot stomped over to the next armored vehicle. The commmbined fire of a mini gun and the chain gun on an Apache finally spelled the doom of the warbot.

A Mini Cooper went sailing through the air trailing lengths of chain behind it. The mini projectile slammed into the side of the gunship and it fell like a stone. There was a small flash when it hit the ground but no big explosion. Go figure.

All around the commmpound, giant warbots started to appear. They outnumbered the Army. As Bradley's and warbots tear about the commpound, nobody noticed a strange little mechanical man sneaking from pile to pile. A warbot came rushing by and knocked him down into a pool of gasoline.

Dr. Brewville struggled to get up, but he was stuck! Suddenly a drone with a torch confronted him. He was going to light the gas and cook himself one doctor.

A .50 sniper rifle went off 600 yards away and the drone was hit square in the chest and fell back away from the gas on the ground. Snipers had been posted all around The Hive ready to pick off anyone who went near the power generators or firetraps. The power had been cut the day before.

A worker drone is trying to attach his bug to Brandy's neck as she hangs upsidedown. She struggles greatly against the wires that bind her and she breaks free and falls the remaining three feet to the ground. She crashes after all, landing on her head. Two drones grab her and try to open the high collar of her jacket. They got her flap open and exposed her tee shirt beneath and went for her collar, but she smashed one of them with a vicious upper cut. The bug scurried up her arm intent on biting her. She grabbed it and threw it to the ground and crushed it under her boot.

The other drone punched her in the stomach with a rivet gun! She doubled over instantly and dropped down to both of her knees. She was holding her injured stomach with both hands. Blood was welling up in her hands. She remembered to close her jacket. He went to hit her again but she caught his arm coming in and stopped it. She wound up to finish him off when another bug bit her and she slowed to a halt.

From there on it was easy for them to open her collar and have the bug crawl up and sting her at the base of her skull. She was theirs, one of them. "Amalgamation commmplete." Seconds later they knew the human's plan.

Two warriors with tridents come rushing at Marshal who is near the rookery in the old foundry building. He catches the first one's fork and uses it to swing him around to knock the other warrior off his feet. Swish! Since the weapon is a part of his body, the warrior can't let go of the weapon. Marshal used it as a handle to smash him back and forth.

Five more come running at him from around the corner. He goes for the shotgun strapped across his back, but before he can bring it into play, he is knocked for a loop by a piece of flying steel. He slides 30 feet across the floor and comes to a stop at the wall.

Standing before him is a 30-foot tall warbot with a mechanical arm swinging a steel bar attached to some chain. FFP, FFP, FFP, was the sound it made as it swung through the air. While sitting there, he pumped his shotgun and let three rounds go into the onrushing drones. Three of them dropped instantly. A fourth staggered off before going down.

The warbot came in to finish the fallen alien. The steel bar came hurtling at Marshal; he used the shotgun to block it. SLAM! The gun broke in half! Marshal grabbed hold of the steel bar before the warbot could start swinging it again and ran under the bot and wrapped the chain around one of the legs. He moved over to another leg and kicked it out from under the mechanical beast. It toppled over. Marshal took hold of the leg and wrenched it out of the skeleton and used it as a great club, smashing the warbot repeatedly until it was just a pile of scrap once again.

A M60 machine gun opens up at close range. Marshal explodes with seven or eight hits. His blue blood goes flying everywhere. He takes one step and falls back.

The warrior walks up to survey the damage. "I regret to inform you that..." He started to report to the Queen but stopped when he noticed Marshal start to move. The deformed bullets fell from his body and he slowly got to his feet. A bug flew off of his assailant and landed on him and tried to sting him. But once again the collar was a problem. Marshal grabbed the bug and smashed it down on to the floor. SPLAT!

The warrior had a belt of 100 more rounds for the M60 and was planning on using them all on Marshal, but the gun jammed after firing just two more rounds which missed Marshal. The warrior started to clear the jam, but Marshal closed the distance before he could and Marshal sent him sailing across the room with one punch.

A pile of four warrior bodies testified to her presence as Superstar peers around the corner and observes the Queen wading in a hip deep tank of warm water. In the water are dozens, maybe hundreds of larvae. Heather realizes that the Queen has gotten bigger since she last saw her. She was now ten foot tall, maybe more.

She eased her shotgun up, but two guards rushed at her. She fired three times and they went down. The Queen was startled and backed off as Superstar turned her attention back to the queen.

She realized there was someone or something behind her. She figured she had better find out what it was before proceeding. She spun astound at super speed. It was Dauntless, her teammate. She let down her guard and turned back to the Queen. Big mistake! WHAM!

Heather was seeing stars and getting a good close look at the dirt on the floor. Dauntless grabbed hold of her collar and picked her up and threw her against the brick wall. Superstar slid down the wall as Dauntless walked up and jerked her up to her feet. Holding her up by her jacket top using only one hand, Brandy used her body to pin Heather against the wall. "You're super speed isn't going to do you any good this time." She smiled a wicked little smile that looked out of place on Brandy's pretty face. She normally looked so sweet and dare I say, innocent, it was quite a contrast from her norm.

Dauntless landed a right to Superstar's face, splitting her lip. "Oh, you're not so pretty any more. Let's see if I can fix that." She went to hit Heather two more times, but each time she stopped because she had squirmed away. Dauntless changed hands and Superstar tried to run away, but Dauntless had a good hold on her and she only succeeded in unzipping her jacket top. Her shoulder, breasts and forearm came spilling out of her top, which remained closed about her waist trapping her arm inside, ultimately prevented her from using her arms. Her bosom bounced and swayed back and forth, now contained only by a lacy black bra. This would have, without a doubt, distracted any man, but Brandy wasn't interested in the least.

Dauntless pounded Heather's face from the other side, relentlessly. Heather took the beating, jerking and flinching with every blow. She was bleeding from both sides of her mouth for a few seconds before they both closed up. Hmm. Not as satisfying as she had hoped but it would have to do. It wasn't important. Heather was out cold and Dauntless had hold of her. She folded Superstar over her arm like today's dry-cleaning and brushed her long wavy hair out of the way, exposing the base of her neck. Seconds later, a bug lands on her and stings her. One again, Heather Carter Superstar was part of The Hive. Really!

At the forward science and Med. center, Dr. Cooly has been watching the events of the last few minutes on the live feed video from the micro cameras in their badges. She may be the only one who knows what's happened and where to go! She has to act! She runs into Tex and gets him to take her to The Hive sight in his Humvee.

The Queen is still standing in what amounts to more or less a heated wading pool filled with the next generation of Harbingers. "You have done very well Brandy my dear, I think I will appoint you as my number two," the Queen said. As she turned to resume her work in the water, she realized the danger wasn't over.

Marshal was standing in the center of the room pointing his sidearm at the Queen. "You have the option of either surrendering and stopping any and all of your hive's activities or I am authorized to use lethal force. Either way, the choice is yours."

She was looking down the bore of the most formidable sidearm on the planet, a .75 caliber automatic plasma pistol with variable capacity. Dauntless and Superstar looked at each other and back at Marshal. Superstar started to move towards him and he cautions her. "Don't force me to shoot! Even you are not that fast."

The Harbingers know what each other knows when they concentrate on it, and the Queen and the two girls were definitely weighing their options. They came up with a plan. Superstar straightened up her uniform so her arms would be free when they would be called for. She heard from the Queen, and dashed as fast as she could straight at Marshal while the Queen ducked.

Marshal pulled the trigger and Superstar smashed into him at full speed. WHAP! They both went tumbling back. They slid back some 20 feet, with Superstar landing on top of him. She stretched out as far as she could in an effort to reach the weapon in his hand. She got both of her hands around his wrist and tried to slam his hand down to make him drop the gun. He was too strong for that.

They were both laid out struggling over the gun when a droplet of red and white striped plasma oozed forth out of the muzzle of the weapon and fell to the floor, plop! A hissing sound accommpanied by a small puff of smoke was all the weapon produced.

They both stopped and she came to a rest lying across his chest. They both just stared at the gun. They looked at each other nose to nose, he said, "I'm going to kill that Doctor Brewville"

She smiled and let go of his wrist and tweaked his nose. "That's right, but you're going to do it for The Hive." Using her super speed, she got off of him before he could get a hold of her.

Heather and Brandy stood side by said between him and their Queen. Superstar turned to Dauntless and asked, "how are we going to do this?"

Dauntless replied, we could gang up on him but what fun would that be? We can always resort to that if we need to. Why don't we try tag teaming him. I'll even let you go first. I want to see what you can do against him."

Heather smiled and wiped her hands on her thighs, Okay, but I warn you, you may not get a chance at him if I go first."

The Queen cautioned them, "remember, I want him alive and unvenomated."

"I guess you're on," Dauntless said as she walked over and leaned against a support pillar. Superstar casually strolled back to the center of the room contemplating her next attack. There were bits of chain and heavy cable scattered all over the place along with jagged pieces of scrap steel and many tools. Many would make effective weapons.

Marshal didn't want to fight them, not Heather, and especially not Brandy. Not that he feared them, it was that he had feelings for them. They were his only friends here on planet Earth.

Somewhere in the background, a generator came to life and the overhead lighting flickered and came on dimly. *Mood lighting,* she thought.

She stopped and turned her body directly facing Marshal, some 40 feet away. She playfully, almost teasingly, tugged on the zipper of her jacket, pulling it down, her breasts seeking to escape the confines of the jacket. She stopped with the zipper half way down. That was enough of a distraction, she thought, "you may as well surrender yourself to The Hive. I've already beaten you once and can do it again. You stand no chance against both of us."

He stood his ground and puffed out his chest and with his hands on his hips he replied defiantly, "it is my duty to defend this planet and its inhabitants. It is you who will lose."

She disappeared from where she was standing! Superstar had started her attack by racing at him as fast as she could. In the short distance she only attained about 200 mph before she jumped and flew through the air with her left foot leading the way to his rock hard chin.

The impact of Superstar drove his head back, arching his back and lifted him off of his feet! They came down 20 feet back with Superstar once again on top, an all too familiar position for Marshal lately. Her left knee was by his ear while her right was by his side pinning down his left arm. She looked down at him with his head resting against her inner thigh. "Just like old times!"

He raised his head to answer but didn't get the chance. She wound up her right and from way behind her body swung with all her might unimpeded to the side of his face. Wham! She continued with the momentum, this time swinging her left from behind her back. She hit him in the forehead Wham! "OUCH!"

Heather stopped her attack and was looking puzzled at her hands. They were trembling and they stung! Then they stopped. She reared back to continue the assault but Marshal's left streaking up at her jaw interrupted it. Superstar demonstrated supreme flexibility as she stretched her body back, way back, out of harms way. His fist zinged harmlessly past her face. The back of her head bumped into his knee.

She lay there for just a second with her hand clenched in fists over her head by his feet. He could see nothing but the inside of her thighs and crotch. Two white mounds rose over the horizon that was Heather. His left arm was across his body; her leg was on top the other.

She arched her back for maximum effect and her body snapped up doing a crunch. Her fist came slamming down on his head like hitting him with a sledgehammer at the carnival trying to ring the bell. WHAP! No bell rang.

"OWW, OWW, OWW! MY hands! She had broken some bones, she could tell by the way her fingers pointed. She started to adjust them when he backhanded her with his returning left. He hit her on her left side knocking her off of him.

She lay next to him on the floor, curled up in pain. He had cracked her ribs. "OHMYGOD! It hurts!" Marshal got up while she was ruminating about the pain. Her ribs stopped hurting but her hands weren't right. She adjusted her fingers, it hurt to do that too. But now she was fine. Almost!

Dauntless grew concerned that her Hive sister might lose before she could tap out and started to approach the contest. Heather seeing this, shouted out to her. "Stay back, I can take him!" Words he had heard before.

Marshal grabbed hold of her by both of her forearms and picked her up off the floor. "Now I have you," he said.

"We'll see about that," was her answer. She reinforced her resistance by kneeing him in the groin. He winced, but continued to hold her. She went to do it again and as she did he held her out at full arm's reach. Her knee came up and hit his chest and got stuck there when her drew her closer.

She worked her other leg up, and with both of her knees against his chest reared back pushing with her long powerful leg in an effort to break free. His grip was like that of a vice, it only tightened all the more, hurting her arms. They both stopped and directed their attention to the far wall.

The wall was vibrating as if a small earthquake was occurring. There was the growling of heavy machinery. BAM! The wall was breached. Ten warbots burst in through the wall and climbed over the rubble. Two of the bots were of a different design, having caterpillar tracks instead of walking on four legs.

Dozens of warriors scrambled in over the rubble followed by the sound of modern warfare. There was an explosion and when the dust settled, an

M1 tank rolled in. One of the warbots ran up to it and grabbed the barrel of the tank's gun with its metal claw and bent the barrel up skywards 90 degrees. The tank turned its turret and tried to knock the warbot over but only succeeded in knocking it to one side when the tank started to pivot in place.

A second arm came out of the warbot with a drill like on a oil rig, and proceeded to drill into the side of the tank. The outside armor of the tank exploded as the drill bit in. Soon the hull of the tank had been pierced and the drill was withdrawn. The operator of the warbot reached out and dropped a hand grenade in the tank. FHOOM! A jet of flame shot out the hole and the tank just sat there with smoke escaping from every little opening.

Heather unsnapped the holster on her utility belt and drew her 9mm. This got Marshal's attention. She brought the tiny side arm up and fired repeatedly at his hand. This broke his grip. She pushed back with her legs and she fell back to the floor free of his grip. He stood towering over her holding his bleeding hand. She emptied the gun into his chest. The bullets had very little effect. His hand stopped bleeding. It still hurt but he could use it. He tried to catch her but she scrambled away. "She's too damned fast!"

A second tank rumbled in and fired its main gun at the warbot. The round hit and passed through the warbot not hitting anything vital. Dauntless walked up to the second tank waving her arms above her head.

The tank commander saw her and stopped. "That's Dauntless, she's with us. She's doesn't have any of that strange stuff grafted to her, she must be okay." She calmly walked over to the gigantic war machine and climbed on top and knocked at the hatch. It opened and the tank commander stuck his head out. She quickly grabbed hold of him and yanked him out of the turret and tossed him to the nearby warriors who made short work of him. She climbed in through the hatch. It was a close fit around her hips and bust. It must have been something for the crew to see her shimmying in the hatch.

Once she was inside, there was the sound of a scuffle and a soldier screamed "NO DON'T!" Snap! She climbed back out and stopped half way and said, "that's how you do it. Now we can use the tank."

"OHMYGOD, OHMYGOD! It hurts, it hurts! Marshal turned to see Superstar fall down to her knees. She was a bloody mess with a three-foot long piece of jagged steel shrapnel imbedded in her side, nearly cutting her in half. She was doubled over holding her side with both arms. There was a large pool of blood with more coming.

"I can't breathe, it hurts!" With a supreme effort, she yanked the jagged steel from her body and dropped it to the floor. Dauntless came over in time to see her wound close itself. Her jacket was shredded and she was covered in blood. But she was moving and she got up! "Are you okay?"

Superstar looked at Dauntless and smiled. "It hurt a lot at first, but now, I'm super!" She took her gun belt off and handed it to Brandy. "Here, I'm not going to need this." She turned to face Marshal and ducked just in time to avoid a freight train like punch. The girls backed away and Superstar took off her shredded, blood soaked jacket and threw it in Marshal's face.

While he was blinded, she moved in and landed three punches on his stomach, with the third one landing just below his belt buckle. He doubled over and staggered back away from her, throwing her jacket down. He was mad. She was stronger now, but she knew she needed to do something different.

She remembered seeing all of the stuff on the floor and thinking how they could be used as a weapon. See darted about and found a length of chain and started twirling it about. Whoosh, whoosh, whoosh was the sound it made as it orbited her.

She swung the chain so fast that you could not see it, only hear the buzzing it made passing through the air. She lashed out at Marshal. SNAPP! He is whipped around, holding the left side of his head. He staggers for a second. There is a deep gash running up and down the full length of his head. He is bleeding profusely.

She gets the chain spinning again and goes in for the kill. SNAPP! And he is down on all fours. She stops and looks back at Brandy, She gives Heather a nod, she was impressed. The Queen commands, "bring him to me. I will take possession of him now."

Superstar walks up behind him and wraps the chain around him several times and puts her knee across the back of his neck and tightens the chains and tucks the ends in underneath. "There, he's not going to get away."

He raised up on his knees, barely able to see with all the blood in his eyes, and turns back to her saying, "I doubt it."

A worker drone operates the controllers in the background and a giant electro magnet is lowered over Marshal. The magnet lifts him up and it starts to carry him over to the Queen who is now by the side of the pool.

POP, POP, POP! He's breaking the chains one by one. When the last one breaks, he falls free of the magnet's hold and lands on his feet. Superstar turns to Dauntless saying, "I'll finish him the old fashioned way!"

She races over to Marshal who is ready for her, POW! She ran smack into his upraised fist. Her unconscious body flew into his and just clung there. Having her body pressed up against his without her trying to pound him senseless felt pretty good. Slowly she slid down his body leaving a trail of her blood all the way.

He paused to wipe the blood out of his eyes, looked up, and there was Dauntless. He threw up his empty hands trying to stop her. "I don't want to fight you Brandy, I can't. Not you! You're better than this, you can resist them." Brandy was marching his way readying her fist. As she got close enough she reared back and delivered a savage uppercut that snapped his head back and lifted him off the ground.

He landed on his feet and staggered back, *Dauntless was normally stronger than Superstar, what was he in for?* He couldn't bring himself to fight her. He tried to block her next punch but really couldn't see where it was coming from. She landed a left cross to his nose. It hurt.

Brandy grabbed hold of his head with both hands and pulled his head down while thrusting up with her knee. Nose met knee and there was a crunching sound and some more blood. His nose was broken. He fell forward into Brandy's body. Seeing stars, on his knees, his face bounced off of her voluptuous bust and came to rest with it buried in her bosom.

He noticed the rise and fall of her breasts as she breathed. He was breathing through his mouth. He would have paid any amount of money if it all would just end right there and leave him there with her, but that was not to be.

As she lifted him up he managed to wipe his eyes on her chest clearing the blood from his eyes. He could see her pretty face and the look of determination on it. He saw, too late, her right fist headed for his eye. Crack! And more stars.

He staggered away from her, but she just came on strong, swinging for the fences with every punch. BAM! A left landed on his jaw stopping his retreat. He stood there dazed, not even defending himself. BOOM! She drove her right deep into his stomach and he went down to one knee protecting his stomach. "Brandy, don't do this, I won't fight you."

His words had no effect. She took a handful of hair and lifted his head, landing a powerful right roundhouse punch that jerked his entire body around and he fell to the floor, laying on his back vulnerable, badly beaten, but conscious.

She thought about stomping on his exposed stomach or jumping on him or possibly both. Now was the time to finish him, but for some reason her heart wasn't in it.

She knelt next to him and turned his face to face her. "Sorry my friend, but it really is for the best, once you're a member of The Hive you'll understand." She drew her right fist up and back ready to deliver the coup de grace. He looked her in the eye, "Please, don't Brandy. I cannot resist you any further, I am yours. It grieves me that I may have caused you any pain. You were always my favotite. I only hope we can be together in The Hive."

A tear welled up and trickled down her cheek. She pulled him onto her bosom and hugged him vigorously. "Kiss me one last time, so I may go to The Hive a happy man."

She held his head in her hands and looked him in the eye. You will know happiness as part of The Hive." She kissed him softly. Then the Queen's voice in Brandy's head commanded her to bring him forth. She kissed him again and scooped him up and started to carry him off to the Queen waiting for him.

She didn't get far when she heard the sound of a racing engine. An open top Humvee came bouncing in climbing over the rubble and debris. Tex is driving with Dr, Cooly riding shotgun and Dr. Brewville is in back with his street sweeper spitting round after round of 12 gauge rock salt. "YAHOO!"

They screech to a stop and Beverly hops out and struggles to lift Superstar into the back of the Humvee. Dr. Brewville is constantly firing his gun, Blam, Blam, Blam! Warrior drones are dropping like flies. Finally, he comes to Dauntless still carrying Marshal. "SHOOT HER!" Beverly yells at him.

"But it's Dauntless and Marshal!"

"But she's carrying him into The Hive, not out! If she's one of ours it will only sting her for a few seconds, but if she's been converted…" BLAM! He was swayed by her logic. Brandy fell to the floor and over Marshal.

The feel of Brandy's luscious body shielding him from further attack certainly had its appeal, but this was his chance to save her, to save them all. He got up and carried her unconscious body over to the waiting Humvee and gently placed her in the back. He picks up Superstar and loads her into the back as well.

As Brewville stops to reload, he tells Dr. Cooly, get them to safety and remove their bugs." He turns back, and she grabs his arm as he turns to go. "Aren't you coming?"

"Not just yet, there's a small matter of the Harbinger Queen to deal with." He wipes the blood from his face, and more determined then ever, he heads for the Queen.

She hops in and says, "Tex, get us out of Dodge." He slips the Humvee into gear and they start rolling. The warbots try to stop them with a myriad of weapons. One had a giant cleaver like blade, another a flamethrower. Tex kept the Humvee out of harm's way as they bounced and darted along running the gauntlet.

They took a turn a little too fast and slide into a pile of steel. A warrior jumped in and began to wrestle the street sweeper away from Dr. Brewville. "NO! MINE MINE!" BLAM! The warrior fell off the Humvee and they got going again. Beverly was responsible for the marksmanship. She sat in the front seat with a smoking shotgun. Brewville was having a magical moment.

As Marshal nears the Queen, a warbot stomps over to him. Marshal has just about recovered from the beating received from the hands of his girlfriends and is in no mood to take another one. A giant cleaver blade chops down just missing him. The blade is caught in the concrete. Marshal takes hold of it and rips it off of the steel arm holding it. He hoists the blade, weighing several tons, over his head and slammed it down breaking the back of the warbot.

Three more warbots ambulate up to join the fight. He pulls the cleaver blade out of his fallen victim and hurls it at the closest warbot smashing it into a hundreds pieces! Next, Marshal takes the back half of the cleaved warbot and uses it to smash the next warbot to approach. He breaks its legs off and it topples down to the floor. He struggles at first to lift it, but after a few seconds, he manages to hoist it up over his head and toss it on to the next warbot causing it to collapse into a pile of scrap metal.

The Queen scurried over to where the other warbots had gathered. She was bigger than before, 10 maybe 12 feet tall now. All black and brown, but her colors had erupted on her back. She was all mottled with green, yellow and red spots and wavy stripes. These are the colors exhibited by a Harbinger Queen when she is ready to mate.

She climbed into one of the warbots and then something started to happen. Marshal wasn't sure at first, but something was definitely going on. He decided not to wait to see what and rushed the Queen. Before he got to the Queen, another warbot came over to the Queen, and the two warbots merged into one.

Just as Marshal reached the Queen, the magnet on the ceiling picked her machine up out of his reach. He jumped up and caught hold of the framework of the machine. The Queen whipped her tail around and thrust at him with it. He dodged it and she lashed out again and again. He lost his footing and was hanging from his hands when she drove her barbed tail into his exposed stomach. He gasped in pain but held on.

There was a SKURNCHING sound as she drove it deeper and deeper into his body. There was a different sound, SHLTH! The stinger broke the skin on his back and stuck out the other side of his body. It had gone all the way through his body. He was wracked by wave after wave of pain. He let go of the machine and tried to free himself from her tail as he dangled like a piece of meat on a kabob. He could not, the barbs were preventing its removal.

He tried to take hold of the tail in front of his body but couldn't get a good grip with all the blood, so he moves another three foot up the tail and took hold and broke it off. He fell to the floor and just lay there. The Queen was in great pain and agony having just lost five feet of her tail. She started thrashing about wildly. Without her tail, she could not take possession of anyone, She would have to rely on others to do that for her. She could even lose her Hive if she didn't repair the damage.

As he lay on the floor quivering and bleeding, the Queen continued the transformation of the machinery around her. The two warbots that had tracks rolled up under her and scaffolding was erected connecting them to the suspended units. They became the feet of a 100-foot tall mechinoid with the Queen in the central drivers seat.

The mechinoid had two arms each, with a large metal claw and several other retractable weapons and tools.

"Can't you hold that light still!" Dr. Cooly commmplained as she worked on Superstar. Dr. Brewville was holding a flashlight in one hand and holding her hair back out of the way with the other.

"How do you like the utility belt I gave you?" He asked while she used the scalpel to remove the last little bit of the stinger.

"Please, not now doctor, I'm trying to concentrate," she admonished him. Soon both Heather and Brandy were back to their old selves and ready to save the world.

Superstar asked, "before we go back can you give me something for pain, this is really going to hurt." Brewville tossed her a shotgun and she slung it across her back.

The good doctor agreed to her request and watched the two most powerful humans on the planet go back to save it. Dr. Brewville asked as he watched them go, "do you think they can do it?"

She then turned to Dr. Brewville and said, "if they can't, who can? And it was really nice of you to make the belt for me, but why brown?"

"Simple," he said, "the black was on backorder."

Superstar, with her shotgun and black bra and Dauntless in her blood splattered uniform returned to save the world. They returned just in time to see a 100-foot tall mechinoid made out of warbots and spare parts pick up Marshal by his head and deposit him on the elevated platform.

"Where did that thing come from?" Heather said with a look of astonishment on her face.

Dauntless had no answer for her.

Next, the giant took one of the huge buckets used to carry several tons of molten steel from the hooks it hung from and placed it over Marshal's motionless body. It banged into the side of the platform and rang like a bell as she lowered it. The Harbinger Queen was in the center chest part of the mechinoid.

"She's killed him!" Superstar exclaimed.

"Not likely, he would be of no use to her dead," Dauntless advised her. "Besides, he's pretty hard to kill. Let's get him out of there." They raced to the giant upturned bucket prison. They reach it, but are unable to move it. "It must weigh 40 tons!"

As they try to find a way to raise the bucket a giant steel claw comes down and grabs Dauntless by her midsection and picks her up. She kicks and flails with no effect. The Queen brings her closer so she can see her better. "You are proving to be more trouble than you are worth." She squeezes and Brandy screams, in pain. There is a sickening crunching sound and Dauntless collapses unconscious and maybe dead. The Queen throws her lifeless body with sufficient force for her to crash through a brick wall and land outside on a pile of steel.

The Queen then turned her attention on Superstar. It was like someone trying to corner a mouse. The 100 foot tall mechinoid was rolling here and there trying to cut off Superstar. Each time it got close, a giant steel bucket would come crashing down, BONG! And Superstar would dash off in another direction avoiding the trap. Superstar was forced to leave.

The Queen now turned her attention to the bucket on the elevated platform and its contents. The giant mechinoid being driven by the Queen bent over and lifted the bucket as if it were unveiling cookies at a tea party.

Marshal was on his knees trying to remove the stinger. There was a great deal of blue blood all over. He looked up and knew it was now or never. He reached behind his back with one hand and pulled the tail on out with it passing commmpletely through his body. "AAAHHUGGH!" The pain was excruciating, too much for him to endure. He collapsed face down, gushing blood, still clutching the business end of the Queen's tail.

She started to reach for him when Superstar came racing in to rescue Marshal. Or she would have rescued him, if the Queen hadn't put the bucket back down over him first.

Superstar had to suddenly change her course to avoid running into the bucket. She runs into trouble instead. The other mechanical claw of the mechinoid catches her broadside and knocks her into the wall. She gets up and staggers forward, but is whacked on the head and KO'd. The mechinoid picks her up and drops her in front of its tracked foot and rolls over her, crushing her legs. Back and forth this continued until the Queen was satisfied that she was crushed commmpletely before moving on.

Superstar feels nothing. She's not sure if it's the drugs or that she has no legs. She tries to move when the Queen moves away but cannot. Her legs are unresponsive. She looks and sees the crushed and shredded remains of her legs. She's too messed up to go anywhere.

The mechinoid returns to the upturned bucket prison of Marshal. She tilts the bucket up on edge to peek in to see if Marshal is, "still with us I see." He is laying face down in a pool of his own blood barely able to move. She lowers the bucket.

The mechinoid picks up the elevated platform with one hand and places its other on top the bucket and begins to shake it vigorously, like making a martini. Marshal's body can be heard tumbling and rattling around inside.

She kept shaking until the noise from inside stopped. Puzzled, the Queen put the platform back down and once again tipped the bucket up on edge to see what happened to him. There was a bloody mess but was that all that was left of him?

The Queen looked around, there were no more threats to her safety, and the humans were as good as beaten. The giant walking scrapyard froze in place holding the bucket tipped up. The Queen got out of the mechinoid and walked over to the bucket to take a closer look, expecting to find puree of Marshal.

There didn't seem to be enough chunks. She looked under the bucket and found her answer. A battered bloody mass known as Marshal was stuck to the bottom, now the top of the bucket. She lashed out with her bloody nub of a tail and he fell to the floor, still clutching the stinger end of the Queens's tail, or at least five feet of it.

She dragged him out and tossed him down onto the old workroom floor.

She leapt down and walked over to where he sat in a heap. "I sssuppose I could still find another human female to mate with you and collect your sssemen, but you have been very troublesssome."

Superstar pushed herself up with both hands. She could see Marshal and hear the Queen, but she could not see the Queen. She took her shotgun from her back. The butt stock was shattered but the gun would still work. Marshal saw her. She flung the gun in his direction. The gun went somersaulting end over end through the air.

The Queen, realizing that something had caught Marshal's attention stepped forward and turned in time to see the gun coming her way. She caught it with one of her human like hands.

Heather collapsed back to the floor. "Game over," she said in dejection.

"WRONG!" He lashed out at the Queen in the only way he could. He used the end of her tail like a whip and caught her by surprise. The stinger slashed her human like arm, she recoiled in pain and dropped the shotgun.

He saw the gun lying on the floor but the Queen kicked it away before he could make a move for it. He started twirling the tail around as Heather had earlier and he lashed out with it again and again. The stinger would only glance off her hard carapace covered insect body. She caught Marshal with her lobster like claw around his chest, and pulled him in close with the intention of finishing him off with her other claw.

But this only brought him in closer and he was able to lash out and get the tail wrapped around her spindly neck. He took another play out of Superstar's book and twisted the tail tighter around her neck with his fist.

The Queen's head jerked around violently as her other claw came in to sever his head. He caught her clawed arm and held it at bay.

He tried to tighten the blood soaked tail into a noose around the Queen's neck, but couldn't. The piece of tail would slip and stretch with every twist. She also tried to squeeze the life out of her opponent, but that wasn't all the Queen could do. Her humanlike hands had claws of their own, wicked looking curved claws like on a big cat.

She slashed and ripped at his unprotected belly, over and over, only doing superficial damage at first. Every subsequent slash of her three inch claws bit a little deeper and deeper into his flesh, sending small chunks and a river of blood flying everywhere!

He was jolted by every slash, his strength faltering with every swipe. The Queen glared at him and kept on disemboweling him. He gritted his teeth and struggled to hang on. His resolve never wavered, but soon, he was coughing up blood and gasping for air.

With each sickening slash, the expression on the Queen's face changed, from one of desperation, to relief, to one of exhilaration and anticipation! Her face and body where splattered with his blood, but it mattered not. She was the Harbinger Queen, more insect than anything else.

Heather, on the floor, had to turn away. She could watch no more. He relaxed his grip and slumped over in her claw. He had succumbed to the loss of blood. The last thing he saw was the evil smile on the Queen's face.

She held him out at arms length and shook him. He flopped about like a rag doll. She tossed his lifeless body away like so much trash.

She unwrapped the noose from around her neck and triumphantly proclaimed, "VICTORY GOES TO THE HIVE! THE EARTH WILL SOON BE OUR NEW HOME! THIS IS THE RISE OF A NEW HARBINGER EMPIRE!"

The end?

NOT!

CHAPTER FIFTEEN

LIFE AFTER THE HARBINGER

There was the whine of jet engines, a flash and everything was dark.

He was awake. Everything hurt, but he was awake. There was a familiar, unthreatening form not far from him in the dark. He could not move. Heavy leather straps restrained him. There were strange alien devices attached to his body and in his arm. He had a clean jacket on.

There was a beeping sound. *Is this The Hive?* He tried to get up, but again failed. An alarm started to sound, and the familiar form started to stir, it was Brandy! She had been asleep in the chair next to his hospital bed.

She moved in over him using both hands to ease his shoulders back down to the pillow. "Easy big guy, easy." Seeing her, and feeling her gentle touch, calmed him and he settled back down. "Linda! Come quick! He's awake!"

"Is this The Hive?" Marshal asked, looking up at her holding him down.

"No, this is the Med. center," she said as the lights came on and Nurse Chapel joined them.

"What happened?" Chapel asked.

"He just woke up."

He also wanted to know, "what happened?"

"When? Before, or after you died?" She said with a little smirk. "The Army and Doctor Cooly came to the rescue."

The rise and fall of the Harbinger Empire spanned but a single breath.

BLAM, BLAM, BLAM, BLAM! Captain Reynolds and the Army had come to the rescue. The soldiers of the 5th special security group pumped more than a dozen rounds of 12 gauge rock salt into the Harbinger Queen. She toppled over, and The Hive fell quiet.

Drones and warbots just stopped and went into hibernation. The open top Humvee pulled up and Dr. Cooly jumped out. She was horrified by what she saw. She reached into the back of the Humvee and pulled out a roll of white and pink cloth. "Where to start?"

A few days later, in the HERO HQ building, the entire crew of the HERO organization comes out of the main conference room. This is the first time they all have been out of the hospital. It was an informal debriefing. General Solo is talking with MaCos Ex about the clean up and recovering any technology. MaCos tries to explain that they were only bugs and that they were only using your own technology against you.

Brandy, in a plaid shirt with blue jeans and cowboy boots, stops Marshal as he goes by. "You said some things back there when you thought you were going to die. Did you mean them?"

He looked back and forth and seeing no exit, had to answer, "I did not lie to you."

"Good, then you had better prove it." She gave him a wink. She had a sly, devilish little smile. She most definitely had something in mind. He was looking forward to finding out what it was. She took his hand and led the big blue alien down the hall. "We've got to get you something else to wear." The other couldn't help but notice, not a word was said.

As Brandy and Marshal went by, Heather, who wasn't in uniform either, stopped Colonel Otis who probably didn't own any civilian clothing. "That brings up something else, I understand you had some rather intense dreams while you were hallucinating."

"Did Dr. Cooly tell you about that?" He asked.

"No, why? Did they involve me?" She had put two and two together and now her curiosity was piqued. She would not rest until she got her answer. "You have got to tell me about that dream you had." She had wrapped her arm around his; he wasn't going to get away, not today.

"What if I said I didn't remember them?" He looked her in the eye. She was very pretty. He could also tell she wasn't buying it.

"You'll have to do better then that. Tell you what, you can tell me over dinner tonight. No uniforms, my treat. They walked off.

Back in the conference room, the two doctors, both in their white lab coats, are picking up their papers before heading out,

Dr. Brewville clears his throat before addressing the redheaded beauty, "I thought we made a pretty good team out there, didn't you Beverly?"

She stopped shuffling papers and looked at him and said nothing. The funny looking man with a ponytail gathered his thoughts and pressed on. "Do you have any plans for tonight?"

"No plans."

"I was wondering, Beverly, would you like to out to dinner with me tonight?"

"Maybe." She resumed adjusting her papers.

"And then after that we could…"

She looked him dead in the eye and slid her glasses down to look at him over the tops of them. "Now you're pushing it."

"Just dinner it is then."

A messenger makes his way through the croweded hallway looking for General Solo. He finds the senior soldier about to exit the building. "Excuse me sir, but we received a message from the VP. He says the international research station in Greenland has been attacked by penguins and he wants a team of heroes on it."

"Attacked by penguins?"

"That's what he said sir."

"Call 'em back."

Captain Reynolds and Sgt. Lopez come down the hall and stop. "And that's how we saved the world from alien mind controlling bugs. If you're wondering whatever happened to that Sheriff and his posse or that beautiful Thugee assassin, that's another story, and you'll have to read the next installment of Marshal, to find out more. Thank you for reading.

THE END for now.